Dear Reader,

Of all the heroines I've ever written, Emma McDaniel may be closest to my heart. Emma first swept onto the stage of *Picket Fence* when she was barely ten years old, abandoned by her mother, angry, hurting, with a talent for getting into trouble. Her greatest treasures were the journal of a child who lived during the Civil War and the antique wedding dress that had survived all those years.

I revisited Emma in *The Gazebo* when she had just won the part of Juliet at sixteen. Emma is a natural-born drama queen with the signature McDaniel temper, and her fierce rebellion in the throes of her first love is the catalyst that unearths her mother's darkest secret.

Now Emma's all grown up, but just when it seems she has everything she's dreamed of, her world tumbles in. At the beginning of *The Wedding Dress* she crosses the ocean to work, intending to bury herself in a world centuries old. She doesn't know she's going to find her own happy ending in Castle Craigmorrigan, her fairy godmother a ragamuffin terrier, her prince anything but charming.

The Wedding Dress is my tribute to family, and to love that through hundreds of years can leave fingerprints, not only on chipped teacups, antique wedding dresses and swords buried long ago, but also on our hearts.

Here's to happily ever after!

Kimberly Cates

Kimberly Cates

THE WEDDING DRESS

HQN™

ISBN-13: 978-0-373-77189-9
ISBN-10:   0-373-77189-4

THE WEDDING DRESS

www.HQNBooks.com

Printed in U.S.A.

To my husband, Dave, who has helped rescue more puppies than I can count. Thank you for twenty-six years of catching frightened strays and breaking up dogfights for me. You are never more my hero than when you utter that long-suffering sigh I love so much and say, "I'll do it. I'll heal faster."

THE WEDDING DRESS

Chapter One

Emma's World Shatters

TWENTY-EIGHT-YEAR-OLD Emma McDaniel winced as she recognized the headline blazing across the tabloid a college-aged girl was devouring in the airport baggage claim. Unfortunately, neither huddling deeper into the enveloping folds of her raincoat nor tugging the brim of her Witness Protection ball cap lower to shadow her face could shield Emma from the pain. She knew the fine print on the glossy cover by heart.

Jade Star actress faces studio insiders' doubts to attempt role of a lifetime… Her beaming ex-husband brings home the baby she refused to give him.

Images in living color flashed into Emma's head: The picture of Drew Lawson, the only man she'd ever loved, leaving the hospital in Whitewater, Illinois, his face aglow as he cradled his new daughter in his arms while Emma's one-time best friend, Jessie, leaned against him, her shy face luminous. The joyous new parents stood out in sharp counterpoint to the paparazzi shots of Emma back in L.A., thronged by reporters clamoring for her reaction to the news about Drew's child. She could still hear them shouting…

"Emma, your fans are dying to know how you feel."

How the hell do you think I feel? She'd wanted to fling back at them. *Read your own damned press clippings and you should be able to figure it out.*

Instead, she'd given an Oscar-worthy performance, forcing a brilliant smile. "I know Drew will be a wonderful father…"

She'd always known he would be. But if she had to pretend one more time it didn't hurt that he'd fathered a child with a different woman…

She shoved her sunglasses farther up her nose, praying no one would recognize her before she retrieved her luggage, found her ride and dropped off the face of the earth. But then, there were times Emma barely recognized herself anymore.

A tight, panicky feeling cinched Emma's lungs as she surreptitiously scanned the crowd of passengers just arrived at Glasgow's airport. And she felt suddenly, horribly exposed.

Emma, traveling alone is a really bad idea, her mother's voice warned in her head. *It could even be dangerous. If someone recognizes you before you meet up with this historical consultant, anything could happen.*

Emma could get mobbed for autographs, pounced on by photographers, stalked by an obsessed fan… God, how had life gotten so insane? And why hadn't she noticed until Drew walked out the door?

I need to get out of here, Emma thought, searching for the man who was supposed to meet her. Dr. Jared Butler, experimental archaeologist—whatever that was. The brilliant scholar who had made Castle Craigmorrigan and its heroic fourteenth-century lady his life's work.

Ever since she'd gotten the call telling her to hop on the

next flight to Scotland, Emma had pictured Butler as a cross between Albert Einstein and her high school history teacher— a single eyebrow crawling across his forehead like a runaway caterpillar, pop-bottle-thick glasses, frizzy white hair and rumpled tweed suits bought sometime in the 1930s. But there wasn't a genius in sight.

A surly dark-haired man in a cream sweater slouched in a plastic molded chair and scowled at a book that looked heavy enough to be used as a murder weapon. A cluster of exuberant American kids on tour crowded around a teacher who was taking a head count. Businessmen with briefcases eyed their wrist-watches as the luggage started spilling onto the conveyor belt.

But no one held the sign Emma's director had promised would be waiting for her when she stepped off the plane. Not a discreet card reading *E. M.* in sight. Nobody even seemed to be searching the crowd with that somewhat awed expression she'd come to know after six years of being swept from movie set to movie set.

"Where the hell is he?" she muttered, peering past families hugging each other and vacationing trekkers ready to wallow in Scotland's wild beauty.

For an instant Emma wished she'd taken her mother up on her offer to accompany her, help her settle in. But Emma had spent enough time grieving for all the things that would never be. It was time she learned how to be alone.

She had to focus on the one thing that mattered now. The sign from God that her luck had changed. The part of a lifetime she'd thought beyond her reach was hers now.

By accident, a voice reminded her. *If Angelica Robards hadn't fallen off a horse and landed in traction, you'd still be trapped in L.A., being hammered by the studio to stick to what you do best. A fifth sequel of Jade Star.*

Okay, so it *was* true what insiders said—that the screenplay for *Lady Valiant* had been written specifically for Angelica Robards. The Meryl Streep of Emma's generation had told the world and Jay Leno the tale of how she had first heard of Lady Aislinn from locals during her honeymoon in Scotland. A pub owner had pointed her to an obscure book this genius Butler had written, and Angelica had fallen head-over-heels in love with the story. The actress had given her new husband, one of Hollywood's most gifted directors, no peace until Barry presented the script to her as an anniversary gift the following year. But no matter what the Robards' intentions had been, the part of Lady Aislinn was Emma's now.

Emma's opportunity to show the world that she was more than futuristic gizmos and special effects. Emma's chance to break out of the role that had left her typecast and her career dead in the water.

Well, not her career, Emma had to admit to herself. The character of Jade Star was still box office gold. It was Emma's creativity that was drowning, her love of her craft, her dreams of playing roles that tested not only her physical strength, but the depth of her heart.

And portraying the Scotswoman who'd defied Scotland's most ruthless villain in 1305 would demand every shred of courage Emma could find within herself. She would have to dig deeper, reach further, strip her emotions so raw that the audience would be as devastated as Emma had been at the end of the script, when the brave lady of Castle Craigmorrigan plunged to her death off the rugged, sea-swept cliff.

And at the end of the ordeal, maybe, just maybe Emma would find herself.

She dove for her suitcase as it whizzed past, wrestling it off the conveyor, the simple black bag so heavy it almost dislocated her shoulder. The ball cap fell off, dislodging her sunglasses, her trademark black curls tumbling down from the elastic band she'd bundled them into an ocean ago. *Cover blown,* she thought miserably as a screech sounded from across the room.

"Ohmigod!"

Emma knew in her gut it was Tabloid Girl. She felt some of the other passengers glance her way, but fortunately most were still too engrossed in retrieving their own luggage to pay much attention.

Tabloid Girl clutched the magazine to her chest and rushed toward Emma, breathless. "It's you, isn't it? It really is you!" Her voice dropped to an awed whisper. "Emma McDaniel."

Emma retrieved her cap, but there was no point in trying to stuff the genie back in the bottle. She shoved the hat in her giant black purse. "You must be thinking of the other Emma McDaniel," she attempted to joke. *The one who could have run through the middle of an airport half naked without anyone noticing. Well, maybe someone would.*

"I adored your last movie," the girl enthused. "The special effects were amazing."

If the glossy tabloid cover hadn't been right in Emma's line of sight, she could have managed to be a lot more gracious. Instead, Emma cursed the man who was supposed to meet her. Where the hell was Butler? A few minutes more and this girl would be asking the pain-and-heartbreak questions everyone seemed to level at Emma these days.

"My name's Sandy," the girl supplied, thrusting out the hand that wasn't clutching the tabloid.

"Sandy," Emma repeated, briefly shaking the girl's hand. "I'm glad you liked the movie, but I can hardly take credit for the special effects."

"Can I ask you a question?"

Emma stared pointedly at the tabloid. "As a matter of fact, I've decided never to answer a question again."

The girl flushed, glancing down at the lurid headline. "Oh, God. You must hate magazines like this. Articles about...well, your creep of an ex-husband. What pond scum!"

If only Emma could relegate Drew to slime level, her life would be so much easier. She gritted her teeth, determined to keep quiet. Sandy just rushed on.

"Running off with your best friend—what a jerk."

"I knew Jessie a lifetime ago, in high school." *Damn,* Emma cursed herself. She'd promised herself she wouldn't rise to the bait. "Listen, Sandy, I appreciate your support, but I really don't want to talk about this."

"And why should you? I say good riddance to the asshole. I mean, who needs him when you get paid to kiss guys like Tom Cruise and Mel Gibson? And your last movie—wow! What was it like? Having Brad Pitt look you in the eyes like that, loving you, knowing he could never have you because he was turning into a werewolf? Women all through the theater were having spontaneous orgasms."

"Actually, Brad wasn't even in the room when we shot that scene. I was talking to a white stick that gave me a focal point so I knew where the computer-generated wolf-guy would be once they put him in."

"Oh." The girl sighed in disappointment.

Emma could just imagine Sandy's reaction if she told the whole truth. That she'd barely noticed Brad, werewolf or otherwise, during the filming because she'd been sick to her stomach most of the time, knowing that with every Jade line she spoke she was digging herself deeper into the creative wasteland where typecast actors lived.

What an odd sensation, the whole world believing she was a roaring success when she could feel everything she treasured slipping through her fingers. If she'd known how much top billing Jade would cost her, would she have taken the part at all?

Emma's heart squeezed, remembering how hungry she'd been to get on stage—fresh out of drama school, newly married, so full of dreams about how wonderful life would be.

Now here she was an ocean away from her life with Drew, her palms sweating with self-doubt as she prepared for her first new role in six years. Feeling so disillusioned that the Emma who'd spent her honeymoon gorging on the Broadway shows she was determined to star in seemed like a stranger.

Sandy grimaced. "I guess sometimes it's better not to know about all that movie magic stuff, you know? It kind of ruins things."

"Maybe you should try reading a book."

The low burr of the sexiest Scottish accent Emma had ever heard sent a shiver of attraction through her. She turned to see who the voice belonged to and found herself face-to-face with the surly dark-haired man she'd noticed earlier. The Scot stared at the tabloid's headline, every fiber of his being radiating scorn.

And there was a whole lot of *being* to radiate. From the time Emma had hit her growth spurt, she had been one of the tallest kids in class. Some of her leading men had to wear risers in their shoes. But this guy loomed over her by at least six inches, one of his big hands holding the "murder weapon" as negligently as if it were a postcard, his cable-knit sweater doing nothing to soften shoulders Brad Pitt would have envied. Wind-tousled mahogany hair curled in thick waves about a face hewn rugged as the Scottish crags she'd seen in books she'd used for research. Two days' worth of stubble darkened a belligerent jut of jaw.

Fierce green eyes burned into Emma's with such intensity she shifted her own a few inches down his face, instinctively trying to shield herself from a gaze designed to strip souls of their secrets.

She knew in a heartbeat she'd jumped straight into the fire. For an instant, she forgot to breathe as her gaze locked on one of God's nastier practical jokes.

This arrogant bundle of raw testosterone had the most amazing mouth Emma had ever seen. Soul-blisteringly sensual, just a whisper sensitive, the left side of his full upper lip curling a fraction higher than the right.

A woman could get herself into big trouble if she spent much time around a mouth like that.

"Ms. McDaniel. You'll have to excuse me," he drawled. "I didn't recognize you without your spandex suit."

Ouch. Too bad the man's personality wasn't as gorgeous as his looks.

"I never wear spandex when I fly," Emma countered breezily. "It seems to distract the pilots." For once she wished she really was armed with the freeze blaster she'd carried in the last Jade Star—she'd point it at this jerk's face and turn him into a giant snow cone.

He turned toward Sandy, then slid the tabloid out of the girl's hand. "I'll be doing you a favor by getting rid of this thing. Between movies like Jade Star and gossip rags like this, it's amazing you have a single functioning brain cell left."

Sandy looked as if the man had kicked her puppy. Okay, so the tabloid *was* trash, but Sandy was already embarrassed Emma had caught her with the thing—utter humiliation wasn't necessary.

Emma pasted on her ice-queen face as she flashed him the glare that had made Robert de Niro back down in *Jade III: Revenge of the Star Demon*. "Actually, I was about to autograph the article for Sandy," she said, digging a pen from her purse. "I wouldn't be anywhere if it weren't for the support of my fans." Emma cringed as the words spilled out of her mouth. So much for keeping a low profile.

"By all means, sign your picture." He held the tabloid out to Emma as if he were disposing of a dead rat. "I wouldn't dream of coming between you and your *work*."

"And I wouldn't dream of coming between you and whatever it is you do when you're not butting into conversations that are none of your business."

She scooped the tabloid out of the man's hand and made a huge deal out of choosing which of the pictures to sign as she waited for the jerk to go away. But he stayed put, as persistent as chewing gum in the tread of her little sister's running shoes. Finally she scrawled her name in red ink across the picture of her brittle smile. Emma the actress, pretending not to care.

Pretending, just like she was pretending now. She handed the magazine to Sandy, who thanked her and fled into the crowd. Then Emma snapped up the handle on her suitcase and started to wheel it toward the exit.

A hard hand flashed out, grabbing her by the arm. She whirled around, heart hammering against her chest. Sexy Mouth was so close she could feel his breath hot on her cheek. Alarm prickled the hair at Emma's nape.

"Take your hand off me," she warned. Her right arm swept up hard. The man swore in surprise and pain as she broke his hold, the book he held in his other hand crashing onto the toe of his scuffed leather boot. If there was a God, Sexy Mouth should have a bruise the size of Manhattan come morning.

"Bloody hell!" Green eyes fired with fury. One second too late, she remembered her stepfather's warning about the defense moves her ex-Army Ranger grandfather had taught her as a child. *The old man's tricks are great, but don't ever pull them on somebody who really* could *kick your ass or you might get a nasty surprise.*

The Scot glanced around, evidently aware people were starting to stare. His rugged cheeks darkened. Jake had been right. Making this stranger mad wasn't the smartest thing she'd ever done. The Scotsman rubbed his arm, hard biceps outlined against the cream-colored yarn as he took a menacing step toward her.

"Do I have to call security?" Emma demanded, searching for a uniformed guard.

"Go ahead. Try it." His gaze pierced her. "*I'm* the one who nearly got a broken arm here. I figure I've already got you on assault, hands down." Too late Emma could hear warning bells that sounded a lot like *lawsuit, lawsuit.*

"Listen, Mr…" She didn't know his name, but he sure as heck knew hers. Not good, Emma. Not good. "I'd like to say it's been nice talking to you, but that would be a lie."

"Isn't that what actresses do for a living?" he asked cynically. "Lie?"

Emma's breath hissed between her teeth. She couldn't remember the last time anyone had made her this furious. Hadn't felt any emotion this sharp since she'd plunged into the haze of regrets and grief, rejection and self-doubt that had plagued her for the past two years…

"Why, you pompous, arrogant…"

"Have you made enough of a scene?" he asked. "Or do you want me to have the PA system announce to the whole world you're here?"

"I don't want you to do a damned thing except leave me alone!"

"That makes two of us. But it looks like we're stuck with each other."

"No. We're not. Because I'm leaving."

The left corner of those wicked lips ticked up a notch. "You want to walk to the excavation site in those ridiculous shoes, it's fine with me. I'll see you sometime next month."

"Excavation site?" Horror flooded through Emma. "Oh, God." So much for rumpled suits bought sometime during the 1930s. The man standing before her hadn't even been born then. And as for *life's work*...how long could that amount to with this guy? All of ten years? "Please," she said, knowing the axe was about to fall, "don't tell me you're—"

"Dr. Jared Butler at your service, milady." He executed a bow dripping with sarcasm, ridiculous in the modern-day airport, and yet strangely suiting him better than a handshake ever would.

Emma's stomach flip-flopped as his eyes narrowed on her.

"I own you for the next six weeks," he growled, "or until you come to your senses and 'cry hold, enough.' Or did you skip MacBeth on the way to your spaceship?"

Emma couldn't help but wince. Kids in high school drama class knew calling "The Scottish Play" by its name was bad luck. But then, could her luck *get* any worse?

"'Lay on, MacDuff,'" Emma quoted the play, challenge in her eyes.

"The bottom line is this," Butler said, ignoring her, "Barry Robards hired me to teach his lead actress how to live, how to move, how to breathe medieval Scotland. How to *be* Lady Aislinn. That's right—it's pronounced *Ash-leen*. You can start by saying her name correctly. You Yanks have been massacring it for two years now."

"Well, *this Yank* looked it up in a Celtic baby-name book the first time she saw the script, so you can move on to more important things."

"Fine. How about this, then? When Barry Robards asked me to take on the role of historical consultant, I figured I'd have a fair chance of success with Angelica Robards to work with. But *you?*" He snorted in derision.

Emma glared. "Why don't you tell me how you really feel?"

"I might as well." He crossed his arms over that impressive chest. "I told anybody at the studio who'd talk to me that you'll never be a believable Lady Aislinn."

This arrogant jerk who spent all his time digging up dead people had been complaining to the studio about her being cast? Who did Jared Butler think he was?

"So now you're an expert on acting?"

His scruffy-looking chin tipped at an angle that made her want to smash it. "I know what it will take to portray Lady Aislinn. Courage, intelligence, tenacity," he asserted, a sudden distance in his eyes, as if he saw a world beyond the Scottish mist. "She held Castle Craigmorrigan for eight months, besting Sir Brannoc with no weapon but her wits. There's a subtlety about her, a…"

"And you know this how? Did you have a chat with her sarcophagus? Or did some psychic channel her for you?"

Butler's eyes flashed and Emma realized she'd managed to strike a nerve, get back some of her own.

But the good doctor was quick, almost as accomplished as Emma at shuttering vulnerability away.

"Why don't you save us both a lot of trouble and just head for some ritzy spa on the French Riviera," he challenged. "Go back where you belong."

"According to Barry Robards, I belong right here. Playing Lady Aislinn. And if that means I have to deal with *you* for six weeks, I guess we'll both just have to suffer. I have to admit one thing though, Dr. Butler. You *are* a brilliant teacher. I've known you all of five minutes and you've already helped me get into character. I can't *wait* to get a sword up to your throat."

Butler rolled his eyes. "I told the bloody screenwriter that part of the legend is rubbish. There isn't a woman alive who could beat a seasoned knight and get a blade to his throat."

If Butler had smacked her cheek with a gauntlet the challenge couldn't have been any clearer. Adrenaline rushed through Emma. She was going to make the man eat his words if it was the last thing she did.

"You're quite sure it's impossible?" she inquired with acid sweetness.

"I'd stake my life on it."

"Hmm." Emma laid one finger along her cheek, considering for a moment. Suddenly her gaze dropped to the bulge in his brown canvas cargo pants. "Maybe I'll just aim a whole lot lower."

Ten minutes in Scotland and she'd already declared war.

Chapter Two

"NOTHING LIKE HATE at first sight to make a lady feel welcome," Emma muttered under her breath as Butler all but rolled his battered Mini Cooper on yet another hairpin corner. The right shoulder of the narrow road plunged down in a boulder-strewn cliff, while a dozen yards to the left, a mountain soared skyward. If it weren't for the biting chill that had whipped her raincoat in the airport parking lot and the lowering thunderheads gathering on the horizon, she might have been tempted to get out and walk to Castle Craigmorrigan.

Her legs ached from bracing herself against the floorboards, her fingers clamped in the upholstery to keep her arm from touching his. For God's sake, could the man take up any *more* room? It was like being wedged in a clown car with MacTavish the Pissed-Off Scot Giant. Not to mention the fact that Butler's testosterone overload was sucking up all the oxygen in the cab of this ridiculously small vehicle.

"Getting us both killed isn't going to do you any good," Emma said.

"You're right." The corner of Butler's sexy mouth twisted. "I'm already in hell."

Before Emma could think of a comeback, a fuzzy brownish-red hill loomed in their path. Emma choked back a scream as Butler swerved with annoying expertise, the car bouncing over the road's shoulder so hard the top of Emma's head hit the roof in spite of her seat belt.

She whispered a Hail Mary, sandwiched for a heartbeat between mountain wall and the weirdest cow she'd ever seen. She glimpsed long horns and terrified bovine eyes all but buried under a shaggy red topknot as the car sped past. Butler wrestled the toy car back onto the road, spraying gravel in his wake.

No doubt about it, Emma thought. She was going to die. But damn if she was going to give Jared Butler the satisfaction of knowing he was rattling her nerves before they'd even reached the castle.

"So, in between trying to give the local rescue team practice with the Jaws of Life rescue tools, why don't you tell me exactly what books I'm going to be reading?"

"Reading?"

"Or do I get to sit around with you feeling the bumps on the old chicken bones you dig up? Archaeology 101: Observe, Ms. McDaniel, this piece of broken pottery we found when Farmer MacSomething was digging a loo."

"I'm not going to have you contaminating my excavation site, do you hear me?" Butler slashed her the look his highland raider ancestors must've fired off when they were about to burn and pillage. "You're not to go near the sections of the castle that are being excavated unless I'm with you. I'll pack you back off to America faster than you can say Hollywood Boulevard."

"And here all the tour books said people in the British Isles were supposed to be charming."

"You want charming, head across the channel to Ireland. I have work to do."

Fat raindrops plopped onto the windshield. Butler flicked on the wipers and, with a low growl of irritation, slowed the car as the drops transformed into a cold, driving rain.

"Part of your job is teaching me," Emma said, easing her death grip on the seat. "So why did you volunteer if you're so all-fired busy?"

"Angelica Robards arrived in April to start training for the riding and swordplay. She was supposed to be gone by the time the summer's work on the dig began."

"But she fell off a horse and landed in traction. Rotten break for you, Butler."

"Right, but it was your lucky day, wasn't it?" he challenged. "Don't you feel guilty at all? Knowing that you've only got the part because the director's first pick is lying in a hospital somewhere? I'd have too much self-respect to—"

"*I'm* not the one who was supposed to train her to ride," Emma snapped, stung. "*You're* the genius who claimed you could turn an actress into the medieval version of an action hero and then put her over a jump she couldn't handle. The press said she fell halfway down a cliff."

Butler's Adam's apple bobbed in the corded strength of his throat. He stood his ground, but Emma could see rawness in his piercing gaze, a dogged sense of self-blame. Fine, Emma thought. Butler had been chipping away at her self-confidence from the moment they'd come face-to-face at the airport. He'd made it clear he'd use whatever weapons he could find against her. She'd just have to hone a few sharp points of her own.

"Considering what a stellar job you did with the actress you thought would do justice to the role of Lady Aislinn, you can surely understand my curiosity about how you intend to handle me. Now that you 'own me for the next six weeks,'" she mimicked in a flawless Scots burr, "exactly what are you going to do with me?"

A muscle in Butler's jaw jumped. "Unfortunately, nobody dared to lock Lady Aislinn in a scold's bridle."

"A what?"

"A metal harness that locked around a woman's head so she couldn't talk."

"And we think we have all the modern conveniences." Thunder rumbled in the distance.

"I suppose there's some chance Lady Aislinn was locked into a chastity belt when her husband ran off to fight. We could give that a try."

"Aw, Butler. I didn't know you cared. But drastic measures are hardly necessary. I'm about as likely to be tempted by you as I would be to fly without an airplane."

Why did an image suddenly pop into her head? Her role in the senior production at drama school—Peter, in *Peter Pan*. It must be the cliffs that were reminding her of that first, terrifying step she'd made into thin air.

Butler swore as he slowed around a corner. Lightning flashed, rain soaking the landscape, making everything slick and shiny. "Maybe you're used to men falling all over you, Ms. McDaniel, but I won't be joining your fan club."

Emma didn't hear a word. She gasped as a castle ruin reared up through the storm like a warhorse frozen by a sorcerer's spell. A single intact tower thrust skyward from the broken curtain wall that had once enclosed all the buildings, livestock and people who owed loyalty to the castle lord: an entire world whose fate had hinged on the courage and wisdom of Lady Aislinn and her husband, Lord Magnus.

White canvas tents smudged the landscape here and there, reminding Emma of costume dramas, tournaments where visiting knights would fight for a lady's honor. But no bold pennants whipped in the wind and the only thing under attack was the mound of earth that had been reclaiming the tumbled castle walls for centuries.

Precise trenches scored the turf like wounds. Even in the rain, the place bustled with activity. People in knee-high rubber boots and rain gear clustered under the shelters, busy with tasks Emma couldn't see. A raised metal viewing platform with a railing around the top had been constructed near the widest cut in the ground. Contemporary machinery and a yellow trailer were situated under a copse of hazel trees.

It seemed strange that anything so modern could besiege this castle's walls. And yet, Emma doubted Castle Craigmorrigan had ever felt at peace. For beyond the intact tower, the ground fell away at the castle's feet, a wildly crashing ocean flinging itself against the stony outcropping below with the singleminded fury of an invading army.

Emma pictured the forces the villainous Sir Brannoc had brought with him—walling off this thin finger of land. What had it been like the day they set up camp, isolating the castle from the rest of the world?

No escape…the sea seemed to whisper, cutting off all hope of flight. Emma shuddered, imagining what it would be like to peer out the tower window, to see her enemy building trebuchets, the great siege machines that would soon start battering at the walls the way the past two years had battered at Emma's heart.

She could *feel* Lady Aislinn, like a pulse, just under the heather-tangled ground, could *see* the castle as it must have been before time and tragedy left its curtain wall broken and all but one of its towers tumbled down.

For the first time since Barry Robards himself had called

to offer her the part, she knew it wasn't a make-believe world she'd inhabit. It was real. The awesome responsibility of telling this story pressed down on Emma like the fallen stones.

What if Butler is right? self-doubt whispered. *What if you dig down into your soul and your best isn't good enough? My God, look at this place. Think of this woman. No one on earth knows more about her than Jared Butler. If he's sure you'll fail...*

Emma's throat tightened, her hand suddenly unsteady. *Don't even think it,* she told herself sharply. *You're not going to fail. You're going to take whatever he can dish out and not give an inch. Think of this as your test. If you can make* him *believe your portrayal of Lady Aislinn, you can make the whole world believe it. And if they see you can play this role, they'll know you can play all the others...* The powerful dramatic roles she'd longed for. Feared were forever beyond her reach even before Barry Robards had made it clear that he'd given her this role chiefly because of her stunt prowess and physical training. But she'd hung up the phone, elated, determined to prove to the world that there was far more to Emma McDaniel than that.

And what if you find out there isn't? Doubt trickled a chill down her spine.

"Why so quiet?" Butler broke in as he pulled up to the intact tower and put the car in Park. "Not quite up to your five-star hotel standards? You're more likely to get a rat on your pillow tonight than a mint."

She should have given him a verbal slap to put him in his place. But she sat, so overwhelmed for a long moment she couldn't speak.

This was the last thing Lady Aislinn had seen—siege engines hammering the walls, inexorably pounding away at the stone. Her home, lost to her forever.

Emma remembered the home she and Drew had shared in

Brentwood, their lives disappearing out of it one cardboard box at a time, just like their promise to love each other forever. But Emma had a life of her own. A career, her gift. What had Lady Aislinn had to cling to when this castle had fallen?

Rain drove against the stone walls like tears from time gone by. Butler opened his door and maneuvered his big body out of the car.

Emma climbed out, rain soaking her hair and sliding down the back of her neck as she made a run toward the door. Too late she realized Butler was ahead of her, intent on getting out of the rain, while her five-hundred-ton suitcase was still in the back of the car.

Bastard. He'd left it there on purpose, for her to manage herself. Fine. Emma slid into the car again and popped the hatch back. Gritting her teeth, she climbed back out into the rain, then slogged to the rear of the Mini Cooper. Heels sinking in mud, she grabbed the handle of the suitcase and pulled. Her knuckles banged against a bolt inside the car.

Emma's eyes stung as she tugged on the case, wriggling it back and forth, working it toward the edge until it slid free. She squawked, unable to stop the momentum, the heavy case falling toward the mud puddle she was standing in. She swore, fought, but the corner of the case crashed to the ground with a miserable splat. Cold mud splashed up under her raincoat, her shoes soaked through.

Sodden hair clung to her chilled, wet face as she heaved the suitcase up out of the mud, staggering under its weight as she made her way toward the dark mouth of the door.

When she finally trudged into the dank chamber beyond, she waited for warmth to envelop her, for lights to blaze on, driving back the dank gray curtain of storm.

It was June, for God's sake, but the place was still freezing. She started to shiver.

Butler grinned at her in the beam of a gigantic flashlight, the jerk. A real barn burner of a smile. "Dragging that out was a waste of time," he said, gesturing toward her dripping suitcase. "Everything in it is off-limits for the next six weeks."

"Excuse me?" Emma knuckled water out of her left ear, sure she couldn't have heard him correctly.

"Call it method-acting boot camp. You don't get to keep anything from the modern world."

He was enjoying this far too much.

Pure devilment pricked at Emma. "I don't even get to keep my stash of tampons?" she asked, itching to get a reaction. After years of marriage, Drew had still blushed when she asked him to pick up a box at the drugstore.

Butler only frowned.

"Come on, Butler. Don't get all shy on me," Emma sniped. "I'll be here for six weeks. The issue is bound to come up."

"I guess you'll have to deal with it when the time comes."

"No. My maid would have to deal with…well, whatever. Even you can't be idiot enough to expect a modern woman to—"

"I expect anyone on this site to do what I tell them."

"Fine. When my time of the month comes, I'll announce it to the whole camp."

Butler's eyes narrowed. "You'd be just bullheaded enough to do it, wouldn't you?"

"You betcha, mister." Emma tried with all her might to keep from shivering. "After all, who died and made you Mussolini?"

"Your director, as a matter of fact." Butler rubbed his chin. "All right, Ms. McDaniel. Keep your tampons if you must. In the end, one small concession on my part won't make any difference. You're not tough enough to survive without all your luxuries. I'll wager there are plenty of other things in that suitcase you'll be missing before your time here is finished."

The glow of triumph she'd felt at unsettling him vanished as the reality of his ultimatum struck her. "There's no way I'm giving up what's… There's something else in my suitcase I…I have to…"

"What? Designer drugs? Your silk knickers?"

"It's none of your business." Emma faced him down, hands on her hips. "It's something I need. Got it, Butler? Isn't there anything you need? Besides a personality transplant, I mean?"

Butler's green eyes blazed even hotter, but something in the taut line of his mouth betrayed him. She'd hit a nerve and damn, it felt good.

"One thing," he snarled. "Got it? You can keep one thing. Agreed?"

Emma tried not to let him see the relief flooding through her. "Agreed." Instinctively she extended her hand to shake on it. Butler gave her a long look, then his large, work-roughened hand swallowed Emma's much smaller one in a grasp that was brazenly masculine, surprisingly straightforward. Her fingers, strong in their own right, tested in countless stunts over the years, felt almost delicate for the first time since she'd left her hometown when she was just sixteen.

Heat pulsed between Butler's palm and hers. The archaeologist's eyes widened just a touch; Emma's breath caught. She pulled her hand away and flattened it on the front of her slacks, as if trying to erase the feel of that strange, hot throb.

"Maybe we'll be able to work together without killing each other after all."

"I wouldn't count on it." Butler folded his arms over his chest, palms against the nubby wool of his sweater, and Emma wondered if he felt the same strange compulsion to buff the feel of her off his hands. It made him seem a tiny bit more human.

"I'll give you this much, Butler. At least we know where we stand with each other. Hate at first sight."

"You have to care enough about somebody to hate them," Butler said.

"Well, all-righty then. That gives me something to aspire to. I assume you have some work to do besides irritating me. So if you could show me where I'll be staying, we can take a break from each other, at least for a little while."

"I thought you'd like to stay in Lady Aislinn's chamber," he said so pleasantly that Emma knew damn well not to trust him. And yet, how bad could it be? Emma reasoned. Aislinn was the lady of the castle. It had to be the best room of all. She'd seen those old movies where the beds were draped in velvet bed hangings and the walls were hung with tapestries and fires blazed in hearths the size of garden sheds.

"Terrific," she said, her teeth starting to chatter. "I don't suppose there are any flashing neon signs to show me the way."

"No. Just take those stairs up to the top of the tower. I guess we'll see what you're made of, Ms. McDaniel. After Sir Brannoc took the castle, Lady Aislinn spent three months in that room. Until Sir Brannoc forced her out. If you can't manage to stay there for six weeks…"

"I'll manage," Emma insisted, her chin bumping up a notch.

"Some even claim that she hid the fairy flag right there."

Emma's eyes widened in fascination. "The one that was supposed to keep the castle from falling to an enemy as long as the flag flew inside its walls?"

"No. The other fairy flag. The one with Tinker Bell on it."

Emma ground her teeth, knowing the man was pulling her chain on purpose, knowing, too, that the less she rose to the bait, the sooner Butler would give up his efforts to torment her.

"What? Nothing to say, Ms. McDaniel?" Butler asked.

"Did you expect me to be impressed that you bothered to read the script? The fairy flag is an integral part of the legend."

"A gossamer-thin piece of cloth brought as Lady Aislinn's dowry," Emma supplied. "A gift of the fairies to be passed down to the most beautiful daughter born to the chief of Clan MacGregor. A hundred suitors filled her father's hall, all vying to win her hand in marriage so they could become invincible."

"A good way to be certain your daughter was well treated once she was married and beyond your care. Husbands had total power over their wives then. The woman who dared put a gold circlet on Robert the Bruce's head was imprisoned by her angry husband for four years in a cage shaped like a crown hanging outside the castle."

"Nice guy. But then, you did warn me to head across the water to Ireland if I wanted charm. What happened to the lady?"

"The countess survived. God knows how."

"A life lesson you should take to heart. Never underestimate a pissed-off woman. She hung on so she could make her husband's life a living hell. But this whole fairy flag thing—obviously you're a pretty big boy to believe in the little people, Butler. So what's the story? Exactly what was the fairy flag really?"

"We'll never know." An intriguing light sparked in Butler's intelligent eyes and for an instant Emma glimpsed an enthusiasm, a warmth, a wonder that transformed his face. "If scientists could get their hands on a piece of it now, we'd be able to test it, hopefully date it, compare it to cloth samples from ancient times all over the world. We might be able to make an educated guess…"

Passion. He radiated it, so hot Emma couldn't help wondering what it would be like to be the woman who inspired that zeal, that intensity. Her tongue moistened her suddenly dry lips.

In a heartbeat, Butler seemed to remember who he was talking to. The stony mask of dislike fell back across his face, leaving Emma even colder than before. "It doesn't matter. The flag was lost forever when Lady Aislinn disappeared."

"Maybe I'll spend my spare time having a look around the room," Emma said. "Find the fairy flag after hundreds of years."

"We archaeologists would really appreciate it. After all, nobody in the past six hundred years has thought to look for the flag in that room. All those treasure hunters over the centuries, countless teams of scholars and experts—we all just wanted to leave it there for you, so you could make the cover of *Hello* magazine."

"There's no such thing as bad publicity." Emma tossed her hair. "Just think what a great promo it would be for the movie." She snapped out the handle of her suitcase and started rolling it across the bumpy stone floor toward the stairs.

"There's no point hauling that thing up three stories," Butler warned. "Just take out whatever you *need* right here."

Emma's cheeks burned. Damn if she was going to let this jerk watch her rummage through her suitcase, let him see…things that were private, things that were precious, things that still made her heart ache. Chinks in the walls six years of living in the public limelight had forced her to build.

No way was she going to open herself up for more of Butler's mockery. She was going to haul her suitcase far from his scornful gaze. She was going to slip out her treasure when she was safe, silent—alone.

If it was the last thing she did, she was going to get her suitcase to the top of the tower.

"Hey, I told you to open the damn thing here."

"So you can sneak a look at my underwear?" Emma said, doggedly hauling the suitcase up the first stair. "Think again, bud."

"I may be the one man on earth who doesn't give a damn what color your panties are, you stubborn little…"

She smacked her bag against the stone as loud as she could to drown out whatever he'd decided to call her. But she hadn't bumped the suitcase up half a dozen stone risers before she wondered if doctors in archaeology knew anything about CPR. The weight of the case was going to leave her with gorilla arms stretched down to her knees.

She heard a growled oath, heavy footfalls behind her. With an unladylike grunt, she was pulling the suitcase halfway up another stair when suddenly Jared Butler grabbed the handle away from her, his hand warm and rough, impatient and un-yieldingly masculine.

For a pulse beat the narrow stairway pushed them together. His arm bumped against her breast. The smell of him—rain and spice and exasperation—filled Emma's head.

"I can handle this myself!" she objected.

"Sure you can. Just like you can play Lady Aislinn." He was already striding up the dim stairs, both his form and the beam of flashlight vanishing in the shadows ahead.

Emma did the only thing she could. Stormed up after him. Her lungs were sucking like bellows by the time she reached her room. But in spite of her vow not to let Butler see her sweat, she couldn't hide the dismay that washed over her as he shone the flashlight over the chamber.

Moisture penetrated cracked walls with the kind of damp-ness that would never really get dry. A bed stuffed with God knew what was blanketed with…skins of dead animals…with the fur still on.

"What…what are those?" Emma asked, unnerved.

"Wolf pelts, stag skins. Whatever you could kill here-abouts in the fourteenth century. Pretty amazing, isn't it? Thinking those skins used to be on some wild animal?"

"Yeah, well, maybe I'm allergic. You can see the feet and—and holes where the eyes used to be in those things. God knows what else might be under all that fur."

"Once we get the hearth burning the smoke should drive out most of the bugs."

"Bugs?" Just the mention of them made Emma's skin crawl.

"I know how important historical accuracy is to you," Butler said. "So if you feel any bugs biting you tonight, just chalk it up to research."

"You're hilarious, Butler."

"Come morning, you're going to find out just how much fun I can be. Meanwhile, I'll send one of the grad students up with your dinner once it gets too dark to dig. Make sure you find your iPod or PalmPilot or whatever is so damned important so that your suitcase is ready to be hauled out of here by then."

"Fine."

"Use tonight to settle in. I'll be taking the flashlight with me."

And then the room would be movie-theater dark. She'd probably break her neck tripping over something. No wonder Angelica Robards hadn't survived the training process without a trip to the hospital.

"Terrific," Emma said, still warily eyeing the animal fur. "It'll be just me and Bambi here." Alone. In the dark. With a whole colony of bugs, no doubt planted by Attila the Scot.

"I'll light up the fire and one candle for you. After that, you're on your own. Everything you'll need for the next six weeks is in that wooden chest over there."

"I don't suppose there's a medieval Porta Potti in it."

"No hot water either. We jerry-built a garderobe in an area beyond the dig site. The student will show you where it is. Starting first thing in the morning you're going to get a crash course in medieval life in Scotland. You're going to eat, sleep and breathe the life of a Scottish chatelaine."

"A chat-a-who?"

"A noblewoman caring for her husband's castle while he's off fighting for his king."

"Isn't that just like a man," Emma quipped. "Running off to play with the other boys, leaving the responsibilities to the woman."

"Despite all the twisted shite people get fed in movies, with fainting damsels in distress needing to be rescued, medieval women were a strong lot. I suppose we'll find out what you're made of."

"Yes, you will. May I give you one little bit of advice?"

"I doubt gagging you with duct tape would stop you."

"Try not to drop me over a cliff, Dr. Butler, no matter how great the temptation. Damaging one actress is an accident. Damaging a second would look downright suspicious."

"Not by medieval standards. Men could go through a half dozen wives between accidents and disease and childbirth. And in desperate cases you could always lock her in prison somewhere."

"Like Henry II did Eleanor of Aquitaine."

Butler looked taken aback. "You read about…?"

"I saw the movie. *Lion In Winter.* Katherine Hepburn won an Oscar in the starring role."

"You're sure as bloody hell no Katherine Hepburn," Butler scoffed, starting for the door.

Cold, wet and tired, Emma sobered. That was what she was afraid of.

THERE WAS NO QUESTION of escape. Jared glared out the office trailer's window to where the mess tent blazed with lights, even more dancing shadows silhouetted against the canvas than there had been when he'd checked the same scene an hour ago.

It seemed that no matter how many times he paced the

narrow aisle between his desk and drafting table, every student on the site was determined to wait out his appearance, no matter how physically and mentally exhausted this day full of mud and rain had left them.

He might as well get it over with, he reasoned, reaching for the cool logic of a scientist. Sooner or later he'd have to face his students and endure their barrage of questions about their famous guest. But damn if he wanted to listen to the kids whose intellect he'd prized raving about Emma McDaniel, dazzled by the glitz and glitter of a world Jared didn't trust.

Having her here is the price you agreed to pay, he reminded himself grimly. He hoped he wouldn't discover that cost was too high. Bracing himself, he stepped out into the night. A hunter's moon sailed the sky, limning the world in silver.

Biting wind, still fresh from the afternoon's storm, tangled invisible fingers through his hair as he removed the battered brown canvas hat he'd hung by its leather cords on the outer doorknob. The wide-brimmed hat dangling there was a signal every bit as dreaded by the students and staff alike as a skull and crossbones would be on the high sea.

Only someone with a death wish would disturb Jared those rare times the hat appeared on the door. But he'd bet that several of his students had considered braving his wrath tonight. Thankfully, nineteen-year-old Davey Harrison, Jared's personal assistant and longest-running team member, had managed to dissuade them.

But damn if Jared was going to waste any more time trying to sort through the feelings Emma McDaniel stirred in him. The anger, the outrage, the sensation of being trapped. Between Angelica Robards' training and accident and Emma's arrival, he'd surrendered too many precious days already. With every hour that passed, the end of summer crept closer. And the end of summer meant the dig had to close.

At least not permanently, Jared reminded himself with grim satisfaction. The university that had sponsored the study for students from around the world might withdraw its funding, move its program on to some site in Greece—just for variety's sake, to give the kids a different kind of experience. And the grant funds he'd hoped for might be promised elsewhere. But Jared had found his own way to keep the dig afloat. By selling the rights to his book to Hollywood, making a pact with the devil. It seemed even Jared's soul had its price. The hard part was forcing his pride to pay it.

He'd imagined celebrity mania would poison the kids when they heard of Jade Star's imminent arrival. The reality was even worse.

From the most insecure undergraduate to his most trusted assistant, they all but stampeded him as he entered the mess tent, the kids barely giving lip service to his questions about any finds that had been made in his absence.

"What's she like?" a breathless kid on foreign study from Northwestern University pleaded.

Too brave. A little wild. Trying to protect that air-brained girl in the airport the only way she could.

"She's a pain in the arse," Jared said.

"Is she really as beautiful as she looks in the movies?" Nigel Sutherland asked.

Jared didn't bother to hide a smug grin as he recalled Emma McDaniel's rain-soaked million-dollar face, with ropes of wet black hair straggling across it. *That* picture made him feel better. The poor wee bairn, going to bed with sodden hair and not a blow-dryer in sight.

"With all those movie tricks they use, Hollywood could make *me* look like Prince William," Jared growled.

"That would be a crying shame," a coed named Gemma whispered to Veronica Phillips, a fresh-talking doctoral candidate from St. Andrews who had made it obvious that the body she hoped to uncover this summer still had plenty of life in it and belonged in her bed, not some museum.

"Why tamper with perfection?" Veronica teased, flashing Jared a sultry grin.

Jared was man enough to be tempted on a purely physical level. It had been a long time since he'd let himself take what a woman offered, but he knew firsthand that the price was too high. The danger too great. That part of him was dead. He'd killed it, as surely as he'd killed Jenny.

Where had that thought come from? He'd buried Jenny, the way Vikings buried their treasure hordes, then tried to forget where he'd left all the memories, all the self-blame.

He'd become an expert at seeming oblivious to women's flirtations, ignoring Veronica's comment as he had all the other glances filled with soulful feminine longing that had been thrown his way over the past ten years. Damn, if they knew how much he hated it, that adoring light that told him what they were thinking—that they fancied him a modern-day Lancelot come to save his fair lady from the stake.

If only they knew that was one quest he'd already failed.

"Emma McDaniel's coming here is quantitative proof that life is not fair," Davey Harrison said at the edge of the crowd. The favorite student Jared wasn't supposed to have shook his head wistfully, then plopped a canvas hat identical to Jared's down on his flyaway dark blond hair.

"Exactly what do you base your conclusion on, Mr. Harrison?" Jared asked.

The kid actually smiled. "In the men's dorms back home, every other room had a poster of Jade Star on the wall and the ones that didn't only took 'em down because their girl-friends made 'em. And what does God do? Dumps the god-dess herself into the lap of the one man on earth who hasn't fantasized a hundred times what he'd do if he could get his hands on her."

"Hey, Einstein's right!" Sean Murphy jabbed his nearest cohort with an elbow. "*That's* what I call a crying shame."

Jared shot both kids a quelling glare. "What's a shame is wasting time on this nonsense when we only have three months before this dig closes for the year," he growled. "Fall term will start faster than you know and then it'll be back to school for the lot of you. Of course, you can read about my brilliant discoveries in *National Geographic*."

Davey grinned, worlds different from the anguished fifteen-year-old who'd first come to the castle on a field trip four years ago. "Internet's faster, chief."

"So you keep telling me." Jared grimaced. Davey was right. The information superhighway put a wealth of research at people's fingertips. And as a scientist, Jared had to learn to access it. But somehow all those flashy graphics never felt as right to him as the solid weight of a book. Computer-generated illusions, everything from dinosaurs to heroines like Jade Star, airbrushed so her body was centerfold perfect the way a real woman could never be. It was one more way to con people into believing the impossible existed.

And yet, there had been a moment when Jared had been struck by Emma McDaniel's charisma just as hard as a green kid like Davey. That stomach-spinning, world-falling-away, dropkick-to-the-solar-plexus awareness that made him cadgy as hell when he'd felt the softness of her breast yielding against his arm.

When she'd defied him, those dark eyes spitting fire, her mouth ripe and passionate and real, without so much as a smear of lipstick. She'd faced him down with the fierce beauty of the wildcats that roamed Scotland's hills. Confronted him with the dauntless courage he'd imagined in Lady Aislinn.

Don't be a fool, man, he warned himself. *She's a spoiled brat with the depth of a rain puddle and she's surly because you didn't hit your knees the moment you first saw her so you could worship at her shrine. There's nothing of Lady Aislinn in this pampered, no-talent excuse for an actress.*

"Chief?" Davey's concerned voice cut through Jared's dark thoughts, reminding him of just how much the boy had had to worry about when he'd first set foot on the site years ago. How lonely Davey had been, isolated, outcast. A kid, troubled about grown-up things in a capricious world he had no control over. Worries that had faded to the back of Davey's mind the deeper the kid was drawn into the history and artifacts, the research and legends that wove like mist about the ruins of Castle Craigmorrigan.

And now, enter Emma McDaniel stage right, to drag the healing boy back to a real world full of things he couldn't have, security he'd never know, a present tense that could only suck him back to barren places. She'd shove Davey aside the way the pretty girls on the site did, giving the gawky kid a dismissive once-over, complete with that scathingly superior plastic smile. And from that moment on, she'd look right through him.

Just the thought made Jared's blood boil.

"Chief?" Davey repeated. "Are you all right?"

He'd be a lot better once Emma McDaniel took her shapely backside across the ocean to Hollywood, where it belonged. "Aye. And since you're all so curious about our new visitor, maybe you'd like to shake out of your tents at five in the morning instead of seven. Make up for the time you're all wasting jabbering about her."

A couple of the girls' faces paled. Others beat a hasty retreat toward the tent flap door.

"Veronica, take Miss McDaniel some food," Jared ordered.

Veronica pouted for a moment. "But I've got some work to catch up on."

"Taking a tray up to the tower will take you all of twenty minutes," Jared snapped. "You can spare that much time."

"Hey, chief," Davey interjected, eager as a puppy. "I'd be happy to do it."

No kidding, Jared thought sourly. Davey would probably be so dazzled by the woman he'd trip on the uneven stone stairs and break his neck.

"I need you to go over the finds you made while I was stuck at the airport. We need to enter them on the site grid."

"Oh. Uh, sure."

"Veronica," Jared said. "After you drop off her dinner, be sure you confiscate that suitcase of hers."

Davey gave Jared the big eyes. "Isn't that kind of heavy for a lady to…"

"As a matter of fact, it was heavy as a rock. Veronica, take one of the lads with you to handle lugging that monstrosity down the stairs. *Not* you, Davey," Jared added sternly. "You I need. To do the job we're here for."

Even as he herded Davey back toward the trailer, Jared knew he was only postponing the inevitable. The kid would have to meet Emma sometime. Jared would put it off for as long as he could.

It was well past midnight when Davey headed to his own cot, still nattering on about Emma McDaniel. By then Jared's very last nerve felt ready to snap. His blood seethed with edginess as he retired to his own roomy tent, dread banishing any hope of sleep.

Emma McDaniel's heart-shaped face swam before him, that pugnacious chin, those flashing eyes. She'd challenged him, fighting to keep God knew what from that elephantine suitcase. *Isn't there anything that* you *need?*

In the beam of a lantern, Jared went to the battered foot-locker where he kept his few, most treasured things. *Never weigh yourself down with more than you can carry...* The thought whispered through him, a familiar refrain.

Jenny had claimed he'd never been the same after studying the excavations in Pompeii. Maybe she was right. The citizens of the doomed city, who couldn't leave their precious things behind when the volcano erupted, had lost the only thing that mattered.

Jared lifted the trunk lid, his fingers running reverently over a flannel-wrapped bundle. Yes, there was something he needed. He'd just have to make damned sure Emma McDaniel never discovered what it was.

Chapter Three

THE WIND SANG its night song to the sea, a centuries-old lamentation of lovers who would never come home. Emma perched on one of the stone benches that flanked an alcove big enough to hold Butler's car. Leaning her elbows on the crude table filling the rest of the space, she peered out the tower window, a view of the rugged Scottish coast that formed the castle's rear defense spilling out beneath her.

Everything about Castle Craigmorrigan seemed ready for war. The soaring walls, the cramped stone stairways in which only a defender would be able to swing his sword. Even the costume she'd wrestled herself into hours ago came complete with a small sharp knife in a scabbard which swung from the filigreed belt slung low about her hips. *It's called a girdle, not a belt,* she could almost hear Butler correcting her in disgust. And he would be right. She remembered the name from a class on costuming she'd taken at drama school.

"Yeah, well, for a genius you're not so smart yourself, arming me with a sharp object the minute I get to my room,"

Emma muttered as if the jerk could hear her. "Next time you tick me off I might be tempted to hand you your family jewels on a platter."

But instead of bracing her, Emma's outburst echoed hollowly in the tower room, leaving it even more melancholy than before. Curling her feet under the yards of saffron-colored linen shift and green wool skirts, she reached across the table.

Emma pulled the cast-iron candlestick closer to the piece of parchment she'd rescued from the trunk, the circle of light spilling over the letter she'd labored over for the past hour. Her fingers were ink stained, her words blotted and awkward at the beginning, but her writing had smoothed out some by the end.

She'd coaxed the crude quill pen all the way to "give hugs and kisses to everyone" before she'd surrendered to the lump in her throat, grateful at least that none but the shadows of Craigmorrigan would know of her tears. And this castle had seen plenty of heartache.

Her eyes burned and she swiped the back of her hand across them, determinedly forcing her gaze out the window to the moonlit night beyond. How strange that for years Emma had yearned for just this sort of quiet time to sort out her thoughts. But she'd barely been sequestered in Lady Aislinn's chamber an hour before she realized being alone wasn't such a great idea after all.

Tempted by silence, her memory spiraled back through years more happy than sad. The incredible sweetness of her first kiss, she and Drew both trying to pretend it was only practice for their parts in the senior play—his Romeo to her Juliet. Before the curtain closed, they'd promised each other their love story would have a happier ending.

She could see Drew's face streaked with tears in the courtroom where they'd eloped. Could picture the garden at March Winds, the guests at the thriving bed-and-breakfast her family ran joining in the impromptu reception her mom and Aunt Finn had thrown when she and Drew came home and surprised the family with the news.

She heard laughter echoing through the cramped New York loft where she and Drew had made their first home. Where they made love on a mattress on the floor, so sure they had forever.

Emma peered out the tower window at the solitary moon adrift on silvery clouds. Butler worried she wouldn't be able to get into character? Emma understood Lady Aislinn far better than she cared to admit.

Lady Aislinn had felt her heart rip as the husband she loved tore away from her to go warring for his king. The medieval lady trapped, pitted against a nemesis she hated.

Both women knew how it felt to be utterly vulnerable, exposed to a world that fed on any weakness.

Emma had come to the wilds of Scotland hoping to find haven from the battering of her defenses, her most private pain stripped bare. But it was already obvious that in coming to Castle Craigmorrigan she'd only leapt from the frying pan into the fire. Jared Butler would like nothing better than to discover the chinks in her armor. And Emma had already proved far too easy a mark for the Scotsman's dirty tricks.

Grimacing, she glanced down at the furs she'd used to cushion the stone bench beneath her. She touched a stray tag the archaeologist had forgotten to snip off. The furs and doubtless the bugs he'd threatened her with "Made In China."

Of course, if she'd been thinking more clearly, she'd never have fallen prey to Butler's attempt to bait her. She'd known from the beginning that the bed across the room wasn't six hundred years old, that the tower chamber was stocked by Butler with replicas of old things. The clothing she'd put on and the parchment, ink and quills she'd laid out on the table were nothing more than props, like the polished metal mirror and the comb she'd abandoned after getting it hopelessly tangled in her masses of dark hair. And yet…

Perhaps the furniture and the accoutrements were merely illusions Jared Butler had created to evoke the fourteenth century. But some things in this chamber were real. Loneliness pooled in the shadows. Isolation bled from the stones. Sorrow ages old plucked with spectral fingers at the hem of Emma's gown.

She couldn't remember a time when she didn't sense things most people were oblivious to. Faint whispers through the veil of time, as if lost souls wanted someone to know they'd once lived, imprinting their emotions into walls and wood, china cups and cloth they'd touched generations before.

Here, in this ancient Scottish castle, those sensations felt as real to her as the treasure she'd placed on the table: her talisman on movie locations all over the globe, her way of bringing *home* with her no matter how far she wandered.

But even in the jungles of Malaysia or while filming in the desert, Emma had never been as miserable as she was tonight. Cold to her marrow, her ridiculously thick hair still damp, she felt more alone than she'd ever been in her life.

That's not true, a child's voice argued in her mind. *You felt exactly like this one other time. Remember? Ten years old, waking up in a stranger's room, your mother gone, leaving nothing but a note…*

Where had that thought come from? Emma shivered as decades-old emotions washed through her again. Terror, anguish, desperation as her uncle Cade raged, furious that his sister had abandoned Emma and vanished, leaving the traumatized child in his care.

Now Emma understood that her beloved uncle had been just as scared as she was that terrible morning. But her first taste of the famous McDaniel temper had shaken her badly.

Between her uncle, her much-adored grandfather and her cousins who'd inherited the family temper, she'd learned how to fight back in the ensuing years. And she'd done her best to bury the pain of her mother's desertion, focusing instead on the fact that Deirdre McDaniel Stone had come back for her.

Emma might be alone tonight in this tower room, but she was worlds different from the outcast child who'd once believed her only friend was March Winds' ghost.

She smiled wistfully, remembering how fiercely she'd clung to that kindred spirit from another century, another girl's hopes and dreams captured within a Civil War era journal. Addy March would have been as fascinated by this castle as Emma was. For if ever there was a place perfect for ghosts, it was this rugged fortress with its soft curls of mist, moonlight on the water and the raging battle of waves upon shore.

Emma scooted closer to the window, the drafts chilling her as she peered out toward the sea, imagining home so far away. But all thoughts of her mother's laughter, her cousins' antics vanished as she glimpsed a quicksilver flash of something on the water. Her heart tripped. No. It couldn't be. She rubbed her tired eyes, struggling to focus, but the figure remained, dancing with death, no foothold beneath him except the churning waves.

A knight, Emma marveled, his armor gleaming in the moonshine, his sword flashing as he battled demons he alone could see.

Emma flattened her palm on the window, trying to remember to breathe as she watched the warrior battle with the sea, swinging his weapon with terrible grace, leaping and dodging, thrusting and parrying, the weight of his unseen world crushing down on broad, phantom shoulders.

A ghost? Emma's subconscious queried. How could it be

anyone else, out there on the waves? Emma of all people knew about ghosts. But whose spirit could it be? Lady Aislinn's husband, Lord Magnus, returned at last from King Edward I's French wars? Trying to fight his way back to her side to rescue her even centuries too late from the foe who had held her prisoner?

As if in answer, a gust of wind rattled the windowpanes. The draft that whooshed through the chamber catching the candle. Its flame leaped wildly, blew out.

Suffocating darkness rolled across the chamber like a sorcerer's spell, the moonstruck window glowing with new life of its own. She could see the warrior far more clearly now.

The phantom knight was tiring. Emma could feel it as if he were inside her, his battles her own. Pain wracked his muscles, exhaustion slowing the swings of his sword as if he were slashing it through air thick as water. He stumbled and Emma wanted to race down the stairs in spite of the darkness, find some way to steady him, urge him not to give up.

Just what are you planning to do? Butler's sneering voice demanded in her head. *Grope your way through the castle in the dark? Even if you didn't break your neck on the stairs, you'd fall off the sea cliffs and drown.*

But how else could she know for sure? Emma's subconscious asserted stubbornly. See if *he* was really there? This warrior trying to fight his way back to the lady he loved even though a chasm of centuries now yawned between them?

And why did it matter so much to her? To prove this phantom was real? A man fighting for love instead of giving up, the way she and Drew had two years ago?

Damn Butler and damn her own good sense! She was going to find out the truth, no matter what....

But she'd barely taken a step away from the window when the warrior made a final wild swing with his sword. She saw the bright blade waver, fall. The knight crumpled to his knees, wind ripping at his silvery hauberk. He yanked a helm from his head, dark hair tumbling about a face she couldn't see. The sea raged in triumph around him, sucked him down under the waves until he vanished, far beyond her reach.

It was over. Emma sank back down onto the bench, her heart a raw wound in her chest. No question who had won both battles tonight. The knight lost to his ghosts from the past, Emma to demons so old she'd thought she'd forgotten them.

But wasn't that the hard truth they forgot to tell you in fairy tales? Emma thought sadly.

Sometimes the dragon got to win.

JET LAG COULD BE a beautiful thing—at least if your goal was to make someone as miserable as possible come morning. And that was exactly what Jared Butler had in mind as he tugged on his Barbour coat to head up to the castle. By his calculations, it must be the middle of the night in Los Angeles. Between the grueling twelve-hour flight with its half-dozen delays and spending her first night in medieval luxury, he figured the pampered Ms. Emma McDaniel must already be running on empty.

Of course, he'd be able to enjoy a whole lot more the prospect of her starting their first day of historical consulting with a bad case of sleep deprivation if it weren't for one minor hitch: he'd barely slept a wink himself.

He ran one hand over the rough stubble on his jaw and glared at his reflection in the shaving mirror nailed to one of his tent posts. He looked like he'd spent the night wrestling a wildcat. His eyes were bloodshot, the lines in his brow carved deep.

And damn if he didn't have a bruise on his arm where

Emma McDaniel had whacked him at the airport. Only because she'd surprised him, masculine pride nudged him to add. He wouldn't give her the chance to do it again.

His mouth hardened with what his father had called the *pure perishing for a fight* look he'd inherited from the mother he'd barely known.

Emma McDaniel might be a third-rate actress, but she'd demonstrated one talent he could attest to. He couldn't remember the last time a woman had made him so mad.

Hell, he couldn't remember the last time a woman had made him feel anything at all. For a heartbeat he remembered how warm feminine fingertips could be, how soft tracing the planes and angles of his body, how delicate the piercing pleasure as they feathered across his skin.

Damn Davey and the rest of the crew for putting thoughts of Emma McDaniel in his mind. *Drops the goddess into the lap of the one man who hasn't fantasized about what he'd do with her...*

Oh, he'd fantasized plenty since he'd gotten word McDaniel was invading Castle Craigmorrigan. Throwing her off the cliff. Hanging her from a tower. Packing her back on an airplane bound for America. But hearing Davey and Nigel extolling the woman's beauty had unsettled him in a new way.

Not that he'd ever been tempted by the nipped and tucked, painted and polished type of woman who spent hours perfecting herself in the mirror. Case in point: Angelica Robards. A woman who was not only drop-dead gorgeous but one of the most talented actresses of her generation. If she hadn't gotten under his skin sexually, then Emma McDaniel never would.

The Jade Star actress and everything she stood for made Jared furious. It wasn't thoughts of steamy, mindless sex that had wrecked Jared's sleep. What kept him up all night was knowing McDaniel would be making a nuisance of herself around the dig site, distracting his crew of students. The thought made him resolve to exhaust the woman so badly this morning she'd crawl up those tower steps begging for mercy, too tired to turn the heads of kids like Davey Harrison.

Entering the castle, Jared blinked, trying to accustom his eyes to the dimness, the dawn's haze that filtered through the arrow loops doing little to relieve the shadows. But he knew this site as well as he knew the rough lines and angles of his own face. By instinct, he crossed to the spiral stairs, taking fiendish delight in the dead silence as he strode up the stone risers. Perfect. His prey must be sound asleep.

As he neared the landing to Emma's tower room, his eyes narrowed in anticipation. No point in knocking. There was no door. One more realistic tidbit from the time of Lady Aislinn that Jade Star would have to get used to. A complete lack of privacy.

An unexpected image stung Jared: the tabloid headlines he'd seen in the airport. And he wondered for an instant what it would be like to have his most personal failures splashed across a gossip rag. When his marriage had crumbled he'd been able to bury himself in his work, lose himself in a past far less agonizing than losing Jenny had been. But the press could've had a field day with what he'd done if anyone besides Jenny's father and friends had cared enough to read about it.

Don't be an eejit. Butler crushed any sympathy he felt. Emma McDaniel had chosen the attention, the fame, the money, the fans clambering around her. What had Davey said? Every men's dorm room had posters of the woman plastered on the wall? Probably poses of her half-naked. What else could Emma McDaniel expect besides this feeding frenzy in the press?

Well, she was about to find out some men weren't impressed by a centerfold-worthy body or a lush red mouth or big brown eyes. The castle history claimed Lady Aislinn was distraught when Sir Brannoc and his mercenaries arrived? By the time Jared was through with Emma McDaniel, she'd welcome an invading army catapulting stones at her tower wall!

Jared crossed the threshold, the larger windows cut in the more defensible top of the tower spilling rose-tinged rays of dawn across the chamber. "Time to get up." Jared let his voice boom against the stone walls. "Can't waste daylight when candles are so expensive." Not to mention the cresset lights, rush lights and candles gave a far fainter light than audiences conned by costume dramas on the movie screen would ever have guessed.

What, not so much as a groan from Her Royal Highness? Jared strode to the bed, gave it a sharp kick to shake it. "This is your wake-up call—" he began, then froze. The piles of furs had barely been touched, the pillow still fluffed, no hollow formed by a sleeping head. The bed hadn't been slept in.

What the hell? Was it possible the prima donna had already taken off for greener pastures? No. He couldn't be that lucky. He hadn't heard a car start and God knew he would have. He'd heard every other damn sound around camp last night. She could hardly have walked all the way to the main road hauling that heavy suitcase.

His brow furrowed with a niggling of worry. Of course, somebody who came from L.A. wouldn't be stupid enough to hitchhike. It would be dangerous for any lone woman and downright suicidal for a celebrity.

There was no way McDaniel had gone that far, he reassured himself. More likely she went for a walk. But he hadn't seen a soul on his way to the castle. And over the years he'd loved this place, worked on it, he'd developed a sixth sense about anyone prowling around the space. He would have noticed. Unless she'd gone wandering around the cliffs in the dark and fallen. Impossible, he told himself sharply. He would have heard her scream.

His father-in-law's white-bearded face swam in his memory, the man who had once been Jared's mentor, so cold, so fragile, aged a hundred years since the last time they'd seen each other. *Don't pretend you even noticed what was happening to my daughter until it was too late. You always were a selfish man, Jared, lost in your own world...*

Last night Jared had been lost in his own world again. Just like he'd been with Jenny.

He rushed toward the window to look outside, but halted at the tabletop that had been empty the last time he'd seen it.

The rough wood now held a cluster of things carefully arranged. The ink and quills he'd packed in the chest, two sheets of parchment filled with writing and one object he'd never seen before, completely out of place with the medieval decor. A cheap purple, glitter-encrusted frame so dinged-up it might have gone a few rounds in the barrel of a clothes dryer. A thin crack snaked across the glass, dividing the photograph the frame held in two.

Jared picked up the frame, held it to the light. Christmas lights glowed against a backdrop of Norfolk pine so fresh he could almost smell the needles. What was obviously a family clustered before it. Two sets of parents wrangled a herd of sugar-overdosed children who were flashing sticky smiles at the camera. A sweet-faced redhead with dreamy eyes nestled close to a tall dark-haired man who looked about the right age to be Emma's father. Another man cradled a toddler in his arms, while a woman with restless blue eyes and a crop of Emma's wild dark hair laughed up at him.

Enthroned in a leather chair, a man of about eighty leveled a hawkish gaze at the camera. Emma, at least twenty in the picture, curled up on the old man's lap, her face so fresh and blooming it shoved hard at even Jared's cynical heart.

Leaning over Emma's shoulder, a young man with features more perfectly sculpted than Orlando Bloom's beamed as he held up her left hand and pointed to the flash of a diamond ring.

This picture with its ugly frame was the thing Emma had fought like a wildcat to keep from her suitcase? A family photograph with her ex-husband front and center? It was the last thing Jared would have expected someone like her to value.

And how had she spent last night? Obviously writing something. Two letters from the look of it. Jared glanced down at the pieces of parchment. Despite a dozen ink blots and painfully cramped script, he could see Emma had worked damned hard with the period materials at her disposal. *Dear Mom,* one page read. The other: *Hey Jake...*

Jake?

Jared hastened to put the frame back down. Hell, he'd almost started feeling sorry for her. But she already had some other man writhing on her hook—besides green college kids like Davey.

He almost walked away. Could hear the grandmother who'd helped raise him scolding from the grave. *Jared Robert Butler, for shame. Don't you even think of reading that lady's mail. Your father and I taught you better manners than that.*

Tried to teach him would be more accurate, Jared amended. He'd been the despair of both of them more often than he cared to remember.

In the end, his insatiable curiosity won out as it always had. But what better way to obliterate any shreds of empathy he might be tempted to feel toward the actress than reading her tale of woe? Line after line of how Jared had abused her. What a bastard he'd been. He'd been generous on that count anyway, given her plenty to bitch about.

Jared picked up the sheets of parchment, scanning Emma's letters. He frowned. Who the devil had written this thing? Because it sure as hell couldn't have been the pampered Emma McDaniel. She'd made her miserable flight sound like an adventure, her arrival at the castle so cheerful and full of enthusiasm Jared had to shake his head to try to clear his confusion. She'd warned this Jake to be on the lookout for a box she'd sent—a surprise for her mom—and promised to bring him back a kilt.

Anybody reading these letters would think the woman was having the time of her life, if one tiny detail hadn't betrayed her. Two watery splotches blurred the ink where she'd scrawled something about "hugs and kisses." Teardrops. Jared stared down at the marks, suddenly damned uncomfortable.

"So the lady cried," he growled aloud. "Why should you care?"

Good question. But somehow, deep down in his gut, he did.

Had he made her so miserable? So desperate that he'd driven a woman to risk… Jared's jaw hardened. Why should that be so hard to believe? His abominable temper had done plenty of damage before.

Guilt a decade old ground like a fist into his stomach. He pushed open the window frame, half-afraid he'd find Emma McDaniel lying like a broken doll on the rocks below.

Nothing. The cliffs were empty. He breathed in a sigh of relief. But he'd barely taken a step out of the alcove when voices drifted up.

He leaned out the window, pain vanishing in cold, clean anger as he took in the scene below him. Emma McDaniel, resplendent in medieval garb, strolled beyond chains that marked places as dangerous and out of bounds, while Davey Harrison stumbled along the precipice after her, his eyes so glazed with adoration Jared doubted he would even know he was dead until he hit the rocks below.

Maybe not, chief, but what a way to go, Jared could almost hear him say. Brash words and yet nothing Davey said could mask the almost invisible cracks Jared knew were inside the kid. Fissures akin to the ones in the medieval clay pitcher Jared and Davey had pieced together with painstaking care on the boy's first stay at the site.

Damned if Jared was going to let someone like Emma McDaniel breeze into the lad's life and carelessly dash it to pieces again.

Hands knotted in fists, Jared charged down the tower stairs, ready for battle.

EMMA BREATHED IN the sweet scent of her first Scottish morning, her thin leather shoes growing damp from the dew clinging to the tussocks of grass and springy moss around her. The cluster of tents at the far end of the broken curtain wall stood dead silent.

Thank God no one was stirring. Especially Jared Butler. Her cheeks burned. She didn't even want to think what the genius archaeologist would say if she told him she'd come out this morning to search for a ghost.

Especially since she'd already broken one of Mussolini the Scot's cardinal rules. *Don't be wandering around where you don't belong,* he'd roared at her in his sardine can of a car. *I won't have you contaminating* my *dig site.*

His? The land had been deeded over to the National Trust before Butler had been born, from what her research had said. And yet the Scotsman acted as if it were his own private kingdom.

Maybe the castle wasn't his exclusive domain, but the dig was. Even Barry had warned her to cooperate with Butler any way she could; the archaeologist's goodwill was vital to the film.

Well, at least she'd hedged her bets by obeying Butler's second warning, she rationalized. Obviously this section of the castle grounds wasn't part of the excavation. There wasn't a shovel in sight.

Of course the danger signs marking the rear of the castle as off-limits were a different matter. Strung at intervals on a thick chain between two concrete posts, the warnings were giant-sized, with big red letters.

"Nobody has to know I came back here," Emma rationalized as she made her way onto the narrow, rocky band that topped the cliff guarding the castle's back. "I'll just nip over to the cliff edge, take a quick look around and then beat feet out of here before anyone is the wiser."

If only it were that simple. Instinct made her want to hurry, afraid with every minute that passed that any remaining clue regarding the apparition might wash out into the sea. But she had to watch every step, gingerly testing each piece of moss-slick stone to see if it could bear her weight.

Breaking her neck on her first day at the castle would be a very bad idea. Especially when she thought of how pleased Jared Butler would be if she ended up out of commission.

But she'd never been able to resist mysteries like this one. Never quite shaken her fiercely held childhood belief in spirits who wandered the night and the gifts they could bring.

Ghosts or fairies like the ones in old Irish stories her Aunt Finn had told her, carrying warnings of impending doom or promising love so strong the person who won it would never die. After all, hadn't a ghost brought Aunt Finn into her life? Aunt Finn, who had brought Emma's mother back to stay.

Who knew what kind of luck the knight of the sea might bring?

Emma swore under her breath as her ankle wrenched, just enough to startle her.

"Ms. McDaniel?" Behind her a worried voice cracked the way Drew's had in middle school. Emma all but jumped out of her skin, tripping over the unfamiliar hem of her dress. The smooth leather soles of her shoes slipped on the damp rock and would have dropped her smack on her backside if a skinny young man of about nineteen hadn't grabbed her around the waist at the last possible instant.

She flailed, fighting to regain her balance. It only took a heartbeat for her instincts to kick in, and she murmured a grateful thanks to the skills she'd gained from stunts she'd done herself in the Jade movies. The beet-red young man couldn't have let go of her any faster if she'd caught his hands on fire.

"You shouldn't—shouldn't sneak up on people like that!" Emma gasped, pressing one hand to her thundering heart. "You scared the life out of me!"

"I, uh, yelled your name, Ms. McDaniel. I can't figure out why you couldn't hear me."

Emma's own cheeks warmed. Rueful, she smiled. "I guess I was…lost in imagining…"

The most gorgeous man I've ever seen… Of course he was gorgeous, and charming and, well, perfect. Because *he didn't really exist.* At least not anyplace except her imagination.

Maybe that was the key, just like her best friend in L.A. often said. *I like my imaginary men best.*

Emma couldn't stifle a smile as she pictured Samantha's eyes alight with her signature biting humor. Of course, the woman wrote books, so she spent plenty of time with imaginary heroes. She was still coming up with creative places to help Emma hide Drew's body.

Emma started, realizing her rescuer was staring at her. Oh,

Lord. She knew that starstruck look, and she absolutely hated it.

"I'm Emma," she said, extending her hand while she flashed him a warm smile.

The youth gave her hand a quick squeeze, then let go as if he expected her to disappear with the pop of a bubble, like Glinda in the Wizard of Oz. "Trust me, ma'am," he said. "There isn't a guy on earth who doesn't know who you are."

"This face is hard to forget." Emma twisted her features into the outrageous grimace she'd perfected to make her mom laugh.

The kid nearly choked on a surprised burst of laughter, coughing and sputtering so badly Emma had to pound him on the back.

"I…I'm David Harrison. Everybody calls me Davey. This is my…fourth summer…working with Dr. Butler."

Nothing like inviting the bad fairy to the princess's birthday party.

She'd pretend he hadn't mentioned Dr. Sexy Mouth. "Davey. Thanks for keeping me on my feet."

Davey's brow furrowed. "I wouldn't wander around back here if I were you. Dr. Butler doesn't like it."

Damn if that didn't tempt her to do cartwheels across the outcropping.

"The rocks are always slick and some are unstable," Davey added earnestly. "One of the undergrad students was playing around the first year the site was open and broke an ankle. Ever since, Dr. Butler has insisted this is off-limits. I'm surprised you didn't, er, well, read the sign. Or notice the chain…"

Emma frowned. "Nobody ever comes back here? But I thought I saw…" A ghost. A warrior. A man. *Oh, give it up, Emma.*

Davey regarded her intently. "You thought you saw what?"

Emma flushed. The last thing she needed was this kid telling Butler she was hallucinating. The jerk would probably call the studio and insist she take a drug test.

"Oh, nothing. I was just thinking…" Emma forced pure mischief into her smile. "Pity the castle doesn't have a ghost. Just think what a great ending that would make, mentioned in the closing credits."

"The script already has Lady Aislinn defeating a battle-hardened knight with a broadsword. Why not add one more ridiculous lie to the story?"

Emma stiffened, glanced over her shoulder. Butler. It wasn't fair that such an asshole should sound so sexy. Not to mention how well he fit into those pants. Thank God he'd had the rotten fashion sense to pull on some kind of olive drab oilcloth coat to hide most of the green T-shirt that almost matched his eyes.

"Here he is at last," she muttered, "the historical genius."

Davey turned, completely flustered as he saw the man charging toward them. "Dr. Butler," Davey stammered, the poor kid looking as if he'd just been caught burying chicken bones in one of the dig site's graves. "I… I was just—"

"Davey was keeping me company."

"Entertaining spoiled starlets isn't in his job description. Last time I checked the schedule, Harrison, you were supposed to head the team sifting through the dirt where we found that intaglio ring. Or do you want me to assign it to someone else?"

"No." Davey looked like Santa had just smacked him. "I'll get right to it." But instead of bolting in the wake of Butler's wrath, the youth squared his shoulders and turned to Emma. "He's not usually like this. He didn't get much sleep last night."

Jared's cheekbones darkened. "What does that have to do with anything?"

The youth gave him a look full of empathy. "When that happens you're a whole lot better dealing with dead people than live ones, I'm thinking."

Jared growled a curse.

"Just remember how you felt after the accident, Dr. Butler."

The archaeologist compressed his mouth into a hard, white line.

Emma tried to get her mind around what Davey had hinted at. Butler suffering guilt over Angelica Robards' fall from the horse? But then, it was only logical he'd feel terrible that the woman was on the injured list. Butler had made up his mind months ago that she made an acceptable Lady Aislinn.

Butler sucked in a deep breath reminiscent of Emma's yoga instructor. "What does the accident have to do with…?"

"It's the only reason I can figure you're acting this way." Davey faced Emma, exuding quiet dignity far beyond his years. "Goodbye, Ms. Mc…"

"Emma," she corrected.

Davey gave her a ghost of a smile. "Emma."

"I'm so glad to meet you, Davey," she said, touching the boy's arm. She hated to send Davey away with that worried expression on his face. Sensed the boy was serious beyond his years. She flashed him her grandfather's ornery grin, made sure her eyes sparkled with mischief as she leaned toward Davey and spoke in a stage whisper Butler was sure to hear. "It's nice to know someone around here gets up at the historically-accurate hour."

David didn't get the joke. "Oh, no, ma'am," he began earnestly, "the chief—"

"The chief can speak for himself," the Tyrant of Craigmorrigan said. "Get to work."

Davey shrugged and headed out of the line of fire, casting worried glances back over his shoulder.

"Keep your eye on the rocks, lad," Jared ordered. "I don't have time to take you to hospital!"

Davey's head snapped forward, eyes fixed front and center.

"Nice move, Butler." Emma tossed her curls. "And now that you haven't got anybody else to bully, maybe you could start the job the studio hired *you* to do. Unless you want to go back to bed?"

Dangerous, Emma. Thinking of Jared Butler and bed in the same sentence was a very bad idea. Especially since, at the moment, he looked all craggy and primitive, like one of those highlanders in the romance novels her aunt Finn loved to read. And with muscles like those, the jerk would have no problem flinging a woman over his shoulder and carrying her up the tower stairs. Of course, Emma would definitely scratch his eyes out the minute he dumped her amidst the made-in-China furs on her bed.

She brought herself up short. How had *she* ended up in Aunt Finn's book? Luckily, Butler didn't have a clue about Emma's unruly train of thought.

"I'm always the first person awake on this site and the last person asleep," Butler said.

"Not this morning, Dr. Sunshine. I've been up since…well, I wouldn't know the time since my Rolex is off-limits. But the moon was just gorgeous out my tower window. I curled up on that charming stone bench and watched the sea for ages."

Butler glanced up at the window Emma knew looked out from her room. Did the man actually look uncomfortable? What was that about? Certainly not concern for her. The Scot had all the sensitivity of her L.A. neighbor's pit bull.

"Everything I read on medieval times said people were up at first light," Emma said. "So I didn't want to miss my curtain call."

Lines carved deep between his brows and Emma was delighted to sense his irritation that she'd actually done some background research.

"So you *can* read then?" Butler taunted. "I was beginning to wonder, considering you obviously passed right by the danger signs I'd posted."

"Yes, well, I've spent my whole career catapulting across volcanoes and climbing sheer rock walls with hordes of natives chasing after me. I thought strolling across a few rocks was no big deal."

"You *thought?*" Butler took a step toward her. Damn if she was going to back away. She leaned deeper into his personal space instead, scowling back with Jade's take-no-prisoners glare.

"Yes," Emma said crisply. "I *thought.* I do it all the time."

"Well you're not doing it here. Do you hear me? No thinking. You do what you're told, when you're told. If I put up a sign that says jump, you ask off which cliff. And there is no ghost. Got it? I don't give a damn what kind of Hollywood candy floss you want to stick all over this story. These are historical figures you're dealing with now. Real people who deserve some respect."

"Respect?" Emma echoed in mock astonishment. "Are you sure you know the definition of that word or did they forget to ask that question on your way to getting your Annoying Genius badge in Boy Scouts?"

"I wasn't a Scout."

"Pity. It's been an amazingly civilizing influence on my cousin Will. Scouting just might have taught you manners. And as for there not being a ghost at the castle, that's something I'd love to remedy. *You'd* make a great ghost, Butler. One little trip off the cliff and my problems would be over. Then I could just have you exorcised or banished—or whatever psychics do to make ghosts disappear."

The corner of Butler's mouth curled, so smug she wanted to slap him. "*Priests* exorcise demons. And *psychics* are a load of codswallop."

Be careful, Emma, a voice inside her warned. Don't let him guess…what? That she'd spent last night imagining a ghost? That part of her would always believe in magic. Even now, after her marriage lay in ashes, she wanted to believe in a love so powerful that even centuries couldn't kill it. She wanted a happily-ever-after for the remarkable woman who had once lived in this castle.

Why couldn't she keep herself from asking? "You don't believe in ghosts?"

Shrewd green eyes flashed. "I'm a scientist. What do you think?"

"I'm not supposed to think, remember?" she reminded so sweetly she hoped Butler would get tooth decay. Rotten teeth. That was the perfect way to defuse the magnetism of Butler's criminally sexy mouth.

White teeth flashed, his smile all crooked. It was flawed, damn it. Asymmetrical. She knew people in L.A. who would have raced to a plastic surgeon to have something like that corrected. Butler should have looked awful. Instead he looked like an X-rated dream.

There's nothing you like about this man, Emma, she told herself. *Remember that. Not one thing.*

Except that libido-blistering smile.

Damn. Butler was watching her as if he knew what she was thinking. Those penetrating eyes swept her from head to toe.

Emma fiddled with the small gilt dagger at her waist. "Don't smirk at me," she warned. "It's irritating."

"Give me a few hours and I promise you'll be too tired to care. Let's go saddle up the horses." Butler leveled Emma an arrogant look. "You *can* ride horses, can't you? In the paperwork you filled out for the audition, you said you were an experienced rider."

"That depends." Emma pressed her hand to her heart, delighting in pulling his chain. "Experience can mean so many different things to so many different people."

"I'm keeping the question at a five-year-old's level since I'm still not convinced you can read." Butler kicked the metal sign with the toe of his boot. "Can you ride? Yes or no?"

"What do you think?" Emma challenged, hands on hips.

"I think I'm in hell." Butler stepped over the chain with his long legs. "But by nightfall I'm going to make bloody sure you're right there with me."

Chapter Four

THE BARN WAS DESERTED. The rest of the horses boarded at the nearby stable dozed in the morning sun as Jared tacked up Falcon, the black Andalusian stallion he borrowed to ride in mock tournaments and the dainty gray mare the studio had leased to play Lady Aislinn's beloved Morgan le Fay.

Jared regarded Emma with a mixture of smugness and irritation. Wary, she hung back just a little, struggling to mask her trepidation, acting nonchalant, but betraying her nervousness in tiny ways. Fidgeting with the end of her girdle, swallowing hard when she thought he wasn't looking, nibbling at her rosy bottom lip as she thrust out a hand for the mare to sniff.

"Don't let her bite you," Jared said. "She'll think you've brought her a carrot."

"Why?"

"Because I… Because horses are forever hopeful and I can't have her nipping off your fingers. The studio wouldn't like it."

"I wouldn't like it either." Emma curled her fingers back into her palm. "I faint at the sight of blood."

"We'll try not to spill any then." He glanced over toward the long canvas-wrapped bundle he'd brought with him, then figured he'd deal with it once he got the duchess up on her horse. Emma would undoubtedly need a few minutes once she was up top to remember how to breathe. "Mount up," Jared ordered.

"M-mount up. Right. I just put my foot in that metal thing and…"

"It's called a stirrup. I've already got it set to about the right length for your legs."

Emma sucked in a deep breath and then edged toward the mare.

"I'm playing the role of groom," Jared said. "He'd help you get up on the horse."

"I can—can do it myself."

"Sure you can. But we're going to pretend we're in the fourteenth century." He closed the space between them, too close for comfort. Her hair smelled delicious, like cinnamon. He linked his hands and crouched so she could put her foot into the cup his palms formed.

"Now just let me boost you up."

Obviously uneasy, she did as she was told, gripping his shoulder in a fingers-of-death hold. Her breast was inches from his face, her hair brushing in silken strands across his stubbled cheek.

Damn good thing they hated each other. Because if they hadn't, they might never leave the barn. "Ready?" he asked.

She nodded.

"One, two, three." He straightened, half suffocating in the folds of her gown as she tried to scramble onto the horse's back.

She gave a nervous squeak as she fought for balance, the mare sidestepping as Emma's arms and legs flailed like a snarl of Slinky toys, limp and useless, her body listing perilously. She seemed ready to slide off the opposite side as she grabbed the leather reins—completely by accident, Jared figured.

Smug as a cat with a mouse in its teeth, Jared started toward her to keep her from breaking her neck. But a split second before he could reach her arm, she nabbed the stirrups with her feet, leaned over the mare's neck and took off at a dead run.

Flashing him a diabolical smile over one shoulder, she left him eating her dirt. Literally. That was the major problem with gaping like an eejit when a horse's hooves were flinging bits of dirt and grass back at you.

Spitting out the grit and swiping the back of his hand across his mouth, Jared grabbed the long bundle, swiftly fastening it on the back of the suddenly restive Andalusian's saddle. He swung up onto the black and gave chase, but Emma had won herself a fine head start.

Reluctant admiration sparked inside him. Emma McDaniel sat on the horse as if she'd been born on one. Her silvery laughter echoed back to him as she splashed through puddles, mud spattering her gown, her hair a wild tangle as she lifted her face to the wind.

She used the mare's delicate legs to her advantage, flying above the ground like a fluff of dandelion seeds carried on the wind before a storm. Falcon thundered after her, the power that made him the terror of the recreated lists where Jared practiced with his lance doing little to close the last dozen meters between the two horses.

But maybe Falcon didn't want to catch them any more than Jared did at the moment. Maybe he wanted to enjoy the sight of two breathtaking female creatures running free. Far enough to the right side to see Emma and her mount in profile, Jared surprised himself, drinking in the sight. For with each stretch of countryside the mare flew across, Emma's smile glowed more luminous, the elegant curve of her cheek a deeper wind-stung pink.

When she'd bolted out of the barn fifteen minutes ago, she'd been showing off—elated to leave him in her dust and shatter his cynical doubt that she knew one end of a horse from the other. But the farther away from the stables they got, the more Emma and the mare seemed to bond, until they both looked as wild and ethereal as the magical creatures Jared's father had told him about when he'd still been young enough to believe in them. Women made of mist and imagination, so exquisite a man only had to look at them to fall deathly in love and pine the rest of his life for the fairy queen far beyond a mortal's reach.

Is that what happened to my mum? Jared remembered the night he'd finally dared to ask. *Did she wander into the mist and vanish to Tir Nan Og just like the fairy queen?*

Tears filled his father's eyes, his callused fingertips tracing Jared's cheek, scratching tender little-boy skin. *She might have done just that, lad. So far above this hard world of mine she was.*

Having a fairy queen for a mum was a lot easier on the heart than the truth his father had never been strong enough to face. But then, by the time Jared had been able to fathom the cold reality of his mother's desertion, Mary Calloway Butler was easier for Jared to understand than any fairy ever could be. After all, hadn't Jared proved that he was just like her?

Jared slammed his mind shut against the memories, drawing on his power to focus so intently on the task before him that his own past disappeared.

Within moments, he'd blocked out everything but the vast sweep of sky overhead and the green, boulder-strewn land below. And Emma McDaniel riding. In the distance he glimpsed an unruly burn, its winding length tumbling over one waterfall and then curving in an exquisite arc to dance down yet another.

The stream marked the end of the land they had permission to ride on.

Snib MacMurray, the farmer whose land abutted the opposite side of the burn, had told the studio to take the money they'd offered him to use his property as part of the set and cram it up their arse. He wasn't about to have a pack of foreigners tramping around, upsetting his sheep and making the cows' milk dry up.

But then, Snib had been surly for as long as Jared had known him. *Don't be taking Snib's insults to heart,* Angus Butler had soothed Jared as a boy. *Snib's the kind of man who took the defeat at Culloden Moor so personal he's determined to make everyone he meets suffer for it two hundred and fifty-odd years later.*

A roguish part of Jared would've loved to have seen Emma McDaniel meet the glen's most cantankerous resident. But the sooner Jared got through the day's training, the sooner he could get back to the dig. If he couldn't wear Emma out on horseback, he'd just use another method.

Jared called out, but if she could hear him, she pretended not to. She and her mare only flew faster, as if the woman was trying to keep her mount as far from his as possible. He got the distinct feeling she was doing her best to pretend he was a tree. Or a rock. Or more likely still, something that had just crawled out from *under* one, he thought with a wry smile.

Not that he blamed her. If he'd behaved so badly Davey felt obliged to make excuses for him, he must have exuded all the charm of a moray eel. Most women he knew would have been appalled by his temper already, but Emma McDaniel gave as good as she got. He remembered how she'd refused to back down behind the castle that morning, challenging him with dark eyes, leaning into his space as if daring him to…to…what? Kill her?

Or kiss her?

Whoa, man. Where had that thought come from? Too many months without a woman beneath him—that's where. A man could wall off his emotions, but defying biology was a tougher matter entirely. Any scientist knew that. The survival of the species depended on the male's urge to mate. And mating was all about the chase.

He squeezed his heels into the big stallion's sides, the animal surging in an effort to close the space between him and Emma's mare. But of her own volition, Emma reined in at the stream. She dismounted and, reins in hand, peered up at the waterfalls, her creamy skin and lovely profile making Jared's chest feel too small.

He drew rein beside her, the mare giving a whicker filled with satisfaction, the equine equivalent of "took you long enough to catch us." But from the mare's come-hither eyes, Jared wondered if the two females had let themselves be caught. One more part of the mating ritual, just to keep things interesting—tempting the male to a knife's edge of desire and then retreating.

But the theoretical analysis that usually took the edge off Jared's sex drive wasn't working nearly as well as it always had before. Not with the way Emma's full breasts curved beneath her surcoat, her slim waist accented by the narrow gold-filigreed girdle. Long nights alone he'd dreamed of a woman's body garbed like that, his hands stripping the layers away as if they were petals, with velvety feminine skin at the center. The only fantasies he'd let himself have since Jenny….

Don't think about her now. Don't think about anything except the job you're supposed to do here.

"So you decided to join us after all, Dr. S. M.," Emma said, her eyes dancing.

Jared knew she was itching to have him ask what she meant by the nickname, but he wasn't about to give her the satisfaction. He swung down from the stallion. Taking both sets of reins, he tied the horses to a low-hanging branch. "Angelica told me it was common among actors to say they ride when they really haven't had much experience. I underestimated you. I won't make the same mistake again."

Emma raked wayward black curls away from her face. One strand stuck to the corner of her bottom lip. Jared couldn't help staring at it.

"Before I read the script for *Lady Valiant,* my all-time favorite horses were the kind with candy-striped poles through their middles so they couldn't go anyplace but around in circles. I'd taken a trail ride once with my stepfather and then there was the pony ride at the county fair back in Illinois."

Jared tried to tear his gaze from the rebellious curl, fought an inexplicable urge to take his own finger and smooth it away just so he could have an excuse to touch that impossibly perfect lip. He reined in the impulse as ruthlessly as he would have reined in a stallion scenting a mare in heat.

"You learned to ride less than a year ago?"

"My best friend back in L.A. is a brilliant equestrian. She gave me a crash course on her Dutch warmblood, Arlie. I think he's the love of my life."

"Davey will be so disappointed."

"Yeah, well, Arlie and I suffered through a lot together during horse boot camp. I figure if Sam ever gets tired of the writing gig, she can be a gunnery sergeant. By the end of the month, my legs were so cramped up I walked like Festus in the *Gunsmoke* reruns my grandfather used to watch."

She demonstrated a bowlegged strut so foreign to her natural grace and elegance Jared was amazed. Never would he have guessed a polished woman like the actress before him would make fun of herself so freely.

Jared found himself smiling back at her. "So why didn't you call 'hold, enough' when Angelica was awarded the part? That was over a year ago. It's obvious you kept riding."

She flushed, impossibly thick black lashes drifting down to hide her eyes. "Know the funny thing?" she asked in a voice he'd not heard before. She laid her cheek against her horse's withers and slid her hand into the silky cove between the mare's mane and neck. "I never expected I would love riding so much. The freedom of it, the feel of the wind. It's not like motorcycles, you know? All noisy and spitting fumes in your face. On a horse, it's just you and the quiet, the peace, of being out in the hills alone." Her voice changed, a little wistful. "You'll never know how much I needed that."

Midnight eyes peered almost shyly into his. He could feel her waiting for him to make some wiseass remark.

Instead, he felt a strange kind of connection, a link he hadn't expected. He spoke to her for the first time without anger or acid wit. "I think I can guess."

How many hours had he spent on horseback with no one but the wind and the sky and his thoughts?

How strange that this exquisitely beautiful woman with her twenty-million-dollar paychecks and the world at her feet should feel the same thirst to escape as he did.

And yet, how hard must it be for her to get that time alone? With the press stalking her and her fans eager to devour any news about her private life. As if she owed it to them to expose her very soul.

Careful, man. Jared's cynical side nudged him. *Remember the lass chose this life. Fame is what she wanted.*

Why did that slick Hollywood existence seem so incongruous with the woman before him, silhouetted against the rugged Scottish landscape, banks of heather and clumps of crab apple trees?

Her eyes drifted closed and she breathed in deep against the mare's sleek coat. A pleased smile tipped the corner of lips more kissable than Jared had imagined a woman's ever could be. Damn if Emma McDaniel wasn't smelling the horse! That comforting combination of hay and leather and sweat that soothed Jared's ragged nerves so often.

"I'd love to have a horse once my life settles down a bit," Emma confided. "I adore Arlie, but…he's definitely Sam's baby. I want a baby of my own."

Strange, Jared thought. Hadn't the headlines on that gossip rag broadcasted that Emma didn't want children to ruin her gorgeous figure and muck up her career? That was why her husband had left her, wasn't it? But then, you could hire a groom to take care of a horse while you were gone for months at a time. And if you got tired of the commitment you could sell a horse. Children narrowed your options forever.

Guilt pinched Jared and he busied himself unlashing the bundle from the back of the saddle. He hated the feeling that he, too, was intruding into parts of Emma McDaniel's life that were none of his business. He had plenty of baggage he'd never want to share. Knew firsthand that suffocating feeling of…

He cut off the thought as the bundle slid free.

"What's that?" Emma asked, eyeing it with interest. "Some really long hot dogs for a picnic lunch…or breakfast. I keep forgetting what time it is."

"I brought the swords along so you could practice here. We're better off away from the site. We'd be a distraction. Here, we can bash around without a soul to hear us but old

Snib. And I'd actually like to irritate him. He's given me plenty of headaches himself."

"Headaches?"

"Putting the fear of God in my students if they dare wander onto his property. Accusing them of everything from sheep stealing to highway robbery when the worst they've done is steal a kiss or two among the standing stones."

"Why not stay right here? This brook would be a lovely place to…well, steal something besides sheep."

Jared chuckled. "The standing stones are supposed to make men more potent and ladies fertile. There's a story that when Lady Aislinn failed to conceive, she left offerings of flowers at the stones in desperation, hoping the spirit there would help her have a child."

"Did it work?"

"No. But I figure it wasn't the fault of the stones. It was more the fact that Lord Magnus was forever running off fighting for the English king."

"I thought the Scots hated the English. Especially…" She paused a moment, her brow furrowing with concentration. "Edward Longshanks, the Hammer of the Scots."

Surprised, Jared smiled in spite of himself. The lady had definitely done her homework. "King Edward didn't get the name Hammer until much later, but say what you will about the man's methods, he was canny as any fox. He gave Lord Magnus wealthy estates in England to buy his loyalty. Quite a dilemma for many Scots nobles. And our own king at that time had sworn fealty to Edward, so there were many who believed honor bound them to take up arms for England."

"And you?"

Jared regarded her a moment, surprised.

"If you'd been Lord Magnus, what would you have done?"

"My idea of honor is a lot closer to Sir Brannoc's. And

speaking of the most notorious mercenary of his time—" He took one sword and handed it to Emma, his hand brushing hers as he transferred the hilt into her grip. He felt the weapon tug her arm down by its sheer weight.

She quickly added the grasp of her other hand. "My Lord! This thing weighs a ton!"

Jared raised an eyebrow. "My point exactly. Think if I ship one over to your director he'll finally give this whole fight scene up?"

"No. And neither will I. It's great conflict. So powerful. And it's a brilliant symbol for all the strength Lady Aislinn has gained by the end of the script."

"Have it your way then." Jared sighed, taking up his own weapon. He ran his fingers down the flat of the blade, drawing from the familiar surface a sense of calm, of power, of invincibility. "Lay on, MacDuff. But when your whole body aches like a boil tomorrow, don't complain to me."

He lost himself in explanations, examples, demonstrating the simplest of fighting stances. He tried not to laugh as Emma's skirts tangled about her legs, inhibiting her stride. In spite of that, she proved to be stubborn as any Scot Jared had ever known. Demanding that he repeat moves again and again, scoffing when even he—bastard that he was—suggested she rest a moment, take a drink from the wine sack he'd brought along.

As it happened, he could have used a moment to collect himself. Clear his mind of the distractions that had surprised him: the soft swells of breasts straining against cloth as she raised her arms to swing, the alluring curve of hip and narrow waist, as time and again he divested her of her sword.

She lunged and parried, thrust and gasped for breath, like one of the Valkyries in legends left in Scotland by Vikings invading ages ago. But time and again, Jared swept the sword out of her hands until at last she didn't have the strength to lift it above her knees.

"See what I mean?" Jared said. "This whole sword-fight scenario is ludicrous. It's impossible for Lady Aislinn to win."

"Nothing…is…impossible." She wheezed, bending over, bracing herself on the sword. "One day I'll find a way to drop you like a rock. Just like Billy Callahan, the school bully."

Jared looked her over. "You look like a stiff wind could blow you away."

"It throws you arrogant caveman types off guard, and then—whamo. I get a perfect opening." She slanted a "damn the duchess" glare up at him, but her eyes twinkled.

"Is that so?"

She straightened, still breathless, her breasts rising and falling from the exertion. "My grandfather served in special forces. When I was ten years old he taught me how to fight. Death shots and everything. Consider yourself warned, Butler."

He grinned. "I'm pure terrified."

"You should be. As soon as I find a way to use all that weight and upper-body strength against you in a sword fight, mister, you're going to be on your butt in the dirt begging for mercy."

A horrible yelp split the air from across the burn, followed by a cacophony of snarling that made the hairs on the back of Jared's neck stand on end. Both horses skittered to one side. Emma caught her breath.

"My God!" she exclaimed. "What is that? It sounds like someone's killing something." She didn't wait for an answer. Damned if she didn't wade into the knee-deep water and slog toward the far bank!

"Emma, stay out of it! It's just old Snib setting his dogs on some poor—"

She stumbled, fell, soaking her left side. Didn't she know how wild the burn could be after a rainstorm? Full of swirling currents that could pull her under. Plunging after her seemed his only option.

That water was going to be so cold it would take care of any problems he might have being attracted to the woman. His ballocks were going to crawl up inside him and hide for a month!

He gritted his teeth on an oath as he plunged in after her, but she was already scrambling up the other bank. Just at that moment, the snarling tangle of what sounded to be canines boiled up over the rim of the valley that had concealed them thus far.

Snib's two border collies were tearing into what looked to be a ball of mange not even half their size, as the crusty farmer with his tweed cap urged them on.

"Take the little devil, Shep and Digger. Snap his fool neck!"

Snib's knobby old head suddenly jerked away from the fight, seeing the soaked woman stalking toward him with all the high dudgeon a straitjacket of wet wool skirts would allow.

"What the devil?" Snib swore. "You're that film star person who—"

"Call off your dogs!" Emma bellowed, grabbing a fallen branch about as thick as her wrist. "They're hurting him!"

"Hurting him? It's killing him they're after. I'll not have a thieving stray sucking eggs in my henhouse!"

Emma thumped one of the collies in the ribs, trying to bat it away. The collie yelped, but with the intensity of its breed kept battling what it saw as a threat to its flock.

"Don't hit the big dog, you crazy woman!" Jared yelled, clambering up onto the bank. "It could turn on you!"

Ignoring him, Emma whacked the second one while old Snib cursed her, but she might as well have been trying to knock out a swarm of bees with a cricket bat. Fangs flashed, tearing at the mangy dog, who fought back as if he were ten feet tall. One of the collies gave a yelp as the little dog launched itself and sank teeth into its shoulder. The bloody little fool held on tight.

Blood streaked the dogs' coats. And for an instant Jared wished Emma McDaniel would do what she'd promised—and goddamn well faint. The woman passing out cold was the only thing he could think of at the moment that might get her out of danger.

Emma flung away her stick, but it wasn't in surrender. Jared knew in his gut she was going to plunge headlong into the nastiest dogfight he'd ever seen and try to snatch the mutt to safety. Fear jolted through him as the image of Emma's hands torn and bleeding flashed in his mind.

He reached her just in time, encircling her waist with his arms, dragging her back against him. The woman kicked and struggled as if he were trying to haul her into danger instead of out of it.

"Don't! They're hurting him!" Her voice choked. With tears? He'd never know. Her heel connected hard with his shin.

"I'll get the damned dog if you settle down," he promised with a fatalistic grimace. "I'll heal faster."

She stilled, her breath catching in her throat, her breasts soft against his arm. He released her. Cursing himself six times a fool, Jared dove into the fight.

Chapter Five

"HAVE YOU GONE daft?" Snib shrilled in disbelief.

Pain pierced Jared's hand as one of the dogs bit him. Probably the little bastard he was trying to save. Another dog ripped at his shirt.

"Call them off, Snib." Jared's hands finally closed about the wriggling mass of fur. Jared booted the collie nearest him and pulled the little dog in to his chest. "Hey," Jared yelped in pain as the mutt snapped his sharp little teeth into the only thing he could reach—Jared's pecs.

"Down, Shep. Digger. Heel," Snib commanded. The collies dropped, shaking from tail to snout as they fought the urge to finish the kill. But if their master had changed his mind, they'd obey him.

Jared's hands dripped blood, the bite in his chest burned, the terrier eyeing him not with gratitude but plain old resentment for ending the fight.

Eyelids peeled back from black button eyes. The terrier showed its sharp fangs and yipped at his attackers as if to say

"Let me at 'em, bloody cowards." For God's sake, with its lip curled like that it looked like an angry rat—the kind who carried distemper and bubonic plague. A rat determined to bite whatever happened to be in reach.

Jared shifted the dog away from its apparent target: Jared's jugular. He didn't need another souvenir from this debacle. Sensing a chance to break free, the little demon writhed in Jared's grasp, flailing its spindly legs, its ribs so sparsely fleshed the bones seemed to grind together.

"Settle down, or I'll strangle you myself," Jared warned, holding on for dear life. Damned if he wanted to go plunging into the creek a second time in pursuit of the dog.

Emma swept off her surcoat, stepping close to Jared to cut off the mutt's hope of escape. In spite of the squirming flurry of dog in his hands, Jared noticed the points of her nipples thrusting against the damp linen of her shift. "Let me bundle him up in this," she said.

"He'll bite." Jared gritted his teeth as one of those razor-sharp fangs slit his knuckle. A thump on the head from God, Jared figured. *That's what you get for staring at a Good Samaritan's breasts.*

"He's just scared," she murmured, moving closer, crooning softly to the mangy creature. But she wasn't a complete moron. She used the cloth to protect her arms as she took the quaking scrap of dog out of Jared's grasp.

"I don't care how many rotten films you've been in back in America, lassie," Snib groused, wrinkling his nose at Emma as if he'd stepped barefoot in dog droppings. "You keep that stray away from my land or next time I won't bother me dogs, I'll just shoot it."

"You'll have to shoot me first!" Emma cried, outraged.

"Don't tempt me." Snib gave a thunderous snort from his bulbous red nose. "I've got no patience for interferin' women.

You tell her that, Butler. Now get on your own side of the burn, all three of you!"

Curving the arm that felt the least like a badly chewed sausage around Emma's shoulders, Jared urged her back toward the water. This time the cold felt good. As soon as he was sure she had her footing, he plunged his arms into the water, letting the chill cool his pain and wash away the worst of the blood. He only wished the water was deep enough to cover his chest.

By the time he joined Emma and the rat of a dog on the shore, the mutt had decided burying his nose in the nice lady's breasts was a far friendlier pastime than being savaged by a pair of collies.

Smart little bugger, Jared thought.

"I suppose we'll have to take the dog with us," Jared said, more to himself than to her. "It's stupid enough to swim right back over there to go another round."

"He's hurt. His ear's all torn. Is there a vet someplace close?"

"We won't be needing one."

"But—"

Jared shot her a quelling look, then shook his head in bewilderment. "You, there. Dog," he addressed the disreputable ball of fur. "What kind of eejit takes on someone so much bigger?"

Emma's grateful smile hurt Jared's heart. "The same kind of eejit who gets between two dogs in a fight," she said as if it were the highest accolade.

EMMA MCDANIEL PERCHED cross-legged on Jared's unmade bed, her shift hiked halfway up her golden-brown thighs so the excess fabric could form a nest for the half-drunk dog in her arms.

She'd protested giving the mutt any alcohol at all, but

since it was the only anesthetic available, she'd given in. Jared's main objection was that the only liquor he had in his tent was the bottle of twenty-five-year-old Macallan Scotch he'd been saving for the day he made the vital discovery he sensed was hovering somewhere in the future of this dig.

But wasting fine Scotch didn't upset Jared's equilibrium half as much as the presence of a woman in his tent did. For six summers the roomy canvas enclosure had been the kind of inner sanctum even Davey was forbidden to breach.

The off-limits rule was a necessity Jared had settled on during the first summer he'd arrived as site director. Nothing like going to bed and finding a leggy blond graduate student naked under the sheets to convince an ethical teacher of the necessity of drawing clear boundaries.

But here he sat, the site's first aid kit open on the crate that served as his bedside table. The spotlight he used to read tiny print late at night aimed down at the most exquisite woman he'd ever seen and a dog who looked as if it had just crawled out of last month's garbage.

Emma filled the spartan confines of Jared's tent like a bright splash of color where there had been only gray. His rumpled bed looked as if it had been put to far more sensual use than a lone man's restless night, the tangled sheets beneath Emma whispering of a night of mind-blowing sex.

And Emma herself, hair tousled, clothes in complete disarray, kept pulling his unruly imagination away from the task at hand and plunging him deeper into a train of thought that could only land him in trouble.

Just because they apparently didn't hate each other anymore was no reason to jump into bed together. Teaching her swordplay was fine as long as he stuck to the kind made of metal, and not the one the sight of her bared legs made stiffen beneath the fly of his pants.

As if a woman like her would let you touch her anyway.

But she watched intently as he tended the dog, observed his every move in a way that made him jittery as hell.

Frowning, Jared gently folded the stitched ear so it lay on the top of the mutt's head. He positioned a bright red button the size of a sixpence on the part of the ear that wasn't tracked with stitches. Might as well put the dog's head to good use, Jared figured, since it was obvious the animal wasn't using it to store any brains.

The dog gave a muffled yip through the gauze-band muzzle around its mouth, as if it understood the slanderous direction of Jared's thoughts. Holding the button in place, Jared slipped the curved needle deftly through the button, the layer of ear and the skin at the crown of the mutt's head.

"You needn't be giving *me* that filthy look," Jared said. "I'd have left you to take your chances with Shep and Digger. *She's* the one who decided you needed rescuing."

"But you're the one who saved the day. Right, Captain?"

"Captain? Oh, no," Jared muttered as he tied off his handiwork and snipped the nylon thread. "This can't be good for either one of us, dog. She's naming you now."

"And you're going to make him the laughingstock of the county with that big red button on his head."

"He'd scratch out those stitches before bedtime if they weren't out of his reach. It's the button or an Elizabethan collar around his neck. He'd like that even less, believe me."

"An Elizabethan what?"

"A fancy name for a big plastic cone that makes the poor beast look like it's tried to squeeze headfirst through the small end of a funnel."

"Oh." Emma puzzled for a moment and Jared could see she was trying to picture the ridiculous image he'd described.

"You're right. He wouldn't like that. It would be hard to watch for sneak attacks."

"Right. You never know when hordes of marauding collies might decide to raid the dig site. That's what every archaeological excavation needs. A troublemaking, digging-obsessed dog mucking about."

"How do you know he digs?"

"That's what terriers do."

"Not this one. He's going to be an angel." Emma unfolded legs Marilyn Monroe would have envied and swung them over the edge of his mattress, sweeping gracefully to her feet. Carrying the dog to the bed she'd made for him by putting her surcoat in the wooden box she'd emptied of Jared's sparse toiletries, she bent over to settle Captain in for the night.

The sight of her shapely bottom held Jared's gaze. After all, what could just looking hurt? Her hair spilled over her shoulder as she crooned to the exhausted little creature, gently removing the muzzle. Jared couldn't stop himself from wondering how that cascade of black curls would feel tumbling over his chest, all silk and fire, this woman a mix of passion and vulnerability more intoxicating than he'd ever known.

No wonder kids like Davey were mesmerized by Emma McDaniel. Jared was a grown man and he had a feeling his pants were going to get damned tight across the front whenever she was around.

"Where did you learn how to do that?"

The question startled him from fantasies so raw he felt his cheeks burn. "Do what?" he managed to choke out.

"Stitch him up. Clean the wounds and all."

The dog. She was asking about the dog, Jared realized with relief. Simple question. Easy answer.

Then again, maybe not.

"My father taught me."

Emma scooped up his razor, his toothbrush and shampoo from where she'd dumped them half an hour before. Feminine hands touched his most intimate objects, arranging them with a woman's eye for order. "Is your father a doctor?" she asked.

"Hardly that." Jared turned his back to her and busied himself putting the contents of the first aid kit back in their white plastic case. If only he could lock his emotions inside the container as well, covering up the sadness, the bitter sense of loss. It seemed he was a better actor than he thought or Emma was still too wrapped up in the dog to know how her question had affected him.

"What are you doing?" Emma asked, noticing the re-stocked first aid kit. "We haven't taken care of your bites yet."

"It's nothing—"

"I would say you saved a damsel in distress, if the dog wasn't a boy." She indicated his hand, the fingers now crusted with dried blood. "The least I can do is patch up the injuries you got while doing it."

"No." Jared fought the impulse to jam his hands into his pockets, knowing it would hurt like fire. "I can handle this myself."

"I'm sure you can. But we're going to play fourteenth century. The lady of the castle did the healing." She brooked no argument, grabbing the bottle of peroxide and a bowl he'd meant to return to the canteen. Indicating he should sit on the bed, she climbed up beside him, cross-legged again, her knees touching his left thigh as she pulled his hand palm-up into her lap. She ran her fingertips over the puncture wounds and Jared welcomed the distraction of pain burning up his arm.

"These are deep. Maybe we should take you to a doctor."

"I'll not be wasting my time driving forty minutes so the man can do what I can do right here."

"All right then. All right." She set the bowl between them. "I'm just going to flush the germs out with peroxide."

Soft, feminine fingers curved gently about his wrist, turning his hand so the worst of the bite wounds were on top. "You might want to have a shot of Scotch yourself before I do this," she said, and he wondered if her fingertips could feel his pulse racing.

"I'm saving that Scotch for an occasion to remember. Today is one I intend to forget."

"Very funny."

Emma tipped the brown bottle. Jared gritted his teeth as the antiseptic seared its way into the puncture wounds. The peroxide fizzed madly as it burned the wounds clean. He felt Emma watching him and looked up to see worried brown eyes.

"Really, they're just a few little cuts," he assured her.

"They're not little. In fact they're…they're rather nasty." Her voice wobbled.

He hated seeing the shadows of self-blame she was trying so hard to hide. Wished he could find a way to drive them from her face. But before he could think of something amusing to say, she spoke with forced brightness.

"You know, human bites are much more dangerous than dog bites." She poured on another dose of peroxide. "They carry a far greater risk of infection."

"And I need to know this why?" Jared reached past the pain to shape his lips into a raider's smile. "You aren't planning to bite me, are you, Ms. McDaniel?"

"Not unless you deserve it, Dr. Butler," she fired back, but her cheeks flushed unexpectedly pink, her gaze darting away as if…what? As if she'd been having the same dangerous thought as he had? *Right, mate. Dream on.*

"Just where did you get your scientific information?" he asked.

"My little sister Hope's pediatrician. You see, Hope is the youngest of all the McDaniel cousins, so when the family got together she'd bite—well, about anyone she could sink her teeth into—until the year she turned four."

Emma dabbed at the wounds with a clean square of gauze. Jared tried to distract himself from the warmth of her other hand cradling his.

"What convinced your sister to stop?"

"My grandfather mentioned at Christmas dinner that—"

"Father Christmas doesn't bring toys to biters?" Jared tried to joke, the image of the dime store frame rising in his memory, the smiling faces silhouetted against the brightly lit tree, the man who'd given this woman a diamond ring. Married her. Taken her to bed on their wedding night. Bad thought. Distracting, yes. But in exactly the wrong way.

"Toys my sister might have been willing to sacrifice for the pure joy of hearing her older cousins howl. Grandpa told her that a girl who bites can never be taught how to fight like a real McDaniel. Hope went cold turkey after that ultimatum, let me tell you! My mom got up from the table and kissed the old man."

Jared chuckled. "It's an unusual family that teaches girls to fight."

"*Unusual* doesn't even begin to describe my family. Of course, you're safe for the moment. Being wounded in action gets you off the official McDaniel hit list."

She bent over her work, so close he could smell the wind, the water from the burn and a hint of wet dog. Who would have thought that combination could smell good? Her brow creased, her hair falling like a curtain around their linked hands as she began to wrap gauze over the wounds. Once all were covered with layers of soft material, she ripped off a piece of white tape with her teeth and fastened the end of the bandage down securely.

"There," she said, patting him playfully on the chest. "That's bet—"

Jared's breath hissed between his teeth. She drew her fingers away, sticky with blood.

"Oh, my God. You weren't bitten here, too!" Full of regret, she touched the hard wall of his chest. "Oh, Jared."

"It's nothing," he said, starting to pull away. But her fingers were already slipping buttons free. The backs of her hands skimmed his skin. He gritted his teeth against the dizzying sweet sensation as she brushed the mat of hair beneath his shirt, spreading the cloth back to expose his skin.

To hell with the measly bite the rat had managed to deal him. A man would have to be having some body part amputated not to react to this woman feathering her fingers over his chest. Even if it hadn't been ages since he'd shagged anyone.

Jared felt his shaft harden. Heard Emma's breath, a little too fast. He dreaded that she'd noticed he was hard as a rock, but her focus was locked on his chest. It had been a long time since a woman had looked at him like that. An even longer one since a feminine touch had wreaked such havoc on his self-control.

What would she do if he closed the space between them and eased her down onto his bed? What would she do if he covered all that feminine softness with everything that was hard and male in him? If he took her mouth in a kiss that would make them both forget to breathe? Forget everything but the primitive need to…

Snib's right. You are daft, man! She'd probably knee you in the groin, and you'd deserve it! Things are complicated enough, having her here. Sex would only…

Feel bloody damn wonderful while Jared was in the middle of it. Trouble was, he and Emma would have to work together for the next six weeks feeling uncomfortable around each other. That is, if the lady let him…and why the devil would she? A woman like her. With a man like him? He might as well try to mate that miserable excuse of a terrier with Cruft's best-in-show.

So say something, dammit, Jared told himself. *Talk about something completely asexual. Like blood.*

"Shouldn't you have fainted sometime in the past hour?" He hoped she'd ignore the huskiness in his voice. "You know. That whole blood phobia."

"IT WAS ALL PART of the act." She seemed as relieved as he was to find something to talk about. "Considering my family, I'd spend half my life out cold if I were that squeamish. They don't call us the fighting McDaniels back in Whitewater for nothing."

He smiled, a real smile this time. Emma's gaze dipped, drawn to the flash of white. Her breasts tingled, a melting sensation in places too dangerous to allow. He looked…feverish. He couldn't be getting an infection this soon, but his eyes…they burned green, hot…intense.

Emma's mouth went dry. Every bit of small talk she'd ever used in conversation flew right out of her head. Lord. She was staring at him like a ninny. She patted the wound on his chest dry, busied herself by taping a gauze pad on the injury.

"You miss them a lot, don't you?"

Emma heard Jared's breath hitch as the edge of her little finger skimmed his nipple.

"Miss who?"

"Your family."

Family… That's what she was talking about. "You'd think I'd get used to it—being gone so much. But like Mom says, they'll always be there to come home to."

"If you like I could send the letters you wrote out with the rest of the post."

Emma froze, a strip of tape snarling around her fingers. "My letters?" Her stomach knotted.

Guilt suffused Jared's rugged features. "I came up to the tower, figuring you were still asleep. You were gone."

"That must have taken one whole glance at the bed to figure out."

"I thought you might have hitchhiked or—"

"Hitchhiked?" Emma's temples throbbed. "You think I'm out of my mind?"

"Or that you'd gone someplace you weren't supposed to," he finished, as if he hadn't heard her. His eyes narrowed. "I was right about that much, wasn't I? I went to look out the window, and...well, you left the thing out in front of God and everybody."

"I wanted to make sure the ink was dry," Emma said with measured fury. "And you forgot to pack any medieval envelopes in the chest. It sure wasn't an invitation for you to read them."

She pressed her hand to her stomach, feeling strangely violated as she imagined the cynical Jared Butler reading through the private, precious thoughts meant only for loving eyes. Oh, God. What had she written? She'd been trying so hard not to cry that she could hardly remember. But Jared couldn't know that, could he? Then why was he looking at her with—damn, a hint of...pity?

"How would you feel if I read your private letters to your family?" Emma confronted him, hands on hips.

"That will never happen."

"I suppose your work is too important for you to be bothered to drop your parents a few lines?"

Jared compressed his lips for a moment. "I don't have any family."

Emma stared at him. His eyes were hooded, dark with secrets. "But your father…you said…"

"He's dead. They all are."

Emma's heart clenched, her fury at Jared's intrusion paling in comparison to her runaway imagination. Picturing just how bleak her own life would be if God obliterated everybody she loved.

Jared held up his gauze-wrapped hand in surrender. "I was wrong to read the letters. I admit it. But don't you think being chewed up in a dogfight is penance enough?"

"Not unless I was the one who got to bite you." She hated the fact that he had a point. He might have read her letters, but he'd also saved Captain.

"What if we make a deal, you and me?" Jared offered. "I'll not invade your privacy again and you'll stay on the right side of the chain barricade at the rear of the castle. No more prowling around where you don't belong."

He looked so damned reasonable, those green eyes fixed on hers as he waited for her answer. But this was one time reasonable wouldn't work any more than indulging his temper had.

One of Hope's favorite phrases rose in her mind: *You're not the boss of me.* Okay, maybe it worked better coming from an eight-year-old, but Emma could at least hold on to the gist of the words.

She walked over to the crate, lifting it up to carry back to the tower room. "I'll just get my dog out of your way now."

"Hold on. I didn't say you could keep it. A dog on a dig site is a rotten idea."

"He won't go near your precious dig site. He'll be with me. After all, they had dogs in medieval times, didn't they?"

"Deerhounds and mastiffs and—"

"I could use some company with manners. Captain won't be able to read my letters or—"

Or look so damned sexy when he was really a nosy, un-principled—

"All right. You can keep the dog. But at the first sign he's digging—"

"Maybe you can sew buttons on his paws."

"Fine. I won't read your letters or give your dog to the SPCA and you won't go poking around the back of the castle. I just don't want the site contaminated. Surely we can agree on that. Do we have a bargain?"

Without a word, she turned and walked out the tent door, the dog's box in her arms.

"Emma?"

She heard Jared's irritated call. He was waiting for an answer. Too bad, she thought. He'd have to wait a long time.

Because there was one more thing she'd forgotten to mention about the McDaniel code. McDaniels kept their word. She had no intention of making Jared Butler a promise she wouldn't keep.

She hadn't forgotten the warrior she'd seen or the strange tug she'd felt in the center of her chest at the sight of him fighting upon the sea.

As if the valiant knight from centuries gone by felt just as lost as she did.

And she was the only one who could find him.

Chapter Six

JARED BUTLER WAS LICKING her neck. Emma could feel it through that delicious twilight between sleep and wakefulness. His warm tongue stroked the sensitive cords and hollows, pausing from time to time to torture her with tiny nips at her earlobe.

His hair could use washing, the thick waves not nearly as soft as they appeared. But who cared as long as she could feel that soul-shattering mouth on her skin at last?

She should make him stop. She would. Just not yet. It had been so long since she'd felt this pulse-racing anticipation, this surrender to needs she'd buried, almost feared.

She moaned, restless against the lumpy mattress, feather quills pricking through the cloth and prodding her to wake. *No. Not yet,* she pleaded. She wanted to feel the weight of him bearing down on her. Wanted him to kiss her mouth.

She didn't want to beg. Couldn't help herself. "Put your hands on me. Jared, please…"

He stuck an ice cube in her ear instead. With a cry of

protest, she started awake. One distorted black button eye stared down at her, a dog's face looming so close to hers it looked as if it were twisted by a funhouse mirror. Captain nudged her again with his cold, wet nose.

"Ohmigod," Emma gasped, struggling upright. "You're not… I mean, he's not…" So much for her night of burning romance.

The terrier tilted its head to one side in query. Still feeling the effects of Jared's Scotch, Captain listed to one side, then toppled into a pathetically thin heap.

Emma gathered the dog into her arms and peered about the room. The sun was setting, shadows painted against the wall. Where had the day gone? She'd brought Captain up to her room so he could rest, but the whole time she'd been changing out of her damp clothes, the mutt had struggled frantically to scratch out his stitches. Afraid he just might succeed, she had finally curled up with him on her bed, holding him so his claws couldn't do any more damage.

She'd only intended to stay there until Captain drifted off. But her sleepless night and the craziness of the morning's adventures had obviously taken more of a toll on her than she'd thought. They'd played through her mind, growing hazier and hazier until…

Her cheeks burned. It would be bad enough if Jared knew she'd slept the day away. If the archaeologist had any idea that she'd been having fantasies about him, her time here would be a complete disaster. The last thing she needed was to reinforce his opinion that she was a pampered little Hollywood…nymphomaniac.

What was she thinking? Having wild fantasies about a man she'd barely met. A man she didn't even like. Well, at least not until this morning.

"It's his mouth's fault," Emma told Captain. "That

mouth is so hot it should come with a warning from the surgeon general."

She'd seen Jared's mouth sulky, angry, reckless. That had been dangerous enough. But smiling in good humor when he'd finally caught up with her on horseback, gruffly tender when he'd stitched Captain's wounds, almost a little shy when she'd returned the favor, drawing his big, blunt-fingered hand onto her lap to clean out the bites he'd gotten saving her dog....

Shy? She brought herself up short. There wasn't a shy bone in that man's body. He was one-hundred-proof testosterone. And Emma hadn't had so much as a taste of the hard stuff since Drew had walked out.

She rolled her eyes as the double entendre struck her. Her middle rumbled in protest, as if to say, "Don't even *think* of a drinking metaphor with a stomach as empty as yours." She supposed the logic was sound. She hadn't eaten all day. Captain rolled onto his back, little legs up in the air, doing the best starving ghetto dog impression Emma had ever seen. Emma grinned, ridiculously pleased. It was nice to see a friendly face, the tower not so lonely anymore.

"Okay, I get the message," she told Captain. "We'll go in search of food. But no more licking my face, got it? And don't you dare tell anyone what I was dreaming or I'll—"

The terrier wove toward the edge of the bed. She caught him by the scruff of his neck just as he was about to fall off.

"What am I worried about? You're in no shape to tell my secrets. At least not tonight." She climbed off the bed, tucked Captain into her arms. He shivered. *Could he be developing a fever?* she wondered, concerned. Holding him in the crook of her left elbow, she wrapped her wide sleeve around him. Captain burrowed under the green wool and heaved a sigh, his shivering fading to an occasional tremor as she headed down the stairs and out the heavy wooden door.

She peered down the length of ruined curtain wall toward the cluster of white canvas tents. The day's work must be over. It seemed everyone was taking a break. A crowd of buff male students showed off their athletic prowess, bumping a soccer ball expertly from one to another with their heads or knees or feet. A bevy of girls sprawled on a blanket nearby flirted outrageously, tossing their hair and laughing as if they hadn't a care in the world.

Emma's chest hurt as her mind spun back in time, remembering how good it felt to be that young, your whole life before you, the handsomest boy in class smiling at you in a way that made your heart threaten to beat its way out of your chest.

We've never officially met. I'm Drew Lawson.

I know. Every girl in their sports conference knew who he was. *I'm, um, Emma McDaniel.*

I know. He'd smiled and Emma felt her stomach drop clean through the floor. *Your audition blew me away,* he'd said. *I just wanted you to know. If the drama department casts any other girl as Juliet, they're out of their mind.*

It's…hard to say what will happen. No it wasn't. Brandi Bates, reigning bitch-queen of Whitewater High, was a shoo-in for the role. Her mom had even ordered a custom-made Juliet costume to "donate" to the theater department. Emma had figured her chances at being cast in the lead were about as slim as the chance that Drew Lawson would ever ask her on a date.

Who would ever have guessed he'd be the first to kiss her, her first lover, her husband, her best friend? Funny, it was her friend she missed the most.

Emma's steps slowed for a moment as the Scottish countryside swirled back into focus, the loss of Drew fresh again. Feeling awkward, she tucked the pain away.

Chin up, she told herself. This isn't the first time you've been an outsider.

But that didn't make it much easier. Everyone else seemed to know where they fit at Castle Craigmorrigan. While Emma…

She'd have to carve out her own place. She'd done it before. Fastening a smile onto her face, she strolled toward the soccer game. Only then did she notice Davey Harrison on the fringe of the game. He looked as out of place as she felt and was stealing wistful glances at a sweet-faced redhead who sat near the blond, homecoming-queen type the other players were obviously trying to impress.

Smack!

A tanned surfer dude sent the ball flying Davey's way. Before he could react, it ricocheted off his shoulder and went careening across the bumpy ground toward Emma. Instinctively, she trapped it with her foot, then wished she'd left the blasted ball alone. Davey's face washed red with embarrassment.

For an instant the group of guys gawked at Emma, awkward as a bunch of seventh-graders peering across the gym floor at their first dance. The girls were almost as awestruck by Emma as the boys. But both sets of students recovered in a hurry.

"Hey, Harrison, go sit down with the girls," Surfer Dude teased. "Let the lady play."

"No thanks." Emma scooped the ball up and lobbed it back into the game. The girls cast Emma green looks as the boys started to play to a different audience.

Only Homecoming Hell Queen seemed not to mind, a superior smirk on her lips. But then, if the angle of her gaze was any hint, she had her sights set far higher. Jared sat in a canvas folding chair outside his tent, jotting notes on some kind of pad.

Emma fought a pang of something that couldn't be jealousy. So a gorgeous grad student wanted to crawl into bed with her site director? So what? That couldn't be anything new. With his smoldering sexuality, the man probably sampled a new lover every dig season while students lined up hoping to be the flavor of the month.

They were sure to be disappointed. Emma had barely known the man for twenty-four hours and she already knew he had too much integrity to sleep with a student, graduate or otherwise.

Irritated with herself almost as much as with the blonde, Emma crossed to the one person she figured felt more out of place than she did at the moment. Davey.

"Is your boss starving me on purpose to get me ready for the whole siege scenario or do you think I could con him out of a little bread and water?"

"Didn't you like what was on your tray?" Davey asked, concerned.

"What tray?"

Davey's brow furrowed. "You mean you haven't had anything to eat?"

"No."

"But I heard Jared tell Veronica to take some food up to you at lunchtime." Davey glared at the blonde, who had grudgingly delivered her a tray the night before. "What's the deal, Veronica?"

Veronica stroked her hand from her throat to her annoyingly perky breasts, stealing a glance at Jared through thick lashes, her voice just a little loud to make sure the archaeologist could hear her. "Oh, I'm sorry. I just got so wrapped up in my work I forgot you were even here."

Sure you did, sweetheart, Emma thought. *Like you'd forget a boil on your ass.*

"God, Veronica, I can't believe you!" Davey exclaimed, outraged. "You sure remembered to eat lunch yourself."

"Jared asked me to sit with him so we could discuss the finds I made," Veronica said, staking claim as certainly as if she'd stuck a piece of tape across Jared's chest that read *keep off.* "We were so engrossed that—"

Emma's sleeve growled.

"My God, is that a dog?" Veronica asked in the tone most people would use to inquire about a poisonous snake.

Captain stuck his nose out of the folds of cloth and blinked at Veronica with drunken-sailor eyes. He showed his miniature vampire teeth, his whole body rumbling. *Great judge of character,* Emma thought.

"Does Jared know you have that thing here?" Veronica demanded, saccharine sweetness not quite hiding a healthy dose of bitchy triumph. "There's no way he's going to tolerate having a dog around the site."

"Actually, Jared is the one who rescued Captain from the middle of a dogfight, then stitched him up," Emma replied.

The soccer ball bounded away, but nobody chased it. The students all but twisted their heads right off their necks looking from the dog to Jared to Veronica.

Jared was listening. Emma could sense it, like the prickle of tiny hairs on her nape just before an electrical storm hit. But she doubted anyone else suspected what he was doing. The big Scotsman acted so absorbed in his work an explosion wouldn't budge his attention.

"I really hate to be a bother, Davey," Emma said, "but if you could point me in the direction of some food before Captain here faints dead away?"

Emma turned toward one of the picnic tables, grimacing as a ray from the setting sun blazed in her eyes. Davey scrambled to help, grabbing the edge of the table.

"You sit down over here, Ms. McDaniel. I'll move this so the sun won't be in your eyes." He started to drag the table toward the shade of a tree. Surfer Dude elbowed him out of the way.

"Don't hurt yourself, Einstein. Let the men take care of it."

She knew exactly what the kid was doing, that pointed banter guys fell into when showing off for girls. The only defense: firing an even sharper smart-aleck answer right back. Unfortunately Davey's arsenal of sarcasm wasn't nearly a match for this crew.

Emma hated the humiliation in Davey's eyes, worse still the resignation. She remembered having that same sinking feeling in her stomach so many times in her own teenage years. Davey didn't even bother to argue. How could he, considering the obvious physical difference between him and the other guys?

All lanky arms and legs, Davey looked as awkward as a newborn colt, his shoulders not yet filled out, his face still a bit too soft, his eyes just a little too sensitive.

Davey stepped back, as if wishing he could disappear, but Emma blocked his path, shining her brightest smile on the embarrassed kid.

"They're right, Davey," she said. "You shouldn't be moving furniture."

The jocks elbowed each other in pleasure. Emma could feel every eye on her.

"Leave the menial tasks to the servants," she told Davey with a wave of her hand. "You've already done enough today, rescuing me on the rocks."

The ringleader of the soccer players swore as he thumped the table leg down right on one of his size-eleven Adidas. "Einstein rescued you?" he asked in disbelief.

"If it weren't for Davey, God only knows what might have

happened. I could have fallen right off the cliff." Emma curt-
seyed to Davey and smiled gratefully up into his eyes. "Would
you do me the honor of dining with me, sir knight?"

The poor kid looked like he was ready to faint. Emma shifted
Captain's weight into her left arm, then linked her other with
Davey's. She gave the boy an encouraging squeeze. "Please?"

"I'd be honored, my lady," Davey finally said.

"I have so many questions about the castle I'm sure you
can answer."

Surfer Dude groaned. "Einstein's already got a swelled
head. Don't make him worse."

Veronica flashed a long-suffering look in Jared's direction.
"Children, children. Shall we just get out a ruler and settle this
once and for all? You know Davey is smarter than the rest of
us, Sean."

Davey gaped as if she'd spoken a foreign language. Emma
ground her teeth, angry that Veronica would use the vulnerable young man in an effort to play to Jared.

Emma was tempted to tell the girl that Davey was certainly
smart enough to remember when he was supposed to bring a
guest her lunch. But this wasn't about Veronica, or even about
Jared. Emma ignored everyone except Davey Harrison as he
led her to her seat.

"Veronica, go get Ms. McDaniel some food from the canteen," Davey commanded, glancing down at his watch. "They
should be serving dinner now anyway." The blonde compressed her mouth into a sour line.

"I'll go," the redhead volunteered. She climbed to her feet,
brushing a twig off of her canvas shorts.

Davey's smile grew suddenly shy. "Thanks, Beth."

Beth. So Davey had a definite crush on the girl, bless his heart.
Not that he'd ever have the confidence to let Beth know it.

Emma felt someone watching her, angled her face so she

could see. Jared Butler's wolflike gaze fixed on her, so inscrutable she shivered almost as much as her dog did. But why should she care what Jared thought? Davey Harrison was beaming as if she'd crowned him king of the world.

JARED WISHED Emma McDaniel would get the hell out of his head so he could get some work done. Even as a lad he'd been able to compartmentalize his life into neat little boxes, lock away his emotions and immerse himself in centuries past.

How many times could he remember his father's wistful face peeking into his room of an evening? Angus Butler had been so fiercely proud Jared was top of his classes that the old man would never have dreamed of pulling his son away from the pile of books that always littered the boy's bed. Yet now Jared understood the price his father had paid for such unselfishness. Jared knew about silences too deep, where ghosts lived just waiting for a chance to haunt you.

While Angus had been silent when Jared withdrew, Jenny had been sad. *I thought things would be different once we were married. But you feel so far away and I can't reach you....*

He'd grown so damned impatient. *I'm right here.*

No. You're somewhere off inside your head.

She'd been right. He'd lived most of his life cut off from the present, building castles in his mind, peopling them with ladies and knights far more real to him than his wife had been. Even students he cared most about—like Davey—he managed to keep boxed up in his head when necessary.

But damn if Emma McDaniel would stay where Jared put her. She kept popping out like some crazed Jack-in-the-box just when he least expected it. Jack-in-the-box? Ha! More like any red-blooded man's hottest fantasy popping out of a cake at some stag party.

No wonder college lads decorated their walls with her picture. She had the kind of beauty that stopped men in their tracks—elegance, grace, a natural sensuality that made men want her, know they could never have her. She might as well be the moon; she was so far beyond their reach.

And now she'd smashed his concentration again. She'd glided across the heath like a princess in ancient tales of magic, about to sacrifice herself to some dragon. But this time no knight had ridden to her aid. The lady had done the rescuing, sweeping into the midst of the football game and transforming Davey from the shy butt of the more athletic boys' jokes to her chosen champion. The boy looked as if he hadn't a coherent thought left in his head.

Jared bundled away the site maps he'd been updating and watched Emma from beneath hooded lids.

So the lad is dazzled by her. At least Davey has the excuse he's not even twenty yet. What about you, Butler? Admit it, man. When the woman carried that disaster of a dog out of your tent, she took your brain as well.

Jared closed his eyes, remembering. The skin exposed when Emma had opened his shirtfront still burned, but not from the wounds her vampire dog had inflicted. Soft, feminine fingertips had blazed invisible trails on his bare chest, leaving Jared so hot, another plunge in the cold burn would've been a relief.

She'd been so warm, so real when she'd pulled his hand into her lap, her red mouth vulnerable with regret that he'd been bitten, her eyes shining as if he had slain dragons instead of driven off a crotchety old farmer and his dogs.

But he'd broken the spell with a vengeance when he'd betrayed the fact that he'd read her letters.

How would you feel if I read private letters of yours?

Letters so emotional he'd actually cried over them the way she obviously had? He'd feel violated, exposed…furious.

But then, he never had poured his feelings out on paper. Not since he'd learned the danger. Once in writing, your words could be used to trap you.

He heard a silvery ripple of laughter and opened his eyes to see Emma, transfixed by whatever Davey was talking about. The woman seemed to relish the fish and chips on her paper plate with the unabashed delight most people of her type would reserve for cuisine from a five-star French restaurant. Yet despite her animated conversation with Davey and her own obvious hunger, she paused now and then to slip her ridiculous-looking dog the choicest bits of food.

Something about the woman hammered at Jared's heart: her ratty dog cradled on her lap, her beautiful smile thawing Davey's shyness, the way the first spring sunshine thawed the heath, coaxing flowers out of winter-barren ground.

In half an hour Emma McDaniel had managed to achieve what Jared had struggled to do for years—forcing the other students to see Davey in a different light. But why had she done it? Questions racketed through Jared's mind.

He saw Veronica slide onto the bench across from Emma and Davey, something sharp in the blonde's gaze. Beth, Sean Murphy and the rest of Veronica's adoring throng crowded into the remaining seats.

It was a strange combination. Curiosity, Jared's fatal flaw, got the better of him.

He rose, took his notebook and a Ziploc bag containing a recent find to the table next to Emma's.

"Dr. Butler, won't you come join us?" Veronica called. "I'm sure someone would be happy to move."

Just like a dog juggling for alpha status in a pack, Veronica was always nudging one of the quieter kids to give up their seat. Usually, Davey would have bailed, but Jared doubted a crate of explosives could blast the boy from Emma Mc-Daniel's side tonight.

Even if Davey *had* started to fall into his old habit of moving, Jared instinctively knew Emma would have stopped the boy. Whiskey-dark eyes had the same protective glint in them Jared had seen when the lady had been a heartbeat away from plunging into the middle of a dogfight after that little scrap of a mutt whose life she'd saved.

"I've got work to do," Jared said, staking out an empty table by spreading his things across it. He drew a magnifying glass from the leather pouch on his belt, removed the finger-length chunk of metal from the plastic bag, then chose the seat where he'd have the best vantage point to keep an eye on the unfolding scene.

For a heartbeat Emma's gaze locked on the find Jared was pretending to study, her avid curiosity surprising him.

But a second later, Jared was sure he'd imagined it. Emma focused on Davey once more. The kid was describing the evolution of castles to her, from wooden motte and bailey fortresses to the grand stone structures like Castle Craigmorrigan. Emma listened with rapt attention, peppering the conversation with surprisingly astute questions, as if her sole purpose was to make Davey shine.

Jared figured it took Veronica about three seconds to hijack the conversation.

"We can talk about castles all summer, Davey," she said, sprinkling malt vinegar on her own fish. "But we'll only have Emma here for a little while. Wouldn't you all rather hear about her?"

A chorus of enthusiastic approval rose from the other students. A resigned aura settled over Emma's features, as if she'd expected to be hit with questions at some point. But Jared sensed a wariness about Emma, too. Smart girl, he thought. Veronica sounded way too friendly considering the glint in her eyes.

"You look so different in person!" Veronica said, nibbling meditatively on a chip. "Of course, women who work out in the real world can't waste hours in front of a mirror. It must be hard for you to adjust, having to dress yourself and do your own hair."

"I'm trying not to crumble under the hardship," Emma said breezily. "I suppose I'll even have to clip my own toenails here."

"I'd be happy to help," Sean offered, elbowing his friend.

"No thanks. It'll be good for me. If I can just figure out how to unfold the little lever thing on the clippers."

Veronica's mouth tightened as everyone at the table laughed, as charmed by Emma as the terrier was. Emma slipped the dog a thick wedge of potato and the animal smacked his lips in pure bliss.

"You don't look nearly as...well, *you* know," Veronica said. "It's amazing what the world's most famous makeup artists can do. I read someplace that there are women who don't go anywhere without one."

"I usually pack Pierre in my carry-on luggage, but these days they barely let you carry on a tube of lipstick. Besides, I couldn't figure out how to declare him in customs."

The kids roared, some sputtering mouthfuls of milk or fizzy drinks. Score one for Emma, Jared thought.

Veronica feigned a laugh. "That's wonderful. But then you obviously get a lot of practice making snappy comebacks, being famous and all, I suppose. Especially lately, you poor thing."

Poor thing? Jared saw Emma's dark eyes glitter.

"Somehow I manage to bear up under the pressure."

"Knowing you're second choice as Lady Aislinn must be tough," Veronica commiserated. "But it's a very complex role. You can't blame Barry Robards for having reservations about giving it to—well, your roles thus far haven't exactly had much depth."

"What a horrible curse," Emma lamented. "Starring in movies that are box office draws when plenty of actresses with a whole lot more talent than I have are waiting on tables and eating stale cornflakes, hoping for their big breaks."

"No way!" Sean exclaimed, a chorus of denials breaking from the other lads.

"Emma's fantastic as Jade! No one looks better in spandex than you do! You sure wouldn't, Ronnie!"

"We'll never know, will we?" Veronica rejected a slightly burned chip. "It's hard enough for a woman to win respect in academia without dressing in some skintight catsuit that…well, you must admit, Emma, it doesn't leave much to the imagination."

Emma selected an even darker chip and popped it in her mouth. "All that exposed skin is pretty risqué. Showing my hands and my face and—that's all, isn't it? You might want to rethink your shorts and T-shirt, Veronica. There's more of me covered in my Jade Star costume than you've got covered right now."

The boys made a swishing noise, shooting their arms up like referees signaling a goal.

"She's got you there, Ronnie," Beth said, stifling a giggle.

"I suppose," Veronica said. "But I'd rather expose a little bit of leg than my whole private life. That must be terrible, Emma. You can't go to a shop without seeing the whole sordid story splashed all over the magazines. Your divorce and all."

Davey flushed, angry. "Veronica! For God's sake. That's none of our business."

"What?" Veronica's eyes widened with poisonous innocence. "I'm just trying to let Emma know we're willing to listen. When my mom got divorced, that's all she wanted to talk about. What a louse my dad was. How he'd screwed everything in skirts. That's one good thing, isn't it, Emma? At least your husband only had an affair with your best friend."

Emma shrugged. "Drew never actually cheated on me. At least physically. He waited until we'd filed for divorce to make his move. Decent of him, wasn't it? I gave him a bonus for that when we settled on his alimony."

"That's so brave of you. Pretending it's funny. But the whole world knows your heart must be breaking. You don't have to pretend here. We all know it's tragic."

"Oh, definitely. My life is right up there with Romeo and Juliet on the tragedy meter." Emma managed to sound bored. "I've got no financial worries, no kids to be devastated by the split. I've got a supportive family and great friends and a career that lets me travel all over the world. When I compare my life with the challenges most divorced women have to face, I feel real sorry for myself."

"That's a great way to look at it," Davey said earnestly.

It wrenched Jared to see the boy, so fragile, damaged by life, trying to offer comfort.

"Dr. Butler always says it's the tough stuff in life that makes you strong," Davey continued. "Like Lady Aislinn. Before the castle siege she was just—"

"Isn't that just like you, Davey?" Veronica patted the boy's hand. "Trying to make her feel better with one of Dr. Butler's maxims when you don't know anything at all about love."

"Yeah," Sean joked. "The only thing Einstein's taking to bed at night is his teddy bear."

"That's very wise of you, Davey," Emma said, just a hint of wistfulness creeping in. Jared's senses sharpened. "Real love is worth waiting for."

"Is that what you had, Emma?" Veronica asked. "With your ex-husband? Real love?"

Irritation fired in Jared, an urge to shut Veronica up. But he hesitated. How could he blame Veronica when he was wondering the same thing himself?

Was real love what Emma McDaniel believed she'd had with the man in that Christmas picture up in the tower room? Or had she found love with one of the dozens of other men who must've spent the two years since the divorce trying to get through her bedroom door? Jared's jaw tightened. For instance, that Jake fellow, whoever he was. The man in the second letter she'd meant to send back to America.

"Veronica," Beth challenged, a little shyly, "I don't think you should…"

"I just want Emma to feel comfortable here, safe," Veronica protested virtuously.

Right. About as safe as Jared's hand had been clamped between the teeth of Snib's collies.

"If we're just open and honest and ask questions straight out, it'll be far better than whispering and speculating, all of us wondering. Just get it over with, like…like having a root canal. She'll feel better after she talks about it. Just because she's famous doesn't mean it doesn't hurt. I mean, really, Emma. Your husband dumped you for your best friend, didn't he? In front of the whole world, no less."

Emma smiled again, a brittle, beautiful smile. Jared wondered if anyone else could see past it to the pain. Before he could second-guess his motives, he shoved himself to his feet.

Chapter Seven

"Ms. McDaniel?" Jared cut in on the conversation. Beth sloshed her drink onto her chips, everyone at the table flustered. Even the least sensitive students had been as uncomfortable with Veronica's line of questioning as he had. Not that they could have stopped her. The other students had learned early not to give her any excuse to aim that incisive sarcasm their way.

Jared leveled his gaze at Emma. "I was wondering if you'd let me take a look at your script?" he asked.

Emma blinked, the pain in her beautiful eyes disappearing. No, Jared realized. Not vanishing. He'd just bought her enough time to hide it away. "My…script?"

Jared picked up his magnifying glass from his table and snapped it back into its leather case. He carefully slipped the metal find into its plastic bag. "Barry Robards said they were going to rewrite the section with that absurd sword duel between Lady Aislinn and Sir Brannoc. I was just wondering if they'd done it."

"They've been editing all along. The latest draft is in my

suitcase. I was hoping to run lines while I was here, before you—"

"That's a grand idea."

She stared at him as if he'd grown a second head.

"Do you have time to show me the revisions now?" he asked, pocketing the plastic bag.

"But, Jared." Veronica pouted. "I thought we'd have time to—"

"Dig up something besides artifacts?"

Veronica stiffened at the edge in his voice. Good. He wanted to be damned sure she got the message.

Jared scowled down at her. "Ms. McDaniel's private life is her own, Veronica. Unless you're planning to do your doctoral thesis on relationships in present-day Hollywood, I'd suggest you start researching something that pertains to your topic. And one more thing. I'm Dr. Butler to students."

Veronica flushed. "I was just—"

Jared looked straight into her eyes. "I know exactly what you were doing. Now," he said, his gaze sweeping the other students at the table. "Any more questions? *I'm* the one you ask."

"Yes, sir." Davey all but saluted, his thin face awash with relief. "I mean, no, sir. No more questions." Jared winced at the glow of hero worship in the boy's eyes. The rest of the students murmured assent, avoiding Jared's gaze. That should keep the lid on their curiosity for the time being.

"Davey, could you look after Ms. McDaniel's dog for a little while?" Jared asked.

"That's not necessary," Emma protested. "Really. Captain is still a bit woozy, and his stitches—he's determined to scratch them."

"The button will hold," Jared insisted. "Trust me."

She regarded him a long moment, her cheeks just a trifle pale, her eyes full of questions.

Trust him? Jared thought. Was he out of his mind asking that of any woman? "The stitches are set in good and tight," he added. That should clarify what he meant. Trust his skill. His knowledge. Never his heart.

Where the hell had that thought come from?

Davey scooped Captain into his arms. The terrier showed his teeth, more on principle than in threat. Davey scooped a chip from the nearest plate and fed it to the dog.

Obviously the terrier's affections could be bought. The dog licked Davey's fingers as Emma looked on, a worried crease between the sweep of her dark brows.

"Don't worry yourself about this cheeky wee fellow, Emma," the lad reassured. "I'll take him for a bit of a walk, then bring him to the tower in an hour or so."

"Just…be careful. He's got a talent for plunging headfirst into trouble."

Jared grimaced. Why should the dog be smarter than a thirty-three-year-old man with a doctorate? Emma McDaniel was nothing *but* trouble. He should be keeping his distance from her, let pressure—even Veronica's brand—drive her closer to seeing that the role of Lady Aislinn was beyond her talent. Better to drive her away before she had the chance to massacre the part, the one chance the rest of the world would have to learn of the legend.

Jared turned back to Emma. "Your suitcase is stored in one of the chests in the great hall. Do you have time to show me the script right now?"

"I don't know." Emma slid from her seat with astonishing grace, considering the voluminous folds of her medieval garb. "You'll have to ask the ogre in charge of the castle."

The corner of Jared's mouth tipped up. "He's decided to open the dungeon door a crack or two."

Jared sunk for a moment into melting chocolate eyes

framed with lashes so curly it seemed impossible that they were real. He gestured with one hand and Emma fell into step beside him. A dozen pairs of eyes burned into Jared's back. He made sure he was out of hearing range before he spoke.

"I'm sorry about the girls' prying. They're not used to—"

"Some other woman barging in and taking all the attention?"

"Something like that."

She winked at him, so mischievous he wondered if he'd imagined the fragility, the pain he'd seen in her features minutes before.

"Don't worry, Butler. I can handle a few lightweights like Veronica and her flying monkeys. I had plenty of practice with Brandi Bates."

"Who is Brandi Bates? One of the paparazzi?"

"No." Emma chuckled. "My nemesis from fifth grade to high school graduation. We hated each other on sight. Of course, she was star pitcher on the softball team, head cheerleader, president of the student council and she looked like a cover model for *Seventeen* magazine, so it was no contest who would win when the rest of the class took sides."

Jared stared, taken aback. He searched for false modesty, but Emma's face was filled with a wry dismissal that was all too real. Jared cocked his head to one side, regarding her with an appraisal that pinched like a shoe two sizes too small. "Some other girl upstaging you? That doesn't make any sense. You had to be a stunner when you were in school. You're one of the most beautiful women in the world." The compliment felt a whole lot more awkward than insulting her had been.

Emma made a face. "I hate to shatter your illusions, Butler, but I'm pretty sure my publicist pays them to say that. Under the table, of course."

"Of course." Why did her refusal to take her beauty seriously make him smile? Damn. It was only the end of their first full day on site and he was actually starting to like the woman. *That* hadn't been part of his master plan.

Dislike her, make her miserable, get her to run back to Hollywood so the studio has to send me a more talented actress or wait for Angelica Robards to heal, he reminded himself.

Well, maybe Emma had surprised him with her bravado, her enthusiasm, her compassion. That didn't mean she was right for the role of Lady Aislinn. He owed it to the Lady of Craigmorrigan to see that her story was told in as worthy a fashion as possible, now that it was being brought to life after so many centuries.

Suddenly the silence jarred Jared, returning his attention to the flesh and blood woman walking beside him. Twilight painted Emma's face in a rosy glow, her mouth a trifle more sober than it had been moments before. "In high school I was a card-carrying geek," she said. "I almost got lynched for winning the part of Juliet in the senior play. I graduated early and headed off for drama school. Couldn't wait to get out of that nest of vipers."

Jared tried to picture Emma McDaniel as anything but this elegant, polished woman. It was impossible.

She shook back her hair, shrugging off her mood as well. "Speaking of vipers," she teased, "I'd say the blonde with the forked tongue has the hots for you, Butler."

Jared glowered. "Veronica is a student—"

"And too full of herself not to realize her obsession with you is hopeless because you're such a stand-up guy."

Unexpected warmth spread through Jared's chest. She'd barely met him, but she sounded so sure he'd never cross that line. "Thank you for that," he said.

"If you've got a girlfriend tucked away somewhere, you

might want to flash her around the site a bit to settle Veronica down," Emma advised.

"There's no one."

"Oh." Did her voice sound a little strange? As if…what? She'd registered the fact he was unattached? *Right, Butler,* Jared thought wryly. *The most beautiful woman in the world is just waiting for the "all clear" before she jumps your body.*

Maybe in his dreams.

Emma tipped her head, regarding him for a long moment. Jared was damned glad she couldn't read his mind. The reel spinning in his head went way past R-rated.

"If flashing a girlfriend in Veronica's face is out of the question, you'll need some other tactic," Emma mused.

Jared's jaw tightened. She talked as if she had plenty of experience rebuffing prospective lovers. Why did the thought make him as itchy as a nosedive into a nettle patch?

Emma tapped her fingertips lightly against her lips, deep in thought. After a moment she spoke. "At the least, you should make sure somebody is watching your back. If I were you, I'd take a couple of the soccer players along when you visit the camp showers at night. Just as a precaution to protect you from any nasty surprises."

Had Emma learned to be that wary the hard way? Jared wondered. Dealing with student crushes was one thing. But someone as high-profile as Emma could find herself in real danger, her safety threatened not only by the clamoring of the press but by some deranged stalker. The fact that Jared's ethics were under siege paled in comparison.

A fierce protectiveness surged through him. He quelled it, exasperated with his own stupidity. She needed him to play guard dog about as much as she needed that ratty terrier of hers! She probably had a mansion in L.A. with thirty-foot walls and a surveillance system to rival Scotland Yard, not to mention a team of bodyguards and security specialists trained to keep celebrities safe. The last thing she needed was an archaeologist running to her rescue.

Jared grimaced. *Put away your lance, Don Quixote. The only dragon is in your imagination. It's just another windmill to make you look like a complete fool.*

Emma's voice startled him from his thoughts. "Really, Jared. It can't hurt to be careful."

"Careful?" He groped for the thread of their conversation. Veronica, he remembered, relieved.

"I can handle myself just fine," he retorted. "It's not the first time I've had to shut a student down."

Emma looked him up and down with a cheeky grin. "I'll bet."

His face heated. What the hell was he doing talking about this? He'd never mentioned his experience deflecting student crushes to a soul. "Ms. McDaniel—"

"Emma. And don't get your kilt in a knot. I just thought I'd give you a friendly warning in case you hadn't noticed Veronica was on the prowl. You looked pretty much in a daze sitting over there in your chair."

She'd been watching him, as well? The thought unsettled him.

"I notice plenty," Jared insisted. "For example, I saw what you did."

She peered up at him, bewildered. "What did I do? Eat dinner? *That* was plenty exciting."

"You swept into that football game and took Davey under your wing." And damned if it hadn't touched Jared to the heart. "The lads were just trying to be the big men on site," he explained. "They all like Davey well enough and don't mean anything by their teasing. But Davey is so bright and so damned young…not in age, you know? But in spirit. He makes an easy target."

Emma frowned. "They're jealous, plain and simple. No matter how good-natured their intentions, it still hurts. As for me taking Davey under my wing, that's ridiculous. He's the only person I've met so far who hasn't tried to bite my head off. I asked Davey to sit by me for completely selfish motives."

"Is that so?"

"Yes. That's so." Her chin bumped up as if daring him to contradict her.

Every instinct in Jared told him to just let the subject go. It would be safer for both of them. But somehow he couldn't make himself be wise.

"For an actress, you're a rotten liar," he challenged. She sputtered a denial but Jared ignored it. "Why did you do it, Emma? I really want to know."

"Why a self-absorbed actress didn't trample over Davey on the way to her makeup call?" She shrugged, self-deprecating. "I did it because I've been right where Davey is in the pecking order. I wouldn't expect you to understand what it's like to be an outsider. Look at you. You're a genius. And with shoulders the size of yours, a bully would have to be suicidal to start picking on you."

"Is that so?"

"Yes, that's so. In fact, if I were judging candidates for getting the soccer ball slammed in their face on a scale of one to ten—ten being no way in hell—you'd be an eleven." She hesitated, caught her bottom lip between her teeth for a moment. Her dark gaze probed his. "I confess it makes me wonder…"

"Wonder what?"

"Why *you* single Davey out. Besides the part about him being brilliant. And sweet."

Jared rolled his eyes. "Don't be calling the lad sweet to his face. You think the crack about teddy bears humiliated Davey? The last thing any man wants is to be known as sweet. Especially in the eyes of a beautiful woman."

"I'll try to remember that. And as long as we're being honest about our Don Quixote impulses…"

Jared did a double take. Hadn't he just been thinking in terms of the Cervantes hero? What the hell was the guy doing in Emma McDaniel's head?

"You don't give a damn about that script," Emma said. "It was pretty obvious you were trying to rescue me from Veronica."

"Partly," Jared hedged, trying not to be completely unnerved that Emma's thought processes seemed so in sync with his own. "But I really *do* want to see the script. Besides, I've been thinking—when Angelica Robards was here, she spent her downtime running lines. Memorizing the script is part of your job, too. There's no reason you shouldn't be able to work on that when I'm busy on the dig."

She gave him a sharp look. "Whoa there, Doctor. Remember, you're supposed to be the villain of this piece. Don't be getting soft on me, Butler."

No chance of that, Jared thought. Every time the woman came near him he got hard as a rock.

Cool shadows fell over them as they reached the part of the castle that was still intact, the crash of sea against shore beating a primal rhythm. Intoxicating salt air filled his head as the wind tousled Emma's hair, one silken curl clinging to the corner of her mouth as it had earlier. But this time Jared surrendered to impulse. He raised his fingers to brush the strand away. Her cheek felt softer than roses, her mouth so velvety moist. He could almost taste her.

Jared's throat went dry. He tried to think of something, anything to break the spell, resist the temptation of those full, red lips.

"Jared, may I ask you a question?" She peered up at him with those eyes a man could drown in.

"What do you want to know?" he asked hoarsely.

"What was that artifact you were studying so intensely? Before you started eavesdropping on my table, that is."

Relieved at the distraction, Jared rummaged in the roomy cargo pocket on the leg of his pants. He drew out the Ziploc bag. "Beth uncovered this find when I was picking you up at the airport. I think it may be a fragment of a coronet a woman would have worn to hold her veil on her head."

Jared snagged the palm-sized flashlight hooked to his belt and flicked it on. He shone the beam on the find. Red enamel reflected the light.

Emma's breath caught. She stared, mesmerized. "The color—it's so vibrant. I thought it must be a gemstone or something."

"Smiths crafted circlets of enameled flowers to help brighten up the long gray Scottish winters. This fragment still has three leaves attached. See?"

Clamping the end of his flashlight lightly between his teeth for a moment, he retrieved his magnifier, handing it to Emma so she could get a closer look.

Jared carefully slid the metal piece out of its container, pillowing it on the layer of plastic he now cupped in his hand.

Emma's eyes widened with feverish interest as she peered through the magnifier. "They look like… Are the leaves made out of gold?"

Jared's enthusiasm dimmed. He slid the flashlight back into his hand. What was his problem? This dragging sense of disappointment he felt was ridiculous. It should come as no surprise that a woman with Emma McDaniel's wealth would be fascinated with riches from another time.

Jared had seen plenty of archaeology students catch cases

of gold fever in his years working on different digs. He always told them that since Schliemann had already discovered Troy most of the things they'd find would be pottery, weapons and hand-crafted tools. People couldn't eat gold. But Emma seemed oblivious to his subtle withdrawal.

"Gold in a circlet would have been rare, wouldn't it?" Emma enthused. "Something only the most important people would wear?"

"Aye." Jared tried not to mind knowing what her next question would be. *How much money is it worth?* Wasn't that how most of the world measured the value of things?

"Do you realize what you have there?" Emma asked.

"I'll know better once we run some tests and get it dated." Why bother trying to explain technical matters, Jared thought with a sinking sensation in his middle. The woman wasn't even listening. She stared down at the tangled bit of metal, mesmerized.

"Lady Aislinn might have worn that circlet in her hair," she breathed.

Jared's stock caution about history being valued beyond mere currency died on the tip of his tongue. "She may well have."

Emma reached out a fingertip, then suddenly caught herself, curling her fingers tight into her palm, like a kid who didn't trust herself to resist. "I'm sorry," she said. "There are probably oils and stuff on my hand that could damage it. Like the antique wedding dress my aunt Finn and I found in the attic at March Winds. The conservators Aunt Finn talked to at the museum said we should never touch it without white gloves on our hands."

An antique wedding dress? Jared couldn't help but wonder what Yanks considered old. The country was in its infancy by European standards. When you'd lived your whole life in a land with walls built by Romans and Neolithic stone circles, the word *antique* definitely became relative.

"This wedding dress," Jared asked, "did experts date it?"

"It was from the American Civil War. In the 1860s. You must have heard of it."

Jared raised one brow, amused. "I think I read a bit about that in some history class I took. Quite rude of you Yanks to fight amongst yourselves, if you ask the English of that time. Played havoc with the cotton mills on this side of the ocean."

Emma tsked. "Thinking of the empire's commerce when higher issues are involved—isn't that just like you English."

Jared scowled. "I'm a Scot. You want to get yourself thrown out of a pub hereabouts, call the locals 'English.'"

Emma laughed and for an instant, Jared forgot to breathe. "I couldn't resist pulling your chain. After reading about the Lady Aislinn legend, I got the picture. The English weren't exactly invited guests in Scotland either."

She tossed that mane of dark hair. The scent of it filled Jared's head, tempting him to grab a wayward curl, press it to his lips. *Bloody hell, was he losing his mind?*

"My family's Irish," Emma continued. "They were forced to emigrate during the Easter Uprising. We consider blaming the English for our troubles an Olympic sport."

Jared studied her face. "You're Irish? It surprises me. I would have guessed some Spanish blood or something exotic—"

Her gaze flitted away from his. She shrugged, taking a step nearer the cliff.

"My mom's family is Irish," Emma said. "I should have made that clearer."

"And your father?"

He wished the words back the instant he spoke them, could almost hear doors slamming shut inside her. What the hell was he doing asking her personal questions anyway? There were plenty about his own life he didn't want to answer.

"My father's not important," she said flatly.

She was avoiding something. Her voice shifted, airy once again. He might have been fooled if he hadn't trained a lifetime to unearth things other people wouldn't even notice.

"Anyway," she continued, "there's this Welshman down at the American Legion where my grandfather takes the family sometimes for the catfish fry on Saturday nights."

Jared tried to imagine Emma eating fried catfish anywhere at all. "The American Legion?" he prodded, just grateful they'd managed to navigate past whatever dangerous waters had made her edgy moments before.

"It's a special pub where military veterans go."

"Right."

"This Rhys Llewellyn was always griping about the English, saying how the Welsh mounted a noble resistance and such. So one night the Captain's finally had enough. He shouts across the room, *You Welsh have got no credibility with me at all.*" She mimicked a booming voice. "*They don't call Charles the Prince of Dublin.*"

Jared laughed. "The Captain? Isn't that what you named your dog?"

Emma's mouth curved in a tender smile. "The Captain is my grandfather. I've called him that for as long as I remember."

"Was he looking to start a fight?"

"He always is. But what could Llewellyn say? At least we Irish kept on trying."

She quieted, peering wistfully toward the sea, and suddenly Jared could see all that was Irish in her, an otherworldliness far deeper than her dark eyes. The rising moon painted her features in mystery, as if she were a fairy lost on the heath.

The flashlight's glare suddenly seemed too harsh, revealing a vulnerability in her that made Jared's heart feel too small. He flicked the torch off and returned it to its leather pouch. He started to put away the fragment of coronet, then stopped and glanced at Emma's woebegone face.

"Emma?" he queried softly, feeling as if he were calling her back from a world only she could see.

She swallowed hard and he wondered what memory had made her so sad. She turned toward him, her smile wobbling. "Don't mind me," she said. "I'm just a little homesick. Silly, isn't it? A simple plane ride and I could be back in Whitewater by morning. When Lady Aislinn came to this place she was so far from her home, she must have guessed she'd never see it again. Especially since her father had just died. Last night as I was staring out at the sea, I could feel her, you know? How alone she must have been. That must sound silly to you."

"No." Moved by instinct, Jared took her hand in his. She stilled at his touch, the pulse in her wrist beating wildly beneath his fingers. Her skin felt so silky, so warm a frisson of awareness went through him.

He forced himself to focus on the task he'd intended, turning her hand in his until her fingers formed a cup. Carefully he slipped the fragment of coronet into her palm. Emma peered down at the enameled flower as if it were a magical talisman that could whisk her away to a world of fairies and moon and mist.

Who knew? Jared thought. Emma seemed like the land of America itself, too new to understand such ancient magic, too willful to recognize echoes that had sounded long before it had been born.

Emma ran her fingertip over the enamel with such delicacy the blood in Jared's veins raced. He could feel her touch as intimately as if it were on his skin. She moistened her lips, her voice unsteady. "It's almost as if it's alive."

Jared's throat tightened. Wasn't that what he felt? Whenever he retrieved some long-forgotten treasure from the earth? A pulse of people long dead. A whisper of voices silenced. A reminder that life was fleeting and he, too, would someday fade away into time.

For a moment he wished that Emma *could* bring Lady Aislinn to life. He'd never seen this glow in Angelica Robards' eyes when she'd spoken of Lady Aislinn, Jared recalled with regret. He'd never felt this unexpected bond with the woman he considered talented enough to play his lady. No. Not his. The castle's lady. The legend's lady. The mystery-shrouded ghost whose secrets had consumed him for so many years.

The brush of Emma's fingers jarred Jared from his thoughts, his hand beneath her fingertips feeling *alive* in a way he'd almost forgotten. Warmth surged through him, as if he were a relic she'd found and held for the first time in centuries to the sunlight.

Emma tipped the enameled flower back into his hand. "Thank you," she breathed, "for letting me touch something so—so precious."

Something cold where she was hot, something lifeless where she was so damned full of passion. Passion for this place, for this legend, for a woman she'd never met and a story he'd always loved. As if she understood....

Jared felt the tug of needs he'd never admit. Feelings he'd never share.

I wish I could make things different, he confessed to himself as he peered down at Emma's face. *Wish I could give you Angelica Robards' skill for dramatic roles, all the tricks in her face and movements that would have made her believable as Lady Aislinn.*

But he couldn't transform Emma into the caliber of actress

needed for the role she yearned to play. Emma McDaniel was all about special effects and fast cars, spandex suits and ray guns. She was fire and storm, as flawed and sensual as Eve after the fall, the opposite of the Lady Aislinn, who seemed too ethereal to suffer the rough touch of any mortal man's hands, despite the inner strength she'd shown during the siege. A woman generations of minstrels had praised as pure and otherworldly as the fairy flag she'd brought with her to her bridal bed.

No, he couldn't transform Emma McDaniel into a believable Lady Aislinn, no matter how much the studio, Emma or even Jared himself wanted him to. But he could share a little of himself, couldn't he? Just this much.

"You wanted to know why Davey is special to me?" Jared asked.

Emma peered up at him. "Why?"

"I used to be just like him."

He expected denial. Expected her to brush off his words.

Instead, her eyes glowed, luminous. She stretched up on tiptoe and kissed him on the cheek. A soft, melting kiss that struck like a lance to his heart.

"Maybe we're two of a kind after all, Jared Butler," she said. Then in a swirl of dark curls and green gown she vanished into the castle, the one place in all the world where Jared allowed himself to dream.

Chapter Eight

IT WAS TORTURE playing Rapunzel when there was a party going on beneath your tower, Emma thought as she looked down at the scene unfolding below.

For the past week she'd done her best to honor the boundaries Jared had set for her. She'd spent her afternoons in her room, not studying her script or searching for the knight fighting invisible demons on the sea, but rather, gazing out the window on the landward side of her room at the dig site. A world she couldn't share.

Not *couldn't,* Emma corrected herself, *wouldn't.* It was a matter of respect, she told herself firmly, honoring Jared's "rule" that she not "distract" the students from their work.

It would have been easy to disregard the dictatorial man who'd ordered her around with such contempt the first day she'd been at the castle. But from the moment Emma had kissed Jared Butler's cheek, the man she had hated on sight transformed like the druids in the Irish tales her aunt Finn loved to tell. Jared: a shape-shifter more elusive than any knight of the sea. Painful secrets haunted eyes too old, in the face of a man who seemed at war with himself every time he looked at Emma.

She swallowed hard, remembering the sensation of his beard-roughened cheek beneath her lips, the heat that had caught her by surprise in a gesture that was only meant as…as what? An apology? A truce? The least terrifying way she could think of to thank him for letting her glimpse what he obviously tried so hard to hide—his world-weary Sir Lancelot heart?

He'd drawn back that night, stunned, as if she'd pierced him with that kiss. Awakened him from some bitter enchantment. But he didn't *want* to be jarred from that solitary world, Emma had known in that instant. He didn't know how to be anything but alone.

Captain caught the hem of her gown in his teeth and tugged, even more restless than she was. She leaned down and scooped the terrier into her arms.

"What?" she demanded. "It hasn't even been an hour since you went outside."

The little dog planted his paws on the stone ledge and strained his head out the window, his pitiful whine now part of their daily routine. At first she'd just figured he wanted to be part of the action below, like she did. But as the days slipped past she'd realized there was only one person he longed to find. Jared.

Captain worshipped the big Scotsman with the same fierce devotion Davey Harrison did and would struggle madly to get free the instant his doggy nose caught a whiff of the mixture of leather and horse, peat and salt air that was Jared's own.

Emma figured it would take the dog about three seconds to track Jared down if she was foolhardy enough to go out into the sunshine and walk the length of the ruined curtain wall to where the excavation hummed with activity.

Visitors to the site watched eagerly as Jared's students worked about three yards beneath ground level, engrossed in whatever cutaway section they were excavating. Emma could feel the intensity radiating from them as the day drew to a close. She spent far too much time ignoring the script she was supposed to be studying, imagining instead what the students said to each other as they bantered back and forth.

The one time she had no trouble translating was when a kid would whoop in triumph. Site visitors would crowd against the rail of the viewing platform built over the excavation, while students in floppy hats and dirt-stained T-shirts abandoned their own square of ground to race over to the location of the new discovery. They'd squabble like a nest full of crows over something sparkly until Jared strode toward them, his long legs so athletic they shouldn't have belonged to anyone with "scientist" listed after his name.

He'd hunker down, broad shoulders hunching forward as if protecting the find from the polluted modern air and the puppylike enthusiasm of the students. He'd examine whatever the student had found, jotting notes in a book he'd dug from one of his capacious pockets. And Emma would watch, wishing *she* were studying under a teacher so gifted that every day she admired him more.

Butler never swooped in on his students, swelled with conceit as he took over the "important" part of the excavation. He'd merely observe the process intently, doling out suggestions and encouragement only when needed, until the student managed to free the find from the ground that had cradled it for centuries.

Then, damn if the man wouldn't smile—that bone-melting, breast-tingling smile that made Emma wonder what it would be like to feel its full force turned on her, without the walls he seemed more determined than ever to keep between them.

She wanted to race down the tower stairs and join the crowd watching so breathlessly. Wanted to be part of the excitement she could feel, even from her tower.

But she wasn't part of the dig. She was an inconvenience that already dragged Jared away for hours at a time from the work he loved. Even so, it was his own damned fault she was chafing to hear every detail of the day's work.

From the moment he'd slipped that enameled flower into her hand, she'd felt like a modern Sleeping Beauty, pricked with a spindle that made her burn with curiosity instead of merely snoring away. She wanted to see more. Know more. Touch more. Wanted her hands in the Scottish turf, coaxing out Castle Craigmorrigan's secrets herself.

Wanted to see Jared Butler's eyes come alive with magic, the way they had when he'd shared the flower with her, when she'd been as awed by touching a piece of history as he had been.

She'd almost shared more with him than the tale of the antique wedding dress. She'd found herself wanting to tell him about the journal she'd also discovered in the trunk in March Winds' attic, the stark childhood loneliness she'd filled with a "ghost" named Addy.

Maybe he wouldn't have laughed at her after all.

But he might have plied her with more questions. Dangerous questions, like the one he'd asked when she'd been trying to make him laugh with the story of her grandfather and the Welshman.

Irish? I would have guessed something more exotic... What about your father?

Captain startled her with a disgruntled yap, as if to say, "Hey, human, when you've gotta go, you've gotta go. What do you want me to do? Tie it in a knot?"

Emma smiled down at the dog. "Fine. I'll take you out. But

you're staying on the leash, got it? No making a break for the big guy, no matter how much we both might want to."

Now there was a thought. Just let Captain slip off the leash, give him a little headstart and he'd lead her straight to Jared as long as none of the students ran interference. Emma was appalled at how tempted she was by the idea.

She fastened on the leash Davey had made out of an old length of rope and with Captain in her arms, headed down the castle stairs. At the bottom, she paused to unhook the thick velvet cord Jared had placed across the bottom, the no-admittance sign supposed to guarantee none of the tourists wandered into Emma's private quarters. Slipping past the gap in the rope, she refastened it with a grimace, imagining just how long that sort of barrier would keep someone out of her condo in L.A.

She didn't bother to set Captain down. The moment she did, he'd yank her arm out of its socket trying to haul her off to find Jared. Instead, she wandered the hundred yards to a secluded boulder beside the sea cliff, the terrier's favorite hydrant spot. It was a good thing Captain had a conniption every time the boulder came in sight since, at the moment, she was so distracted by the bustle around the dig she might have walked straight off the cliff.

The two groups of visitors Jared had told her about during sword practice now wandered the property. A busload from Elderhostel crowded along the rim of the excavation, while a pack of schoolboys, adorable in their blazers, shorts and knee socks, reveled in a day away from the classroom. A smaller cluster of tourists ranged along the curtain wall, taking pictures with the cameras slung around their necks.

But they could wander anywhere they wanted looking at all the fascinating stuff. *They* hadn't been officially labeled distractions. Frowning, she turned her back to them, unable to shake the feeling she'd had as a kid, when she was the only one not invited to the biggest party of the year.

She plopped Captain on the ground, but instead of getting down to business, he started scrabbling in the direction of the dig, showering the hem of her dress with tufts of grass. "Jared doesn't want either one of us down there. Got it?" she warned sourly. "I'm a distraction and you're the demon digger from hell."

Captain tilted his head in his best angel imitation.

"An Oscar-worthy performance, dog," Emma said. "You might even have convinced me if the dirt from your early-morning digging spree wasn't still sticking to your claws."

Captain flopped down on the grass in puppy exasperation. He might as well have demanded to know why she'd bothered to bring him outside in the first place if neither food nor jumping on Jared were involved.

"I hear what you're thinking," Emma said. "There's hardly any point in Rapunzel breaking out of the tower if the witch still won't let her play with the other kids, is there? Although technically, I suppose Jared would be considered a warlock."

Captain's button-free ear perked up at Butler's name. The terrier grabbed the leash in his teeth and tried to pull Emma in the direction of the dig.

"Dumb dog. You think Jared is more like the prince since he rescued you from the dragons. But trust me. I know a thing or two about princes. I used to be married to one. Princes are supposed to be charming. And Jared Butler is way too danger-ous and sexy to settle for a glass slipper at the end of the ball."

Suddenly Captain went off like a string of firecrackers, snarling and yapping at something behind Emma. She wheeled to see what the fuss was about, then stumbled back a step as a barrage of camera lenses were all but jammed in her face. She tried to smile, figuring that the local kids who had pestered her for autographs a few days ago must have shown off their prizes to the folks in the little town she was still trying to con Butler into loaning her a car to see.

Or were these tourists who'd somehow recognized her? Her gaze locked on the mini tape recorders in the intruders' hands. No. Not fans. Reporters. Her heart sank.

Not yet, God, a voice inside her cried. *Not yet.* But there was no escape as the cluster of journalists started snapping off questions.

"So, Emma, what's this about Prince Charming?" a burly man with a shaved head demanded. "Got some new man on the line, eh?"

Emma searched the repertoire of smart-aleck answers she'd grown so skilled at firing back, but came up empty. Knowing these men had overheard her thinking aloud tumbled her off balance. "Sorry to disappoint you," she said. "But…there's nobody new in my life except my dog."

"You were just telling Fido here you think somebody's way too sexy. Who's the lucky guy?"

Emma's cheeks burned as she scooped Captain up into her arms. "I just told you. There isn't anybody." She pushed past them, racing toward the castle as fast as her tangled skirts would let her. But the reporters kept pace, pounding after her, bellowing questions. A shark-eyed man in the lead cut in front of her and shoved his miniature tape recorder at her, keeping his hand just beyond Captain's snapping teeth.

"What was that name she said, Feeny?" a man with a bulbous nose demanded, looking at Shark Eye as the others tried to block her escape. "It started with a B… Burns? Barry?"

"Butler!" Shaved Head shouted.

"No!" Emma denied, so rattled she knew damned well it had to show.

"Bingo!" the shark named Feeny crowed in triumph. "We've got it!"

God, what was wrong with her? Emma thought wildly as she bulldozed her way toward the castle. She was making an absolute mess of this.

"How about an exclusive, Emma?" Feeny urged in an upscale British accent far too proper for a sleazy job like his. "It's way past time you grant the wishes of men everywhere and put that world-class body of yours back into circulation."

Emma shoved her way through the castle door, hearing a chorus of oaths behind her as the intruders tried to jostle in after her. She couldn't breathe. She felt vulnerable, raw. Sick to her stomach as she yanked the velvet cord out of her way and snapped it back in place.

Up the stairs. Just get up the stairs, she told herself. How many times had she sought safety behind closed doors? Put barriers between herself and the clamoring press? Barriers they couldn't cross. But this time was different she realized as she reached her tower room. There wasn't a sturdy wooden door to lock. Nothing to disappear behind. Only Jared's rope with its no-admittance sign at the foot of the stairs. A warning not much different than the one she'd ignored to explore the rocky cliffs on her first disastrous morning at the castle the week before.

A cacophony of disgruntled voices echoed up to her, the journalists grousing in disappointment as their prey vanished. She sucked in a shuddery breath of relief one heartbeat too soon. Heard footsteps approaching.

She groped for composure, struggling to paste a blank expression onto her face. But it was too late. Feeny charged into the room, scenting blood.

Captain's lip curled, threatening Feeny with those doggy vampire teeth. Love welled up in Emma for the scrappy little dog.

"You're not allowed up here," she said, confining Captain in his wooden box. "The castle is private property."

Feeny smirked as the terrier tried to dig its way through the wood. "Try again, sweetheart. Castle Craigmorrigan is part of the National Trust. It's open to the public."

"Parts of it might be. But the door to this tower has a sign saying no admittance."

Feeny shrugged, pacing toward her. "Funny, but I didn't see a damn thing."

"Then I'd advise getting your eyes checked, because—"

More footsteps hammered up the stairs. Emma's stomach plunged. Oh, God. Were the rest of the reporters following Feeny's lead? All she'd managed to do by fleeing to the tower was trap herself with Feeny and whoever else was stalking her.

Captain scratched frantically at the edge of his box as broad shoulders filled the doorway—a man, all sinews and shadows.

Jared. Emma's heart leapt as he charged into the room, his chest heaving beneath his faded blue Celtic shirt, his hair wind-blown. He must have sprinted all the way from the dig site to the castle. "Emma," he demanded, breathless. "Are you okay?"

It was all Emma could do not to close the space between them, put Jared's big body between her and the journalist. Good Lord, when had she turned into such a coward?

"I'm fine," Emma said. *At least I am now.*

Green eyes slashed from Emma to Feeny. "Davey said he'd seen some men following you into the castle." Jared frowned. What were those questions clouding his brow? He couldn't possibly think she'd *invited* Feeny and the rest of the harpies to ambush her, could he? "You didn't mention any press engagements this morning."

This morning… Emma winced in dismay. Perfectly innocent words a reporter could have a field day with.

In spite of herself, her voice wobbled a little. "This gentleman was about to leave."

But Feeny had used the time Jared was focused on Emma to gain the advantage, insinuating himself deeper into the room—a strategy Emma knew would make it harder for Jared to evict him. "Hey, Emma, is this the guy you were telling me about?" Feeny probed.

Jared rounded on him, glaring. "Who the hell are you?"

"Joel Feeny, *Independent Star.* And you are?"

"That's none of your business!" Emma started to protest, but Jared cut in.

"I'm Dr. Jared Butler. I'm the site director here."

"Well, what do you know?" Feeny's eyes glittered in triumph as he snapped off a camera shot. "If it isn't the prince himself."

"Prince?" Jared snarled, glancing back at Emma. "What the hell is this about?"

Feeny's busy gaze snagged on the purple glitter frame perched on the table. He picked it up with sausage-like fingers, his eyes raking the picture with rapacious curiosity.

Emma lunged toward him, but Jared was quicker.

He grabbed the frame out of the reporter's hand, thumping the picture facedown on the table, then turned to collar the man. But with skills honed in countless journalism-by-ambush ventures, Feeny dodged Jared and thrust the whirring tape recorder at Emma. "Hey, Emma, nice family you've got there. We never hear anything about your daddy, though. What's the story?"

Emma pressed her hand against her stomach, feeling like she was going to throw up. "There is no story."

"Ballocks!" Feeny gloated as Jared grabbed him by the arm and hauled him toward the door. "I know damned well there's a front page byline in here somewhere! It may be a story about your daddy or it could be Butler, here. You and the doc having a fling, Emma?"

Emma groped for scorn, her scathing ice queen tone. "Give me a little credit for taste! I don't even like him!"

Jared's green eyes locked with hers for a moment, turbulent with emotions too fierce, too plain. Surprise? Surely not hurt?

She could explain to him later, Emma assured herself, bile rising in her throat. *Explain what?* a voice mocked her. How the tabloid reporter would be frothing to cast Butler as her latest lover? *That* would confirm every reservation Jared had had about opening his precious castle to the media, prostituting the legend he'd spent his lifetime studying.

Don't let them see, Jared, Emma thought helplessly as the two men disappeared into the shadows. *Don't let Feeny know my words cut you.*

But who was she to be handing out advice? She'd given Feeny plenty to write about in the past few minutes, plenty of dirt to try to dig up. She might as well have pointed Captain in the direction of a T-bone steak.

There's nothing for Feeny to find, Emma reassured herself firmly. *Jared isn't my lover. And as for my father, the only people who know the truth would never tell.*

But since when did the truth have anything to do with tabloid headlines?

Emma flinched, her memory filling with the ominous smack as Drew slammed the latest rag sheet onto their kitchen counter, the headlines blaring—Emma McDaniel: "I don't want your baby!" Husband shattered, sobbing.

For God's sake, Emma! Drew's voice echoed in her head. *I didn't sign on for this. Who in their right mind would?*

She crossed to the table in the alcove and picked up the purple frame, carefully smoothing her fingers over the glitter as if to brush away any trace of Feeny's intrusive hand. She gazed down at the family she loved, their faces frozen in time. Forever happy, their demons laid to rest. So sure they were safe at last.

But the world could change in an instant, secrets spilling out that could never be reclaimed and buried once more like the wedding dress tucked deep in its trunk in the attic.

Emma's throat tightened as she caressed her mother's face, sheltered beneath the glitter-speckled glass. Deirdre McDaniel Stone, so strong now, beautiful and fierce with a love Emma tried to believe no blow could ever shatter.

Again.

How can you be sure? a child voice whispered inside Emma's head. *She fell apart when you were ten. And at sixteen when you made her tell you about him... What if the reporters find out because of you? It would be your fault....*

Emma's eyes burned. "No," she told herself sharply. "I won't let that happen. I'll never let that happen. She's safe."

Safe? Drew's anguished cry pierced her memory as he flattened his palm on the latest story. *Don't you get it, Emma? As long as anyone's name is linked with you, their life will never be their own. It'll be open season on any secret, any flaw....*

But even Drew hadn't told her the most painful truth of all.

Maybe Emma McDaniel's husband could divorce her, marry another woman and remove himself from the public eye.

Emma's mother never could.

JARED FOUGHT THE URGE to ram Joel Feeny's head into the stone wall as he dragged the reporter down the tower stairs. It wasn't as if the fool was using his brains anyway. Even Emma's eejit of a dog would have had the sense to get the hell out of Jared's reach before the last tiny threads holding his temper in check blew the roof off the whole damned castle. But Feeny was trying every trick he could think of to feed Jared's fury.

"Listen, Doc," Feeny pressed, using his body weight to slow Jared down. "I know you've got a prime deal going on here doing the horizontal bop with a lady any man in the world would like to be screwing. But the hard truth is she'll be dumping you out of her bed before your car needs its next oil change."

Emma's sneer flashed in Jared's head, her scornful words raking him. *Give me a little credit for good taste... I don't even like him....*

Why did those words sear his pride so badly?

"I'm not *in* her goddamned bed," Jared snarled, giving Feeny a brutal yank. "Don't you understand English?"

"Actually, as a rule, you Scots garble it up so badly, you make it damned hard. But I hear you, mate. Loud and clear."

Feeny staged a stumble against the wall, the rough stone rasping the skin off Jared's knuckles. Jared swore.

Feeny sagged toward the nearest step. "I'm trying to help you, mate!" he insisted, resisting.

"Sure you are," Jared snarled.

"I can be your bloody fairy godmother if you let me. Do you have any idea how much money you can make? You can cash in on these rolls in the hay for hundreds of thousands of dollars if you play it right."

Jared cocked his fist back, imagining how damn good it would feel to break a few of Feeny's teeth. "You filthy son of a—"

"You really want to be front-page news, Butler? Hit me," Feeny warned, survival instinct finally kicking in.

Damn Feeny. The slimy worm was right. Jared forced his fist back to his side. The reporter scrambled to his feet, starting down the stairs under his own steam. "Right then, mate. I'm leaving. Just think about what I said. Someone is going to make plenty of quid selling news about Emma McDaniel's love life. It can be you or the next lucky bastard she hops into bed with."

"Go to hell," Jared growled.

Feeny groped in his suit pocket as Jared herded him to the door. "Here's my card," he said, shoving it at Jared. "Ring me up. Night or day."

Jared crumpled the rectangle of paper in his fist and hurled it to the ground. "Stay away from my dig," he warned. "Or next time—"

"You think it'll be clear sailing for the goddess up there if you scare me off, Butler?" Feeny jeered. "I just got lucky enough to draw first blood. If it's not me, it'll be some other reporter hammering at her in hopes she'll break down and spill something that'll make us a fortune."

"What kind of a parasite are you? Hounding a woman like this?"

"Act all high and mighty if you want, but don't kid yourself, Doc. Reporters like me made Emma McDaniel famous. She knows that, no matter how much she recoils from us now. She owes us."

Jared's fist lashed out, but someone caught his arm, giving Feeny time to dodge out of the way. Jared wheeled, expecting to see Emma.

Instead, Veronica's face swam into focus. "Don't!" the student cried, holding on for dear life. "Are you crazy?"

Jared yanked himself free, his chest heaving, his jaw clenched. "Go get some of the lads. I need them to get this piece of garbage off the property. Now."

"I'm going. I'm going!" Feeny backed away, hands up, his tape recorder still whirring in one, camera swinging from its strap around his neck. "Just remember what I told you, Doc.

You can ring me up any time. All three numbers are on my card. Office, mobile and home."

Jared ground the card under his boot sole. "I'll see you in hell before I'd ever call scum like you."

"I've heard that before," Feeny said. "We'll see what happens once the sex burns out and Emma McDaniel throws you in the shite heap."

"S… Sex?" Veronica echoed faintly, turning even whiter as her gaze flashed to Jared.

He couldn't stop himself from taking a menacing step toward Feeny. But Veronica dove between them.

"Please," she begged. "Mr.…Mr.…"

"Feeny. Joel Feeny, *Independent Star*," the reporter supplied.

"If you'd just follow me." Veronica stared at Jared as if he'd gone insane. Maybe he had.

"Uh, Dr. Butler," she said, glancing over her shoulder. "After I escort this gentleman to his car, we need to talk right away. There's a…problem at the site."

"It'll have to wait," Jared snarled. He turned and stalked back through the castle door.

Chapter Nine

JARED STRODE UP the stairs, his knuckles burning, his temper boiling, feeling more shell-shocked than he would have believed possible. The most disturbing thing in the whole nightmarish encounter was the fact that some of what Feeny had said was true. The press and celebrities did feed off each other. And even if Jared ever was lunatic enough to give in to what his body clamored to do every time he thought of Emma McDaniel's lush curves, Feeny was right. She'd dump a man like him quicker than last month's garbage.

Not that she wanted anything to do with him anyway. She'd made that plenty clear. So why the hell had it hurt? Yes, damn it—hurt. But more than his pride. Something far deeper, in the place where her fleeting kiss had buried itself.

Anger and confusion roiled inside him, mingled with a fierce protectiveness that scared the hell out of him. One more joke. He sneered at his own stupidity. As if the lady needed him to jump between her and this particular dragon. She'd been handling scenes like this one for six years without him. What if Feeny was right about that whole *the lady doth protest too much* attitude and Emma was actually using this encounter for her own benefit somehow?

No. Emma *had* been genuinely shaken, Jared told himself. He wanted to believe that and yet…wasn't it possible he had just imagined that hunted light in her eyes because that's what he'd needed to see?

Jared stalked into the tower room, expecting the ice queen. His heart tripped as his gaze locked on the figure huddled on the bench by the seaward window, her knees curled up like a child's, her face haunted as she peered down at the glitter frame in her hands. So lost, so alone she didn't even know he was there.

"Emma?" Jared's voice, almost tender, sounded strange to his own ears.

Her head jerked up. Before she turned toward him, she scrubbed one hand across her cheeks.

"I got some…some glitter in my eye," she said. He cleared his throat, wishing he were the kind of man who could close the space between them, comfort her.

"Feeny's gone."

"He'll be back." She swallowed hard. "They always come back."

Jared clenched his hands, wishing to hell he could think of something to say. "Not on my watch," he murmured at last. "I won't let anyone—"

He'd meant to say he wouldn't let anyone hurt her. But before he could squeeze that absurd promise from his throat, Emma cut in.

"I know. You won't let anyone like him trample through your dig site, shaking things up, distracting the students."

A muscle in Jared's jaw jumped. "Right."

Emma set the frame back up on the table and stood, brushing glitter off of her hands. But her cheeks still sparkled with tiny flecks of purple and traces of tears. "I'm sorry this whole mess dragged you away from your work," she said, squaring her shoulders. "I don't blame you for being angry."

Did she really think work was the reason his nerves were so bloody raw?

"I don't know what's wrong with me," she said, turning her back to him, walking toward the bed. "I usually handle reporters like Feeny much better than this. They won't catch me off guard again."

Jared couldn't stop himself from going after her. He curved his hand over her green-clad shoulder. Emma stiffened, but damn if he'd let her go.

"They won't catch you at all," Jared swore. "Not in my castle." *In my castle?* His cheeks warmed. He sounded like a raving lunatic. What was he doing? Playing the knight, vowing to guard his lady?

His hand slid down Emma's arm as she turned toward him. He drowned in eyes so vulnerable it broke his heart.

"I'm grateful, Jared. Really. For...for your help today. But you mustn't get tangled up in this. It would be better if you kept your distance. People...get hurt when they get too close to me."

"I'm not." *Not too close. Never will be. I'm broken inside...* One corner of his mouth crooked up in a smile as he tried to hide how much he wanted to kiss her. "Give me credit for *some* taste, McDaniel. The truth is I don't even like you."

He hoped to stir up the fire in her, the bravado he'd seen in her every morning they'd crossed swords. Instead, her lips trembled.

"Most of the time the truth doesn't have anything to do with what tabloid reporters write. You want a case in point? My divorce. All that blather about how coldhearted I was. Refusing to give my husband a baby. My career was more important—playing Jade fucking Star. And God forbid, I risk getting stretch marks or lose my figure for something as inconsequential as having a child."

Jared stood silent, helpless as pain wracked her. But she peered up at him with honesty so relentless it took his breath away.

"You want to know the truth? I begged Drew to let me have his baby."

She *had* loved her ex-husband. Loss ravaged her beautiful face. Why did the knowledge knife deep into Jared's gut? He let his hand fall away from her.

"I wanted a baby so much, I even offered to give up acting in such high-profile movies. I'd try the stage, stay in one city doing theater. I'd be home every night, just…just like his new wife, Jessica." She choked on an anguished laugh. "You know what Drew said?"

"No." *Don't tell me. Don't trust me. Don't.* He was no man to share secrets with. He had too many of his own.

"Drew told me it was too late. The media would always track me, hunting for any kind of news, any failure, any secret. Drew wouldn't risk a child of his suffering through what he had because of me."

Jared wanted to reach for her again, but his hands felt too rough, too awkward to handle such honest, openhearted grief. "You can't change yourself into something you're not. Even for a husband or wife you…care about."

Why couldn't he just say the word? *Love.* Because of Jenny? Because even when she'd been his wife, he hadn't been sure…his feelings so jumbled he couldn't tell what emotions lay beyond the hard crust of his resentment.

"But I wasn't just trying to tell Drew what he wanted to hear," Emma insisted. "Jared, I *meant* it. I would have given up—"

"Who you are? Work you love? A life you've struggled for years to build?" Jared gave an impatient wave of his hand.

"Before you and Drew married, did you tell the man you wanted to be an actress?"

Emma blinked. "Of course I did. He even moved to New York while I was in drama school so we could live together."

"So what was his gripe, then? You were honest about what you wanted to do. He supported you in it. Then he…what? Changed his mind?"

Emma shrugged. "People do it every day."

Jared's face hardened. "I'll tell you what happened. He thought he'd play the role of supportive husband until you crashed into the wall. He counted on the probability that you would fail, like ninety percent of the kids who head into drama school with stars in their eyes. And when you had the gall to actually succeed, he yanked his support for your career, cheated on you and divorced you because he couldn't handle your success."

Emma gaped. "That's not… I mean, Drew didn't—"

"Didn't he?" Jared crossed his arms over his chest. "Maybe it's a good thing he left you when he did. You'd have ended up hating him."

"No. I could never…" She nibbled at her lower lip. "Maybe after a while I would have felt…"

"Cheated? There's no maybe about it. I know damned well you would have. All those ugly feelings between you and the person who's supposed to be your w— I mean, your husband." He'd betrayed more than he'd wanted to.

Her eyes flashed, belligerent. "Yeah, and my career thus far is so spectacular it's been worth blowing off my marriage? I wanted to be…so much more, you know? I wanted magic and brilliance and…to touch people's hearts. Change them. To leave some mark on the world after I was gone."

Wasn't that what Jared wanted as well? To discover something brilliant, something historians would be studying centuries later? To win his own place in the legend of Castle Craigmorrigan and its courageous lady? But he would never tell a soul about those fantasies. Leave himself vulnerable. While Emma...

So many dreams shone in Emma McDaniel's eyes, battered dreams, broken ones. What was she thinking, sharing her wounds with him? A man who had scoffed at her talent, who had dismissed her as shallow, a waste of his precious time?

Hell, Jared thought, his chest tightening. There were emotional depths to this woman he'd never have believed possible just by looking at her exquisite face. Considering what she'd been through the past few years, it was a miracle she was still standing.

Jared reached deep inside himself for the gentleness he rarely allowed himself to reveal. He drew out the memory of other pain-filled eyes, another heart he'd seen broken. His father's face, too soft beneath his craggy features, waiting, forever waiting for his highland Mary to come home.

"It's only human to want...things that are far beyond our reach," Jared said at last. "There's nowhere in the world that truth is plainer than it is right here in this tower. People died on this ground to possess something that couldn't even exist. A magical fairy flag."

"But the legend. All the years you've studied it." Emma tilted her head to one side, a puzzled crease between her delicate black brows. "I thought you believed—"

"That the fairy queen got lost in the world of mortals and fell in love with a beautiful warrior slumbering beneath a tree? That she stayed with him, made love with him for a year and a day, though they were from different worlds?" The words rasped on Jared's tongue, his throat dry as he stared into Emma McDaniel's face.

Emma spoke softly. "And she bore him a child, then wrapped the wee lass in her robe woven of spun moonlight, the queen sorrowful because she had to return to her kingdom. She left the babe with the man she loved. Swearing no castle that flew the cloth once bound about her tiny daughter would ever fall to an enemy, just as the fairy queen's love would never fall to another, though the handsomest men in the fairy realm should lay siege to her heart until the end of time."

Her lips curled in a smile so piercing it lodged in Jared's heart. "It's a beautiful story, Jared."

"Aye, but a story for all that. The cloth held power only because people believed a flight of fancy to be true."

"So things haven't changed so much after all in five hundred years. People will believe what they want to, whether in a legend or in one of Feeny's tabloids. And as for sieges— we'd best prepare for a real one in the next five weeks."

"What are you saying?"

"There are bound to be other reporters." She sighed. "I suppose I should have expected it. But…I was so careful. I hoped they wouldn't track me down here for a while. I wonder how…no, *who* tipped them off this time."

She was right, Jared reasoned. Someone had to betray her whereabouts for the press to find her here, in the middle of nowhere. But the airport had been plenty crowded with people who might have recognized her and Jared hadn't made a secret of his displeasure when he'd heard she was replacing Angelica Robards. He'd grumbled plenty—at the pub, the shops, over the phone to the studio and to the kids on site. Had *he* brought Feeny and the rest down on Emma's head?

Emma laughed wearily. "I don't suppose there's any way to attach a nice galvanized steel door at the bottom of that staircase? One with a very big lock?"

"No."

"Then maybe I should call Jake."

Jake. The man she'd written to in the letter Jared had read. Irritation gnawed at him.

"Jake could arrange a bodyguard." Emma kneaded her temples. "But then he might come running over here himself. It would be heaven to see him, but—"

"I'm not having your boyfriend tramping through here, creating even more chaos," Jared growled.

Emma's hands dropped to her sides. She stared at him, incredulous. "My... Jake isn't my boyfriend. He's my stepfather."

Jared took a step back, telltale heat flooding up his neck. "Your stepfather?"

"Despite what you might think, I didn't spring fully grown out of a producer's head like some Hollywood version of Athena. Jake was a private investigator when Mom met him, but he handles celebrity security now."

"I see." Jared did see. Exactly how big a fool he'd just made himself look. And yet, even the thought of Emma McDaniel's stepfather on site didn't sit well with Jared. This was *his* site, damn it. Keeping people safe here at Castle Craigmorrigan was his responsibility. And Emma McDaniel was part of that responsibility for as long as she was here.

You're supposed to be trying to make the woman miserable, remember? So she'll quit?

Maybe so, Jared told the voice in his head. But he'd do it on his own bloody terms. Showing her how impossible it was for her to play this part, not having her driven away by parasites like Joel Feeny.

Why should it matter why she goes, as long as her name isn't on the credits of Lady Valiant *when the movie is released?*

I don't know why it matters, Jared argued with himself. It just does.

"Listen, Jared," Emma interrupted his thoughts. "I promise I'll make sure Jake sends somebody who understands that they can't get in your way."

"That won't be necessary."

"Jared, you don't understand. It'll be open season—"

"I'll stay with you." What the hell? Jared couldn't believe the words that fell out of his mouth.

Emma gaped. "You?"

"Consider it more coaching in medieval life. After the siege, Sir Brannoc slept across Lady Aislinn's door, to make certain none of her loyal retainers could spirit her away."

"Yes, but—" She flushed, looking about as thrilled with his suggestion as he felt. "But how would you explain... I mean, the students...what would they think..."

"Universities send them here to think about archaeology, not my personal life." Jared scowled, imagining all too clearly the buzz of gossip this arrangement would start with the students. Not that any of them would dare say anything to his face. Not even the brazen Veronica. Hell, who was he kidding?

"But even if—if you did stay close by at night, that won't fix things during the day while you're working—"

"You'll stay with me during the workday." *Right, genius. Brilliant idea. You'll be getting a world of work done with her flashing that centerfold body around. Discipline, Butler. Discipline.*

"Jared, I can't stay with you day and night. The media will get wind of this and I can tell you how they'll interpret it. They'll say that you're my lover."

"Anyone who knows me at all will know that's ludicrous." He thrust out his chin, wishing someone would take a swing at it. If only to shut him the hell up so he'd quit making these absurd propositions. "You're the last kind of woman I'd ever fall for."

"Of course." Emma turned away. For an instant Jared thought he saw something fragile in her smile. The next instant she was wisecracking again. "And yet, a hot affair with Jade Star would do wonders for your reputation down at the pub. Even if we both knew it was imaginary. You'd never have to buy your own drink again."

"Thanks, but no. I'd rather take my chances with the worm."

"The what?"

"Never mind. Listen, we got the tenor of our relationship just right in the airport when I picked you up. The whole Aislinn and Brannoc mutual-loathing society. We'll just keep it at that, shall we? It suits the legend perfectly."

"All right, then," Emma agreed, going to the crate to pick up her menace of a dog. "Captain and I will be thrilled to come to the dig site with you."

"Oh, no," he started to protest. "Not the dog!" But he knew perfectly well that Emma wasn't going to leave the terrier locked away all day long. She treated the thing like a goddamn baby.

"Captain's been missing you something terrible. I thought he was going to jump out the tower window when he saw you walking to your tent this morning."

"I should be so lucky," Jared grumbled under his breath.

She snuggled the dog against those incredible breasts. The lucky little bastard. "Look on the bright side, Butler," she said. "With the two of us together constantly, day and night for the next five weeks, we should be back to wanting to kill each other in no time."

He should have found that prospect comforting. But it only cinched the knot of wariness in his chest even tighter.

Wanting to kill Emma McDaniel would be far preferable to what he wanted to do right now.

Crush his lips down on that cheeky mouth of hers. Kiss her deeper than he'd ever kissed any woman in his life. His tongue in her mouth, his hands on her breasts, tumbling her back onto the bed where those incredibly long legs would open to invite him in....

"Jared?"

"What?" He jerked out of a fantasy he'd been having far too often lately.

"Are you all right? You look so..."

Hard as a rock?

"I look so what?" he challenged, chin jutting out again.

"Grim."

Grim? He felt like he was being burned at the stake, every ounce of his will focused on what he had to do. Endure the flames without recanting everything he truly believed. About himself. About her. Maybe if she wasn't constantly looking like his fantasy—dressed in clothes Lady Aislinn might have worn—his blood would cool down.

"I'll bring up your suitcase," he said sharply. "I don't suppose you packed jeans and trainers?"

"Yes, but...but you said—"

"You can still wear Lady Aislinn's garb while we're riding or training with the sword, but you'd stick out like a sore thumb in those clothes at the dig site. Our goal for the next five weeks is to keep you low-profile. Though God knows how we're going to manage it."

Maybe he could use her as a teaching exhibit for ancient Celtic body art. Paint some nice blue streaks on her face, put lime paste in her hair....

But damn if he wasn't aroused just thinking of stroking blue woad on her skin.

Show a little self-restraint, man. Discipline. Get her in some regular clothes, get her hands dirty and that should help put out the fire. If the woad painting was over the top, maybe he could find a more subtle way of muffling his attraction to her. He could find an excuse to give her one of his old T-shirts. Faded and shapeless enough for her to swim in. If he couldn't see her body, he wouldn't want it, would he?

Aye, and you wouldn't want to touch the fairy flag if the ghosts here dangled it before your nose, lad, his father's voice mocked him. *The heart is willful and a man's body more rebellious than any highland clan. Rabbie Burns said love is a red, red rose, but it's fire far too fierce to control....*

He was on fire inside with wanting...not the Emma McDaniel on the tabloid covers, not the Emma McDaniel in the Jade Star posters Davey and the lads talked about. But rather the Emma whose face had lit up as she ran her fingertips over the centuries-old enamel flower, the Emma who'd been so damn sweet when she'd bandaged his hand. The Emma who would have leapt into a dogfight to save a mutt she'd never seen before.

But it was this new Emma who scared the living hell out of him. If he lived to be a hundred he knew he'd never forget the vulnerability in her face and the courage as she revealed the most painful secrets of her heart. How her husband had rejected her. How her life had fallen apart. The bravery she'd shown had terrified Jared, made him fear that her ruthless honesty might change everything between them.

This Emma was dangerous. So real, so warm. So damned human in ways the rest of the world could never know.

Captain yipped, wriggling to get out of Emma's arms. The dog was too stupid to live, trying to get away from those gorgeous breasts.

"If that mongrel of yours is going to be running around the dig site, maybe we should take him to the surgery after all."

"For shots?"

"Aye. And to get him fixed. He'll be nothing but trouble

until we do, trying to get loose, wanting to chase after any female in heat."

Captain's tufted eyebrows lifted as if to say: *You're a fine one to talk, mate. I'm not the one who's swelling out the fly of his jeans.*

Not for just any female, Jared defended himself silently. *Only one in particular.*

One is all it takes. Captain cocked his head to one side. *Besides, ruining all my fun is going to solve your problem how?*

Ballocks, Jared thought. He really was losing his mind, having imaginary conversations with a dog. But damn if the beast didn't have a point.

Jared glanced from the terrier to Emma, her dark hair wind-tossed, her mouth so enticing he could almost taste it. No question about it. The next five weeks were going to make the siege of Castle Craigmorrigan seem like Sunday tea at his gran's house.

He'd just have to make damn sure at the end of it all the walls that lay in ruins weren't the ones around his heart.

Chapter Ten

HE WAS WATCHING her again. From the moment Emma made the trek from castle to dig site, Jared's temper had grown sharper, his patience shorter until even Davey Harrison was diving for cover.

The only person who *couldn't* escape the line of fire was Emma, lucky girl. Jared never let *her* get more than thirty yards away from him. She actually might have enjoyed getting a closer view of the excavation if it weren't for the fact that Jared bit her head off every time she asked a question, the good-humored tolerance she'd seen him extend to his students obviously not to be wasted on his hostage.

Hostage? That might be a little overdramatic. The man *was* doing her a favor, Emma tried to remind herself. And yet she was beginning to think she'd rather take her chances with Feeny.

Jared glared across the site with wolf eyes, so piercing she felt like a rabbit just waiting for him to pounce. *And it isn't even bedtime yet,* a voice in Emma's head mocked. Awareness set every nerve cell in her body tingling as she tried not to think of Jared Butler's mouthwateringly sexy body sleeping anywhere within her reach.

So close she'd hear his every breath, every shift of his long legs against the sheets. That is, if there were any sheets involved at all. When it came to medieval bedtime rituals, she was a little vague. Maybe when Davey got close enough, she could ask him.

Hey, Davey, what does your boss wear to bed? Is the doc a boxer man or is he into tighty whities? That question would give the students something to talk about besides the World Cup.

Her imagination ran wild, remembering. Uncle Cade had worn old blue boxer shorts for the nine months she'd lived at his cabin. Her stepfather, Jake, had never recovered after her little sister announced to the entire McDaniel clan over Christmas dinner that Jake saved Mommy laundry 'cause he didn't wear even a stitch to bed. Poor Jake still hadn't lived it down.

Drew had always worn pajama bottoms, "in case there was a fire or something." But Emma would bet her entire financial portfolio Jared Butler had never even owned a pair of pajamas in his life.

Jared definitely seemed like an if-there's-a-fire-the-neighbor-lady-is-going-to-get-one-hell-of-a-show kind of guy. Yeah, Emma chided herself, *and wouldn't you just love to be in the front row when the curtain rises on that scene?* The prospect of a naked Jared Butler running amok was enough to induce a woman to consider arson.

She didn't even have to close her eyes to picture how magnificent his bare chest had looked as she'd swabbed the tiny wounds Captain had caused in Jared's sleek, tan skin. Hard planes of muscle, dusted with dark hair that had teased her palm, tempting her to touch longer than she needed to, trace the lines and angles, satin-sheathed steel.

"This train of thought is positively not helpful," she

scolded herself. "You should be thinking of anything but a giant-sized naked Scot—"

"Emma?"

She jumped as if Davey had hit her with a water balloon instead of merely saying her name. Where had he come from? She glanced over to see the other boys ambling toward them from the table where they'd been cleaning the day's finds.

She pressed a hand to her thundering heart, a guilty flush burning her cheeks. She could just imagine the teasing mileage those boys would have gotten if they'd overheard her grumbling about naked Scotsmen. Thank God Davey wasn't a mind reader; he'd be scandalized at the R-rated thoughts she'd been having about his hero. She played her best *nonchalant.* "Hey, Davey. How's the work going? Find the fairy flag yet?"

"The only thing I'd like to find is Dr. Butler's sense of humor," Davey complained. "I haven't seen him in such a rotten mood since the day he found out the site's funding had been yanked."

"Why did they yank it anyway? It seems like you're still finding artifacts."

"Budget cuts. There's only so much money. And one of Dr. Butler's colleagues discovered a treasure horde that might rival Sutton Hoo. This terrific burial site that—"

"I get it. Great news for archaeology. Rotten news for your boss, eh?"

"That's pretty much it. Add to that what happened this morning and well…" Davey shrugged. "He wasn't thrilled about the media showing up."

Not to mention the fact that he must be looking forward to the shift in sleeping arrangements as much as I am, Emma almost said. No. Don't do it, Emma. Don't mention the fact that the man is surly as a grizzly because he's going to sleep with you—well, not *with* you. Just in the same general area.

A doggy yelp split the air, followed by a string of curses. "Bloody hell, woman, will you keep *your dog* out from under *my feet!*" Jared bellowed. But Captain only held up one paw pathetically, and gazed with adoration into Jared's eyes.

Emma raced over to snatch the little traitor out of harm's way. "Right. *My* dog. That would be *my* dog who curls up at *your* feet every time you sit down and trails after *you* every time *you* move. *My* dog who climbed up on *your* bed when we had to go in your tent."

"No doubt for the pleasure of infesting the blankets with fleas," Jared growled, tossing the trowel he'd been using to the ground. "You'd think he understood me when I mentioned that trip to the surgery and is trying to charm me out of it."

He sounded as if the poor stray were the canine version of Machiavelli! Emma's chin hitched up. "How would you feel if Captain had been plotting to slice off your manly bits, Dr. Mengele?"

Davey's eyes almost popped out of his head. "His what?"

"Jared thinks we should get Captain neutered. I know I'll have to do it eventually, but after all the trauma he's been through already this week—talk about inhumane! He was almost chewed up by those horrible collies and that awful Snib man threatened to beat him with a stick! And as if that wasn't bad enough, he has to wear that gigantic button on his head so he looks ridiculous. Talk about humiliating!"

"I couldn't make that dog look any worse if I tried," Jared defended.

"Captain would have to disagree with you there." Emma sniffed. "Males of any species tend to be touchy when somebody talks about slicing off—"

Jared glared. "It's a little different, wouldn't you say? Whether you perform the operation on a man or a dog?" He stomped away, muttering under his breath. Emma strained to hear. "*Although with you around the site I might just consider it an act of mercy...*"

Davey's jaw nearly hit the dirt. "Dr. Butler...what did you say?"

Jared rounded on the kid, green eyes blazing. "I said—"

Emma waited, relishing how embarrassed the doc was going to be when he blurted it out. But Butler checked his tongue at the last minute. "Move the mattress from my cot and the rucksack I packed up to Ms. McDaniel's room."

"Your, um..." Davey faltered.

"That's right. I'll be staying up at the castle from now on."

A hoot of appreciation echoed from the approaching lads. Sean fired off a low whistle. "Way to go, Professor! Smooth move. Real smooth."

Jared turned on the boys. His eyes narrowed. "You have a better idea for keeping the press out of that tower?"

"Of course not!" Sean splayed his hands, obviously taken aback by the expression on Jared's face. The other boys looked ready to dive into the castle moat. "I was just joking," Sean soothed.

"Well...I...have a better idea." Davey's Adam's apple bobbed in his skinny throat. "I could do it instead of you, Dr. Butler. I mean, sleep with...um, up there."

"Great idea, Einstein," one of the other kids teased. "The lady's virtue would be safe with you."

Jared shot them a glare that sent the soccer mates scrambling off in the other direction. Only Davey held his ground.

"And wouldn't your mother just love that situation?" Jared asked. "Her nineteen-year-old lad alone with the woman he had hung on his dormitory wall. Not to mention the fact that this *is* still a working dig site. I need my assistant to be alert, on task. Not staying awake all night fantasizing about—"

"Now, hold on there just a minute!" Davey exclaimed, his face brick-red.

Jared regretted his harsh words. Emma could see it in his eyes. But the archaeologist crossed his arms over his chest, determined not to back down.

Davey squared his shoulders with heartbreaking dignity. "At least I wouldn't be yelling at Emma or blaming her for things that aren't her fault. Besides, I don't think of her that way anymore. Emma is my friend. Not just some glossy poster that doesn't have any feelings." His voice choked, and for a moment Emma was terrified the kid was fighting back tears. She couldn't bear the thought of him losing face because of her.

She crossed to the teenager and handed Captain to him. The terrier licked his neck, but the dog's eyes were still on Jared. "Don't let Attila the Scot here bother you," Emma told Davey. "I'm a lot tougher than I look."

Jared looked almost sheepish, and Emma felt her own cheeks sting, knowing he was remembering those all too brief moments in the tower when she'd let her own guard down and told him about Drew. What on God's earth had she been thinking, confiding something so personal to the man? She must've been out of her mind.

In any case, whatever truce they'd tried to strike up in the tower room was obviously over as far as Jared was concerned. What was it she'd said? *We should be back to hating each other in no time?*

She'd meant it as a joke. Her attempt to lighten things up when ghosts grew too real and old pain too fresh. Why did losing the bond that had sprung up so tenuously between them make her sad?

Sad? *No,* she told herself sharply. *Be mad. Don't you let this man know he hurt you.*

Emma glimpsed a rainbow of girly T-shirts and bouncing

ponytails meandering toward them. Just when she thought things couldn't get any worse: Veronica and the rest of her flying monkeys.

Ever since Emma had followed a stormy-tempered Jared down from the tower, Veronica had acted so solicitous that every time the blonde got near her, Emma had the urge to throw up—preferably all over Veronica's purple sandals.

It was almost as if the witch knew....

Knew what? About the whole media disaster? And the effect it had had on Jared? It wasn't as if anyone with a pulse could miss the fact that things between Emma and Jared had gone from bad to worse. Even so, the last thing Emma needed to deal with was more of Veronica's gloating.

"Listen, Davey," Emma said to the lad. "How about if I help you carry Simon Legree's junk up to my prison. And in return, you can answer some historical questions I have."

Jared's jaw clenched. "I thought I made it clear—"

"Look around, Butler," Emma said briskly. "There's not a soul on site except your students. I'm perfectly safe. Besides—" she gestured to Veronica, the girl's avid little ears all perked up "—I'm sure you could use a little time to explain our new sleeping arrangements to the ladies. You did such a stellar job explaining it to the guys. Meanwhile, Davey can answer some questions that have been gnawing at me the past few hours. I'm positively dying of curiosity."

Mistrust clouded Jared's rugged features. "About what?"

"Nothing you need concern yourself with," Emma said with an airy wave. "You just…flit about doing whatever it is you do."

"I don't 'flit.'"

Jared was right there. Anything as brawny and big and male as he was couldn't flit if his life depended on it. Too bad he didn't have some deep dark secret photos hanging around somewhere—blackmail-worthy ones like those her mom lorded over Jake. Deirdre still loved to taunt her husband about the Jacob shrine his grandmother kept on display in her Easter egg pink house. A teenaged Jake in tights, starring in Baryshnikov-esque roles: chick bait to keep his beloved grandmother's dancing school in business.

"I'll take good care of you, Ms., I mean, Emma." Davey's voice startled her from her thoughts.

The lad almost seemed to grow taller, making it clear to everyone, the girls and Jared included, that Emma was under his protection. The sweetness of the gesture touched Emma's heart.

"What is it you want to know?"

"Know?" Emma asked blankly, her train of thought shattered by images of Jared Butler in a pink tutu—or kilt, as the case might be.

"You said you were curious about something."

That's right! She was, she remembered with relish. "I was just wondering about poison."

Davey's brows arched up in confusion. "Poison?"

"Didn't someone kill Lady Aislinn's father that way? At least, that's what the script hints at."

"Legend says Sir Brannoc gave him a hawking gauntlet painted with something toxic inside," Davey explained.

"Would that work?"

"You could absorb it through your pores, I suppose, but it's probably just part of the myth. Dr. Butler doubts that part of the story is true."

"Does he now?" Emma tossed her curls back over her shoulder. "Well, I'm sure the genius doctor is right. Of course, it does make a person wonder…if somebody *did* want to poison someone else, what kind of potion would she brew?"

"She?" Jared snorted.

Davey didn't even notice. The boy nibbled at a hangnail, lost in concentration. "Some mixture of herbs, I'd imagine," Davey mused. "Nightshade or foxglove could do a lot of damage."

"How lovely." Emma slanted Jared a pointed glance as she swept Davey away. "*Please* tell me those still grow in Scotland."

EMMA THUMPED JARED'S ten-ton backpack onto the stone landing outside the arched entry to her room. She frowned at Davey. The boy, who had so chivalrously insisted on going up first to make sure there were no rogue reporters running loose in the tower, was already unrolling the mattress from Jared's cot on the stone floor. *Inside* her room. No way was she letting Butler intrude that deeply into her personal space.

"Wait just a minute, there," she protested. "Your boss is sleeping on this side of the imaginary door." She tapped the slab of stone pointedly with her foot.

"Emma, it's way too narrow," Davey explained. "If he rolled over in the middle of the night he wouldn't stop until he hit the bottom."

Emma glanced over her shoulder at the steep spiral staircase, the uneven stone risers one of the more ingenious defenses Castle Craigmorrigan's builders had devised. Damn if Davey wasn't right. She shifted her feet, restless, irritated. The thought of Butler invading her bedroom set her nerves on edge. "Then I suppose he'd better not roll ov—" She swore as the backpack toppled under its own weight, thudding ominously downward. It disappeared around the corner of the spiral stairs, then after a moment landed at what must be the bottom with a resounding smack.

"Listen, Emma," Davey began.

Emma held up her hand to stop him. "Just give me a moment to enjoy this. Imagine all kinds of breakable things in that backpack—you know, aftershave and cologne and shoe polish and God knows what else—soaking into your boss's clothes."

"Cologne draws gnats that bite something awful. Dr. Butler never wears any."

The man smelled that good all on his own? That should be illegal.

Davey straightened, shoved his hands in his pockets. "Listen, Emma, I don't blame you for being...well, angry with Dr. Butler. Every time you're around him, he starts acting like a real jerk."

"Not every time," Emma admitted. Her memory flashed to images of Jared diving into the dogfight. Jared tipping the enamel flower into her hand. Jared listening as she told him about Drew's defection—how Jared had taken her side, made her feel at least a little better.

"If you just knew him the way I do, maybe you could cut him some slack."

"Davey, I know you adore Dr. Butler. I promise I won't roll him down the stairs in the middle of the night. Fantasizing about it is good enough."

Davey chuckled.

"I'll even go fetch the backpack, though the wreckage inside it is bound to be a disappointment."

"Wait."

She paused, tipped her head in query.

He wouldn't meet her eyes. "I've been wanting to ask you... I read somewhere that you...your mom raised you alone."

"That's right." Emma tried not to show her surprise at his abrupt personal question.

"I don't mean pry into your private life. It's only...it's always been just my mom and me, too."

She could see how much those words cost Davey. She reached out and touched his arm. "Your mom must be a remarkable lady to have raised a son like you."

Davey paced to the window, shrugged, his shoulders stiff. "Mom...did the best she could. I never really knew my dad."

"That's hard," Emma said. *Sometimes knowing him is even harder.*

"We moved a lot. Mom worked three jobs, cleaning people's houses, waiting tables wherever we were. The flats got shabbier and smaller, the neighborhoods more dangerous. Lots of crime and such. And the schools…they got so bad I…it was desperate. Pure hell, you know?"

Oh, yeah. Emma knew, all right. The knot you got in your stomach when you walked onto the playground. The sick dread when you entered a bathroom or a corner of a schoolyard out of the teacher's sight. Where anything could happen.

"I moved to Whitewater when I was in fifth grade. The other kids…well, let's just say tormenting the new kid was their favorite hobby. It stunk."

She expected Davey to react like Jared had when she'd told him about Brandi Bates. Incredulous. Disbelieving. Davey just nodded sadly. "That's where the dark places come from. In your eyes sometimes, when you're acting. I wondered."

She hesitated, surprised. "You see dark places in my acting?"

"Sure I do. Anybody who really watches you can tell. You've got so much more depth than you get credit for."

"Your boss would disagree. Not to mention my own studio."

"Well, once you play Lady Aislinn, the whole world will know how terrific you are," Davey said, so certain it boosted Emma's spirits. Still, his praise made her uncomfortable. Davey was a starstruck kid who liked her, not exactly an impartial judge.

She changed the subject back to his question of moments before. "You asked me about how I channel dark places into my acting. Maybe…you had plenty of your own?"

"My dark places were all over back then. School or holiday. It didn't matter. I got beat up pretty much whenever I went outdoors. So when summer came, I stayed inside. Alone."

Emma remembered smoky clubs, feeling invisible curled up in a corner with her books until her mom was done singing. She knew how alone felt.

"When I was fifteen, we came to the castle for a field trip just as school was letting out. Dr. Butler was so amazing. Made the middle ages seem so real. I kept asking all these questions. For once, I didn't care that the other lads were making fun of me behind the teacher's back."

"It feels good to be thinking about something that enthralls you, people or places where the other kids can't reach you."

"You did that, too?"

"My best friend was a ghost, a fact I didn't bother to hide from the brats at school. You can imagine their reaction to my little fantasy. Bet you could sell that story to the tabloids for a bundle. I'm surprised nobody's already done so."

Davey chuckled.

"I guess that's why that first night I was so sure I saw…well, a knight fighting with a sword out on the sea. Not such a big leap from one fantasy to another. Anyway—not that it matters. Tell me more about your first day here at the castle."

"We'd brought boxed lunches on the field trip. During break, I took mine off under this tree, alone. I always ate alone."

"Me, too," Emma said. "Until Jessie moved to town." And at ten years old, Emma finally learned the magic of having a real-live best friend, instead of a ghost who couldn't talk back, couldn't laugh out loud, couldn't share a treasured copy of *Little Women,* giving Emma a glimpse into the kind of family she'd always dreamed of having.

In hindsight Emma wouldn't trade her family for anything in the world. But back then, the fictional Marches had seemed heartbreakingly perfect.

And if anyone in Whitewater had told her that Jessie would

steal Emma's husband someday, Emma would have laughed in their face. Emma's heart twisted as she remembered Jessie showing up at March Winds after she'd gotten engaged to Drew.

Em, I didn't mean for this to happen... Jessie's voice echoed in her head. *But you were gone so much or in the middle of some crazy schedule on some other continent, and Drew...needed someplace quiet where he could be himself.*

And you were right there waiting, weren't you?

We didn't touch each other until after you were separated. Drew needs you to know that and so do I.

Of course you wouldn't. You're both too damned nice *even to be honest enough to—* Even then Emma had known she was being absurd. Had she wanted them to commit blatant adultery so she could hate them both? Would that have made it easier somehow?

Stay away from me, Jessie, she'd warned. *I never want to see you again.*

But forever was a long time, and there were moments she missed Jessie's generosity, her understanding, the simple way she faced life. It had been hard enough for Emma to lose her husband, but the divorce had shattered her two longest, most precious friendships as well.

"Emma?" Davey's voice pulled her back to the present.

"I'm sorry," Emma said, trying to cover up thoughts too private to share. "What were you saying?"

"I was telling you about the first time I came to the castle," Davey said with a thoughtfulness that reminded Emma far too sharply of the friend she'd turned away. "The popular lads had a place all set for Dr. Butler at their table. But he came over and sat by me."

Emma swallowed hard, imagining how much that must have meant to Davey.

"We talked about history and archaeology and I asked him

for a list of books I could read that summer. Great, huge non-fiction tomes, you know? Like the *Oxford Encyclopedia of Archaeology* and all kinds of stuff."

"Murder weapons," Emma supplied.

"I'm sorry?" Davey cocked his head, confused.

"When Jared met me at the airport he was carrying this book thick enough to be a murder weapon."

"Exactly. Somehow, he got me talking about home, you know? When I *never* talk about home to anybody." Secrets haunted the boy's eyes. He looked away. "He said his personal assistant had just gotten his doctorate and had run off to supervise a dig in Colombia. He asked if I'd like the job."

A fifteen-year-old kid replacing someone with a doctorate in archaeology? What had Jared been thinking? Emma's heart squeezed. She knew exactly what he'd been thinking.

Jared's voice echoed in her head. *I used to be just like him…*

"Anyway, Dr. Butler promised I could have free rein in his library. You wondered why his rucksack was so heavy? It's probably full of books."

Emma thought of her own suitcase, the books she'd hauled from L.A. She'd packed too many, as usual. But she'd never gotten over the terror she'd had as a kid, that she'd end up somewhere without anything to read.

"About the third week I was on site, Dr. Butler caught me raiding the research books again, more books on scientific method, Scottish history, stuff like that. He asked if…I ever read poetry."

"Poetry?" Emma echoed, surprised. Imagining Jared Butler reading poetry was like imagining Attila the Hun drinking a piña colada with a pink paper umbrella on top.

"Dr. Butler loaned me this book he kept on his bedside table all the time. A thin little ragged copy with pages held in by a rubber band. Told me to try it."

"What was it?"

"The works of Robert Burns."

Butler a romantic? All right, so he'd managed to surprise her. Again. At least the man's choice of poets made a twisted kind of sense. From what Emma had read, Burns was a hot-blooded plowman poet who'd sizzled his way across the Scottish countryside, leaving a trail of little Burnses in his wake. And that innate brand of blistering sensuality seemed to be Jared's stock and trade. If he ever decided to make a sweep across Scotland, he'd probably have women lined up in every village, eager for a taste of what he offered.

"Burns, huh?" Emma prodded, praying Davey wouldn't notice how flustered she'd suddenly become.

"Dr. Butler told me his da had carried that book with him everywhere."

"Jared's father was a scholar?"

Davey bit his hangnail and avoided her gaze. "That's for Dr. Butler to say," he hedged. He turned back to Emma. "At the end of the summer, when I was going home, I was miserable. The summer had been brilliant. Work I loved. And Dr. Butler—he didn't tolerate the other lads bullying me. I can't tell you what it felt like. All that respect and the way he trusted me. I wasn't just that upstart scholarship kid who threw off the grading curve at school."

"Leaving the castle must have been awful."

"It was like dying. Felt like the end of the world. See, Mum had written to tell me her latest boss promised to hire me the next summer at the stable where he kept his horses. I'd make enough to help Mum with bills. And in time, I could manage the place. I wouldn't have to waste any more time on school. I could work full-time."

"Oh, Davey." Emma tried to imagine him leaving school.

No more books. No more learning. After a summer with Jared's library to devour and all of archaeology to explore.

"The worst thing of all was my mum. She was so happy. I'd be secure for life. The night before we closed down the site, I showed Dr. Butler the letter. I couldn't just blurt it out, tell him like a man. I was afraid I'd cry." Davey grimaced. "In the end, I bawled like a baby anyway."

Emma could only imagine how humiliated Davey must have felt.

"Next afternoon, Dr. Butler drove me to the train station. Said he expected me back at the dig site the minute school was out. He'd found a scholarship that would pay me even more than my mum's boss would *and* I'd get credit from his university while I worked for him. I swear, I nearly fainted."

"No wonder. At your age."

"Age had nothing to do with it. It was when he talked about university. As if there was no question I'd be going. No one in my family had even graduated from what you would call high school. Then he reached in his coat pocket and…" Davey's voice cracked. "He handed me his copy of Burns. Said his father always told him that Burns was proof that a man didn't have to be stuck in the rocky earth where fate had planted him. He can be a poet or a doctor or a dreamer—be anything he chooses—as long as he believes in himself."

Emma's eyes burned. *Oh, Jared…*

"I didn't want to take the book. Told him he should keep it for his own kids someday. I mean, it belonged to his father. If I had the kind of father who would have given me something like that, I'd never, ever give it away. Dr. Butler just clapped his hand on my shoulder and said his father would have been proud for me to have it."

Emma sighed, trying to disguise how moved she was by

attempting to joke. "So much for my devious plot for revenge. Maybe I won't poison Jared after all."

Davey's mouth crooked in a lopsided smile. "You and Dr. Butler are…are two of the nicest people I've ever known."

"As long as we stay on opposite sides of the dig."

"I just wish…if he'd watch you in the Jade movies, maybe he'd change his mind about…well…"

"The fact that he thinks I'll butcher the role of Lady Aislinn?" Emma offered.

Davey winced, obviously groping for something to say. But how could he possibly deny it?

"It's okay, Davey. It's no big secret."

"But it's hardly a fair judgment. If he'd just watch even one of your movies, he'd—"

"See that they're techno-garbage," Emma admitted reluctantly. "I'd hate to prove him right."

"No way! You were fantastic in the first two movies. You played the strongest woman I'd ever seen. It was only later that the director got all caught up in special effects. That's his failing. Not yours. Dr. Butler is a smart man. He'd see how terrific you are."

Jared, with his murder-weapon books and his genius degree from University Of Davey's Dream. A dream Jared had made come true. If anything, the confidences Davey had just shared about the man made Emma want to buy up every copy of Jade from here to Glasgow and bury them under the castle wall.

But Davey looked so hopeful, so earnest, Emma couldn't very well tell the kid his taste in movies stunk. Instead, she hugged the boy.

"I'm grateful. Really, for how you keep trying to defend me," she said. "But Jared Butler watching my movies? That's one thing that will never happen."

"Emma, just—"

"Dr. Butler will never watch Jade Star." Her voice dropped low with painful honesty. "And frankly, Davey, neither will I."

The sudden heavy thud of the outer door echoed up the staircase.

"Speak of the devil." Emma gave herself a mental shake. "Looks like your boss is here."

Davey fidgeted. "Listen, don't tell him...well, that I told you about the book and all. He gets real touchy about..."

"Letting anyone know he's a poet at heart?"

"He's just not as hard-edged as he acts. He's got...soft places, too."

Not so Emma had noticed. At least not on that amazing body. But his heart...

"He's like...did you ever read *Le Morte d'Arthur?* Remember when Morgause trapped the king behind an invisible wall?"

"I remember."

"Sometimes I think all his life, Dr. Butler's been waiting for someone to care enough, be stubborn enough, to knock it down."

At that moment, Butler himself strode into view, scowling like a highland raider, his backpack slung over one broad shoulder, his sword in its scabbard balanced on the other. "What was my rucksack doing at the bottom of the stairs?"

"I dropped it," Emma confessed, knowing she'd dropped plenty of other baggage as well since she and Davey had climbed up to the tower room. "I'm...sorry."

Jared stared at her as if she'd lost her mind. "Are you suffering from multiple personality disorder, McDaniel? Half an hour ago you were threatening to poison me."

"Yeah, well, I changed my mind. You can live for all I care. At least until I can kick your butt with a sword. After that...

well, poison does seem a little extreme. I mean, after my training is over we'll never have to see each other again."

Oh, God. Maybe Jared was right. She was going crazy, babbling like the village idiot. Worse still was the sinking feeling she got, knowing her final observation was true. Once these few weeks were over, she and Jared Butler would go back to their separate worlds.

The thought should have soothed Emma's ragged nerves. But it didn't. Her gaze flicked to Jared's mouth, so sexy, so compelling. Something more clung to his lips and hid within the glen-green depths of his eyes. Pain. Compassion. Sensitivity. A soul-deep loneliness that called to Emma's heart.

She turned away, closed her eyes, but this time she saw Jared, not in his canvas cargo pants and scruffy T-shirt, but as Davey had described him.

Exhausted, trapped behind an enchanted wall, his body battered as he fought a young lad's demons, more valiant than any knight could ever be.

Chapter Eleven

NO WONDER SIR BRANNOC went stark raving mad after months of guarding the most beautiful woman in Scotland a mere ten paces from her bed. Jared had only been trapped in the tower room for three hours and already he—an archaeologist, for God's sake—was beginning to think installing a door in six-hundred-year-old castle walls wasn't such a rash idea after all. As long as *he* got to stay on one side of all that lovely galvanized steel and Emma McDaniel remained on the other.

Even that demon dog of hers would have offered a welcome distraction. But Davey had taken the animal with him when he'd fled down the stairs as if his bum was on fire. The kid had looked almost guilty. But then, it had to be tough for Davey, torn between his loyalty to Jared and his understandable fascination with the first beautiful woman ever to lavish attention on him.

What chance did a raw lad like Davey have of resisting Emma McDaniel's allure when the actress had shattered even Jared's laser-like concentration?

Jared prowled Emma's tower room like a lion in a menagerie at feeding time, the air thick with a hunger that rattled the hell out of him. Every nerve in his body strung tight as a longbow about to be fired. What the hell was wrong with him?

Lust. Pure and simple. And the woman, curled up on her bed for the past two hours, wasn't helping defuse his predicament a damned bit.

Emma draped herself across the furs like a medieval goddess, a circlet of silver flowers gleaming in her hair, her brow furrowed with concentration as she studied her script. She'd surprised the hell out of Jared when he'd returned from walking Davey downstairs, her modern khaki capri pants and white blouse banished somewhere out of sight, her lush body once again garbed in a flowing gown Lady Aislinn might have worn.

I told you that you didn't have to wear those clothes unless we're training, he'd snapped, his voice harsh even to his own ears as he imagined the silky bare curves he might have seen if he'd returned to the room a little more quickly. Hell, he probably could have set an Olympic record in sprinting with that kind of motivation. If he'd allowed his baser instincts to kick in. Which he would not. Could not.

She'd smiled at him—disarmingly shy—all but driving him to his knees to beg for mercy. *It just feels right to wear these clothes here. Makes me feel closer to Lady Aislinn, you know?*

Then how about if we keep this whole thing historically accurate? Jared was tempted to say. *Tonight you sleep the way Lady Aislinn did.*

Naked.

But naked might be easier for him to resist than the way she looked now. A tousled stowaway from another century, as out of place in modern times as he was. Jared ran his tongue over lips parched with a thirst all the water in the world couldn't quench. God, she was so beautiful.

Bloodred velvet pooled along one smooth golden-brown leg, bared to the knee when she had shifted position on the furs. Her surcoat slipped low to expose one graceful white shoulder. The cloth was embroidered with an interlaced design of St. George's dragons and Scotland's wildcats tangled together in what should have been battle, yet kept twisting in his mind's eye to something far more sensual.

Candlelight dipped shadowy fingers into the cleavage her shift was meant to conceal, the drawstring that should have gathered the wide neckline to a more decent height obviously tied too loosely in her haste to cover herself before he returned to the room.

Jared could've saved himself plenty of agony if he'd just told her to refasten the thing, but damned if he could make himself do it. Every time he tried to say something, he imagined his own fingers tracing the elegant line of her throat, the delicate ridge of her collarbone, the ripe swell of breast.

His mouth went dry as he pictured himself drawing her to her feet, snagging the end of that wayward drawstring, tugging it until the loop of the bow came free. Palms on her shoulders, he'd skim the fabric down her arms....

And then Emma McDaniel would rip his eyeballs out.

At least that would have been the outcome if he'd tried to seduce her a few hours ago when she'd been threatening to poison him.

But now...

He glanced over at her, caught her looking at him with eyes dark as midnight and twice as mysterious. That red mouth glistened, so kissable his shaft swelled against the fly of his cargo pants. He hoped like hell the pockets stuffed with the tools of his trade disguised the fact that he was once again hard as the rock on Craigmorrigan's cliffs. But damned if he was taking any chances of her seeing how she affected him. He searched for a way to distract them both.

"You haven't turned the page for almost an hour," Jared accused. "If it takes you that long to memorize a part it's a miracle you ever finished a movie at all."

She flushed, moistened her lips with her tongue. "I...I can't seem to concentrate."

Neither can I. At least, on anything except getting my hands all over you.

"I usually bribe someone to run lines with me. Drew or...or since he left, Sam."

"Sam?" Jealousy poked Jared with a pointed stick.

"My best friend back in L.A. She taught me to ride."

Sam was a woman. Jared clenched his teeth, irritated at the relief that surged through him. First he'd been jealous of her stepfather, now this Sam person? Even if they had turned out to be her current flames, why should he care?

Hell, he hadn't felt so much as a twinge the semester his wife had set the whole campus talking, running to one-on-one poetry critiquing sessions with the English professor who'd fancied himself a modern-day Byron. Even when the sessions had lasted half the night, Jared had been relieved she wasn't waiting at home for him. That finally she'd found something she was passionate about. That delusion shattered when she'd finally thrown her sheaf of poetry in the garbage, admitting she hadn't cared about anything besides getting Jared's attention.

If there was one thing Emma McDaniel had proven in her three weeks at the castle—the woman was passionate about her work. One more driving force Jared couldn't help but admire.

Emma grimaced, oblivious to the thoughts racing through Jared's mind. "I thought about asking Davey to run lines with me," she mused, "but he takes everything so seriously. Somehow the idea of him playing the conqueror of Craigmorrigan was—well, out of character. And I've got such a wicked sense of humor that I was afraid I might laugh by accident and completely humiliate the poor kid."

"I could do it." The words fell out of Jared's mouth before he could stop them.

Emma's gaze sprang to his, a frozen, almost deer-in-headlights expression on her face for a fleeting moment. "No. I couldn't. I mean, you already have to teach me riding and swordplay and whatnot. And you made it clear the script drives you crazy. Why torture yourself?"

"Torture is pacing around this tower with nothing to do." *Except imagining having hot sex.* "Besides, I have a completely selfish motive. If I run lines with you, I can see how badly the screenwriter has mangled things since last time I read the script. I made such a pain in the arse of myself in the early days, Robards told me to back off."

"You? A pain in the arse? Hard to believe, Butler." Her eyes danced. "You've been a regular Dragon Prince...I mean, Prince Charming since I got here."

Jared laughed. "Sir Brannoc *is* the villain. A Dragon Prince seems to be just what's in order here."

"Then you should be spot-on. You've already got that growly look down to an art form. But the lumpy cargo pants—well, let's just say it's a good thing I have a brilliant imagination. I can dress you in something more appropriate in my head."

Her gaze swept from his face down his body. He hoped like hell she wouldn't notice the extra ridge straining the fly of his canvas pants. But her cheeks reddened. She turned her face away, obviously scrambling to find a distraction for them both.

"About the script—Robards expects me to improvise here

and there. Actors do it all the time. If something feels wrong to you, we could fix it together."

"You'd let me do that?" he queried, surprised.

"Nobody knows what Lady Aislinn and Sir Brannoc would say better than you do. Or at least nobody could make a better guess." Emma frowned. "Don't you wish we really could know what they said to each other? How they felt inside? Where Lady Aislinn got the courage to fight him? I'm not challenging your scholarship. It's only…" She glanced around the room, wistful, as if searching the shadows for ghosts or clues. "Sometimes I feel like there must have been so much more."

Kinship. It sank deep in his bones, more alarming even than the pull of sensual attraction. "That feeling is what keeps me here at Craigmorrigan," Jared confided. "What makes this dig so important to me. A puzzle with missing pieces only I can see. And once this movie is filmed, I'll lose the chance to get it right."

"That's not true. Your book—"

"How many people are going to read it?" he challenged.

"Once the movie comes out—*plenty.* And they'll be as fascinated as I was."

"You read it?" Jared asked in surprise.

"Yeah. The moment I finished the script I raced over to the UCLA library and snapped it up. I would have ordered it on Amazon but I couldn't wait that long, even for the speediest delivery. My stepfather says that when God was handing out patience, we McDaniels thought He said 'pasties' and ran screaming in the opposite direction."

"Pasties?" Jared echoed, nonplussed.

"He spent his childhood backstage in Las Vegas with a bunch of showgirls. Sometimes things just slip out."

"Another family trait," Jared quipped, but he was still trying to imagine Emma racing to the library, hauling his massive book down from the shelf. He could almost hear her choking on the cloud of dust she must have unleashed.

"Reading the book must have been a jolt for you," Jared sympathized. "Going from potential soundbytes in a movie script to dry academic fare."

"Are you kidding? I stayed up all night, read until my eyes felt like they were going to roll out of my head. The book took my breath away. No wonder the script was driving you crazy, trying to squeeze all that action into a few hours of film. And God knows what Robards is going to leave on the cutting-room floor to bring it in at two and a half hours."

"I doubt anybody will miss it."

"I will. But if this movie is our one chance to reach them, help me convey as much of the story as possible through the words I say and the way I say them. I really do want to get this right, Jared. She matters to me. Lady Aislinn. That's why I keep pestering you with so many questions, why I'm wearing her clothes." She shrugged, her shift sliding down her shoulder another inch. "I want to be a part of this story. A part of this place. It haunts me."

Jared's mouth went dry as he once again lost himself in those velvety-brown eyes. Of all the words in the world he could have chosen to describe his link to this castle and its long-vanished lady, *haunted* was almost eerily apt. Haunted by a woman who had so loved her husband she'd endured captivity, outsmarting the vilest of mercenaries to protect his holdings, his people. A woman willing to stand with those she loved no matter how unbearable things got, day after day. A woman who would never have deserted her husband.

Or her son….

Jared winced inwardly at the shard of insight that buried itself in his consciousness like a sliver of glass, leaving him bleeding.

"I'll be back in a minute," he said, needing to get away from Emma McDaniel's far-too-penetrating gaze. Impulsively, he snagged his rucksack and headed down the spiral stairs. He sagged for a moment against a wooden bench, wondering why he'd never thought of his bond with Lady Aislinn in that way before. Remembering his grubby child's hand clamped in his father's callused one as Angus Butler helped him explore the castle ruins.

And she wouldn't leave, Da? Even when the bad knight made her fight with swords and he beat her again and again?

No, lad. For her love was more stalwart than the cliffs. As true love should always be….

Do you love me that way, Da?

Angus had rumpled Jared's hair. *Not even Sir Brannoc's whole army would ever chase me away.*

Jared had known his father expected a laugh. But he couldn't help himself. *Mam didn't love me that way. Gran said no decent mother would ever just leave her boy behind like that.*

Angus had knelt down, folding his big workman's frame until he could look Jared straight in the eye. *Your mam's coming back, Jared. I know it.*

But Gran said—

Your Gran is a fine woman, but she doesn't believe in magic like you and I do. Maybe…maybe your mother is in a secret cave guarded by a dragon, or lost in a castle's maze. Or maybe she wandered into a fairy ring, and the sidhe carried her away on a white horse. You know, six hundred years ago, the folk hereabouts whispered that is what happened to the lady of this castle.

Jared had fidgeted, torn between Gran's practical world and his father's fanciful one. *That's not what my book says. It says that Lady Aislinn hid the flag so it wouldn't fall into evil hands and Sir Brannoc pushed her right off the cliff.*

His father had seemed to consider. *No one witnessed her fall, did they? Not one person in all the records of that time.*

But they think—

Nobody knows for sure what happened at Castle Craig-morrigan on that fateful day. The people who write your books just study and try to guess, but that doesn't mean their story is true.

But Sir Brannoc was the evilest man in all Scotland, Da. And Lady Aislinn's husband was coming back from the wars. They found her crown of flowers on a branch halfway down the cliff and a piece of her gown.

Ah, but hadn't Lady Aislinn already proved herself clever, and the fairies, they'd sworn to protect the keeper of their magic flag. I think the fairies carried Lady Aislinn away to their world, where there is nothing but joy. Only the one who finds the fairy flag someday will know the truth. It might even bring the lady of Castle Craigmorrigan back to the world hundreds of years later. Can't you see her, boy? In your mind? Brave Lady Aislinn stepping out of the mist in her fairy gown, a crown of gold on her head?

Jared had quavered, hardly daring to hope. *Maybe she'd bring all the people the fairies stole away to Tir Nan Og. If I found the fairy flag, do you think I'd find Mum?*

You just grow into the finest lad you can be. Make sure when Mary walks back in that door you'll be a son she can be proud of.

A thud of something heavy struck Jared's boot. His rucksack, slipped from memory-numbed fingers. Jared bent down to retrieve it. He'd vowed to be steadfast when he became a man one day. Swore he'd never run away. How strange to realize now that in so many fights with Jenny a lifetime ago he'd been just like the mother he'd never known. Jared hadn't hid in a fairy rath or the far reaches of the globe.

Instead he'd chosen a place even more unreachable—the vastness of his own mind.

Somehow, he sensed Emma McDaniel would understand the reason why.

Shaking himself inwardly, he unfastened the rucksack and delved to the bottom of the bag, dragging out a bundle of clothing.

He unrolled the garments he wore at the medieval fair held at the end of every dig season, bringing the castle to life for the schoolchildren who swarmed Craigmorrigan to taste its former glory. He'd instituted the fair as a way to make history come alive, to inspire people and to intrigue them. Now, Emma had offered him a more far-reaching gift: the opportunity to shape the words that would come from Lady Aislinn's mouth on screen. Did she have any idea how precious such an opportunity was to him?

Yes. Emma knew. She understood in ways the more talented Angelica Robards never could have. And she'd offered him this chance with the same generosity of spirit she'd shown Davey Harrison and her mangy stray.

Was it possible that with Jared's help, Emma could make this movie what he had dreamed it could be the day Barry Robards had bought the rights to *Lady Valiant?*

What had Emma said when Jared had returned to the tower room to find her a vision in scarlet? That it felt right to be garbed in the clothes Lady Aislinn might have worn here. She was right. The costumes were one more way to lay fingers on the soft pulse in the veins of the past that flowed beneath Castle Craigmorrigan's surface. One more echo of voices long stilled.

Jared stripped off his shirt and hesitated, glancing at a chest across the tower hall. No. He turned his back resolutely on the trunk. The scientist in him would feel enough of a fool as it was. He shook out a forest-green tunic and pulled it over his head.

EMMA GAPED AS Jared filled the doorway, his dark hair tousled in silky waves around a face hard and masculine as the blade of a sword, his powerful body draped in a green tunic, the color faded just a little across the tops of his broad shoulders where sun and rain had obviously battered the coarse wool.

A leather belt ornamented in silver cinched his waist, a sword carriage dangling to his left side, the sheath of a dagger glinting in the candlelight. His eyes, unfathomable as a druid wood, burned her despite the veil shadows cast across his rugged features.

Something earthy in him called to Emma, primitive, like the moon's pull on the tide. The last vestiges of modern civilization stripped away with the canvas pants and shirt he'd shed somewhere in the stone chamber below.

"Wh...where did you get those?"

"We keep some stray period costumes around to use with the schoolkids. Helps hold their interest, being able to see history come alive."

"I can imagine why," Emma murmured. Butler had certainly gotten her attention. And then some. "But you didn't have to go to so much trouble for me. I'm, uh, pretty much a sure thing. A captive audience, you know? You've got me here for another...three weeks or so."

"You wanted to run lines."

"Yes. But dressing that way..." She waved her hand toward him, trying to remember how to breathe. "You didn't have to..."

"You didn't have to either."

"I told you. I like the clothes. Uncle Cade says I only became an actress so I still had an excuse to play dress up."

She was blabbering. But then, how could she help it with Jared standing there, oozing all that testosterone and wearing an outfit any red-blooded girl raised on a diet of fairy tales couldn't wait to get her hands on. Or *under,* as the case may be. Sensitive palms skimming that mouthwatering expanse of chest Emma had seen when she'd been stitching up Captain's bites.

She licked her lips, remembering the contrast between Jared's warm skin and the prickle of chest hair, the way her finger had skimmed his nipple and his breath had hissed between his teeth. Not from pain. She'd known even then it was something else entirely—an excruciating jolt of desire.

Jared crossed to her bed, picked up the script she'd left open in the middle. Not to some innocuous page. But rather, to the page where Sir Brannoc was using every power at his disposal to batter down Lady Aislinn's reserve, to win his way into her bed.

"One more irritating touch of Hollywood romance," he scoffed.

"I thought so, too," Emma said. "They were enemies."

"Right."

"But Brannoc was a man and Lady Aislinn a woman… A beautiful one by all accounts. Wild and spirited. Maybe it's not out of the realm of believability that Sir Brannoc would be tempted to tame her."

"That's a far cry from love. Sir Brannoc was nothing but a battered, forsworn mercenary, while Lady Aislinn's husband was honorable, so fair the legends say women mourned the day he wed. There was no hint of romance. Even Hollywood couldn't find enough evidence to support that."

Maybe not, but Emma thought that if Sir Brannoc had looked or sounded anything like Jared Butler, even the sainted Lady Aislinn might have been at least a little bit tempted.

"Maybe running lines wasn't such a great idea," Emma said. "I'm a little tired." As if a blow from a sledgehammer could make her sleep right now. Every nerve in her body was tingling.

"I see. Well." Jared glanced down at the printed page with another kind of longing. Emma wondered if this brilliant, proud man had any idea he'd let her glimpse just how vulnerable he was when it came to this story. How much he wanted to be a part of things that were now so far beyond his control.

"I suppose we could try a scene or two," Emma caught herself saying. "I really would like your input."

"No one else has wanted it." His eyes held hers. "Not since the first time I told them…"

"Told them what?" she asked.

"That the sword fight was impossible."

Emma groaned. "Not *that* same old story again. I'm not finished with you yet." She tossed her curls, teasing. "Know what my family motto is, Butler? *Never surrender.*"

But damned if she wasn't seriously under siege. One corner of Jared's mouth crooked in a smile more devastating to a female heart than a trebuchet to a castle keep. Emma's mind flashed to an image of the catapult's stones battering barriers that had kept her safe since Drew walked away. A dizzying mixture of elation and fear shot through her as walls tumbled down, leaving her wide open for Jared Butler to charge in.

"No man in Scotland would dare to defy me!" Sir Brannoc's words rolled off Jared's lips, emotions far too real surging through him, possessing him as if the knight's black soul had seeped into his own sometime during the past half hour. "Not your husband! Not your own clan! Yet you, a woman barren through ten years of marriage, believe that you can stand against my will?"

"Perhaps my father is dead and I know not if my husband lives." Emma's face swam before him, otherworldly in the candle-shine, her hair a wild tangle, the silver coronet gleaming above eyes that blazed with courage. "Perhaps my womb is cursed, cold and dead as you claim. But still I will stand against you. These people are my people now. Craig-morrigan will never be yours."

"Take down the fairy flag. 'Tis simple enough—give me that treasure and I'll not harm a soul in this accursed place."

"If 'tis so simple to steal the fairy magic, then why don't you take the flag down yourself?"

"You know that a man cannot."

"Or his shaft will shrivel and his seed die. He'll never mount a woman again."

Jared felt the torment Sir Brannoc must have endured, the dread of losing his manhood when a woman like no other stood before him, seeing what he stood to lose.

And Emma *was* rare, fiery, more convincing as Lady Aislinn than he'd ever have guessed she could be.

"So you believe in the legend the fairy flag carries?" she mocked him. "You, the most vile and dastardly knight in all of Scotland, who swears he doesn't fear eternal damnation?"

"Not that. Never that."

"Nay, for I'd wager your soul has belonged to the devil these many years past. But the hell the monks whisper of, 'tis mere child's play in comparison to a fairy curse. You should be afraid, Sir Brannoc. Be very afraid."

"Do you know what I could do to you? Right here. Right now. Fling you back onto this bed and ravish you." Jared's hand flashed out, clasped her throat.

Emma froze, her pulse racing, her very life force terrifyingly fragile beneath fingers that could snap her neck with a mere twist of his arm. Jared could feel her desperation to tear free of his grasp, could sense Lady Aislinn's realization that escape was impossible. No, not Aislinn's. Emma's.

Even so, Jared drowned in warring emotions, torn between his physical power over the woman in his grasp and his own strange helplessness when matched against her indomitable spirit. He hung on tenterhooks of indecision, mesmerized by feelings Sir Brannoc must have felt, opposing needs battling in his chest. The primitive instinct to possess clambered through his veins. He had the strength to take from her what he wanted and yet he knew in his darkest depths that unless she came to him willingly he'd lose far more.

His one chance at redemption....

What the hell? Jared tore his hand away as if Emma had burned him, his mind a jumble of confusion, the story of Lady Aislinn's courageous stand seeming more real to him than ever before. As if he really had stood for a moment in Sir Brannoc's skin, felt vulnerabilities, the hellish flaws in the mercenary knight's heart. A heart filled with cynicism, bitterness, secret despair. A heart suddenly far too similar to Jared's own.

Emma seemed to fight for balance a moment, her voice breathless. "So why didn't he?"

"Why didn't he what?" Jared snapped.

"Rape her."

"I don't know."

"That was standard operating procedure after you overran a castle from what I read, along with pillaging and such. Maybe Sir Brannoc had a war wound or something and he couldn't—"

"If his man parts were already shriveled he could bloody well have marched up and taken the flag down himself, remember? But no. The man had to suffer the tortures of the damned, wanting..."

"Wanting what?"

"What any man wants when he's been locked in a room with a beautiful woman this long." Bloody hell! Heat burned into Jared's face, his own man parts doing the opposite of shriveling. And since he'd pointed the dilemma out, Emma could hardly escape noticing.

She bounced up from the bench, putting a safe distance between them. "Want to fight?" she asked.

Jared shook his head in an effort to clear it, his imagination still filled with the scene they'd just altered, the sizzling undercurrents that had spurred Jared to reach for Emma's throat the way he'd suddenly known Sir Brannoc would. The dark knight threatening her, adoring her.

Strange, Lady Aislinn had always been the character who fascinated Jared. He'd found himself in her head—her heart— far deeper than he'd ever been in Sir Brannoc's. But as he and Emma had revised the lines, honing them to biting sharpness, something astounding had happened. Jared empathized more than he would have believed possible with the villain who had guarded another bold lady centuries ago in this chamber.

All of that glorious defiant woman just within Sir Brannoc's reach and yet totally beyond his touch. All that passion just a kiss away, and yet knowing that even if he did what his body clambered to do, ground his mouth down on those ripe red lips, he'd still never touch her, really touch her, inside where her soul lived. The way Jared could never touch Emma....

Not that he wanted to, Jared warned himself. He'd found out long ago the problem with secrets: Once you possessed a person's deepest secrets, you had no choice. You had to keep them forever.

"Jared, are you listening?" Emma demanded even more sharply, her breath catching just a little. He gritted his teeth, trying not to stare at her breasts welling above the neckline of her shift, the damned garment clinging ever more precariously to the curves glowing white against the scarlet surcoat. "You've spent five minutes staring at me as if you were the big bad wolf and I was...well, the medieval version of Red Riding Hood," she complained. "It's making me nervous."

"I was just trying to figure out what Sir Brannoc would have said next."

Said next? Brannoc would've been on the brink of *doing* something. Not talking about it. And yet, the fairy flag had to be surrendered willingly. It couldn't be taken. And woe to the man who attempted to take by force either the flag or the virtue of the lady it protected. If Lady Aislinn was anywhere near as alluring as Emma McDaniel, it was no wonder Sir Brannoc had lost his mind in the end.

"I guess I didn't hear you," Jared added, suddenly wary. "What did you say?"

"Do you want to fight?"

"Fight?"

"You know. To, uh, break things up a bit."

Like the sexual tension that held them both in an iron-fisted grip.

Jared brightened. Yes, that's what he needed. A nice sharp battle to remind him of all the reasons he couldn't let Emma McDaniel burrow any deeper under his skin.

"I mean...you, um, brought your sword," Emma insisted, "so...you must've intended to practice."

Of course that's what she'd think. He glanced at her purple-framed picture, then quickly looked away. Swordplay was a damned fine excuse to get his mind out of Emma McDaniel's bed. "We'll practice. Grand."

She unfolded her long legs, tantalizing him with glimpses of pale ankles, slender calves as she stood up and shook her skirts into place. She went to fetch her own weapon, the re-production sword leaning in a corner. A week ago she'd graduated from wooden wasters to a sword forged of far heavier metal.

Still, Jared hadn't supplied one of the lightweight props she would use in the choreographed fight scenes in Lady Valiant. The aluminum swords might be a practical necessity so she could endure take after take of the grueling sword match when Barry Robards wanted to film all day. But Emma had clung with such dogged determination to the notion she'd prove Lady Aislinn could have gotten a medieval blade to her enemy's throat that Jared had provided her with one from his own collection. A sword balanced and weighted as authentically as possible to test theories about battle he'd experimented with for years.

He'd known damned well the added burden exhausted her the first few days but she hadn't complained once. She'd just bulldozed through each practice with a tenacity that made him feel like a beast, and each time he'd been the one to call a halt.

And tonight? If Jared was lucky he'd exhaust himself as well, until his own arms ached so badly he could hardly lift them, until his mind blurred and he could close his eyes, find nothing but a blank, blessed oblivion when he finally fell asleep.

Emma's hand closed about the hilt with an easy familiarity that might have impressed him if he could have stopped staring at the top curve of her breast like a cadgy lad. How could she help but notice?

Her breath tripped, her left hand hastening to her shoulder, easing the neckline back into place. He should have been glad.

"I've been practicing the moves a lot," she said, hefting the sword, shifting the hilt until it settled into her hand. "And yet, no matter what I do, I can't seem to break through your guard. I keep trying to think what Lady Aislinn might have done, you know, to even the odds. Maybe if I dressed like a boy as the heroines in Aunt Finn's romance novels sometimes do…"

"In medieval times a woman could be put to death for that."

Emma's jaw dropped. "Just for wearing pants?"

"They weren't pants," he corrected automatically. "They were called hose."

"And men might as well have been wearing dresses during that time, according to the pictures I've seen," Emma huffed, outraged. "That's male chauvinism at its finest. It's hardly fair."

"Is that what you think medieval swordplay was? Fair?"

"Sure," she countered. "King Arthur and the round table, Lancelot and all those guys—I thought nobility and honor and fair play were what the whole knight-in-shining-armor bit was supposed to be about. At least that was the story in the musical version."

He must've looked glazed. She chuckled.

"*Camelot,* Butler. You know. Vanessa Redgrave. Richard Harris." She launched into a few bars of song.

Jared couldn't help but smile. "You sing, too?"

"Sometimes with the most nefarious motives. My mom's the one who really has a kick-ass voice. I sing off-key around her on purpose. Drives her absolutely raving mad."

"Nice to know I'm not the only one you have that effect on." The words slipped out before Jared could stop them. Emma laughed, obviously as relieved as he was at the break in the tension between them—sun breaking through a raft of lowering storm clouds.

She flounced to the open space in the tower room. "So, if dressing like a boy means you get to eat my liver in the marketplace, what other options should I consider? Even you have to admit this whole sword fight business is stacked in your favor."

"Playing fair is where your problem lies," Jared explained. "You want to be a female version of Sir Galahad? Get used to losing. Sword fighting in the middle ages meant life or death. Even in practice or during tournaments, knights died. Warriors who survived stayed alive any way they were able. By fighting dirty."

"You sound like my grandfather." She made a stern face, her voice a low growl. "'Don't diddle daddle around, Emma. A girl can't afford to fight like a fluffy. If you're going to fight, fight to win.'" Imps danced in her eyes. "I don't suppose you'd mind if I gouged your eyes or kneed you in the groin, would you, Butler?"

The corner of his mouth ticked up. "You can try."

"Aw, Butler, bad move. There's a cardinal rule in Whitewater. Never dare a McDaniel. We never say die." She slid into fighting stance so naturally he couldn't help but admire her. "At least my arms don't feel like they're going to fall off when I go to bed anymore."

Bed. Not that word again. Heat surged through him. He clenched his jaw, fighting arousal. *Damn,* he thought, his cheeks warming, *don't let her see....*

But her gaze was locked on his face, not the place far lower where he was burning.

"Fight dirty, fight dirty." She repeated the words like a mantra as she raised her blade. "All right, Butler. Bring it on."

Steel clashed as their swords slammed together in a dance becoming far too familiar. Jared tried time and again to catch her off guard, knock the sword from her grasp, but she changed mid-battle, clutching the heavy blunted blade in a two-handed grip far harder for him to break through.

Quicksilver fast, she dodged and parried, ranging about the

tower chamber, aware of every piece of furniture, every wall, never distracted by them, but always mindful of the terrain, just as he'd taught her.

Blast if she wasn't good at this, Jared thought with a surge of pride as she scrambled backward over the bed, putting a barrier between them and earning herself a moment to catch her breath, to ready herself for his next onslaught. She pressed the fingers of one hand against her chest, and Jared wondered if her heart was pounding like his was, a primitive rhythm that surged white-hot through his veins. No, she was yanking at that troublesome drawstring, trying to keep her shift from slipping.

He started to lunge over the fur-covered mattress, stopped himself. Damned if he dared get any closer to that bed. He might not be able to resist the temptation of catching her by the wrist, dragging her down, pinning her beneath him— sword be damned.

A ragged groan escaped from his throat as he rounded the bed. *The sword. Keep your mind on the sword,* he warned himself. *Or you could bloody well hurt her....*

Concentrate, man. Put an end to this before it gets any more out of hand.

But for the first time he could remember since he'd picked up his first sword his arm wouldn't obey his command. Jared's breath caught as his gaze slid past her weapon, to where her shift ran amok. Instead of helping matters with her hasty fumbling, she'd made them worse. Embroidered scarlet surcoat and creamy linen shift cascaded down her arm like the waterfall he'd shown her on their first wild ride. Desire seared through him as a swell of breast rose like a pale moon above the cloth.

A gentleman would have called a halt, let her rearrange herself. But Jared had never felt less like a gentleman in his life.

Oblivious to the bounty she was displaying, she leaned

toward him, just the rim of her aureole peeking above the cloth, her nipple so close Jared could almost taste it. One tiny tug and he could take her in his mouth....

Jared froze as something cold kissed his throat.

The blunted edge of Emma's sword.

Chapter Twelve

"GOTCHA." EMMA GRINNED, infuriatingly pleased with herself as she tugged her shift back into place.

"You did that on purpose!" Jared accused.

"Give the boy a gold star. Come on, Butler. I'm waiting."

"For what?" He glowered, not sure who he was more irritated with—her for tempting him with female wiles or himself for falling headlong into her trap.

"Admit it," she challenged. "It *is* possible the sword fight in the legend is true. I got my sword to your throat. There's no reason Lady Aislinn couldn't have done the same thing."

Outrage flooded Jared. "Lady Aislinn never would have flashed her breast at Sir Brannoc!" He bristled, as defensive as if Castle Craigmorrigan's lady were standing shamefaced right next to him. "She wouldn't have lowered herself to such a cheap shot."

He expected Emma to come out swinging, snapping some cutting rejoinder, clashing with words as fiercely as they'd just battled with swords. But instead of striking back, she suddenly sobered, her eyes misty, her expression far away as if she were trying to peer back through time to find answers six hundred years old.

"Really, Jared?" Emma queried softly. "You're so sure she wouldn't show a little bit of skin to save her castle? If the survival of everyone I loved hung in the balance, I'd do whatever I had to do to protect them. Everything I've read about Lady Aislinn tells me she would have, too."

Emma rested the blunted tip of her heavy sword on the ground, her eyes searching his. "But you know her better than anyone else in the world, Jared. What do you think she would have done?"

Emma was waiting for an answer. But for once he couldn't fire one off, weighted with the authority he'd earned through years of research. Research close to obsession.

He'd been so sure of himself when it came to this castle and the lady who presided over it. But now... He wasn't sure about anything anymore. Not ancient legends. Not Emma McDaniel, gazing up at him as if he held all the wisdom in the world. Would Lady Aislinn have risked exciting Sir Brannoc's lust in such a reckless manner? Might she have hoped that her body would earn the survival of the people of Castle Craigmorrigan?

What if her beauty was the only coin she could trade in?

Emma is right, instinct told him. The medieval lady he'd come to adore would have displayed the same courage, the same resourcefulness Emma had shown. She would have braved Sir Brannoc's desire to win the lives of innocents and get him to leave Craigmorrigan. Though she'd be damned for it in the end.

How strange that Emma should be the one to unearth that facet of Lady Aislinn's character, one Jared in all his years of study had never suspected. And yet, it fired his imagination with other possibilities, new theories fascinating him, daring him to prove…

What? That Sir Brannoc had fallen in love with Lady Aislinn? Dark to her light, night to her day?

Would Emma's interpretation explain the other facet of the legend that had always troubled Jared? The part that claimed an infamous scoundrel like Sir Brannoc had actually fulfilled his end of the devil's bargain he'd struck? *The day you get a sword to my throat is the day I leave this castle….*

Nothing and no one could have held him to it. He'd forsworn himself so many times before, broken oaths he'd made on his honor as a knight. There was no reason on God's earth why Lady Aislinn should have trusted him to keep his word. Brannoc had nothing left to lose.

Yet he'd been preparing to leave Castle Craigmorrigan when a trembling squire had brought him the dread news. Lady Aislinn and the fairy flag had vanished. Instead of taking his rage out on the castle folk, he'd raced out into the night, half-mad, wandering Scotland in search of them both.

Jared had been so sure it was the fairy flag the black-hearted knight sought, but now as he peered into Emma McDaniel's face he wondered.

"Jared?" she prodded, questions in her eyes, shields she'd held up to him for so long lowered, leaving her soft parts with no defense. He thought he'd taught her better than that.

"I suppose anything is possible," he said, taking refuge in science. "There's no way to prove your theory either way."

"I'm not asking you to prove it. I'm asking what you feel."

"My feelings are immaterial. I deal in facts."

"I don't believe that. Maybe your science depends on carbon dating and luminescent whatever-you-call-it, that stuff Davey told me about. But you…you feel this legend as deep in your bones as I do. The magic. The mystery. Things you can't touch or taste or write down as fact in that little notebook of yours. So tell me. Do you think Lady Aislinn might have tried to seduce Sir Brannoc into surrendering or not?"

If the castle's valiant lady had been even half as beautiful as Emma, Jared admitted to himself, it wouldn't have taken any effort at all to turn Brannoc's head from war to far more dangerous pursuits.

Had Sir Brannoc's breath rasped like Jared's did now? Had the knight's heart hammered in his chest? Desire welling up inside him so hot, so ferocious, that he couldn't stop himself from touching, tasting…taking.

Jared's hand itched to bury itself in black curls, pull Emma's mouth to his. Could she see it? Feel it? Alarm flared in Emma's eyes, as if she suddenly realized she'd let down her guard. He felt her shields slam shut.

"Oh, well. It doesn't matter. Like you say, we—we couldn't prove it anyway," she stammered, breathless.

Hefting her sword again, she turned away from him, hastening back to the middle of the room. Jared knew damned well the woman was trying to put space between them. As if that tactic would cool his blood at all. Didn't she know it was the oldest aphrodisiac in the book? A woman tempting a man to madness, then retreating before he tasted her?

"Listen, I don't think I quite had that last maneuver right," she said, tossing her hair back over her shoulder. The glimpse of her graceful throat made Jared want to bury his face in the silky column, kiss the fragile skin until it made her moan. "Do you think we could try it again?"

"Try what?" Jared jerked his mind back from the tantalizing image.

"Sword fighting. That last maneuver."

Jared scowled. "You've already won the damned bet."

"Right." Her face clouded. "I bet you're just itching to head down to your trailer, fax the studio and tell Barry Robards you were wrong about me. That I'll make a brilliant Lady Aislinn. That was our deal, right?"

"Right," Jared said between gritted teeth. Nothing like the prospect of eating crow to irritate the hell out of a man. For an instant he wished he were more like Sir Brannoc. Could say the hell with the deal. So Emma *was* turning out to be better than Jared had expected. He still thought Angelica Robards would make a more believable Lady Aislinn.

Even so, he couldn't stop remembering Emma's face when she'd told him the castle's lady would do whatever necessary to save the people she loved. Angelica Robards hadn't come up with that insightful bit of characterization. And neither had he. "I said I'd call Robards," he grumbled. "I will. At least I'll have *something* to say for a change when I answer the endless faxes and phone calls he's been pestering me with."

"Robards has been contacting you to see how my training is coming?"

"He's—" *Scared his pet project is going to crash in a ball of flames. Has far too much time to imagine Jade Star playing opposite Oscar winner Liam Neeson leaving Robards an industry laughingstock.* But Jared couldn't say that to Emma, wound her that way. Not anymore.

"He's...worried," Jared finished lamely.

"Listen, I know exactly how he feels about me. And I don't want any praise I don't earn. And I certainly don't want anyone to lie about how they feel my performance will be. So don't."

"What?"

"Don't call. I already have the role and you still don't think I'm right for the part." *Do you?*

The question shone in her eyes, but she didn't ask it. He couldn't answer. His gaze dipped down to where her pulse beat in the hollow of her throat. Her fingers fluttered up, covering that vulnerable spot as if he'd kissed it.

"You won the fight," he said. "What more do you want?"

He'd expected her to turn away, hurt. But she seemed to appreciate his honesty. Her eyes flashed with a challenge old as time.

"What I want is to make the fight scenes in Lady Valiant as realistic as possible," she said. "I want people to share her triumph, feel her passion, just like I do now."

Passion? Jared thought. *She seemed as turned on as he was and he hadn't even touched her.*

She moistened her lips. He bit back a groan. "I mean, really, Jared," she taunted, the husky note in her voice betraying her. "Do you have any idea how spectacularly the scene would film if I could disarm you—I mean, Sir Brannoc—completely?"

He barked a derisive laugh. "That will never happen."

Sparks of all-too-familiar stubbornness lit her eyes. "Butler, Butler, I would have thought my little triumph a few minutes ago would have taught you never to tell a McDaniel something is impossible."

"This time it is. Because after that little feminine trick of yours, I won't be holding back."

She latched on to his verbal thrust as if it were a life raft in stormy seas. Her eyes glittered. "Oh, so now you *let* me win. Is that your story?"

"We'll see soon enough. Woman or no, you'll be getting the full power of my blade this time."

The double meaning raked at Jared's self-control, and he imagined how she'd feel beneath him. Emma caught the full curve of her lower lip with her teeth and he wondered if she was thinking the same thing.

Dream on, man. A woman like her wanting a man like you?

And yet, he couldn't deny the magnetism between them. "Let's get on with it, then," he ordered, voice low. "I've just remembered a crucial bit of training I forgot to pass on."

Her eyes narrowed with that incredible intensity he'd come to admire, the dedication she brought to anything having to do with her craft. What must it be like to work that hard, be that devoted to acting and suspect somewhere in your heart what Jared already knew—that your best would never been good enough? Your talent would never measure up to the genetic accident that made you almost too beautiful to be real. Empathy welled up in Jared, filling him with emotions he didn't want to feel.

She was getting too close, burrowing into him too deep, past defenses that meant survival.

She raised her blade to the ready, balancing lightly on the balls of her feet. "So, quit looking at me like the big bad wolf, Butler. Let's see this crucial bit of training that's going to help me kick your butt even more magnificently than I did the last time."

Jared crossed his sword with hers, each swing precise, graceful in what his sword master years past had called his dance with death.

Emma met him blow for blow, new confidence making her eyes shine. But this time his focus couldn't be shattered. He narrowed his gaze, determined to use the one weapon at his disposal—the single blow he was dead certain would dissolve the perilous connection between them once and for all.

"I'm...aging here, Butler," she taunted, breathless. "You planning to...show me your...new move any time...before my next birthday?" she dared him. "Or can't you get past my...guard? Come on...sword boy...hit me with...your best shot. What's this...crucial bit of strategy?"

He drove her sword wide to the right. Before she could whip it back to defend herself, he caught her wrist with his other hand, leaving her body open. But instead of bringing his own weapon to bear, he shoved her back against the tower's stone wall. "I fight dirty, too." His mouth crashed down on hers.

Emma reeled, struggling to keep her knees from buckling as Jared's hot, hard kiss set her body on fire.

She could have stomped on his instep or kneed him in the groin and given the man any of the lessons in self-defense her grandfather had taught her. Instead, she did the unthinkable. Kissed Jared Butler back.

Her sword dropped from numb fingers.

He felt so good as his lips devoured hers, that rock-hard body pinning her against the rough stone wall. She could feel his heart thundering, his breath rasping as he angled his face to ravish her mouth more deeply. His tongue traced her lips, demanding entry, and she let him in, her own tongue dueling with his, tasting all that was male and primitive, a desperation far too deep, mingled with sudden anger and confusion.

Her fingers delved into the thick, dark waves of his hair, silk against the white-hot sensation of the powerful cords of his throat against her skin.

Oh, God....

She'd never felt so wild. Never known a kiss could burn her up inside and she'd only want to plunge deeper and deeper into the heart of the flame.

She jumped, startled, as Jared pulled away from her. A clatter of metal against stone jangled her nerves. Both of his powerful hands closed on her arms, his nostrils flaring, his breath hot, ragged, emotion raging in those glen-green eyes.

Shame washed through Emma. Had he just been trying to get back some of his own? Salvage his pride after she tricked him? And she'd fallen for it, big-time. Kissed him, really kissed him...like she meant it. As if she were easy....

One of the sexiest women in the world, the tabloids had called her. She'd given him reason to believe those rumors now. God, if he only knew the truth.

She tried to bounce back, think of something to say. But she felt stripped bare.

"What do you know? I *am* a bloody genius," Jared growled, his hands sliding roughly up her arms. "I've invented a move that doesn't just disarm my opponent. It disarms me as well."

Emma marveled at his confession. Her heart swelled as she glimpsed real passion and surprise on his rugged face.

"So, the question is, what the hell am I supposed to do now?" Jared's voice, whiskey-warm, caressed her as he ran his hand up to her throat, skimmed her cheek with his thumb.

"I suppose there's no help for it," Emma breathed. "We'll have to resort to…"

"To what?"

"Hand-to-hand combat."

She pressed her palm to the rugged contours of his jaw, slid her fingertips across the light stubble on his cheek to where his lips tempted her, so sensual, unyieldingly masculine and yet sensitive in a way far more dangerous to her heart.

"This is a bad idea." Jared caught her finger lightly between his teeth. His tongue touched the responsive pad, hot, wet, melting Emma deep inside. She moaned softly, pulling her finger away. "We're going to be stuck together in this tower for at least three more weeks," Jared warned.

"Actually more like twenty-four days." She twisted his wrist to see the watch he'd forgotten to remove. "Six hours and…seventeen minutes…"

He smiled just a little. "Enjoying our time together so much you're counting the seconds before you can get away from me, are you?"

"You've been so charming I couldn't help it. But there's still time. You can try to change my mind."

"Emma…" Jared cleared his throat. "I know this is…nothing new to you. Having a man want you like this."

"Like what?" The fragile part of her curled inward, trying to protect itself.

"For sex."

Emma tried to shrink back into the wall, but the stone held her, trapped her. She wanted to push past Jared, but she wouldn't let him see he'd left her bleeding.

"Sex," she echoed.

"Where you come from…it doesn't mean a damned thing. In Hollywood."

"Of course not." A steel band clamped around Emma's chest.

"I know you've had your choice of blokes."

"Whole armies of men. You should see the line at my bedroom door."

"I don't mean to hurt you. I just…if we're going to do this, I want it to be real. Honest."

"That's the Butler I know and love. A regular Sir Lancelot."

"Damn it, Emma, I just…" Something naked shone in his eyes, something that kept her from slapping him in the face, stalking away, freezing him out the way she'd frozen out men so many times before.

"Just what?"

"I've never wanted a woman so much. I've never…hell…I can't tell you how many nights I've lain awake, thinking about us in this bed together."

She peered up at him, mesmerized, silent.

"The only thing that kept me sane was…knowing it was all a mad fantasy. You'd never want me. A woman like you couldn't possibly…"

"And you know me so well. Probably researched me the

way you do everything else. Or had Davey look up my name on the Internet."

"Damn it, aren't you listening?" He gave her a little shake. "You weren't supposed to want me."

Her chin hitched up a notch. "Maybe I don't want you. Maybe I'm a better actress than you thought. First I get the sword to your throat and now…now I trick you into believing I want to fall into bed with a—a virtual stranger."

Except he wasn't a stranger. Not anymore. Davey had shared too many of his secrets.

"You're angry."

"Why would I be angry when I've just given the performance of a lifetime?" she said, suddenly brittle. "I obviously had you fooled."

"Is that the way of it, then? It was all an act?" Jared's jaw clenched. "I don't believe you. The way you kissed me back. It was real."

"Of course it was." Emma rolled her eyes, trying to forget the piercing awareness that had stunned her, sensations sharper, sweeter than anything she'd ever felt before—even with Drew.

Jared winced, but damned if pride would let her back down.

"Gotcha again, Butler." She licked her index finger, then scratched an imaginary point in the air inches from Jared's nose. "Score two for the rotten actress."

Jared searched her face as if trying to put the lie to her words. Emma felt his gaze hammer against defenses she swore she wouldn't let him see beyond.

Did she imagine it? Or did she see him draw back, too, behind the barrier Davey had told her about—Morgause's invisible wall holding King Arthur prisoner, separating him from the world.

"I'll not be troubling you that way again," Jared said, dead quiet, dead certain. The words somehow sharper because they were.

"Good," Emma said, chin jutting at a stubborn angle. "After all. I do have my standards."

Sure you do, Emma, a voice mocked in her head. An empty bed. An empty life. If Jared only knew.

There'd never been any man but Drew. Her first. Her only. Until she'd almost let Jared Butler…

Thank God they'd both come to their senses. She crossed to the fur-draped bed, plopped herself in the middle of it. She pounded her pillow once with her fist, then turned her back pointedly toward the man who still stood watching her.

If this were the Middle Ages, she could name a champion, have someone make Jared Butler eat his words. The knight of the sea she'd glimpsed her first night in the castle. The warrior wouldn't be a ghost. He'd be real and alive, a noble man who'd fight for a lady's honor….

But her only champions were a ragged dog and a boy who worshiped the ground Jared Butler walked on. No, she thought, remembering all Davey had told her. She wouldn't put Davey in a position where he had to choose sides. After all, in a few weeks she'd be gone. Jared would still be part of the boy's life, Davey's hero, his mentor, his friend.

Emma's chest ached with a loneliness so fierce she wished she hadn't let Davey keep Captain for the night. What good was finally having a dog of her own if she couldn't hide a few bitter tears in its coat? But who was she kidding, anyway? Her dog would probably be on the other side of the room licking Jared's hand. Captain had fallen almost as hard for Jared Butler as she had.

At least Captain had an excuse for making a complete fool of himself over Jared, Emma told herself sharply. The idiot dog had tried to fight two rabid collies. It was obvious Captain had rocks for brains.

So what's your excuse?

I wanted to be like any other woman for just one night. Wanted to make love with a man who...who could see me. Really see me. Just Emma....

Oh, he'd seen her all right. As some hot Hollywood babe who fell into bed on a whim.

I know you're used to this...a man wanting you... It doesn't mean anything....

At least he doesn't know how much he hurt me, Emma tried to comfort herself. But that didn't change the truth.

She'd let Jared Butler slip past her guard with far more than his sword, and he'd managed to cut her.

To the heart.

Chapter Thirteen

JARED GROUND HIS FINGERTIPS into his burning eyes, trying for the hundredth time to clear them enough to actually bring the site map on his desk into focus. A forlorn hope, after what he'd suffered the past three nights.

Sure, he'd researched torture devices, as any archaeologist excavating a castle site should. But he'd never expected to become an expert in a technique that didn't require thumb screws or iron boots filled with boiling oil. Didn't require anything at all except keeping the poor son of a bitch awake until he'd confess to any crime in the world just to get a decent night's sleep.

And to add insult to injury, while he was in here trying to work, Emma was curled up in a chair in Davey's tent, sleeping with her infuriating little dog.

Jared swore, burying his face in his hands. Not that it did any good. Emma's image was still branded into his eyelids, her eyes wide with anticipation just before he kissed her.

He shifted in the uncomfortable chair he'd hoped would

keep him awake. But no matter how cramped his position or how badly his muscles ached from nights on the damp stone floor, he could still feel her gasp of pleasure as his tongue slipped into her mouth, her breasts yielding against the wall of his chest, her hands on his face—so feminine, so eager.

And what had he done when that incredible, sexy woman had been melting in his arms, as hungry for him as he was for her? Had he stuck to kissing her mindless? Stripping all those irritating clothes out of the way? No. Jared Butler, genius, had to strike up a bloody conversation.

And ruin everything.

Why? Because he'd wanted to get the parameters of this nonrelationship straight before he had what promised to be the best sex of his life. Jared groaned. It wasn't as if Emma was some starry-eyed twenty-year-old ready to rush off and buy *Bride* magazine the morning after. True, she had admitted to wanting children someday. *That* should have been enough to cool his blood once and for all. The last thing on earth Jared Butler wanted was a child.

The better part of his nature *should* have kicked in, hoped she would realize that dream in the future with some other man after the passion keeping Jared awake burned out, as it inevitably would. But the dragon inside him felt a killing urge every time he imagined another man's hands on her body.

It's only because you've never had her, he told himself. *It's nothing but science. A throwback to primitive times when a man's biological purpose was to spread his genes with the most perfect female specimen possible. Once I've had sex with her, the urgency will fade. For both of us....*

Odds were, she'd be as relieved as he was once the compulsion to shag each other blind passed. They were two consenting adults whose pheromones flung their animal attraction meters off the charts. Once they got it out of their systems…

He rubbed his fingertips against his eyes, trying to blot out the images of just how much fun they would have had in the process.

Maybe I didn't want you…maybe I just gave the best performance of my life… her denial echoed.

But the words no longer stung. No matter what she'd said, he knew damned well if he'd handled things differently, they would've spent that night in the tower together exploring every curve and dip and hollow of each other's naked bodies.

Instead, he'd taken the long road to hell until now he was sure he could write a whole new doctoral thesis on the misery of sexual frustration. *If* he could stay awake long enough to find the shift key on his laptop.

"You're brilliant all right," he muttered. "A real—"

A knock on the trailer door made Jared grind his teeth. The last thing he wanted was company, but barring the students from his office until Emma left Scotland was hardly an option. "Come in," he called.

Davey. The kid had been tiptoeing around him lately as if he were walking blindfolded through a minefield. But whatever mission he was on at the moment must be stronger than his instinct for mere self-preservation. The lad clutched something in his hands.

"I was going over office stuff and found a few things you missed. Some order forms you need to sign, and some faxes from Mr. Robards asking how Emma's training is coming along. I, uh, wrote something that should keep him off your back for a while—about how you're running lines with Emma and—"

"You're answering *my* correspondence?" Jared demanded.

"Well, you sure aren't at the moment! You keep forgetting and—well, I thought maybe I could help."

Jared checked his aggravation. Davey was right. "I'll read these over. You can send them in the morning. That should buy us another few days."

"That's what I thought." Davey fiddled with the other objects in his hands. If Jared didn't know better, he'd think the kid was trying to keep him from seeing what they were.

"Davey," Jared said, more gently. "Thanks."

The lad lit up at the praise. Nothing like those puppy dog eyes to make Jared feel like a real bastard.

"Chief, is there sometime we could talk?"

Jared sighed and gave the kid a rueful smile. "Might as well do it now," he conceded, closing his aching eyes. "I'm not getting any work done."

"You look, uh, tired. The floor up in Emma's room is pretty hard, huh?"

Not as hard as my... Stop it, Butler, he warned himself. Don't tell the kid your hormones are in charge.

"Know what I do sometimes to help me go to sleep?" Davey asked. "I watch...um, movies."

"Thanks for the suggestion, but the shite you kids watch would probably make me brain-dead. Now, did you come here to measure the bags under my eyes or did you have a question?"

Jared hadn't thought he could feel any worse. Davey's defiant expression dashed that theory. "I didn't use to need a reason to talk to you, before you turned into Attila the Scot," he accused.

Jared chuckled wearily, trying to put the boy more at ease. "Attila the Scot, eh? An apt description. But why don't I think it's a Davey Harrison original?"

"Emma came up with it."

"Of course she did. And probably a few hundred more nicknames that would have had my gran coming at my mouth with a bar of soap."

"You can't really blame her."

Ouch. That stung. Jared looked up at the lad who'd regarded him as hero for far too long. That was the problem when you put someone up on a pedestal, Jared thought as a sunburned, white-bearded face flashed through his memory. It hurt like hell when they did the inevitable and tumbled off. Trouble was, Jared had never experienced that tumble from the hero's perspective, hadn't known how much it hurt the fallen idol as well.

"Davey," Jared began, running his fingers back through his hair. "Emma and I...well, it's complicated. I know I'm being an ass, but this castle...my work...it's everything to me."

"I know. It's the same way for me." Hurt faded from Davey's face. The lad smiled, that terrifyingly innocent old soul smile that had moved Jared from the first moment he'd seen it. "It's like...wandering in a dream where the world outside can't...hurt you. But at the end of the summer, we still have to go home. And all the stuff we hate is still out there, waiting."

What could Jared say? How could he describe the panic that had jolted through him when he'd realized his funding was being yanked? Davey's face had haunted him, filling him with stone-cold terror.

"Remember the first summer I came here?"

Jared's chest squeezed. He glanced at Davey's thin wrist. A two-inch scar marred the lad's pale skin.

I didn't even have the guts to finish. Davey's small voice echoed in Jared's mind. *But I wanted to....*

"It was a long summer." Jared tried to keep a tremor from his voice. "Want to be more specific?"

"The books."

Jared warmed. "I remember." How could he forget? The kid had gobbled up books as if he expected them to be sucked into a black hole once summer was over. He'd soaked up knowledge, asking so many questions, transforming right before Jared's eyes from the pallid, shy ghost of a kid who had almost given up on life to the finest student Jared had ever taught. "By the end of that first summer you could have tested into a master's program in archaeology."

"Right. But you said there's more to life than archaeology. Remember?"

"You were fifteen years old. There was a rich world out there for you to discover. I didn't want you to limit yourself. Hell, you'd never seen an original painting by Van Gogh or studied Homer's *Iliad*. You'd never read Yeats or Robert Burns."

Davey fingered whatever he clutched, hidden in his hands. "I told you poetry was a waste of time. There was no point to reading it. You told me to try it before I threw it in the rubbish bin."

"I was right, wasn't I?" Jared said with satisfaction. "You and the immortal Rabbie became fast friends, as I remember."

Davey's eyes held his. "The poetry was brilliant and I almost missed it because I'd closed my mind to it before I'd even tried it."

Jared's heart sank. "Oh, Lord. This is going somewhere, isn't it, lad?"

A guilty flush flooded up from the collar of Davey's shirt.

Jared sighed. "If my skull wasn't pounding I'd let you get to whatever you're trying to say in a roundabout way. But I'm begging for mercy. Just come to the point before my brain explodes."

Davey unfurled his fingers from a stack of plastic DVD cases and thumped them down on the site map. Emma, heart-stoppingly beautiful, adorned the cover, while scenes of space battles wreathed around her.

"Oh, no," Jared said, shoving the discs back toward the lad. "The woman's already in my head all the… I mean, in my way all the time. I'm not about to put her on a television screen as well. Besides, she's supposed to spend the night immersing herself in the fourteenth century and I'm supposed to be watching her."

Watching her…every move, every expression, every agonizing moment of sexual frustration…

"You don't have to worry about her tonight. She was asking me about some castle stuff and I promised I'd help her research," Davey said. "Then the kids invited her to play Trivial Pursuit."

"Grand." Jared rubbed his hands together, eager for the distraction. "What time should I be there?" Not that he'd be any use to anybody, his usually sharp brain reduced to mush.

Davey regarded him solemnly. "You're not invited."

"What?"

"We only let you play because we need someone to even out the teams, and you, you're so smart it isn't fair. Might as well save ourselves the trouble and not play the game at all since your team always wins."

Jared couldn't deny the surprising sting he felt at that. "Why didn't somebody mention it before?"

Davey shrugged. "Because we like you. I mean, we really admire you. And…well, there is the problem of evening out the teams." Davey paused. "Dr. Butler, do you ever wonder why kids like me love working with you so much?"

"Because you get to play in the dirt?"

"Because you don't talk down to us. You don't tell us to do one thing while you're off doing the complete opposite. You walk the walk, you know? Show us…how to be."

"Why do I think this isn't going to play to my advantage at the moment? I really hate it when a student hoists me on my own petard."

Davey grinned at the archaic expression, but his eyes

darkened with pleading. "Just watch the movies and I promise I'll never do it again. I know you think it's worthless fluff. Truth is, Emma thinks the same thing. But there's more to Jade Star than meets the eye." Davey's voice softened. "There's more to Emma McDaniel, too."

LONG AFTER SUNSET, Jared sat alone in the pitch-dark trailer, the screen of the small television set casting its spell. Or maybe it wasn't the set at all, but rather the enchanting young woman frolicking in the outtakes, bloopers and director's cuts.

Emma, fresh-faced and painfully young, doing her own stunts, her good-humored endurance as some kind of contraption flung her out of swampy water, seaweed clinging to her hair. Her courage as she did stunts that would have terrified any sane woman—or man, if the truth be told.

She plunged headfirst off a cliff, snowboarded through glaciers on some frozen planet, came within chomping distance of a very real-looking shark. She practiced intricate fight scenes with the same tenacity she'd shown while training with the sword.

But most painful of all were the extra clips from the first movie, where she played with the pack of kids who costarred as children marooned on an obscure planet, waiting for their parents to come and reclaim them after the war against evil forces was won.

One clip showed Emma twirling a tiny dark-haired girl in the harness Jade used to fly, then setting the deliciously dizzy mite down in soft grass to stumble about. Emma caught the girl just as her wobbly legs gave out, cushioning the fall by plopping the little girl's bottom on her own lap as the child giggled madly.

Jared couldn't stop replaying the clip, imbedding it in his memory where he could press on it, like a wound, if he were ever foolish enough to believe there was a place for him in Emma McDaniel's life.

Hell, whenever he was around anyone under the age of twelve, the kids looked at him as if he were a dragon in disguise. He scared them on purpose, subtly bullying them into keeping their distance. Because every so often, when he looked into a soft, vulnerable child's face, the guilt still seared him.

But Emma...she was a natural with kids. So...free. Had her ex-husband ever bothered to watch that cut? The man from the purple-framed picture. Mr. Father of the Year, if the tabloids could be believed.

Jared seethed inside. How could anyone watching Emma with those kids ever think she didn't want children of her own?

Or that she was some kind of shallow Hollywood sexpot who just fell into bed with whatever man she happened to be with at the time....

She'd only been divorced two years. And this Drew Lawson guy...they'd been married since she was in drama school. That's what Emma had said, wasn't it?

Jared hit the remote, selected a scene from the middle of the last installment of Jade Star. "God, look at her," he whispered to himself. "She's still acting her heart out, but it doesn't matter. The director's sold his soul to the special effects department instead of banking on Emma's talent."

And she *was* talented. Gifted in ways Jared had never imagined. Because he'd never given her a chance to show him what she could do.

A knock on the door made him hit the power button, turning the telly off as guiltily as if he'd been watching porn. He grimaced, knowing he must look ridiculous, sitting here in the dark. He groped his way to the door of the trailer, banging his elbow on something in the process.

He opened the door.

Emma. She stood there, flushed with pleasure, her hair tousled, a smile on her face. A far sadder, far wiser smile than the young actress in those outtakes should ever have owned.

Jared's voice felt tight in his throat. "Guess I don't have to ask whose team won."

"That's right, Butler. We creamed 'em. God, I love to win."

But she'd lost where it mattered most, hadn't she? Been left with her career instead of her husband's love, nasty lies instead of the truth. People believing the worst about her, thinking they knew her when they didn't have a clue who the woman really was beneath all that glitter.

Maybe it was time Jared tried to find out.

"Davey was helping Beth put the game stuff away," Emma explained. "I figured I could walk the twenty yards to your trailer by myself." She flipped Jared a teasing salute. "Prisoner McDaniel reporting for lockup, sir."

Jared searched her face, wondering if that might be the most honest thing she'd ever said to him. It made him ache thinking of that free-spirited young woman on the DVD, now unable to walk through an airport without being recognized, being stalked by the press even here in the wilds of Scotland.

He locked the trailer door and they walked to the castle in silence, Emma's face turned up to the stars.

When they reached the tower room, he lit the branch of candles on the table, his gaze straying toward the purple frame. He picked it up, turned toward her.

"Nice picture."

Her mouth softened, wistful. "Yes, it is."

"It's the last thing I expected you to choose the night I told you that you could keep one thing from your suitcase."

She wiped the softness from her face, pulling down a brittle, devil-may-care mask. Her armor against him during the days since he'd all but called her an easy lay. "Yeah, well," Emma said. "I'm just full of surprises. Of course, the folks back home don't know my black leather bondage side. You know, that whole Hollywood swingers scene. You should see what I can do with a riding crop."

"Don't."

She stopped, peered at him, off-balance. "What do you mean, *don't?*"

"Act. I know I'm the one who cast you in that role, but…it doesn't fit you at all, does it? While this…" He trailed his fingers over the glass, touching her face, frozen forever, happy. "This seems to suit you a whole lot better. You want to tell me why it's so special? I mean, besides this…er, positively elegant, exorbitantly expensive designer frame?"

He smiled, displaying the purple glitter clinging to his fingers.

Still wary, Emma approached him, sliding the frame from his grasp as if it were too precious to let careless hands touch. "This Christmas was the last time I truly felt at peace," she said with an honesty that seared his heart. "Everybody was so happy. All of the family, together. Drew and I had just gotten engaged."

Ouch. Jared tried to keep the sharp jab from showing on his face. Why the hell should that hurt? Because the son of a bitch had broken her heart? And *Drew* hadn't exactly been ringing up the reporters to set things straight when that whole "Ice Queen Freezes Out Husband, Denying Him Children" story had broken.

I'm sure Drew will be a wonderful father….

Emma's quote burned through Jared's head. The lady showed more class than her *GQ* cover model of an ex-husband deserved.

"My sister Hope was scared I was going to forget her when I got famous. She gave me this and made me promise it would be the first thing I put out whenever I got to a new movie set.

It's been all over the world. I keep a paper in the back of the frame where I write down all the countries it's been to. I figure I'll give it to her when it's her turn to wear the wedding dress."

"The wedding dress?"

"The Civil War era one we found in a trunk in March Winds' attic."

The preservationist inside him kicked in, hard. Jared choked, horrified. "You'd actually wear an artifact?"

"My Aunt Finn wore it. My mom—well, dresses aren't her style, antique or otherwise. But ever since I was a little girl, I dreamed someday…well, you know. When Aunt Finn packed it away in that trunk in the attic, she promised she'd keep it for me."

"Did you? Wear it?" Why the hell did he want to know? Wedding dresses—real or imaginary—made a better signal than a bloody plague cross on the door to send him running in the opposite direction.

Emma made a wry face. "I grew to roughly the height of a Los Angeles Laker. You ever see period clothes, Butler? They're so small, they look like they should barely fit on dolls."

"Too bad." *Yeah, boyo. The fact that she hadn't worn the dress she'd cherished for Drew the Asshole just breaks your heart.*

Emma seemed to shake herself, as if suddenly aware she'd let her guard slip just a little. "One of the producers at my studio showed me a great picture of Emma Thompson's wedding here in Scotland. Her groom was wearing quite a lovely dress of his own."

"A kilt," Jared corrected.

"If you say so. Apparently the bugs had a real good time biting his bare…assets." Her eyes twinkled and he wondered if she was really amused or resorting to acting for self-protection. "You know, Butler, this is the last subject I thought you'd be interested in. Wedding dresses and my family and such. What about yours?"

"My what?"

"You'd look pretty silly in a wedding dress. What about your family? Your father and…oops." She looked like she'd swallowed a raw egg.

"My father?"

"Uh, obviously you had to have one," she stammered. "I mean, it's a scientific necessity. Unless you came from a sperm donor, but I hardly think he'd be able to squeeze a book of poetry into the test tube."

"Davey." Jared's hands clenched.

Emma pressed her hand to her breast, obviously rattled. "Listen, this isn't Davey's fault," she began. "I mean, I wasn't supposed to tell but my family is really crappy at keeping secrets. I suppose I should have warned him."

Jared scowled. "What did he say?"

"Nothing, really. That you gave him your dad's book of Robert Burns. It meant the world to Davey." Her voice disarmed Jared, suddenly so hushed, almost tender.

"Da would have loved him."

"Loved. Past tense." Emma's eyes filled with empathy. "Your father…he's dead?"

"Years ago. My whole family is dead."

"I'm sorry. I bet he was so proud of you."

"He didn't know any better." Bitterness crept past the edges in Jared's voice. He hadn't meant to let it.

"You don't mean that!" Emma pressed her hand to his forearm, her touch warming places he'd kept cold far too long. He pulled away, unable to bear it. "God, Jared. Look at you. You're brilliant! Any scholar who loved Burns that much must've been overjoyed with a son like you."

"My da was a simple working man, with hands like iron,

all battered and scarred. If only his heart had been half as tough. But it was far too tender. Life…hurt him. But I was too wrapped up in my own world to care."

Why was he telling her this? Things he never spoke of to anyone. Not even Jenny. He'd tried, the night after his father's funeral, tears streaming down his face when he'd hidden himself away by his father's favorite trout stream. The place where Angus Butler had gone on a Sunday, his one day off from grueling, spirit-breaking work, to read poetry and dream. But Jenny had recoiled in horror, frightened by the sobs that had racked Jared's body when he was supposed to be the strong one, the one who sheltered her from sadness, from life.

Maybe he'd known even then that their marriage was doomed. She was more child than wife, determined to shut her eyes to anything hard or painful that demanded of her a strength she didn't have.

It's up to you to make her happy, Jared, Jenny's father had said on the day they'd married. *It's your responsibility to take care of my baby girl….*

Jared had been too young to realize then that you couldn't "make" anyone happy. And too arrogant to know there were times he'd need someone to care for him as well. A woman with a heart big enough and brave enough and strong enough to endure the dark times, the haunted times, in a life far too full of secret pain.

"Every child is self-absorbed," Emma murmured, seeming far away, her thoughts fixed on some distant point she alone could see. "We think we're the center of our parents' world. It doesn't even occur to us that they have their own wounds, their own scars. The year I turned ten, my mom left me on my uncle's doorstep. I didn't even know him and…well, he was about as thrilled to have a little girl dropped in his lap as you were when Captain came on the scene."

She'd been abandoned by her mother? The knowledge jolted Jared. He crossed to the picture, picked it up. "Your mom is the dark-haired one, isn't she?"

"Yeah." Emma smiled tenderly.

"You don't look much alike. But she has the same determination in her eyes."

"Jake calls it our 'dead stubborn' look and thanks God she has it. Otherwise, he figures she'd have given up on him."

Jared stared at the images as if trying to unravel something foreign, full of mystery. "Strange. Looking at this picture, it's hard to believe your family was ever anything but happy. From the way you and your mom were smiling, I thought…"

That you'd been together always, had bedtime stories and lullabies and that soft mother smell of talcum powder and perfume swirling around you when she tucked you into bed…all the things I can't ever remember….

"There are no perfect families, Butler," Emma confided. "They all have their flaws, their vulnerable places. But we McDaniels figured out the hard way things have a way of healing, as long as you've got the courage to bring them into the light."

"My mum left when I was a year old. I…don't remember her at all."

Emma reached out. Touched his cheek for just a heartbeat, then let her hand fall away. Silent understanding shone in dark eyes that didn't look away from his.

"My da spent his whole life waiting for my mother to walk back in the door," Jared confessed, his voice frayed on edges still sharp in spite of the fact that they were decades old. "Sometimes I despised him for it."

"You must've been waiting for her as well," Emma said. "I mean, if your father thought she'd come back, how could a little boy not keep hoping?"

Jared turned away, pressed his palm against rough stone wall, as if to scour away the pain of it, that waiting, that hoping he'd denied forever, even to himself. "Every Christmas my father would slip a present under the tree for her. Just in case. Sometimes I heard Da and Gran fighting about it. *She's gone, Angus! And good riddance to her, flighty baggage that she was. Let her go then find that poor lad of yours a mother!*"

"God, I hate it when grown-ups yell like that, completely oblivious, as if somehow being a kid makes you deaf or stupid. When I have kids, I'll never—" She stopped, fresh pain in her face. "*If* I have kids, I won't ever do that."

Jared would have wagered his life she was right. Emma would never indulge her temper in front of a child. But Jenny wouldn't have bothered to hide her emotions from anyone, even her own children. She'd been brittle as a weather-battered Ming vase, ready to crack at the slightest pressure once her father had passed her into Jared's care.

He remembered their last fight, her voice, on the edge of hysteria, crackling over the international telephone line. *I'm flying out to the site in the morning to talk about this....*

I'll be back in the States in two weeks, Jen. Time enough to settle this then.

You mean time enough for you to close me out! Ignore me! This is your problem, too, Jared....

For Christ's sake, Jen! You think I don't know that?

And it had been. The end to all of his dreams until he was too old, too tired to care. A prison where he'd be locked too deeply into a world he'd never wanted to inhabit.

Emma slid onto the bench and leaned her face toward the open window as if giving him privacy, letting him sort out memories she sensed were better handled alone. After a long moment of staring at the sea's moon-sheened surface, she spoke. "My mom would love this place. All those crashing waves and twisted trees and stone cliffs. It's wild, you know? So…so free. Just as long as you never took her to a pub where she'd have to listen to suicide music."

"Suicide music?"

Emma chuckled. "My Aunt Finn is Irish. Instead of normal lullabies, she sings all these haunting ballads to her kids, you know, where everybody dies or—worse still—leaves Ireland. One particular gem always kicks my mom's blood pressure into overdrive. *I'll dye my petticoats, I'll dye them red and round the world I'll beg for bread until my parents would wish me dead…* Mom says it's a wonder the kids don't have nightmares."

Jared heard strains of his own, haunting music carried on the wind. "My da always sang one of Burns' songs," he confided softly. "But it was more for my mum than for me." Jared shifted into his baritone, his voice filled with his father's longing. *"Ae fond kiss and then we sever, Ae farewell and then—forever. Deep in heart wrung tears I'll pledge thee, Warring sighs and groans I'll wage thee. Had we never loved so kindly, had we never loved so blindly, never met or never parted, we had ne'er been broken hearted."* The melody drifted into silence, joining the sea's timeless mourning.

Emma swallowed hard. Her eyes shone up at his, over-bright. "That's beautiful."

"I never thought so. Romantic rubbish and all that. My da said he hoped I'd fall in love someday, deep enough to understand it. Hopeless that, wasn't it?"

Emma smiled, as if she sensed humor was safer. Too much tenderness might undo him. "You're not in the grave yet, Butler," she said. "Besides, I think you've been in love a long time."

"Me?" He frowned, incredulous.

"Yes, *you.* But you were born six centuries too late to woo your lady fair."

A flush burned into Jared's cheekbones. "That's absurd."

But Emma brushed his protest aside. "Of course, if you ever *could* manage to surrender your grand passion for Lady Aislinn, there are plenty of real live women who'd be happy to take her place. Veronica Phillips, for example."

Jared grimaced. "I think that might be taking Burns' 'loving blindly' thing a little too far."

Emma laughed. "I guess you're right. Maybe that's why fate threw us together, Butler. We're both hopeless. You're in love with Lady Aislinn and I've got it bad for some knight in shining armor who doesn't even exist."

Jared sucked in a breath, feeling suddenly, unutterably old, tarnished and battered beyond help. "Ah, so that's your secret. Emma McDaniel, on a quest for the proverbial fairy-tale knight."

"Nope." She turned back to the window, the pale curve of her cheek fragile with dreams that could never be. "My knight looks like the dragon won. Beaten down and exhausted, as if he'd been fighting his way forever through a million seas."

Jared stilled. "Seas?"

She glanced over her shoulder at him. "That's where I saw him. Out there." She gestured out the window to the rugged coast beyond. "He looked so tired, so sad. I wanted to…help him. Tell him it's alright to lay down his sword." She looked at Jared. She seemed so tender, bruised by life, as if kissing her might break some dire enchantment. "I know it's silly."

"I'm not laughing," Jared said hoarsely, groping for the right words. "Maybe the only thing a knight knows how to do is fight. If he stopped…" *He might have to learn how to live. Might have to listen to poetry. Might know what he's missed all those years at war. He might face the most terrifying dragon of all, without his sword to defend himself. A dragon named Loneliness….*

Emma fiddled with her hair, obviously shy having confided

far more than she meant to. "Well, tomorrow morning will come early enough." A worried cast clouded her eyes. She cradled his face with her hand, her fingertips soft, sweet magic. "You look tired. You should get some sleep. Easier said than done when your mattress is on a stone floor, right?"

"We knights are used to sleeping on rocks. It keeps us from going soft." He wanted to curl his fingers around her wrist, bury a kiss in her palm, see what power she held to break dark enchantments. Instead he crossed to his cot, knowing he'd never sleep. Only mark his time until her breath came, gentle with sweet dreams, and he could take up his sword once more.

Chapter Fourteen

EMMA WOKE TO UNNATURAL silence, the steady, all-too-familiar rasp of Jared's soft snoring from across the room gone. She sat up in her bed and peered to where his mattress lay across the arched doorway. The candles kept lit for emergencies glimmered, casting weird shadows across tumbled blankets thrown back onto the stone floor. It was far too easy to imagine Jared kicking them away from his long legs in restlessness or frustration. Picture him climbing to his feet to pace, scowling darkly. But Jared gone altogether? That seemed unthinkable.

"Jared?" she called, drawing her blankets up to her chin as her gaze tried to pick out his silhouette in the shadowy recesses of the room. "Jared, are you there?"

Silence. Unease rippled through her. The man had been guarding her as fiercely as Sir Brannoc had guarded Lady Aislinn. What in the world would make Attila the Scot desert his post?

Maybe you drove him off, a voice whispered in her head.

*Flinging yourself at him like some desperate crazy woman.
Really, you were every bit as bad as Veronica and the other
girls. Maybe worse. You don't have the excuse of being a kid
with a crush on the teacher. You're a grown woman who
should know better....*

Stupid. Emma hugged herself. Stupid, stupid, stupid to get
carried away like that and worse still to let Jared know how
hot she was for his body. No wonder the guy had fled the
bedroom. He was probably afraid she'd jump him in his sleep.

"For heaven's sake, Emma, get a grip," she told herself
crossly, kicking off her covers. "Talk about playing the drama
queen. There are plenty of reasons Jared might have left the
tower. Reasons that have nothing to do with the way you
tried to pounce him. It isn't as if you're the first woman who
put the moves on him. With a body like his, he's probably
turned avoiding unwanted passes into an Olympic sport."

But if that was the case, then why had he left the tower?
He'd been so furious the night she'd dared slip out to the loo
without waking him, he'd started sleeping across the doorway.

"Emma McDaniel, girl genius," she muttered, grateful for
the distraction of cold stone on bare feet as she climbed out
of bed. *That* was the solution to the Jared Butler disappearing act. He'd just slipped out to relieve himself. It was that
simple!

So how come he hadn't taken the candles with him? And,
more to the point, how come he wasn't back? Every move the
man made was layered through with a restless energy, an
ability to seem like he could be in three places at once. She
should barely have known he was gone before he reappeared.

She cocked her head to one side for a long moment, listening for his footsteps on the stairs. Nothing. Emma caught
her lip between her teeth. What on earth was the matter
with her?

She should be glad he was gone. After all, it wasn't that long ago she'd been ready to sell her soul for a few Butler-free moments. But now, well…his absence made her edgy somehow.

Stockholm syndrome, she heard Samantha's voice quip in her subconscious. *You remember that Patty Hearst thing? Hostages forming some psycho attachment to their captors? Next thing I know, you'll be telling me you've fallen in love with the man.*

"I have not!" Emma's cheeks flamed. "Don't be ridiculous, Sam! I—" She grimaced, swiping her hair back from her cheek. "Maybe I am crazy. Flinging myself at Jared like some sex-starved idiot and then arguing about it with someone who isn't even on the same continent."

A ray of moonlight creeping through the tower window pulled her gaze. Maybe a lungful of sea air would clear her head. She started toward the moonbeam, then froze in her tracks.

A distant roar set the hairs on the back of her neck prickling, the raw cry reverberating from somewhere in the night. Alarm shot through her. Had Jared fallen on the cliff? Or a wildcat…hadn't Davey said there were wildcats in Scotland? She raced to the window, banging her hip into the edge of the table as she peered out, her gaze sweeping from stony cliff to moonlit sea.

But Jared was nowhere in sight. It was another figure that made her press her hand to her lips, her stomach plunging in disbelief.

The knight of the sea battled on the violently thrashing water, his sword flashing in the moonlight, his face a pale blur.

She scrubbed at her eyes with her knuckles, expecting him to disappear. But when she opened them again, the knight still battled on the waves. Emma's heart leapt. He was there! Her ghost knight! He was real!

She'd always believed in spirits wandering the earth. Since

the summer she was ten and Addy March had been her best friend, she'd found comfort in imagining souls still linked to people or places they loved. Addy bonded to March Winds by the journal Emma had found, the nineteenth-century girl real in spite of the fact that the rest of the McDaniels thought her an imaginary friend Emma had concocted to ease her loneliness.

Although Emma had grown up and left Addy behind, she still believed Addy had been real. That the little girl who once longed for her absent father during the Civil War had spoken to Emma through time, helping Emma endure the months without her own mother. Addy a guardian spirit to help Emma navigate the most painful time in her life, until now.

So if Addy had come to her for a reason, why did this Scottish ghost call to Emma now? What drew her so fiercely to her knight of the sea? Her heart squeezed, understanding to her very marrow his battle with an enemy he couldn't see.

Loneliness… Emma's soul echoed his.

The knight, searching all eternity for a lady he would never find, his love and dreams lost…not so different from Emma's own.

He's not real, doubt and logic prodded her. Then why did she *feel* the knight's pain so sharply, *sense* his isolation so deeply. *Need* with every fiber in her body to reach out to him across time to comfort him….

It was time to put an end to all her wondering. Prove to herself once and for all whether she was right about the spirit wandering Castle Craigmorrigan or whether she was simply losing her mind.

Fearful that at any moment her knight would vanish once again into mist, she didn't bother to slip on her shoes. She merely grabbed one of the candles flickering on the table and raced down the tower stairs.

She plunged out into the night, rounding the tower exterior and clambering over the chain to the forbidden area beyond. Cold winds bit through the fragile cloth of her shift. Slick stones bruised her feet, slowing her down. She picked her way across the ankle-twisting expanse in spite of pain and danger, hot wax from the candle splashing onto her knuckles.

Her eyes swept the seascape, searching, desperate for the apparition she'd seen from her room, half-expecting she'd be too late. He'd already have sunk deep into his watery grave.

She gasped as she saw him. Her gaze locked on the lone figure battling atop the waves. Her memory filled with fairy tales she'd read as a dreamy little girl, battles she'd pictured and foes knights had vanquished. No fearsome dragon writhed across the waves, and yet that didn't diminish the wonder of the scene before her, a magic far too real.

The deadly blade of the knight's sword flashed—his battle cries battering against the night wind—a silvery coat of chain mail gleaming on his chest.

Thunder crashed as clouds conquered the moon. Or was that terrible pounding sound Emma's heartbeat raging? The warrior vanished in darkness as black as sin.

"No!" Emma cried in protest. "Don't leave me!"

As if at her command, a moonbeam pierced through a break in the clouds, limning the warrior in an ethereal glow. The knight wheeled toward her across the wave's divide. His image seared into her mind in that frozen instant, moonlight ruthless as dragon flame illuminating Jared Butler's face.

Jared? Emma's mind screamed denial. No! That was impossible! The knight was fighting on the sea. How could any mortal…

But she knew the crags and hollows of Jared Butler's face almost as well as she knew her own. She knew the shape of that mouth, with its crooked grin and its sin-dark secret: the sensitivity he tried so hard to hide.

Jared stood—his sword flashing, his powerful body dripping silver—as if he were Sir Lancelot come real.

She didn't see the vast emptiness beyond the cliff's edge until it was too late. Her foot stepped into nothingness.

The candle flew from her grasp, an arc of light against the darkness tumbling to the sea. She flailed, fighting for balance, screaming as she groped for something, anything to grab hold of as she fell. Her fingers snagged the branch of some scrubby underbrush clinging precariously to the cliff's edge and she held on with all her might.

"Emma!" Jared shouted, flinging his sword away. "Hold on!"

Her hands slipped, rough bark tearing at her palms. She glanced down at the waves hurling themselves with bone-crushing force against the foot of the cliffs far below, foam-crested currents that would drag her beneath the surface forever if she fell. Oh, God, Jared would never get to her in time!

She scrabbled with her feet, searching for purchase. Her toes dug into a small hollow. The tiny outcropping of rock helped bear some of her weight.

She shut her eyes, her mind filling with faces she loved. Her mother, once so restless, glowing with joy in the gazebo as she'd married Jake. Her uncle Cade and aunt Finn…their twins and Deirdre Skye. And Emma's very own little sister, Hope. Chattering over the phone about her very first dance recital come September. Hope dancing as Red Riding Hood, with her daddy playing the big bad wolf. Emma planned to order the most extravagant bouquet imaginable to give her little sister when Hope came off stage. Who would do it if Emma wasn't there?

No, she told herself, clinging even more tightly. She couldn't fall…couldn't leave them….

And yet, they'd all get through it—the grief her loss would bring. There was only one McDaniel who'd never survive if she fell. Her grandfather. Sure, the Captain loved all his rebellious family. But Emma had always known she was his favorite. His "diamond in the sky." She remembered the Christmas she'd gotten engaged, the troubled crease in the Captain's brow when they'd stolen a moment alone together.

What's wrong, Grandpa?

I just want to know you're happy before I die. Drew… he's…

Perfect! Emma had provided with a bride-to-be's bliss.

So he is. Maybe that's what scares me.

What would the Captain think if he ever met Jared Butler?

The sound of footsteps clattering on the rocks yanked her back to the present. Jared's voice urging her, "Hold on, Emma! Hold on!"

She strained her neck back to search for him, saw his face appear over the ledge, his jaw rugged as the cliff, set and unyielding. "Don't you let go!" Chain mail clattered against rock as he flung himself down on his belly and reached for her.

Strong, hard, real, Jared's fingers clamped around her wrist. "Give me your other hand," he urged. "Grab on to me."

For an instant, terror flooded her at the thought of releasing the branch. His fingers were too damp, her wrist too slippery. How could he ever hold her? She glanced down at the raging sea.

"You're not going to drag me over. Emma, look at me," he ordered. "Trust me."

She peered up into his face, his world-weary eyes, his stubborn jaw. His mouth. So fierce, so tender. Her knight, a light in her darkness. And she knew he would never let her fall. She released her hold, her right foot suddenly sliding out from under her. She dangled by one arm for a terrified moment that stretched out forever. Then she flung her other arm up and grabbed on to Jared, holding on with all her might.

Ever so slowly, he edged his body back from the brink of the cliff, pulling her with him inch by painful inch, her stomach raking against the stone. She tried to help him, pushing against whatever surface she could reach with her feet. But it was Jared's strength that held her, Jared's will that moved her up onto solid ground.

The instant he could manage it, Jared caught her under her arms and rolled himself beneath her to cushion her from the rocks. He crushed her hard against him. "Thank God," he growled low, his hands roving up and down her back as if trying to assure himself she was really there. "You're safe now. Safe."

Emma clung to him, links of chain mail biting into her breasts. She didn't care about anything except being in Jared's arms. "You…you're the knight of the sea. But the water…fighting on the water…impossible…"

"A sort of bridge of rocks sweeps out to a stone platform from the east. You can't see it unless you know it's— What the hell does it matter?" he demanded in a shaky voice as he maneuvered them both to their feet.

He swept her up into his arms, carrying her like a child as he picked his way with astonishing sure-footedness across the maze of tangled stone. He smelled of sea spray and spice and dark fairy magic as he stepped over the chain with one long stride. "Emma, you could have drowned!"

"For the s-second time in my life," Emma said, burrowing closer, remembering another near disaster—her fall as a child into the river near her uncle Cade's cabin.

She'd left the castle door wide open. He shouldered it shut behind them and started up the stairs. "What the hell were you doing out there?" he growled.

"My knight. Thought…thought he was Lady Aislinn's husband trying to find her. I was scared he was giving up."

"He wasn't giving up. He was working out his frustrations. Hell, what am I talking about? *He* doesn't even exist. It's just me, an archaeologist with a bugger of a temper trying to let off some steam so I won't kill anybody. Working with my sword out there, in chain mail and all the trimmings until I can't lift my arms—that's my release valve when the pressures get too intense. It…centers me."

"But the knight sank into the water that first night. I saw him."

"Must've finally exhausted myself and fell flat. Only time I ever got that frustrated was the night you first came to Craigmorrigan."

"The dragon was winning."

"Don't tell me there was a dragon out there and I didn't even notice! Some knight I am," he said, but his attempt to tease her fell flat. She could feel him shaking.

She felt vulnerable, raw, terror from her fall still rippling through her. She smacked her fist against his shoulder, the metal links tearing a stinging cut in her knuckle. "Don't make fun of me!"

"I'm not. I was just trying to make you laugh." He squeezed her even more fiercely against him. "I promise you this, sweetheart. There are no dragons here."

He set her gently on her feet and grabbed a blanket from her bed, wrapping the plush fur around her.

He peeled the heavy coat of chain mail over his head, his leather jerkin damp with sweat, plastered against his skin. But even as he let the mail slither to a pool on the floor, he still looked every inch her embattled knight.

"You p-probably think I'm being ridiculous," she accused, her lower lip quivering. "My head full of ghosts and—and dragons."

"Reckless, maybe," he said, closing the space between them again. "Hardheaded and damned disobedient. This is the second time you've ignored my danger signs. And you're blasted lucky to be alive." He swept a tear from her cheek with the pad of his thumb and gazed at the glittering drop of moisture as if it held some kind of enchantment. "But the knight you saw was real. Well, sort of. And when it comes to believing in dragons, well…" An almost sheepish aura blunted the chiseled power of his face. "I'm the last man who would ever laugh at you for that."

"You? The—the great scientist?" She sniffed back the rest of her tears, the fur not half as warm as she knew Jared's arms would be. "You can't fit a dragon under a microscope."

"No. But when I was a boy I would have bet my life one could fit under my bed." The corner of his mouth curved ruefully. "The year I turned nine I had nightmares. I'd been devouring *Lord of the Rings* for weeks. Those orcs, they're damned scary."

"Tell me about it," Emma said, shuddering. "I didn't discover Tolkein until I was fourteen and the ring wraiths creeped me out."

Jared stared at her as if one more veil had been torn away between them. "Don't tell me you're another Tolkein freak."

"Oh, yeah. My aunt Finn gave me a boxed set of the books for my birthday. The whole time I was devouring the trilogy Mom thought I was just having one of my reading orgies and fell asleep with the light on. Truth is I left the lamp burning on purpose. Every time my room got dark, I could hear those Nazgul things breathing down my neck."

"I know what you mean." Jared's eyes warmed. "My gran was beside herself, a great lad like me afraid to go to sleep in his own bed. One night I woke up screaming. When Da came in to comfort me, I told him if I had a sword…a real sword like Aragorn's sword of Elendil...I could keep the dragon away from him and Gran and me. Three days later I found one leaning next to my bed."

Emma slipped her arms around him, seeking comfort, warmth. His chest felt warm and solid, powerful enough to slay a whole army of dragons. "So that's how your fascination with pointy objects started?" she teased. "A nice plastic sword to use in dragon taming? I should pick one up for my little sister before I go home. The neighborhood boys would never forgive me." She smiled, imagining Hope's glee.

"The sword wasn't plastic. It was real. A reproduction medieval sword." Jared chuckled. "I could barely even lift the thing."

"A real sword, huh?" Emma nestled in closer. "That must have made you sleep a whole lot better."

"Aye," he whispered into her hair. "Want to hear something funny? Your turn to laugh at me if you've a mind to."

"What?"

He leaned back, crooked her that bone-melting smile. "I *still* can't sleep without the damned thing in my bedroom."

She gaped up at him. "You mean the sword you brought up here? The one you fight with?"

"That's the one. My magic sword. Elendil North, so to speak."

Her heart ached at his honesty, the incredible sweetness of him confiding in her about a time when he'd been small and powerless and afraid. She cradled his cheek in her hand. "Your secret's safe with me, sir knight."

He leaned deeper into her caress. "Remember that first night you arrived here at Craigmorrigan, when you were so damned stubborn and defiant? You asked if there wasn't something I needed, one thing I couldn't do without?"

"I remember."

"I thought of my sword, and…well, that's the first time you managed to do it."

"Do what?"

"Slip past my guard and get your blade to my throat. I would have been the worst kind of hypocrite not to let you take whatever you needed out of that suitcase. A grown man who sleeps with a sword under his bed can hardly object…"

Jared looked out the window to the sea, something sudden and heartbreaking showing in his eyes.

"Maybe you still need the sword because the dragons are never far away. I…" She stopped, understanding the expression on his face, so solemn, so still. "Oh, God, Jared. Your sword. Where is it?"

"I heard you scream. Saw you fall. I let go of it midswing and…"

"It's got to be out there on the rocks where you were fighting." She started toward the door in alarm, but Jared caught her arm. She wheeled toward him.

"I heard it hit the water, Emma," he said, his voice roughened, low.

Emma felt as if she were about to throw up. "No! We'll go look. It has to be…"

Green eyes caught hers, held hers. "It's gone."

"The sword your father gave you! No! How can I ever replace it?" She pulled away from him, pressed her hands to her churning stomach. "Oh, Jared. It's my fault. If I hadn't gone storming off where you told me not to…"

He stopped her words gently with his hand. "Didn't you ever read the old legends? How the fair maiden's life had to be bought at a price? Mountains of gold or a knight's blood or some magical fairy treasure like Lady Aislinn's flag? Maybe my sword was the price for saving you. Like you said, what does a scientist need with magic anyway?"

"Don't try to make me feel better. It won't work."

"Emma, I lost the sword. It could have been worse. If I'd dropped you off the cliff…" His voice caught, or had she imagined it? His teasing smile looked forced. "What would I have told the studio? I not only injured the first actress, the second I lost entirely?" He ran his thumb across the curve of her lip. "I'd rather lose a hundred swords than let something happen to a woman like you."

"Why don't you come clean, Butler." She gave him a tremulous smile. "Even if you *did* want to get rid of me, you wouldn't want me falling off a cliff. You'd much rather have the fun of drowning me yourself. With me out of the picture they might even have waited for Angelica to heal."

"Angelica Robards could never play Lady Aislinn with the power you will."

Emma froze. "Wh-what did you say?"

"You heard me, woman," Jared growled, tousling her hair. He grimaced. "I've a confession to make. Want to know what I did while you were decimating my poor unsuspecting students in Trivial Pursuit?"

"Polished up your chain mail and plotted new ways to torture me?"

"I watched your Jade Star movies."

Dismay flooded through Emma. "Oh, God, no!"

"Davey coerced me into it."

She pulled away from Jared, appalled. "I'm so sorry! I told Davey not to."

"And he used to be such an obedient kid. Lately he doesn't listen any better than you do. It's just as I expected, you're starting to rub off on him. That's what comes of keeping bad company."

"Jared, this isn't funny."

"That's the strange thing about it. I figured he was just misguided and I'd watch the damn films to humor him. But it wasn't a joking matter to the lad. He seemed to think I'd find the films enlightening. Maybe change my attitude toward your acting."

She snorted in disdain. "I'm guessing your opinion went from bad to worse."

"Hardly." Jared caught her arm again, turned her toward him. "Davey was right, Emma. You were fantastic. Talented. Just like he said. You amazed me."

She angled her face away. Why did Jared's praise suddenly hurt more than his scorn had? Because it couldn't possibly be real. "Don't patronize me."

He grasped her chin between his fingers, turned her face back to his. "You should know me better than that. I wanted nothing more than to prove I was right about you. One more thing we have in common. We both love to win."

She managed a wry smile.

"I was wrong about Angelica," Jared insisted. "And I was wrong about you. This is probably the one and only time you'll ever get to hear me admit I'm wrong. I'd rather be stretched on the rack."

"Me, too. Imagine that. Another way we're alike."

"You're nothing like I expected, Emma. Maybe the reason I growled at you like a bear all the time wasn't because you weren't my ideal for the role. Maybe it was more like…sour grapes because…" He hesitated, a vulnerable light in his eyes.

"Because why?"

"Because the moment I set eyes on you I knew. A woman like you might as well be the moon, you're so far out of reach for a plain Scottish boyo like me."

Emma's heart stopped, mesmerized by the naked longing in Jared's eyes. A longing just as deep, just as fierce, just as terrifying as what she felt for him.

She'd never felt any man's hands on her body except Drew's. Never even been tempted by casual sex. Because she'd known from the beginning sex should mean something deep and real. It should change her.

Go to bed with Jared and you can never take it back, a voice in her head warned.

And yet…

She closed her eyes, suddenly carried back to three months after her divorce. She was lying on her stomach on the rug in front of Samantha's fireplace, her friend's beautiful English cocker spaniel offering Emma yet another of her eighty-seven identical stuffed yellow ducks for comfort.

"This twisted affair you've got going with my dog's ducks has got to stop," Sam insisted. "Even Chamois thinks you need a man. This isn't the 1950s in freaking Whitewater, Illinois. You're divorced, Em, not dead. You're a young, talented, intelligent single woman with guys hitting on you every three seconds. What are you waiting for? Prince Charming?"

"I already had Prince Charming. It didn't work out so well. Another shameless case of false advertising."

"Too bad for him, losing someone as fantastic as you are. The question is what are you going to do now? Take Hamlet's advice and *get thee to a nunnery?*"

"I'm just not ready, Sam."

Sam's eyes filled with empathy. "I know it's hard, sweetheart. But this whole divorce thing will get easier in time. Once you get past that first time making love with some other man, you'll be getting on with your life, you know? Drew will really be past tense. Just close your eyes and jump."

"But I want sex to mean something. I want…"

"The glass slipper to fit, the beast to turn into a prince. The whole goddamn fairy tale?" Samantha asked.

"Sounds silly, huh?"

"No. Although if that's the criteria, I probably would have better luck dating one of these things." She examined a particularly badly-chewed version of duckzilla.

"I'll know when it's time, Sam," Emma had insisted. "I'll know."

"How?"

Warm firelight, gold travertine marble and a soulful spaniel's gaze faded.

Emma opened her eyes, Jared's rugged features swimming again into focus. *So what is different this time?* Emma asked herself. *Why let down your guard with this man? In this place? You'll not be acting here. It's not one of Aunt Finn's romance novels. This is real, this night. This choice.*

And yet, would it be the worst thing she ever did to take what Jared Butler offered?

Yes, her common sense told her. This falls under the heading of BIG MISTAKE. To go charging into the dark, plunging over a cliff for the second time tonight. But this time there would be no Jared to pull her up.

He was going over the cliff with her.

She swallowed hard, scraping together every bit of her courage as she peered up into his eyes. "You say I'm out of your reach. But I'm not so far away now. All you have to do is stretch out your hands. See?" She twined her fingers in his. She prayed he couldn't feel her trembling. Or was it Jared trembling? Those strong, sure hands as unsteady as her own?

"Emma, this is…probably a bad idea. You being who you are, while I…I'm no fit man for a woman like you."

"A woman like me?" she echoed sadly. "And who is that, Jared? The Emma the rest of the world sees? The one who smiles that plastic smile for the camera even when her husband leaves her? I see her picture sometimes when I pass newsstands and, God, it's so strange. I don't even know her."

Neither did he. The sudden realization hit Jared like a fist to his gut. No. The woman clinging to his hand wasn't the actress of Jade Star fame, every man's fantasy shag. She was Emma. Just Emma. Savior of mutts with more bite than brains. Defender of gawky teenaged boys with scars on their wrists and pasts too full of pain. Emma, who knew in her blood and bone what it meant to have your mother abandon you, that horrible thirst no one else could slake, the void no one else could fill.

Emma, the lovely young woman from Whitewater, Illinois, who carried a glitter-laden photograph of her family everywhere she traveled and refused to surrender to Jared in battle, no matter how impossible the odds.

His Emma.

No. Not his. She could never be his.

Bloody fool, Jared warned himself sharply. *What do you think, man? If you take her body tonight you'll be able to keep part of her soul? That light in her nothing could vanquish? What have you got to give her in return? Your foul temper. Your obsession with this castle, people dead six hundred years. The work that locked Jenny out, left her crying alone outside the door to your heart.*

What heart? He could almost hear Jenny wail. And she'd been right after all. He didn't have a heart. He was broken inside from watching his father all those years. Jared had killed the tenderness inside him one impulse at a time, forever haunted by the grisly reality he'd lived with as a boy—love no saving grace, no sweet, stunning glory. Love only the twisting knife in Angus Butler's chest.

No. Jared was a scientist. A realist. Through the years he had come to know himself far too well. He was nothing but a giant intellect, so ruthless it didn't care if it devoured anyone in its path.

And yet, he'd told Emma that, hadn't he? The first time they'd come close to making love? She knew he hadn't anything to give her except sex. The skill in his hands, the power of his mouth, the passion even his mighty will could no longer deny her. The first, the only time he could ever remember his body overruling his mind.

"Jared?"

He stiffened, wanting too much, needing too badly.

"Don't…don't think so hard. It's easy, really. I only need one thing from you tonight."

"What's that?"

"See *me*. The real me. Don't make love to some woman I could never be."

Jared's throat tightened at her courage, her honesty, the vast, terrible isolation in her that he understood far too well.

She trembled as she drew his palm to her breast. Her cheeks flooded with color as if no man had ever touched her there before, as if it were her first time.

Her sudden shyness enthralled him. Jared stared at his hand, dark, powerful, relentlessly male against the fragile swell of her breast, his touch burning through the thin fabric of her shift.

"It'll only be you and me in this bed tonight," she said softly. "No expectations. No masks or facades. Just us. Swear to me, Jared. On your father's sword."

Loss swept through him, and longing, for the missing sword or for other things forever beyond his reach. He raised his gaze to hers, carried to another time, another world where Emma belonged as much as he did.

"I swear it."

Emma's mouth tipped in a quavering smile. "You sure you

don't want to run the way you did last time, sir knight? There's still time to escape."

Jared threaded his hand back through her waves of hair, wrapping the dark tresses around his wrist. "Escape chains like these?" He smiled, his gaze intent on the strand of raven black hair, so silky around the sinewy power of his arm. "Don't you know, lady? No knight who ever breathed could be that strong."

Chapter Fifteen

EMMA MELTED INTO Jared's arms, her mouth eager beneath his, her hands threading back into the unruly waves of his hair. He groaned at her response, his tongue laying siege to the crease of her lips, demanding entry. She surrendered and he thrust his way inside, invading her body, invading her soul.

In that instant, it felt so right to let him breach her last defenses—inevitable, as if this night had been their destiny as much as the fairy flag had been twined into the destiny of this castle and its lady. For a heartbeat Emma felt a frisson of foreboding, wondering if their story would end sadly as well. But she shuttered the thought away, losing herself in this moment when there was nothing but her hands in Jared's hair, his tongue leaving fiery heat wherever it stroked her own.

He kissed her as if he were starving for the taste of her, as if part of him feared he might come to his senses at any moment, be wise instead of reckless and pull away from feelings too stormy. Emotions beyond even his power to control. She reeled under his sensual onslaught, sensation piling on sensation, harder, hotter, higher as he fumbled with the tie to her shift. The cord knotted under his fingers. With an oath, he pulled away, started to pick at the knot, meaning to untangle it, his brawny workman's hands almost absurd matched against a task so delicate.

"Break it," she begged in a voice she didn't even recognize. "I need your hands on me. Now."

Feral heat blazed in Jared's eyes as he wound the cord around powerful fingers and snapped it with a yank. Emma gasped as the gathered neckline cascaded off its string, the shift sliding past her shoulders, down her body to pool like sea foam at her feet.

Jared's nostrils flared as his gaze swallowed her up from the crown of her dark curls to the tips of her toes. "Jesus God, the sight of you," he murmured, his Scottish burr rougher, low. "You're so damned beautiful. 'Tis a miracle I can still breathe."

"Don't," Emma drew away, pleading. "I don't want to hear…"

"Hear what?"

"About…what I look like. About the other Emma. I'm not—"

"I'll say you're goddamned beautiful if I want to, woman," Jared growled. "This isn't one of your scripts where you get to revise however you choose. That painted-up woman on the covers of all those magazines—she couldn't hold a candle to you, standing before me right now! Do you hear me?"

He surprised a laugh from her. "Oh, I hear you. In fact, the whole dig site probably hears you. Why, the students should be racing up here at any moment to make sure we haven't killed each other. Didn't anybody ever tell you you're not supposed to growl at somebody you're making love to?"

"Guess I'm a bit out of practice," he said, a hint of color staining his cheekbones.

She was stunned at how glad his admission made her.

"As for the kids intruding on us, they wouldn't dare. They're scared to death of me." He flashed his highland raider's grin. "You would be, too, if you had any sense, woman. I could eat you alive."

"I dare you to try. I've been waiting forever to feel your mouth on my skin." But suddenly she chuckled, astonished at how easy it was.

"If you're so carried away with passion, would you mind telling me why you've got the devil dancing in your eyes, Ms. McDaniel?" Jared's brow furrowed in suspicion. "You find the idea of my making love to you amusing?"

"No-o-o," she hedged. "Well, not exactly." It felt so good to laugh with him, to *play*... She'd never had any idea that the man even knew how. "It's about your...well, I *have* had a bit of a joke on you and—"

"And that joke would be?"

"Do you remember when I first came to the castle? How I called you Dr. S. M.?"

He arched his brows. "You called me a lot worse than that, if I remember rightly."

"Didn't you ever wonder what the initials stood for?"

"I figured it was a comparison to the Marquis de Sade or something equally flattering. Being a sadomasochist or some such. Am I right?"

"That's exactly what I wanted you to think," she said, inordinately pleased with herself. "Truth was it stood for *this*." She reached up, touched his upper lip, the right side arching a fraction higher than the left. "You have the sexiest mouth God ever put on a man, Jared Butler."

"You've gone daft, woman."

"It's your fault if I have," she said, tingling as she ran her finger along that hot, tempting curve. "Do you know how long

I've been thinking about this? Your mouth on my neck, on my breasts…even lower."

Was she insane, saying that aloud? Breaking through her "no sex" barrier was one thing. But making a complete idiot of herself?

Still, she couldn't seem to stop the truth from spilling out. The man burned with a raw sexual tension that took her breath away. The upper lip she'd found so damned alluring curled in blatant male arousal.

He caught her fingertip between his teeth, worried it for a moment, then when her knees were threatening to buckle, released her finger and buried his mouth in the sensitive hollow of her throat, nibbling that fragile skin. Pleasure speared through her nerves, setting her nipples burning and starting a hot, hungry melting between her thighs.

"I've imagined my mouth on you, too," he confessed. "But I never imagined it would be anything but a dream."

She shivered, feeling naked down to her soul.

He pulled back, cupped her cheek ever so gently in his broad palm. "What is it?"

For a moment she thought about brushing the question away, distracting him somehow. But then she looked into his eyes and knew. The truth. She needed to tell him the truth. Maybe this wasn't true love, but honesty mattered to her. *He* mattered.

"I'm just…I guess I'm afraid, that's all."

"You? Afraid?" Jared asked in tender disbelief. "You're the bravest woman I've ever known. What are you afraid of?"

I'm afraid of wanting more than you could ever give. Afraid of feeling the way I felt the day Drew walked out the door, the loneliness, the pain. Only worse, because this time I knew it wouldn't last before it began and I jumped anyway….

Most of all, I'm afraid this night won't be enough.

Saying that aloud would be insanity. Emma hid her bitter-sweet thoughts away and forced herself to meet Jared's searching eyes.

"I'm afraid you're never going to get naked," she tried to joke, and thanked heaven when her subterfuge worked, swirling them both back into currents of raw heat. "Let me see you, Jared," she urged. "All of you. I've been wanting you for so long."

He shifted away, just far enough to shed the leather jerkin he'd worn beneath his chain mail, leaving his broad chest layered with only the linen undergarment beneath. He took her hands and put them on the laces.

"You do it, Emma. Take it off."

Emma slid the fabric off his tanned body and knelt to free him of leather boots and rough linen hose, her unbound hair burying his bare feet in silken curls. Her heart pounding with a desire fiercer than any she'd ever known, she kissed the inside of his knee, the corded strength of his hair-roughened thigh. Jared's breath hissed between his teeth as she rose higher, her cheek brushing his arousal, his shaft heavy and hard with need for her.

Her breath feathered against its length as she drank in the beauty of him, the power, breathing in the scent of salt spray and pine and musky male.

She reveled in the sight of him, such deliciously uncharted territory, so different from Drew. Every sinew of Jared's body had been hewn by the hard physical labor of wresting the past from beneath the stone-strewn ground. The callused hands, roughened by work and weather, only accented the untamed aura that defined the Scotsman's powerful body, awakening an answering, primitive beat in Emma's own.

Drew's sleek runner's muscles, polished by daily workouts at the gym, seemed delicate in comparison. Drew's constant self-control never breaking like the waves on Craigmorri-gan's cliff, transforming into that over-the-edge dragon-fierce hunger Jared radiated now.

"Emma?" Jared's voice, deep with concern, jarred her.

She looked up the length of his body to his eyes peering down at her, suddenly solemn, still.

"You seem a million miles away, lady. What is it?"

"Nothing." Emma lowered her head to hide her face. Jared's powerful thighs blurred before her gaze as she shoved her ex-husband determinedly out of her mind. "I'm just glad you're..."

Strong enough to know what you want...reckless enough to take it.

She moistened her lips and leaned forward, kissed velvety smooth skin, the skeins of her hair brushing his belly, his thighs.

Jared's whole body jerked in response. He growled an oath, grabbing her under her arms, dragging her up his body. "Much more of that and it'll be over before I've begun. I'm not made of steel, woman."

His gruff honesty drove the last of her ghosts away.

"Not steel, eh?" Emma teased. "You could have fooled me. You're so hard all over. So...hot. Let me look at you."

His green eyes lured her off a lifetime's safer paths into wildernesses only he could explore. His mouth whispered of enchantments so filled with forbidden pleasure, no woman snared in such dark magic would ever wish to be free.

Golden specks of candlelight caught in the fine net of dark hair spanning the steely muscles of his chest and arrowing down in a narrow ribbon past his navel. Emma splayed her hands against his narrow waist and slid her fingers up through his feathering of chest hair, traversing the swells of his pecs to the hard points of his flat nipples.

He made a ragged sound, low in his throat as Emma kissed him, soft, wet kisses on the scars Captain had left what seemed a lifetime ago. The first time Jared had let her glimpse the man who lay hidden beneath the armor he showed to the rest of the world.

He caught her around the waist with one powerful arm, urging her up on tiptoe as he crushed her against him, skin to skin. His mouth sought hers, ravenous, as if he could never get his fill of her.

Scooping her up in his arms, he carried her to the bed and laid her back on luxurious furs. The tower room spun above her like every fantasy she'd dreamed since she'd first read of the lady who once dwelled in this place.

A love so fierce, even time and terror couldn't quell it. Yearning flowed through her, a sorrow that she and Jared didn't have that kind of love. And yet, hadn't Lady Aislinn's love ended in tears? Heartbreak that echoed through centuries to come?

Emma wouldn't have to endure that. Only an ache she alone would feel. Or might Jared feel it, too? A soft echo of regret?

No. No regrets. Not now. Not yet. She'd stay in the moment, drink in every sensation, every touch tonight had to offer.

He followed her down onto the bed, covering her with his big body, crushing her deep into the straw ticking with his weight. She felt delicate, feminine and strangely more powerful than she'd ever been in her life.

Jared tangled his fingers in her hair and angled her face to meet his kiss. Emma snapped the last thread of caution, opened herself to him, soaking in every swell of muscle, the delicious contrast his mat of chest hair made to the silky smoothness of her breasts, the way his hard shaft burned its shape into her inner thigh.

She arched against him, delighting in the pressure, wanting more, wanting it all. Jared, hot and hard inside her. All that passion, all that fierceness driving her wild. She let her thighs fall open and Jared kissed her harder, deeper, arching against her center, teasing her, making her whimper in need.

Oh. Had that sound come from her? Emma's face burned. But the noise only made Jared's hands rougher, more insistent.

He pulled her head back, baring her throat to his lips, his teeth, claiming the delicate arch of her collarbone, the faint rasp of his whiskers sensitizing the place where her breast began.

He edged his long body down, breaking the maddening contact between her slick center and his shaft, leaving her bereft until suddenly his mouth closed on the straining bud of her nipple, suckling it deep into the cavern of his mouth.

Fire seared through Emma, stunning in its intensity, driving her to knot her fingers in the lengths of his hair, holding him to her, arching her back so he could draw her deeper, spiral her higher than she'd ever imagined possible.

She looped her leg around Jared's thigh, holding him even tighter against her the only way she could as he kissed his way to her other breast, licking it with his rough tongue.

She was burning, melting. The man reducing her to ash with his sensual skill. He shifted slightly, his callused fingers hungry as they searched the soft swell of her belly, circling her navel, then spearing lower, through downy curls to find the place fairly screaming for his touch.

Emma's body bucked against him as the rough pad of his finger claimed the nubbin of flesh between her damp folds. She cried out, feeling as if she would shatter if he slid his touch away. The sound seemed to reverberate through the room, too loud, too wild.

"Oh…oh, J…Jared," she stammered, horrified. "I…don't think… I can't…"

"Can't what, angel?"

"Can't stop… I'm not usually this…this…"

"This hot?" he asked, his finger stirring that burning ember. "This wet? This sexy? I don't believe it."

"This…noisy," she confessed, closing her eyes in embarrassment. "Out of…control."

She expected him to laugh. Expected him to tease her. Instead he gave her a rough shake.

"Look at me!" he demanded. "Now, Emma. Open your eyes!"

Stunned at the fierceness in his command, she let her lashes flutter open, unable to deny him anything, even it seemed her complete humiliation.

"I *love* it that you're out of control. You were made for this, Emma. For a man's hands, a man's mouth. Made to drive a man out of his mind. Drive *me* insane," he added darkly.

"No. You don't know."

"I know, all right," he challenged roughly. "Don't tell me *he* didn't like it. Your bloody fool of an ex-husband. Did he want you quiet, Emma? Tame?"

Emma bit her lower lip, too hurt inside to answer.

"Drew Lawson was a fool! You're a wild thing in my arms. You hear me, Emma? Wild and beautiful and so bloody strong no man could ever conquer you. Nay, no more than any man ever conquered the Lady Aislinn."

Tears trickled down Emma's temples into her hair, a strange mixture of gratitude toward Jared and the first real stab of anger at Drew. That in all the years they'd been together Drew had never known her even half as well as the man strewing kisses down her body.

It touched her to the heart, scared her to her soul, Jared comparing her to his medieval lady. A woman he idolized. Loved. A woman who would always be perfect because she didn't exist, except in his imagination.

"All those noises you make?" Jared murmured against her stomach. "Bloody hell, they turn me on! Trust yourself to me, Emma. Give me all that passion I see when you fight me with your sword. Let me make you scream."

"I couldn't…hold back if…I…wanted to. Not with you. Oh, Jared…"

He leaned to one side groping under the edge of the mattress, confusing the life out of her until he emerged with a foil packet in his hand.

Grateful, she took it from him, sheathed him inside it.

Jared bracketed her hips with his big hands, settled his weight between her legs. She felt him there, blunt and hot, every muscle in his body rigid with need for her. His eyes captured her gaze, held it.

"Don't close your eyes, Emma. Look at me when I take you."

He thrust deep, touching places Drew had never touched. Could never reach. Parts of her soul Drew had never wanted to see.

"You feel so…so right underneath me," Jared murmured in amazement. "God help me."

Jared was the one who pulled his gaze away. Heavy dark lashes settled on the blades of his cheekbones, shutting out every sense but touch and taste and sound as he kissed her, setting a wild pulsing rhythm that echoed deep in Emma's soul.

The edge sharpened as her body tightened around him. She felt the cry forming at the back of her throat. She couldn't stop it any more than she'd been able to stop herself from stumbling over the edge of the cliff.

Jared gave a raw cry of triumph as her body quickened around his shaft, a white-hot fulfillment, blinding her, burning her.

He drove himself deep, kissing her so fiercely her lips stung. She didn't care, only held tight to his hard warrior's body, glorying in his rough loving, somehow more beautiful than any tenderness she'd ever known. He stiffened above her, cried out in his own searing climax. But the whisper Emma heard was her own.

I love you.

She reeled at the truth of it.

Oh, God. She'd wondered what made Jared different? Made her choose this night, this man? She'd wondered why her defenses had come tumbling down?

She loved him.

Her adversary. Her foe. Her battered knight fighting dragons all alone.

She loved him.

The truth shattered its way into her heart.

Emma held him long moments as he lay against her, his chest heaving, his face buried in her curls. What if he couldn't look at her because he was as stunned as she was, by feelings he hadn't expected? What if love had…well… She couldn't help but smile as a purely Jared Butler smart aleck description flashed into her mind. *If love had sneaked up and bit him like her damned terror of a dog?*

It was possible, wasn't it? Emma couldn't keep from hoping. That's what happened to McDaniels, Uncle Cade had always claimed. No warning. Just a sneak attack and then, wham, next thing you knew, there you were facing down a sour-faced minister in the gazebo, no escape in sight.

Sometimes, Jared seemed almost more McDaniel-esque than Emma was.

What if she just told him the truth? Blurted it out right here, right now? *Hey, Jared, funny thing happened when you were screwing my brains out…*

Don't be crazy, Emma, her common sense warned. *Just…just test the waters. See what Jared says. Maybe…well, you can see if this meant anything more to him than just sex.*

Right. And won't it just smash your little heart to bits if it was no big deal to him?

Had a riot making you scream, Emma. Have a nice life...

Blessedly, Jared rolled away from her before she could think of any more cheery farewells. He turned his broad back to her, busying himself disposing of the condom. A simple act that took the king of multitasking far longer than necessary.

Was it possible he was feeling as awkward as she was? What did people say to each other after they made love the first time? Drew had been almost apologetic, sure he'd hurt her, treating her like some fragile, delicate thing. That kind of chivalry would seem ridiculous after the fireworks that had happened here. But Jared's silence was driving her slowly insane.

Emma groped for something to break the tension, settled on humor. "Nice touch, Butler," she said, trying to keep it light. "Ye old medieval condom. Did they have those in the Middle Ages?"

"Actually, condoms were invented in—"

"Never mind! Never mind! I was just teasing you! I really meant to congratulate you for being a good Boy Scout."

"What?"

"You know, the old motto. *Be prepared.*"

He still didn't look at her, his shoulders far too stiff. Emma's stomach tightened.

"I planted this when you weren't looking," Jared explained. "Just in case I lost my mind."

"Is that what just happened?" She tried not to let the sudden hurt she felt bleed into her voice. "You lost your mind?"

He ran his hand back through his hair. "I don't know what the hell else to call it. You have a way of making me lose control. Of my temper, my, er, baser instincts."

"Your *baser instincts?*" They were already down to *instincts?* Oh, God, he wasn't turning scientist on her already? "Maybe that's the reason Lady Aislinn never had any children," she said, her voice sounding brittle. "Her husband kept a stash of birth control hidden under the bed. Of course, I doubt they had nice tidy little foil packets from the chemist's down the street. Blows your whole theory of historical accuracy."

"Historical accuracy is one thing," Jared insisted. "Being reckless is another."

Stubbornness fired up in Emma. "What if I told you I *like* being reckless when you're around? What if I told you I've never had so much fun? In sword fights. In bed."

"That's just grand. You almost dropped yourself over a cliff tonight, and now...this. I'm not sure this little stunt wasn't even more dangerous."

"What the hell is the matter with you?" Emma demanded, hurt and confused. "I know this was a...was a big step for both of us. It's natural to feel some...well, awkwardness after. At least, I think it is. Not that I really know. From experience, I mean."

Jared pressed his hands to his temples, as if she were giving him a headache. The jerk. She hadn't wanted to kick him this badly for weeks. Drawing her tattered dignity around her, she reached for her shift, drew it over her head. She caught the gaping neck closed. Told herself it was to cover her breasts, not somehow protect her heart.

"Whatever you think of me, Jared, know this. My making love with you wasn't any stunt, reckless or otherwise."

Jared swore under his breath, and she could tell he was struggling for patience. "Emma, I'm not trying to hurt your feelings here."

"Oh, don't worry. You're not. You're just making me mad as hell."

"Don't tell me we're back to normal again already? Are we?"

"Maybe there's something I *should* tell you," Emma fired back, McDaniel pride kicking in. "Something *you* need to know."

"And what would that be?"

"I'm *anything* but reckless when it comes to sex, Dr. Butler. Drew wasn't just my first lover. He was my *only* lover."

Jared wheeled toward her, his face going pale. "You mean you've never—"

"Give the boy a gold star. He guessed it in one. I've never made love to any man but Drew. And now you."

"*That's* a bit of information you might have shared earlier!" Jared grabbed up a fur, wrapped it around his hips. He stalked to the window, looking more wary and wild than ever before.

"I'm not expecting you to marry me or anything," she shot back. "You don't have to build me a house with a white picket fence and raise a passel of kids."

"You picked the wrong man if that's the job you're offering! And that's a dead cert."

She folded her arms across her chest. "I don't expect anything of you."

"Maybe not. But I can see the wanting in you. You're supposed to be an actress, for God's sake. But I always saw it. So why the hell didn't I stop myself before…"

"It was my right to choose."

"And you're thinking so clearly, aren't you? You were vulnerable after the divorce and I took advantage—"

"Don't you dare pull that chivalry bullshit on me!" Emma scrambled out of bed, her fist knotting even tighter in the folds of her shift. "Don't you cast me as some helpless damsel who fell victim to your charms! Charms which, I might add, have been sadly lacking in your follow-through."

"Oh, is that right?"

"As a matter of fact, you're being a real bastard!"

"You knew that before you slept with me. It shouldn't come as any big surprise."

They faced each other down, breathless, quivering with emotion, as angry as they'd been in any previous battle. And then Emma glimpsed it—beyond the rage, beyond the stubbornness, beyond the snarled words and steely glares. Icy cold, paralyzing fear.

Oh, God, what had put so much hopelessness in her bold warrior's eyes?

She drew in a steadying breath, stepping away from the shield of her own fury. She looked Jared straight in the eye. "You *are* a bastard," Emma observed softly. "But when you turn into the beast there's always been a reason. I might not find out what the reason is until later, but it's always there."

Jared kicked the bench with his bare foot. He swore, but she knew he was glad of the pain. "Don't tell me," he snapped. "You played a psychiatrist in some movie I've never seen, and now you're going to analyze me? Poor boyo from a broken home. He's got commitment issues, and never dealt with—"

"Don't make something complicated out of this," she broke in, determined not to rise to his bait, the anger that would make him feel safe. "This thing between us is far too simple for that." She raised her chin, quiet, defiant. "I know you, Jared. You may not have meant for it to happen. You may not like it a bit. But I do."

He flinched back as if she'd struck him. "You don't really know me. No one does. If you could only see, you'd be sickened by the kind of man I am."

"I don't believe that."

"It's true. I knew it from the moment I watched those director's cuts, you playing with that bunch of kids on the set.

Laughing with them and swinging them 'round in that harness thing of yours—"

"You mean the cuts from the first Jade movie?"

"Any man with a brain could have seen how much you loved them. What a…a fine mother you'd make someday." His eyes darkened with sadness, an awe that made her ache inside. "How did you learn that, Emma? When your own mother left you the way she did?"

Emma's mind filled with images of Deirdre McDaniel Stone's catlike face, all edges and restlessness and self-blame, her blue eyes hollowed out with regret. "I forgave my mom a long time ago. She was gone for nine months. She spent the rest of her life trying to make it up to me. She even stopped singing. Some kind of twisted penance."

Emma shrugged. "Maybe it sounds hokey, but I just try to remember the good things that came out of the time she was gone. I got my family back, my uncle Cade and the Captain. And Aunt Finn…if I hadn't been in Whitewater to stir things up, Uncle Cade would've scared her off for sure."

"There you go again. Making it sound like fate."

"It's the only thing that gets me through. Believing something better is just around the corner, that there's a plan, you know? And things will work out in the end." *But they hadn't always worked out,* a practical voice in her head challenged. Things hadn't worked out with Drew. "Maybe you've been studying Lady Aislinn's story for too many years, Jared. It has such an unhappy ending."

"Most of the stories I've known do."

Emma swallowed hard, trying not to look away from the stark honesty in his face. And she wanted to reach beyond the chain mail of his defenses, to where he was vulnerable. To real flesh and blood beneath. To where the hurting lived.

She crossed to him, laid her hand on his arm. "Won't you

tell me?" she asked softly. "What is it, Jared? What's wrong? This...weight I can see you're carrying deep inside you. Maybe it's not as bad as you think."

"Not bad?" His face contorted in misery. "It's fecking hideous, Emma. Makes any other life impossible. *Us* impossible. Don't you see?" Jared sucked in a deep breath, blew it out, his features drawn, so raw it hurt her to see. "You want...things I don't want." His jaw clenched. *"Ever."*

He crossed to the window, staring out to the sea. And Emma sensed he was about to tell her what kept his heart as locked away from life and laughter and love as Lady Aislinn had been in her prison tower. Then maybe, just maybe for the first time since she'd met this enigmatic man Emma would understand what he'd been fighting out on the waves, all alone.

"You know I have a dead wife," Jared began. "If I didn't mention it, I'm sure Davey must have."

Emma hadn't seen so much as a picture of the woman, any hint of her memory in Jared's tent. "I remember hearing something about her," she said evenly. "Not much."

"That's because I don't talk about her. To anyone. Ever."

"You weren't happy." It was a statement, not a question. There wasn't any joy in Jared's eyes. Not even bittersweet echoes of joys remembered, like the memories she still had of Drew.

"Not happy?" Jared scoffed. "That's an understatement of epic proportions. We were... a disaster from the day I put my ring on her finger."

"I'm sorry."

"Me, too." He ran his fingertips over the edge of Emma's purple frame, glitter clinging to his fingers. "Before Jenny and I got married we never talked about the important things. What we wanted. Who we were."

"Things like…kids?" Emma hazarded, remembering his reaction to the kids in Jade Star.

"Jenny always joked that she wasn't about to share my attention with anyone else. There was a twisted kind of logic in it. She was a child herself, really, needing someone to take care of her."

"A real damsel in distress, huh?"

Jared grimaced.

"I'll bet that was pretty irresistible to a man with his head all stuffed with tales like Sir Tristan and Isolde," Emma said.

"I fell in love with the idea of her. And she… God knows why she thought she loved me."

It was all too easy to imagine the young man Jared must have been: so strong, so talented, so bright, with those knee-meltingly sexy, dangerous good looks that would have turned any young girl's head. And the secret sadness in him Emma wished she could heal.

"I was always ambivalent about parenting," Jared continued, "but somewhere in the back of my mind I figured that in time kids would be…natural, you know? The next step. I'd just have to get through it. There were kids on the dig sites I interned at during both my undergraduate and graduate studies. Archaeologist's families. The families would spend summer holidays together on this grand adventure, then the kids would go to boarding schools the rest of the year."

"Boarding schools." Emma knew some of her dislike had leaked into her voice.

Jared bristled. "I know you Yanks think it's terrible to send your kids away from home most of the year, but plenty of people in Britain do it."

"Yeah, I read *Harry Potter*," Emma said. "No offense, Butler, but unless I'm going to Hogwarts, it doesn't sound like such a great idea to me."

An old yearning shadowed Jared's face. "I would have killed for a chance to get away from home like that as a boy. Nothing but books and classes and learning."

"No watching your father's heart break every Christmas when your mother didn't come home," Emma probed gently.

"Perhaps," he confessed. "In the end, I learned to bury myself so deep inside my mind I might as well have been two hundred miles away in some ivy-walled school. And as a man, I fully intended to do the same thing. But as long as I had what I needed to survive—the work like a shield to keep the painful bits from showing—I figured I could make an adequate father a few months a year."

Emma listened, aching for him, this man, so sure he didn't know how to love.

He shrugged. "First time I met Jenny I was on a dig with her father. He was a world-renowned expert in medieval history. Had made discoveries that—it doesn't matter." Jared paused, shrugged his shoulders. "Hell, he was my hero, you know? Everything I wanted to be. If I was ever going to make a go of this family thing, I figured it would be by marrying his daughter, seeing his example before me all the days of my marriage. Sounds naive, doesn't it? Planning life out that way. But then, I was only twenty-four."

Emma didn't want to think of Jared, young and full of enthusiasm, his face softer, far less careworn than it was today. She didn't want to think of another woman smiling up at him, didn't want to picture his hands on this Jenny's body, didn't want to imagine his rough Scottish burr repeating wedding vows, promising to love, honor and cherish this Jenny forever and meaning it.

She imagined that lost, lonely boy Jared had been, wanting the kind of family his friends had, with a mother at the table, smiling and pouring tea. Had he hoped to recapture a bit of his own childhood by marrying Jenny? Or had he feared it?

"It wasn't until after we were married that Jenny came clean," Jared said, old bitterness tingeing his voice. "She told me she hated spending her time in the field with her father. She always had. She was willing to endure it for a time, because she loved me so much. And she knew I'd be fair, because I loved her. She'd be perfectly happy in the field as long as I gave her my solemn word that once we had children I'd take a job at her dad's university."

Emma tried to imagine Jared confined in a classroom year after year, no excavation sites, no fresh air, no dirt from the past under his fingernails. She might as well have imagined a dragon at the chalkboard, giving students exams. That kind of life was Jared Butler's definition of hell.

"It was the first time she'd mentioned having kids at all. But once it was on her mind, she was obsessed by the idea. Imagining what our life would be like. Jenny wanted our kids to have stability, she insisted, not be dragged from one malaria-infested site to the next."

"Don't they have vaccines to prevent malaria? Most strains, anyway. When I was filming in… Oh, never mind." She stopped herself. It was ridiculous to argue the point, as if she were reasoning with the dead woman. She settled for the obvious, cutting straight to the point. "Sometimes compromise sucks."

Emma didn't add what she'd learned from Drew. That sometimes no matter how hard you tried, compromise wasn't enough.

Jared's face darkened. "I'd be a bastard if I didn't agree to her plan, right? I mean, she was my wife. I'd made a commitment."

"From your tone it sounds more like a jail sentence."

"She was so…young. She acted like it was a game, getting me to write my promise down. I felt like an idiot, but I did it just to please her. After we sealed our little agreement, Jenny was…" Jared made a rough sound, low in his throat. "The sex…"

"Don't want to know, Butler," Emma cut him off, holding up one splayed hand. "*Really* don't want to know."

"No," Jared agreed grudgingly. "I suppose I wouldn't want to know either if I were you. But it is…well, pertinent to the story."

Emma pursed her lips. "Go on."

"Later that month I was chosen for an internship with another world-renowned scientist on this amazing dig site in Kenya. It just blew me away. The man said he had no intention of taking on someone so inexperienced, but something about my application got his attention, made him think I had the potential to be…" Jared broke off, looking uncomfortable.

"I already know you're brilliant. And I'm not a world-renowned scientist. It's not bragging for you to say the guy figured it out, too. Jenny must've been so proud of you." Emma would have been. Bursting with pride.

"That's the strange thing. I expected her to be upset. She was usually resigned at best when something like this happened for me. I was going to Kenya for six months and she hated Africa. This may sound petty, but I expected to pay."

Irritation jabbed Emma, this woman she'd never met annoying the blazes out of her. Sounded like Jenny had tried to suck all the joy out of Jared's achievement. "Well, she did promise she'd buck up and deal until you had kids, didn't she?"

"She didn't want to come with me." He still sounded amazed. "Said she'd stay with her father, visit friends. This time she packed me off without a single tear. I hoped that maybe we were finally growing up."

Emma sighed. "Call me psychic. You were doomed to be disappointed, weren't you?"

"She called me from the States three weeks later. She was pregnant."

"Oh, God." Emma's stomach fell, imagining how Jared must have felt, hearing that news over the phone. "But there hadn't been that much time! I mean, she couldn't have expected you to just quit. How did it… Scratch that question. I know how it happened. The biology and all. But still…"

Jared kneaded his brow with his fingers. Emma could almost feel his head throbbing. "I don't know how the hell it happened. She was on the pill. Just to be sure, I was using condoms as backup."

"This isn't…any of my business, Jared," Emma faltered. "Your private arrangements with your wife."

"I just want you to know I wasn't leaving the whole birth control thing up to Jenny. Abdicating responsibility."

"No. I'm sure you wouldn't." If there was one thing she'd learned about Dr. Jared Butler in her time in Scotland, it was that he had an incredible sense of responsibility. How many men would have bothered to be so careful if they'd known their wife was on the pill?

"It just…" Jared rammed his fingers back through his hair. "It wasn't supposed to happen, you know? I felt…"

"Stunned?"

"Trapped."

Trapped. The word hung between them. Hard. Ugly.

"You think she did it on purpose?" Emma asked in a small voice.

"Went off the pill? Tampered with the condoms? I'll never know for sure. But I'm a scientist. I know the odds of both methods failing at the same time. They're slim to none. Hell, when she called to tell me she was pregnant it was like being kicked in the stomach. She insisted on holding me to my promise, saying her father was overjoyed at the thought of a grandchild. He had already arranged a position for me at the university and they'd picked out the baby's crib."

"Ouch." Emma imagined just how that must have cut him. "Her father knew before you did? That must have been hard."

"She wouldn't even give me any time to process it, you know? She insisted on flying out to the site to get things settled between us, even though I promised to come back to the States in two weeks. I asked her to stay away. Hoped to buy myself a little time to... I don't know. Sort out my feelings. She was my wife. That was my baby she was carrying. I didn't want to resent it. But, selfish bastard that I was, all I could do was think how much I was going to miss the smell of dirt on my hands. Never knowing what the next moment might bring."

"It must've hurt so bad, thinking of losing the work you loved. Work she knew you loved before she married you." Realization struck Emma, the memory of Jared's face the night he'd soothed her grief about Drew. "That's why you said what you did the night I told you I offered to give up my career for Drew. You said a person couldn't turn their back on work they adore even for love. You can't change who you are. Because you had already tried."

"No." Self-loathing and bitterness twisted his beautiful mouth. "I never had to make that sacrifice. Fate stepped in and swept my slate clean. A nice, convenient sandstorm blasted Jenny's plane out of the sky. She died and so did my baby."

Emma wanted to slide her arms around him. Knew she didn't dare. He seemed so brittle, as if one touch might crack something inside him she could never repair, something even more irreplaceable than the sword her recklessness had cost him.

"I'm so sorry." It sounded so lame, her sympathy so useless.

Jared's throat convulsed. "Know what's hardest of all for me to live with?"

"What?"

"I'm still not sure if *I* am. *Sorry.* Deep down, underneath, where I felt so damned hurt and angry and trapped." He turned away from her, paced into the shadows. "What if…if somewhere in my subconscious I was glad that crash took the whole mess out of my hands?"

"I don't believe that."

A ragged laugh tore from his throat. "No offense, but you believe in knights fighting on the sea and fairy flags and little girl ghosts that live in deserted mansions."

"I believe in you."

"Don't!" He wheeled on her, fierce, but she didn't back down.

"In time you would have come to terms with the baby. You would have loved your little boy or girl, the way you do Davey and the other kids. Even if you didn't want to."

"Or maybe I would have walked away, like my mother did," Jared countered, despair in his eyes. "Maybe I simply would have turned my back on my child and—God, what a nightmare. My worst fear, being like *her.* But I'll never know for certain what I would have done in the end, will I? And neither will you."

"Maybe I can't prove it, but…"

His fierce gaze raked her. "When I buried Jenny I swore to myself that there'd be no more mistakes. No wife. No child. Not ever."

Tears burned Emma's eyes, her heart breaking with love for this wounded, wary man. "Time heals, Jared. People grow. It's not betraying Jenny's memory to change your mind."

"I won't be changing my mind, dammit! There won't be

any little boy waiting for me, putting a present under a god-damned Christmas tree for someone who's never coming home. I won't risk being a parent who wishes he could wave a magic wand or cause a plane crash and make my own kid disappear."

Tears brimmed over her lashes, fell down her cheeks. He grabbed her by the arms, gave her a gentle shake.

"Emma, do you understand what I'm telling you?"

She caught her lip between her teeth and nodded.

"There's no place for us. Do you hear me? No future."

She nodded again, touching his face, his jaw, his mouth.

He swore, groaned, running his palms up her arms. "I just wish to hell I could stop...stop wanting you so damned bad. We just made love and all I can think about is how to get you back into that bed."

She didn't think twice. She let the shift bunched at her breasts go. It cascaded down her body to form a snowy ring on the floor.

"This is madness," Jared groaned.

"Mad as a fairy flag and a knight on the sea," she said softly. "Mad as believing in dragons and magic swords."

"Emma, it's doomed before it starts. We both know it. Better to get the ending over with before it hurts...hurts too much. Forever is...beyond our reach."

She wanted forever. She wanted so much more. The kind of love Lady Aislinn knew, that would live on in legend for six hundred years.

"Maybe we can't have forever." God, it hurt to admit that, down in the very center of her soul. "But our part of the story won't be over until the music swells, until the closing credits roll. Wouldn't it be wrong to waste..."

"Waste what? Heartbreak? Loss? I don't want to hurt you."

Her chin bumped up a notch, the fierce determination of

generations of McDaniels reflected in her eyes. "I'm stronger than you know."

"You're sure as hell stronger than I am if you're ready to charge into this without armor, without any defense, knowing it will end in tears."

"Then trust me, sir knight. Give me just one more gift."

"The holy grail? A fairy flag?"

"Something far more precious than that," she said, drowning in his eyes. "Let's make the most of whatever time we have left."

Chapter Sixteen

EMMA SHOULD HAVE GUESSED Jared Butler would hog her bed. From the moment she'd met him he'd taken up too much space—in the car, in her head, in the room. The man's big body sprawled across the mattress until she was forced to balance on the edge where one little nudge from his hip would send her tumbling to the floor. He'd kicked off blankets and furs, leaving them both naked to the chill night air. Emma should have been cold. Would have been, if Jared hadn't been so deliciously warm, heat radiating off him long after they'd finally sated each other.

Taking care to keep her balance, Emma propped herself up on her elbow, chin in hand as she watched Jared sleep, sooty lashes curled on his cheeks, one arm flung up over his head. He snored ever so softly, lips parted, his slightly crooked teeth delighting Emma to an absurd degree. Everything about him was rougher, more natural, somehow more real than any man she'd ever known.

Shadows and light from the rising sun painted the landscape of his naked chest in gold. He should have appeared exhausted after the night they had just shared. Instead he looked like a Roman gladiator who had finally reached the Elysian Fields. Peaceful, after a life of battle. A little bewildered as if he couldn't believe his good fortune, even through the haze of unconsciousness.

How long had it been since the man had actually slept? Emma wondered. A deep, restful sleep, instead of tossing and turning and waking every few hours. Since he'd moved into the tower room with her? Or had she kept him awake long before that, even when he'd been able to escape the sizzling tension between them, his bed still located in his own solitary tent? Had he battled there against the attraction he couldn't deny, the woman he couldn't avoid?

And when temptation to give in to his "baser instincts" had grown almost too strong to resist, had he taken out his memories of Jenny? Crushed them tight in his hand so they would cut him like broken glass, remind him of all the reasons he couldn't…

Lose his mind.

His description from the night before echoed through Emma. *At least you didn't lose your heart….*

But how could she have helped it? If she hadn't loved Jared already, she would have fallen hard during those anguished moments when he had bared the most tortured secrets of his soul to her, tried to make her understand how flawed he was, how hopeless. A man so monstrous he'd wished his unborn child dead.

Except that he hadn't. He'd been reeling, drowning in shock. Before he'd been able to surface, Jenny's plane had crashed and he'd lost the chance to discover all the potential Emma could see beneath his gruff exterior. It was clear from the way he loved young Davey Harrison, warily, reluctantly and yet with every bit of his battered heart.

If Jenny had lived—his child had been born—wouldn't Jared be living a nightmare right now? Locked away from the life he was born to lead, forever haunted by his suspicion that his wife had trapped him into selling the most genuine part of his soul?

After the pain of his childhood, would Jared ever have been able to leave Jenny? No matter how miserable he would have been? Emma doubted it. But at what cost to his heart? His sense of honor? Living forever with a wife who had deceived him in the most intimate way? And Jenny Butler *had* deceived him. Jared was sure of it. Emma had seen it in his eyes.

But in the end it didn't matter what Jenny had done. How miserable their marriage would have been. All Jared could see was the instinctive recoiling he'd felt when he'd learned Jenny was pregnant. He didn't realize it was Jenny's betrayal that had sparked such horror in him. A man like Jared, possessed of an honesty and honor so fierce they seemed to belong to another age.

Jared moaned in his sleep, his hand groping across his pillow for a moment until it closed on a lock of Emma's hair. He curled his fingers around the strand and drew it toward his face, breathing in the scent. Emma's heart squeezed as he sighed, relaxing again into that bone-melting slumber she sensed was so foreign to his nature.

Oh, God, would it be so terrible to stay with him? Maybe he could get used to the idea of a relationship with her, as long as she gave up the idea of children. What if Drew had been right? Being a mother wasn't fair when you'd bring your child into the press's spotlight.

Emma imagined years stretching out before her, loving other people's children. Her cousins, her sister. Their kids someday in the future. Couldn't that be enough?

No. The denial rang like a death knell in her heart. She couldn't change who she was for Jared any more than she could have changed it for Drew. Without blaming him deep down in the secret places of her soul. Without resenting him eventually. That hollow ache in her chest growing bigger and bigger until it crowded out the love she felt for the brawny Scot sleeping beside her.

"Emma?"

Jared's voice pulled her from her thoughts. She looked down at him, knowing she'd lost the chance to hide the sadness in her eyes.

"The look of you," he murmured, so vulnerable just awakened that it broke her heart. "Are you already regretting us? If that's what putting the dark in your eyes, we can go back, pretend…"

A lump formed in Emma's throat. "Don't you know that's the magic of you? I don't have to pretend. I can…" She lost her focus, started teetering on the bed. Jared's arm flashed out, his reflexes amazingly sharp for a man whose eyes were still heavy with sleep. He pulled her tight against him. He felt hard and hot, solid and dangerous in the most delicious way.

"You can what?" he encouraged.

"I can…be who I am." It sounded so simple, so basic. But she could see from the understanding filling Jared's eyes that he knew just how rare it was. He pulled her mouth down for a kiss, surprisingly tender, bittersweet with a parting they both knew they could never avoid.

"In just the few weeks since I've met you, you've learned more about me than my ex-husband ever did," Emma marveled. "Who would have imagined it was possible? Drew and I went to the same school from the time we were in fifth grade. At sixteen, we fell in love. And in all those years, he never understood…"

"What?"

"The wildness in me."

Jared smoothed back the curtain of hair that fell across her cheek, listening the way only he could, with such intensity Emma felt it in her very soul.

"I was such a quiet kid when he first met me, right after my mom left. But once I got my family back, I...how can I explain it?" She shrugged, searching for the words. "There was this...the other Emma inside me, the one I was supposed to be." She locked on to a memory. "On our first visit home after we eloped, Drew and I were out in this gazebo my uncle Cade built in the garden at March Winds right before his wedding. It's the most romantic spot in the world. Besides here in bed with you, of course."

Jared smiled. "Of course."

"Every couple in my family has, well...christened it, so to speak."

"Christened it," Jared echoed, drawing a slow figure eight on the small of her back with his fingertips.

"There we were, the two of us, newlyweds all alone, with the flowers blooming and the butterflies dancing and the river shining a little ways away. Couldn't have been a more perfect setting if it had been in one of Aunt Finn's romance novels. I turned to Drew, unbuttoned my blouse and..."

Jared's eyes dipped down to the shadowy valley between her breasts. His lids narrowed. His gaze heated. "No translation necessary. The lucky son of a bitch."

"That's just it. Drew didn't think so."

Jared snorted in disbelief. "You should've called in the paramedics. The man must've been dead."

His reaction warmed Emma, soothed the sting that still lingered from Drew's rejection.

"Actually, he was sort of...horrified that I would want to

make love there. He said there was a chance somebody might walk by, see..."

"And wouldn't that be half the fun of it, then? That little spice of danger."

Emma grinned at him. "I knew you'd understand."

"If I ever got you in that gazebo, Emma McDaniel, you'd best be ready for sure. If somebody walked by, they'd get a grand show."

Emma shivered as if she could already feel the soft river breezes on bare skin, hear Jared's husky murmurs of arousal. "Just imagine what the paparazzi could do with those pictures," she teased.

Jared's smile died. His face thunderous, a fearsome protectiveness in his rugged features that would have made even the most tenacious photographer turn and run. "I'd break the camera over their bloody heads. Stalking any woman of mine like that."

Emma's heart turned over at the possessiveness laced through his whiskey-warm Scottish burr.

Any woman of mine... But he'd told her there hadn't been any women in his bed for a long time. Even when he'd talked of his wife, he'd sounded as if she were someone distant, as removed from him as if they'd been on opposite sides of a stone curtain wall. The rough protectiveness in his voice told her as nothing else could that even if he didn't love her, she'd somehow edged her way inside to where the real Jared dwelled, believing no one could see him.

Emma closed her eyes for a moment, imagining light filtering through the gazebo's gingerbread trim, drizzling liquid honey over Jared's back as he covered her body with his, every atom of his concentration centered on her moans, her sighs. Sighs? No, sounds far louder than that.

She chuckled.

"What is it?" he asked.

"I was just thinking it's probably a good thing you'll never come to Illinois. It's one thing to steal a quickie in the gazebo, but another thing to announce it to…" Her cheeks burned, but not with shame. "Well, I guess we *could* try it in winter, if everybody in the house had their windows closed. And the stereo was on full blast."

He growled, pressing a hot kiss to her throat. "I wouldn't give a damn if the whole world heard us. They'd either be jealous or be getting ideas of their own." He sobered, his voice a little wistful. "But then, I'll never come to Illinois."

"No," Emma agreed, knowing it was true.

This castle was their place. Now was their time. This tiny, jeweled fragment of their lives, too brief to sully with wishing it could be more. She swallowed hard. "I just wanted to…to thank you for understanding the…the rebel in me."

"I'm honored that you let me know you, Emma," he said, touching his lips to hers with a tenderness that stunned her. "I always will be."

She threaded her fingers in his, her hand feeling lost until he enclosed it in his bearlike grip. She pressed his hand upward, over his head, held it there as she shifted to lie atop him. She reveled in the contrast. His hard against her soft, his rough against her smooth, need even more urgent because reality lay in wait beyond the castle's wall to snatch it all away.

Emma's hair tumbled around them both, wreathing Jared in a waterfall of living silk, closing out the rest of the world.

JARED HAD BARELY buttoned the fly of his olive drab cargo pants when the door in the great hall crashed open, the bang of the heavy oak panel against the castle wall below echoing warning up the winding stairs. Grabbing a white T-shirt, he blocked the entrance to the chamber to give Emma a moment to pull herself together before the tower was invaded.

He glanced over to where she'd stood, gloriously naked a few moment's ago, saw that she'd managed to clothe herself as well. Jeans hugged her curves, her glowing face hidden by folds of the loose knit green sweater she was pulling over her head. He should have been remedying his own state of undress, but pale slivers of Emma's midriff tantalized him as she wrestled the hem of the sweater over her breasts, the dimple of her still-exposed navel reminding him of a dozen wicked things he wanted to do to her once darkness fell again.

Emma tugged her tousled hair from the cowl neck as the sound of footsteps rushed toward the tower stairs. He pulled his own shirt on, emerging a moment later to see her turn toward him. Something twisted in his chest. Possessiveness. Awe.

She looked a little shy, a lot satisfied, like a woman who'd been thoroughly made love to. Jared wondered if any of his students would be perceptive enough to notice the whisker burn he'd left on the tender curve of her cheek. Damn if Jared hadn't finally found a reason for bothering to shave more than once every week or so. More amazing still, for the first time in his life he couldn't wait until the day's excavating was over.

But the impatience flaring inside him vanished as Davey Harrison's voice bounced up the spiral staircase, the sound punctuated by the pounding of his running feet.

"Emma…Dr. Butler…" the boy gasped, as if he'd sprinted the whole way from his tent. "Oh, God, I'm so sorry." Davey burst through the stone archway into the room. Jared caught him by the arms to steady him. Any concern that the boy would guess what Jared and Emma had got up to the night before vanished as he glimpsed the lad's stricken face.

"Easy there, mate." Jared gave Davey's biceps a bracing squeeze. "Calm down now. Nothing can be bad as all that."

"Oh, yes it can." His eyes darkened with guilt. "I can't believe I could be so—so stupid."

"Davey," Emma soothed. "You're anything but stupid." But her comforting words only deepened the grooves desperation carved in the youth's brow.

"I *was* stupid." Davey ripped himself away from Jared's grasp. "Stupid, stupid, stupid, just like the other kids said."

Dread crackled along Jared's nerves. He hadn't heard Davey so rattled since the day the lad announced that his mother was making him take that blasted dead-end job. But at the moment, Davey barely knew Jared was in the room. He rushed toward Emma, his voice quavering. "It's just that he looked so pathetic, I figured if I let him sleep with me…"

"Lad, you're not making any sense." Jared fought to keep the alarm from his voice. "Slow down and—"

"It's Captain," Emma cut in evenly. Only the tiniest loss of color in her cheeks betrayed her dismay, but Jared felt it in the center of his chest.

Davey nodded miserably. "Captain dug his way under the side of the tent." The boy's voice broke. "I only hoped he'd…he'd come to find you… You'd hear him barking…"

"No," Emma faltered, giving Jared a pained glance. "We…didn't hear anything."

Hell, Jared doubted either he or Emma would've noticed a cannon being fired off under the tower window last night. They'd been engrossed in each other, the rest of the world a million miles away. Trust that wretched dog to ruin the morning after. Probably punishing Jared for moving into Emma's bed. Well, Captain's ploy had worked. Emma might be putting up a good front, but behind her actress mask, Jared knew she was scared as hell. *That* was one bit of mischief he'd see the terrier paid for.

"The wee devil must be around here somewhere." Jared

stalked across the room to look out the window, hoping he might catch a glimpse of dingy fur from the vantage point. "He's probably off digging somewhere he shouldn't."

"That's what I thought," Davey said, "but everyone's been looking and he's nowhere on the site. If something happens to him, I'll never forgive myself."

Sunlight glinted on the white of Davey's scar, or was it just Jared's imagination? Or his own secret terror of the fragility he still feared in the boy?

"Don't worry, boyo. Losing that dog would be impossible as losing a blister on your heel. He'll turn up, if only for the fun of annoying the hell out of me. Saddle up the horses for Emma and me. We'll be able to cover more ground that way."

"Right." Davey bolted toward the stairs, so recklessly Jared yelled after him. "Breaking your neck won't solve anything, lad!"

But Emma intercepted the boy, hugged him tight. Her brow clouded with fear for the boy that echoed Jared's own. "Davey, this isn't your fault," she said fiercely. "No matter what happens, you're much more important to me than a dog."

Davey hugged her back, a stifled sob breaching his lips, but even the vulnerable boy couldn't doubt Emma meant what she said. Jared clenched his jaw against the pain of awakening to her in yet another way, a sharp-edged coming to life in his heart he hadn't asked for, didn't want.

Davey fled down the stairs. The instant Jared was sure the lad was back on level ground, he turned to where Emma was fumbling to get her feet into her trainers. "You—you go on to the dig site," Emma said, frantic now that Davey couldn't see. "You have work to do. I'll look for Captain."

"Alone? I don't think so."

A shoe popped out of her hand, skittered across the floor. Jared retrieved it before Emma could.

"Jared, I'll be all right."

He knelt down, took her foot in his other hand and slipped the shoe into place. "Sure you will," he said as he tied it to spare her shaking fingers. "But if that terror of a dog comes to anybody, it'll be me."

"He…he's just so little…"

Jared scowled, mad as hell at the terrier for distressing her so. "He's a black curse and a wee devil and why the hell you're determined to love him, I'll never know."

"I can't—can't help it," Emma choked out, tears pushing against her lashes, her heart in her eyes. "He needs me."

Like I need you, a voice inside Jared whispered in ruthless honesty. *Need you to make me laugh, fight with me, make love with me. Make me feel alive.*

Jared wanted to fold her in his arms, but he knew that was the last thing she needed. She'd never forgive herself if she wasted time crying. Instead he resorted to his gruff dragon's voice to help brace her.

"Think you'll get rid of me this quick now you've had your way with me, eh, woman? I don't think so. I'm not about to risk that pretty backside of yours getting snapped by a camera or spattered with buckshot."

"Buckshot?"

Jared grabbed her hand, hauling her down the stairs. "If I were that mongrel of yours, locked out of your bed, I know exactly what I'd do."

"What?"

"Go straight to the one place in all the world I shouldn't, just out of sheer contrariness," Jared said grimly. "Snib Mac-Murray's farm."

EMMA'S THROAT BURNED, already hoarse from calling for Captain as she and Jared neared the length of stream where they'd first run across the scrappy dog. But they hadn't heard so much as a yip or seen a flash of dingy gray fur.

Jared reined in his horse, signaled Emma to a halt as well on the stream's rocky bank. "We'll have to stay quiet," he warned. "No telling where Snib might be. We don't want to let him know the mutt is missing or he'll set the collies on him."

"Right. I won't…won't…" Emma swallowed the lump in her throat, trying not to imagine her brave little Captain, torn and bleeding. If they were too late…

Jared's expression softened. "I'm not meaning to scare you," he said gently, "but with their sense of smell they'd find Captain before we could, sure. And I intend to have the pleasure of ringing the little scamp's neck myself for worrying you this way."

Emma nodded, knew her fear still shone in her eyes.

"Whist, then, lady," Jared soothed. "Have a little faith. What kind of knight would I be if I let something happen to your dog?"

Images flashed into her mind. Jared garbed in chain mail, a warrior from another time. Jared appearing over the cliff's edge, pulling her to safety like a shadow from hero tales of long ago.

Emma tried not to think of his sword, fallen beneath those crashing waves because of her carelessness, tried not to imagine fate somehow evening up the score between them by snatching Captain away. The little dog meant so much to her. She'd never known how hungry she'd been since Drew left, hungry not to be alone.

Jared urged his mount across the stream and Emma followed. As they crested the first hill, a crazy quilt of meadows spilled out below them, piled stone fences hundreds of years old dividing one pasture from the other. Where would they even begin?

She felt lost, anchorless as a rowboat in a storm. Overwhelmed by the enormity of trying to find one tiny dog in so much space. But Jared wound his way from gate to gate with an instinct that surprised Emma, as if he knew every rock and tree on the property.

Deeper and deeper they plunged into the forbidden grounds, whistling softly in hopes that Captain would hear them and the collies would not. From the height of the horse's backs, Emma and Jared searched among the black-faced sheep eyeing them with mild curiosity. With every minute that ticked by, Jared's face grew more grim, his shoulders stiffer as Emma's own hope dimmed.

"Maybe he went the other way," Emma said as Jared expertly maneuvered to open another rusted gate from the back of his horse. He motioned her through and she followed him, drawing rein long enough to catch his answer.

"There's one more place to look. It's too close to the farmhouse for my liking, but it would be just like that dog of yours to make this rescue as difficult as possible. Not to mention digging in the one place in all Scotland I'd sell my soul to excavate." Jared glanced at his watch. "Damn. We're running out of time. Snib will be sending the dogs out for the sheep any time now. Go back, Emma. To our side of the stream. I'll keep looking for Captain on my own."

"I'm not leaving either one of you. Just…just hurry."

Swearing under his breath, Jared kneed Falcon into a run, his gaze sweeping the landscape all around them. Emma glimpsed a smear of run-down cottage in the valley as she kept pace, the yard overgrown with weeds like some haunted house in a child's book of ghost stories. Like March Winds before Aunt Finn had loved it back to life.

What if Captain had caught a whiff of some kind of food set out to cool in the cottage's kitchen? Or wanted to torment

Snib out of pure orneriness? The doggy equivalent of her sister Hope's "Na, na, na, boo, boo." If her grandfather was on the loose anywhere in this vicinity and someone had set dogs on him, that's exactly what the old man would do.

But Captain was a dog, not a person, no matter how much intelligence shone in the terrier's eyes. She'd just have to hope he wasn't smart enough to know where his tormentor lived.

"There's a ring of standing stones atop that rise," Jared called to her. But Emma could already see the slabs of gray against the horizon. Completely unexpected, a cloud of mist snagged about the base of stones so heavy they seemed a giant's playthings. Neolithic building blocks set with the same careful precision her little sister had used arranging the hand-cut wooden blocks Uncle Cade had made for her third birthday so long ago.

Despite Emma's distress, she felt the ancient site's pull deep in her core, a world of untold mystery, ageless magic. A faint sound echoed from the mist. Emma's heart leapt. Was it an excited yip or just her own wishful thinking?

A heartbeat later, a far more piercing whistle reverberated from the direction of the farmhouse below. Emma raised up on tiptoe in the stirrups and glanced over her shoulder, seeing a tweedy brown figure emerge from the cottage's door in the distance, splashes of white and black fur tumbling out in his wake.

Snib….

But Jared was already rushing into the sheltering mist. Emma plunged in behind him, praying the farmer hadn't seen.

Inside the stone circle the mist thinned and Emma gave a choked sob of relief as she glimpsed a gray ball of fur digging against one of the stones in puppy glee. Sprays of dirt flew up behind his wriggling little body, his nose thrust into a freshly-dug hole three times his size.

Jared started to dismount, but Emma was already on the ground running toward the dog. She flung herself down on her knees and scooped the little scoundrel into her arms. Captain snarled around whatever he held in his mouth, and writhed in frustration until he caught her scent. He gazed up at her with black shoe-button eyes, wondering what all the fuss was about as she buried her face in his fur.

"Bad dog! Bad, bad dog!" she cried. "What were you thinking, running away to this awful man's place?"

"If he'd been one of my undergrad assistants he couldn't have found a likelier site to dig." Jared loomed over them, like some guardian of old. Emma surfaced from her reunion with Captain to see the big Scotsman peering around the circle of stone with unabashed longing.

"What is this place?"

"The stone circle that figures in the Lady Aislinn legends."

"The one I read about in the script?" Emma clung to Captain's collar and looked at the site around her, awed. "If there's room for it, Barry's got a wonderful flashback of their parting just before her husband left. She'd stolen off alone to leave flowers and such—making offerings to the old ones, hoping they would give her a child. Lord Magnus finds her there and she cries, wanting his baby with all her heart, saying that then if he died in battle, at least she'd have a part of him to hold, a child of their love." She felt the tug in her own womb, the vast emptiness in her arms despite the terrier she held.

"That's how the legend goes." Jared frowned. "A woman who couldn't give her husband a son in medieval times was seen as cursed by God. As if barrenness were her fault. Not ever that of her husband."

"I would have thought she'd have gone to the church instead. Didn't I read somewhere that desperate women bought religious relics from priests?"

"One of the favorite cures was vials of milk, supposedly from the Virgin's breast. But the church couldn't wash all the old ways from these hills. A woman like Lady Aislinn would have tried anything for the chance to provide her husband with an heir."

"Maybe she didn't see a child as an heir at all." Emma snuggled Captain closer. "She'd been taken away from her own family, her father dead. Maybe she just…just wanted someone of her own to love."

"Whatever her motive, she never conceived."

"Hard to do when your husband's off running amok in France, fighting the English king's battles," Emma scoffed. "What did the guy expect? If I'd been Lady Aislinn, I'd have given him a piece of my mind. Written him a letter that burned his socks right off!"

Jared chuckled. "I doubt the Lady could read or write. There's no record of it, at least. But if *you'd* been at the castle, I doubt the letter would be necessary."

"Right. He wouldn't have gotten past the gates before I—"

"He wouldn't have gotten past the gates at all." A shadow fell across Jared's beautiful face. "I doubt any knight bewitched by the likes of you would have been strong enough to ride away, to leave you behind."

Except you… Emma thought sadly, turning her face away.

Jared kicked dirt back into the hole with the side of his shoe.

"How did you know how to get to this place?" Emma asked. "It seemed like you knew every curve, every gate."

"I do." Jared busied himself forming a makeshift leash out

of his belt and fastening it around Captain's collar. "This used to be my grandfather's farm. My da grew up here. When my grandfather died, Gran wrote to Da, told him the property was his for the asking. But da had already fallen madly in love and my mother wasn't the type to bury herself in the hills. Da told Gran to sell it. No matter how he loved the place, he was never coming back."

Emma felt the hollow ache, the sacrifice gentle Angus Butler had made for a woman who would leave him far too soon. "You grew up around here? I didn't know."

"Just a nice walk of a Sunday from gran's house in town to here." Jared grimaced. "When I was a lad, Da and I would steal across the fence and he'd show me..." His voice trailed off. "This is where I fell in love with the legend of the fairy flag. The stories my father could tell...as if he'd lived every moment himself. Kid that I was, I still felt as if this place was mine."

Emma reached up to him, squeezed his hand.

Jared drew her to her feet, Captain held captive in the crook of her arm. "One of the stones has a hole in the center," Jared said. "God knows how it got there." He led her to where a stone sat off-kilter, a perfect circle cut in the middle of the slab.

Fascinated, she paced around the stone, examining it from different angles. Unable to resist, she ran her fingertips over the smooth worn edge of the opening.

"I wouldn't do that if I were you," Jared warned from the opposite side of the slab. "Legend claims that if you put your hand through the hole and clasp a lover's hand, it will bind you to each other forever."

Emma peered at him through the opening, noting the sudden husky timbre to his voice. "No matter how far you wandered," he said, "your hearts would be melded into one for all eternity."

A subtle movement of his hand caught her eye, the callused

fingers, as roughened by life as his heart, drifting toward hers as he finished. "Any woman reckless enough to link her heart with the wrong man would be cast adrift forever. But then who would be reckless enough to dare…" His voice trailed off. Emma was sure she could hear his heart pounding.

"You should know better than that, sir knight."

"Than to believe such a story? I suppose—"

"No," she cut him off. "You should know better than to dare me by now." Emma reached through the opening in the stone, twining her fingers with Jared's own. He stunned her, making no effort to pull away. They stood staring at their linked hands, frozen in time, palm to palm. The whole world was suddenly still.

"Don't say I didn't warn you," Jared murmured after what seemed forever. "About the consequences…"

"I'm not afraid." She let her eyes speak words he couldn't bear for her to say. "Don't you know, it was already too late for me long before we came here?"

His beautiful green eyes answered her, a wealth of desperate love trapped inside his heart. His hand tightened around hers until her fingers ached. She welcomed the pain of it, the fierceness.

"This doesn't change anything," he warned, his face darkening.

"I know."

"Still and all, I'm glad of it. I can't help myself."

A sharp whistle pierced the air. Jared let her hand fall free. She felt the loss of his touch to her soul.

"Snib," he said, suddenly alert. "We'll take the back way down. The road is a hundred meters to the north. We should be able to reach it before he sees us." Jared rounded the stone, grabbed her around the waist and flung her up onto her horse's back. Something sharp jabbed her in the middle, where

Captain's teeth still clung with the tenacity of his namesake to whatever he'd found.

The terrier scrabbled against Emma's thigh with his back paws for a moment, as if to launch himself to the ground, but a sudden menacing woof that must be MacMurray's collies made him prick his ears to listen. Emma could almost feel the confusion in her little dog, Captain trying to decide which was more important: struggling free to fight with his sworn enemies or hanging on to his recently found treasure. The treasure won.

Jared swung astride his own horse, reined it down the hill with Emma's mount close on his heels, the mist and magic fading behind them.

It wasn't until they reached the stables and Emma handed the dog down to him that Jared noticed the terrier had something clamped in his mouth. "What the hell?" Jared exclaimed. He fastened the dog's makeshift leash to a board in the stable, then carefully pried the object free of Captain's sharp white teeth.

Emma slid down from her own mount on trembling legs. "Don't tell me, he stole part of the collies' secret stash of bones—they'll be out for blood for sure the next time they see him."

"Emma, this is no bone." Jared thrust it into the light from the stable window, where dust motes swirled around it like will-o'-the-wisps.

"A stick then or an old slipper—" She stopped, struck by the intensity in Jared's face.

"Damn it, I *knew* there was something under there," he muttered. "I felt it."

"Felt what?"

Those green eyes flashed to hers. "This is a piece of a knight's gauntlet."

Emma froze. "What?"

"A gaunt—"

"I heard you the first time!" she interrupted, crowding him in her eagerness to see. She reached out to take the segment of metal from him, then snatched her fingers back guiltily. "Shit!" she said. "I mean, shoot. I probably shouldn't touch it, right?"

"It's been chewed on and drooled all over by your dog." Jared laughed, placing it in her hand. "You're not going to hurt anything." Captain's drool had washed away some of the dirt. Jared wiped the worst of the muck away with his thumb then blew softly against the corroded metal surface, obviously hoping to get a better look.

"There's some sort of…of engraving on the edge, here. See?" he said, pointing it out. "We'll have to clean the piece up before we can see clearly."

We. The partnership implied by the word touched Emma deeply. She looked at the treasure cupped in her hand. "You're telling me that my dog stole a valuable archaeological artifact from that terrible man's farm?"

"Right out from under Snib MacMurray's nose. Truth is, that mutt of yours may have uncovered the best find we've made in years." Jared hustled Emma toward his lab, barely pausing to order Veronica to call off the search for Captain and get the troops back to work at the dig. The blonde stomped off, expression sour with envy.

At the lab, Emma and Jared huddled together over the find, his big hands impossibly deft as he cleaned away centuries of grime. "This seems to be from the fourteenth century," he judged. "I'd guess within a hundred or so years of the siege."

"Do you think some knight lost it fighting by the lover's stone?"

"I doubt it. It was probably a token of the heart, buried so close to the stone. I'd have to completely excavate the area to tell."

"So let's buy it, rent it!" Emma exclaimed. "I'm not exactly hurting for money. We could pay Snib oodles of money to let us—"

"Money wouldn't matter a damn to that old bastard. He hates me, in case you haven't noticed. Never forgave me for the traffic mucking up his own private kingdom."

"Traffic? This is in the middle of nowhere."

"School buses clogging up the roads, college students taking over his neighborhood pub. When word got out hereabouts that I'd lost my funding, the old miser got so excited he bought rounds of whiskey for half the village and danced on the bar at the pub."

Emma tried to imagine the crusty old man dancing anywhere at all. "He'll have to retire sometime, won't he?" she inquired hopefully. "He looks like he's a jillion years old!"

"Five jillion, at least." Jared grimaced, plying his softest brush to clear the metal of the last few crumbs of dirt. "But I figure Snib is going to live forever just to spite me. There." He frowned at the find in satisfaction. "I think we're ready to stick this under the magnifier."

He scooped up the tool, held the piece of gauntlet under a glaring bright light. "It seems to be from the right time period. From what I can tell."

"Right time period for what? Tell me! Is it linked to Lady Aislinn somehow?" Emma prodded, unable to wait another second. "Did it belong to her husband?"

"Impossible," Jared muttered, examining it again. "This makes no sense."

"What? Tell me!"

He thrust it practically under her nose. "Read the engraving."

"You've got to be kidding me!" Emma skimmed the etched letters. "It's Latin, isn't it?"

"Right." Jared flashed her a bemused glance. "I forgot you can't read it. You fit so perfectly here. It seems as if you should be able to…"

Emma jabbed him with her elbow. "Just translate, boy genius! Before I lose what little patience I have left!"

He turned toward her, his rugged features clouded with confusion. "It's the knight's family motto. *I conquer all.*"

"But that's not Craigmorrigan's motto. It was something long and flowery, wasn't it? All full of death-before-dishonor garbage. Took up half of the family crest. So if it's not Lady Aislinn's husband's, then whose motto is it? Was some other chick off leaving love tokens in Lady Aislinn's secret place?"

"The stone circle wasn't secret, remember. The legend had to be known all over this area. And yet a knight's armor was valuable. Meant survival in the medieval world. They'd hardly have scattered pieces of it about."

"You mean sir what's-his-name couldn't pick another gauntlet up at the medieval version of a convenience store?"

"That's right." His grin flashed white. "We'll have to date the metal properly to be certain. Do some more tests."

"Don't go all scientific on me! I can tell you know more than you're saying! If the gauntlet isn't from Craigmorrigan, then who did it belong to?"

Jared ran the pad of his thumb wonderingly along the edge of the artifact. He looked up at Emma, the thrill of discovery still burning in his eyes. "If I were to hazard a guess, I'd say this gauntlet belonged to Sir Brannoc."

"That creep's stuff in Lady Aislinn's magic place?" Emma sputtered, outraged. "No way! His motto said something like… Sir dirty bird the ruthless."

"That's right." Respect flared in Jared's eyes. "Nice job on the research." Emma felt a warm glow of pride in her chest.

"After Lady Aislinn and the fairy flag vanished, Sir

Brannoc was so hated that people all across Scotland added a postscript of their own." Jared's gaze caught Emma's, held.

The nape of her neck prickled as if touched by a ghostly hand from another age. "What was it?" she breathed.

"I conquer all...without mercy."

Chapter Seventeen

JARED LOOKED UP from his site notes as his office door swung open, the whole trailer jiggling as Beth Murphy and Davey Harrison jostled their way inside, all but dropping the mounds of packages weighing down their arms.

"Post just came," Davey said, jamming his chin down on his topmost parcel to keep it from falling. "The man apologized all over the place. That big storm that came in from the east the other day held things up over the Atlantic."

"A storm?" Jared shook his head, trying to clear it of all too vivid images of Emma laughing as she wrestled him down in one of her grandfather's famous self-defense holds the night before. "What are you talking about?"

"Whoa, chief. You've been out of it all week, ever since you and Emma found the gauntlet. The phones have been out for two days." The kid was talking to him as if Jared's brain had gone missing. Maybe it had.

"Right," he said. "The phones."

"What Davey's trying to tell you is that these were supposed to be delivered yesterday," Beth explained.

"It's hardly a crisis," Jared said, in a downright sunny mood. "I don't even remember ordering anything."

"These aren't for you." Beth slid her load onto his desk. "They're for Emma."

"Emma?" Jared echoed, brow furrowing. "Don't tell me Robards has revised the script again? Or God knows what this time."

Instead of relaxing as Jared had hoped, the director had become more difficult than ever since Jared had begun to praise Emma. Robards kept firing off terse questions about Emma's abilities, something about the man's attitude making him edgy.

"No, it's not from the studio," Davey said. Strange, Jared thought. Then what could it be? Had Emma conned Davey into helping her order more research materials from some obscure book site on the Internet? She'd been more obsessed than Jared since they'd found the section of gauntlet two weeks ago.

The woman had been reading everything she could get her hands on, including copies of actual medieval texts written in Middle English. Not exactly fare for an intellectual lightweight. Another assumption he'd made about Emma that she'd proved dead wrong.

Beth helped Davey shift his batch of packages onto the desk. The girl touched his hand a little too long, setting Jared's nerves on edge.

"We figured Emma would be in here with you," she explained when she finally drew away. "You two have been joined at the hip the past two weeks. If we kids in the dorm tents didn't know better, we'd think something was up."

Beth laughed breezily, but a slow flush burned its way up Davey's throat. No matter what the rest of the students knew or didn't know, the lad was far too intuitive to miss changes all too visible between his two favorite people on site—next to Beth Murphy, that was.

Emma had even urged Jared to give Davey a few tips to help the lad make his move on the girl. After all, Emma insisted, summer wouldn't last forever and Davey would spend the dreary schoolyear kicking himself for missing his chance to kiss Beth.

Jared had all but snapped Emma's head off, fearing the fragility in the boy, what rejection might do to him. But Emma hadn't backed down an inch. She'd just pinched Jared's thigh and asked how he would be feeling right now if he'd stayed all by his lonesome on the other side of Lady Aislinn's tower room.

That would be easy enough to answer, Jared thought wryly. *I'd be so frustrated every student on site would probably be diving for cover any time I walked by.*

Unfortunately, realizing that didn't change his opinion. Jared was a grown man. He could take it when the breakup came. Hell, he *expected* it. He'd just bury the inevitable pain in his work and get on with his life. He wasn't looking for some fairy-tale ending, didn't believe such a thing even existed in real life.

But Davey Harrison brimmed with such desperate hope, such dangerous innocence that every time Jared saw it, it struck him through with a cold, biting terror, a foreboding he just couldn't shake.

Jared lifted the topmost bundle and squeezed it: small, soft, definitely not the familiar heavy weight or shape of a book. "Why don't you two see if you can wrestle Emma away from her research. Tell her these just came from…" He scanned the address label, felt like he'd taken a punch to the solar plexus.

To: Ms. Emma McDaniel… From: Andrew Lawson… Whitewater, Illinois, USA.

"Hey, Dr. Butler?" Davey's voice sounded a long way off. "You okay?"

"What the hell is her jerk of an ex-husband doing sending her…" Jared bit off the rest of the sentence, not wanting to betray Emma's vulnerability. But his outrage rushed on. What was in the package, anyway? Some baby picture Drew the asshole hadn't had the chance to rub Emma's nose in yet?

Hell, if it were up to Jared, he'd burn the thing. He nosed through the rest of the pile. The bottom package, wrapped with enough duct tape to reach from the castle to Edinburgh, was upside down. He flipped it over and its sparkly surface all but blinded him. Scrawled all over the brown wrapping paper with some kind of glittery marker were childish block letters that read: HAPPY BIRTHDAY. DO NOT OPEN TIL…

"Son of a bitch," Jared growled.

"Dr. Butler?" Beth took a step backward, as if he were one of Snib's collies ready to bite.

"Yesterday was the blasted woman's birthday!" he snapped, stung.

"You're kidding!" Davey exclaimed, Beth gasping in unison.

"Why the devil didn't she say anything?" Jared demanded as if the two stunned kids actually knew the answer.

"She seemed a little, well…pensive yesterday," Davey said. "When she thought no one was watching." Jared winced. Trust Davey to use an adjective that shouldn't roll easily off a teenager's tongue. A word that described exactly how Emma had behaved the day before.

But then, Jared hadn't been feeling so terrific himself yesterday morning. Veronica had been flashing some glossy fan magazine around the breakfast tables picturing Emma, a veritable goddess on some red carpet three years ago. Veronica jabbering on to the other girls about how shallow a life was when defined by designer dresses and caviar.

Not that Jared had heard much of the conversation. He'd been trying too hard to get the magazine image out of his head. Emma, swathed in scarlet satin, her curls smoothed into sleek waves, rubies flashing at her throat, her ex-husband smiling beside her, as smooth and polished as a pair of million-dollar shoes.

Jared had wanted to tear the page in half, ball up ol' Drew the asshole and toss him in the nearest wastepaper bin. *And then what?* a voice in Jared's head jeered. *Paste your own picture there beside her? That would be a hell of a sight. You and Emma McDaniel on the red carpet. Your hands dusty from digging, your ratty cargo pants bulging at the pockets with tools, your attitude surly as Snib on a rampage?*

What was it Jenny's father had said when he'd drunk a little too much champagne at their wedding? *It's a good thing Jared spends all his time with people who've been dead for centuries. They're a whole lot harder to insult than the living.*

Veronica had finished off her little recipe for indigestion by firing off a stream of biting questions about some charity event Emma had coming up. Jared's gut clenched with something akin to panic at the idea of Emma's real life intruding into their already too brief time. Had it been his own sense of loss that kept him from paying more attention to Emma's wistfulness?

Later that night he'd caught her peering down at that picture of her family, looking a little forlorn. But he'd figured she just missed them. He'd grabbed her from behind, growling into her neck in an effort to distract her—distract them both from the specter of her leaving Craigmorrigan. Damn if the woman didn't flip him onto his back, straddling him.

Gotcha...she'd teased, the shadows fleeing from her eyes. *The only question is, what do I do with you, now that I've got you at my mercy?*

He'd been happy to bring her back to the present moment with his mouth, with his hands, making them both forget anything but sensation.

"Find the woman and send her in here. Right away," Jared ordered. Davey and Beth rushed to do his bidding. Jared levered himself up from the chair, pacing. What kind of woman ignored her own birthday? Hell, if Jenny's celebration hadn't gone on for a week, the woman had acted as if she'd been cheated. Truth was, he'd come to dread her birthday, knowing he'd screw up somehow.

Of course red roses are just as pretty as yellow ones...why, I'd much rather have chocolate cake than white...it's wonderful you made dinner yourself instead of spending all that money taking me to the restaurant we went to last year....

Emma had stomped square on one of his personal buttons without knowing it.

The door swung open and Emma breezed in, her curls in bad need of a brushing, her face clean of makeup, her eyes sparkling with excitement. She didn't even notice the packages, every fiber of her being was so centered on him.

"Davey and Beth said you wanted to see me." She smiled. "Did you find something new about Sir Brannoc's gauntlet?"

"No. I found out something about you." Jared blocked her view of his desk, hands planted on his hips. "Yesterday was your birthday," he accused.

"Oh. Yeah, well..." She looked a little crestfallen. Walked over to the tiny window to try to hide the fact that it hurt her to think no one in her family had remembered. "It's no big deal," she said, more to herself than to him.

"Then why didn't you tell me?"

Emma shrugged her elegant shoulders. "Mostly I try to ignore them. If you have too many birthdays in Hollywood it's the kiss of death. Besides, we've got lots more important things to worry about right now. Like getting the rights to dig on Snib MacMurray's land. God only knows what else might be buried in that stone circle. Davey says Snib has this favorite fishing spot."

"It's my da's fishing spot," Jared corrected, irritated beyond belief. "*He's* the one who found it."

"All-righty then," Emma said, obviously getting the message loud and clear. "What matters is that Snib is probably in a good mood when he's there snagging trout. I thought if I could just catch the old curmudgeon at the right moment, I could convince him to—"

"What part of 'trespass on my land again and I'll shoot you in the arse' don't you understand?"

"He won't really pull the trigger!" Emma scoffed. "Well, maybe he'd shoot my dog, but me? Come on!"

"I absolutely forbid you to—"

Emma's eyes all but popped from her head.

Damn, he cursed himself. *Bad move, Jared. Very bad move. See what a mess you make when you lose your temper?*

"Emma, I…care about you. I'm not willing to take the chance that Snib might try to get back at me by—"

"Shooting me in cold blood?" Emma arched her brows in disbelief. "I'll admit you can be annoying, Butler, but you're hardly worth going to prison over."

"The man hates me," he attempted to explain. "Not only did I bring all this traffic to his private kingdom, but the whole village knows my grandfather was ten times the farmer Snib is. And Da…everyone loved him. Everyone but my mum." How the hell had that slipped out?

Emma's attitude ebbed. She crossed to him, touched Jared's arm. "I doubt Snib would win any Mister Congeniality trophies, even if the rest of the contestants were crocodiles with toothaches."

Gratitude welled up in Jared. He smiled, pushing back the old pain. "Speaking of toothaches, there's one more bit of the story I've neglected to tell you. Before I left for university I was sharing a pint with my da when…well, Snib got in his face and… Damn, it was making me crazy, the things that bastard was saying to Da, trying to needle him into a fight. Da said I should feel sorry for the man, so sour and alone, but I…"

"You what?"

"I kind of knocked Snib's front teeth out."

Emma choked on a stunned gasp, laughing. "Oh, Butler! You didn't!"

"How was I to know I'd want to excavate the bloody fool's land someday?" he crabbed. "Anyway, save your breath arguing with the man. He'd suffer the tortures of the damned before he'd give me permission to dig there."

"When I first arrived at Craigmorrigan you thought *I'd* turn out to be the tortures of the damned, remember? And now I've got you wrapped around my little finger. And, er, other far more interesting parts of my anatomy."

Looking far too full of herself, she edged past him and boosted herself up on the corner of his desk, causing a major avalanche. She squealed, flinging herself on the jumble of packages in an effort to stop them from falling.

"What on earth?" she cried.

Lawson's package was the only one to hit the floor. Jared resisted the urge to kick it under his desk before Emma saw it. "They're for you," Jared said. He gritted his teeth and fished the runaway parcel back out, banging his head in the process. "They were supposed to be delivered yesterday, but there was a storm."

Why was he bothering to explain? The woman hadn't heard a thing he'd said. She shrieked with delight, falling on the presents like a barbarian bent on pillage. "I thought they forgot!" she cried, tears of joy spilling down her cheeks. He wished to hell he'd been the one to put them there.

Wrapping paper flew as she wrested out her treasures, none of them the sort of fancy things he would have expected when he'd first met her. A homemade CD with something scrawled in magic marker was clasped to her breast. "It's Mom! Jake promised he'd have her cut a new CD for me!"

Some kind of candy in orange wrappers rained around her. "Reese's Peanut Butter Cups!" She ripped one package open and shoved the palm-sized circle of chocolate into her mouth. "Oh, Lord! Take me now!" she moaned around the chocolate, sounding orgasmic in her delight.

"React like that over a piece of candy and you'll give me an inferiority complex," Jared protested.

She laughed out loud and offered him the second piece. "You don't know what you're missing."

Thrusting Lawson's package on a shelf behind him, he took the candy with his other hand and eyed it suspiciously. "I can tell you this for nothing, woman. This won't taste half as good as you." He took an experimental nibble. "Everybody knows Americans can't make chocolate. Of course, if I smeared this all over your body and licked it off…"

He had hoped for a big reaction, major heat, maybe a quick birthday shag behind his desk, but she'd already gone on to the next parcel. Something heavy in a plastic case tumbled out and landed on the toe of his boot. He swore as a piercing siren shattered his eardrums.

Emma lunged for the monstrosity, laughing as she poked at wildly flashing buttons on the thing. It gave a pathetic bleep, then fell silent.

"What the hell is that?" Jared demanded, rubbing his sore right ear.

"The latest in modern technology, no doubt. Let's see…" Her brow furrowed as she scanned the official-looking lettering on the top of the packaging. "Hotel Door Alarm… Far from home? Don't trust hotel locks! The Sleep Guardian stops intruders in their tracks… Jake's always afraid some crazy is going to break into my room."

Jared scowled, remembering Feeny, the nasty reporter who'd followed Emma up the tower steps what seemed an eternity ago. No wonder Emma's stepfather was scared for her.

"I suppose I can see Jake's point," Emma said, shooting Jared a considering glare. "If he knew what you'd been up to, Butler, he'd probably feel honor-bound to kick your ass."

"He could try," Jared scoffed.

"Oh, he'd do it, all right. He's a black belt in martial arts. Once he took a baseball bat to the car of…" Something suddenly shadowed her eyes.

Protectiveness flared in Jared. His fists clenched. *"And?"*

"And nothing." She waved her hand, dismissing the subject. "It doesn't matter anymore. Especially not while I'm opening presents on my almost-birthday." She took up the glittery package. "My little sister, Hope," she said, running her fingertips over the block letters before she ripped it open. "Probably full of Twinkies. They're her daddy's favorite treat, so she thinks everyone in the world should adore them. Once she made Jake's whole birthday cake out of them. Stuck them together with toothpicks. Uncle Cade missed one and speared the roof of his mouth…"

Jared tried to wrap his brain around the kind of birthdays Emma was used to. Her whole family gathered around. Presents. Twinkie cakes sabotaged with toothpicks. His chest hurt.

Emma set the Twinkies aside and ripped open the biggest box of all. She unearthed a book, its cover a little worn, with soft illustrations of Victorian girls in watercolor skirts. "It's the Tasha Tudor edition of *Little Women!*" Emma clutched it to her, her voice all quavery.

"It's a lovely book," Jared said. "But it's not a first edition or anything. You could probably afford the first book off the presses if you wanted…hell." His cheeks burned. "I must sound like a real ass. That didn't come out the way I meant it."

"Jared Butler, king of tact."

"I just want to understand why you're so excited by it." Why the devil should it matter so much to him? He didn't know. It just did.

"My aunt Finn was a librarian when I first met her. She turned me on to *Little Women*. On the first Christmas we were all a family, she found me a copy in an antique book store. I brought it with me wherever I traveled. A piece of home, you know?"

Jared nodded, surprised by the lump in his throat.

"Somebody stole it from my hotel room right before Drew and I divorced and I never got another. I guess I knew it wouldn't have the same kind of magic unless it came from Aunt Finn."

Jared scooped up a pottery box hand-painted with clouds and the names *Deirdre Skye* and *Emma* in bright pink letters. The lid had cracked in two during shipping.

Jared retrieved the broken piece from the packaging, turning the box on its side to see if he could mend it. Something jingled and fell into Emma's lap. Jared retrieved it. "A key ring?" He held it out to her. A miniscule red corvette dangled from the chain, a note impaled where the keys should have been. *"In case you need any ideas in the future. I will be sixteen this year,"* Jared read aloud. *"Amy wants a bug like Mom's old one.* This sounds more like an order form than a present."

"It's from my cousin Will. Now all I have to do is convince Uncle Cade to let me give his kids their first cars."

Jared started at Emma's mention of her wealth. He'd almost forgotten it. She seemed so much more the woman from small-town Illinois who loved Twinkies, the niece who cherished antique books, the daughter who still longed to hear her mother sing. He stared into the jumble of gifts as if trying to dig up the secret to Emma's genuineness, her down-to-earth aura, her loving heart.

He glimpsed a tiny velvet jewelry box still nestled at the bottom of the package, looking for all the world as if it could hold an engagement ring. Jared felt himself bristle instinctively. "Don't tell me you've got a phantom boyfriend back in the States and he's decided to propose long distance."

She laughed as he took the box out, laying it in her hand. He wondered what it would be like if it *were* an engagement ring and he were the man giving it to her. Something exquisite and antique…maybe an emerald or…

Don't be mad, man. You'll not be offering her any ring and she'd not be daft enough to take it. Where the devil would the both of you live? In Beverly Hills or in a tent?

Emma snapped the box open. It was a necklace, a delicate gold star, rimmed with tiny diamonds and suspended on a chain. Hell, it was so small nobody would even see it.

"There's no card," Jared said.

"I know who it's from." Emma fastened it around her throat right away, pressing the star against her skin as if to imprint its shape in her heart. "The Captain…my grandfather always called me his diamond in the sky. Isn't it beautiful?"

"Beautiful," Jared echoed. But it was the woman before him he was speaking of. She took his breath away—the joy in her, the strength, her courage, her wide-open heart. God in heaven, the man who won her would be a lucky son of a bitch.

Jared's hand clamped hard on the package he'd slid onto

the bookshelf, desperation rising inside him, the need to
remind himself he wasn't that man. Never could be. "There's
one more package left." He hated the edge to his voice. "This
one's from your ex-husband." He'd meant to warn her. Instead
he figured he'd just made it worse.

Did she pale a little or was he just imagining it?

"From Drew?" she said, fiddling with the flap of the
package. "Why would he be sending me a present?"

"I was wondering the same thing, after letting those rag
sheets print such lies about you. It would take some nerve for
him to contact you now."

Emma gripped the package as if it held a bomb. "We've
talked a couple of times since the divorce. Drew said how—
how sorry he was."

"And that fixed everything right up," Jared sniped. Damn,
he wondered, why was he feeling so surly? Because he'd
missed her birthday and now it was too late… Or because of
the wariness and vulnerability Drew Lawson could still bring
to Emma's eyes?

"It's not Drew's way to grab guys like Feeny by the collar
and throw them off the property. Drew was always too much
of a gentleman for that."

Jared swore under his breath.

"He'd hoped someday we could all be friends again. He
and Jessie and me. But I…it felt…"

"Ridiculous? Stupid? An exercise in sadomasochism?"

Emma gave him a weary grin. "Something like that. It still
hurt too much for me to imagine a time I could see Drew without
pain. But now…" She shrugged. "It's funny. The present surprised me, but it didn't…lacerate me inside, you know?"

"It didn't?" Jared was stunned to realize just how much
he'd wanted to shield her from that hurt. "What's different?"
He couldn't help asking.

"You." She turned the full force of those melting chocolate eyes on him, eyes dark and beautiful and full of feeling.

He must have gotten pale. She actually grinned. "Don't panic, Butler. I'm not going to make any mad undying pledges of love or anything to ruin your day. It's just that, you made my body feel more than I ever did while I was with Drew. So now I can hope someday my heart will feel more, too."

Dangerous ground, Jared thought, his pulse jumping. Better to change the subject. "So what did the asshole get you?"

She laughed out loud, obviously as relieved as he was to break the tension at least a little. "So much for that tender little moment," she said.

Then slowly, intently Emma loosened the tape, unfolded the paper. When she emptied the contents into her lap, Jared stared, completely flummoxed.

Socks.

A gorgeous woman like Emma, and the idiot had sent her a bunch of chunky gray wool socks? He couldn't wait to hear her slam the jerk's present.

She extracted a small card and read it aloud. *"Sent you these so you won't get cold feet."* She blinked hard against what he knew were tears.

Jared felt jealousy gnaw inside him. "Your feet aren't cold," he complained. Hell, Drew Lawson had been married to Emma for years. He should know the woman was red-hot.

"He's not talking about my feet feet," Emma said. "He's talking about my career feet. The first rumblings that Barry had bought the movie rights to *Lady Valiant* were rippling through the industry when our marriage was getting rocky. I wanted the part of Lady Aislinn so badly but the role also scared me to death. It was taking such a chance. I didn't know if I could do it. Now I wonder if that's the real reason I thought I could give up my career to have a baby. Because then I'd never have to know I couldn't do it, you know?"

She sighed. "Drew's right. I married him for the wrong reasons, too. I took the safe way out, but I didn't understand what it would cost me. I wanted security, but not predictability. He was too tame. I needed excitement, adventure. Someone I could fight with who wouldn't walk out the door whenever things started getting uncomfortable."

Jared tried not to remember they'd been fighting since the moment they'd met, and coming back for more. Fighting, laughing, loving.

"I've barely known you a month and I can tell you even if you'd quit acting and had a dozen babies that relationship would never have lasted. He would have driven you crazy if he couldn't stand up to a good row."

"You're right about that. Maybe Drew knew it, too."

"I doubt it," Jared snapped before he could stop himself.

The toe of one sock crackled as she started to set it aside. "Something's inside this," Emma said. She pulled out an old photograph, one corner crumbled.

"Don't tell me," Jared groused, looking down at three teen-agers squeezed into a wooden booth at some kind of shop. Even as an awkward teen Emma had been one hell of a heartbreaker.

"It's me and Drew and Jessie at Lagos, this little soda shop back home."

Jared ground his teeth. "What a jerk, reminding you of this after the divorce. I wonder if his wife knows he's sending things to another woman."

Drew had written on the white border around the snapshot. *I'm sorry loving you wasn't enough. I wanted an ordinary life but married an extraordinary woman. Be happy, Em.*

"You can't possibly buy into this—" Jared sputtered but

Emma seemed a million miles away, her attention focused on a line squeezed in the white blur where the photographer's thumb had apparently covered part of the lens.

In neat block-printed letters the message said: *I miss us.*

"Jessie," Emma murmured, running her fingers over the line. "I miss us, too," she confessed softly.

Suddenly Jared wanted to dash away the images clouding her thoughts, wanted to make new memories for her, memories of *his* world to drive back the shadows.

"Listen," he said. "I've kept you a virtual prisoner here these past weeks. What would you say we see a bit of Scotland for a change?"

"But reporters—there could be…and I thought you didn't want to encourage the town's kids to come around and muck up the excavation."

"I changed my mind. How about we all go to the pub tonight? You, me, the kids."

"Great idea, Butler. We can pile everybody into the family station wagon and try to keep Davey and the soccer boys from fighting over who gets to sit by the windows."

"I mean it. A kind of…well, impromptu birthday thing. It *could* be fun."

"It *could* be disastrous. I'll let you in on a little secret. Me and alcohol…we don't mix. All those galas and premiers? I'm drinking tonic water with lime."

"You're kidding."

"All that time I spent in clubs as a kid kind of wrecked the drinking scene for me. And then after my grandma died, my grandpa kind of went on a binge. I wasn't around for it, but I've heard enough to get the picture. I don't want you to think I'm a killjoy or anything. I just want to warn you that if you're plotting to get me drunk and have your way with me…it ain't a-goin' to happen."

Jared's mood improved as he considered the possibilities. "I can have my way with you anyway. All I have to do is find that sweet spot on your throat, the one that makes you moan, and rake it with my teeth…"

He could see her shiver of response, just thinking about it. It made him hot as hell.

"You're getting way too arrogant for your own good," Emma said, giving him a measured glance. "Maybe I should get a headache just to take you down a peg or two."

"Flora, the pub keeper, will take care of cutting me down to size. She puts every man in town in their place, except one. Come on, McDaniel. Let's go to town. The kids will love it. And you can't go back to America without taking in the local color. Scotland's pubs are famous."

"*In*famous, don't you mean?" She grinned. "All right. We'll go to town. Maybe I'll be able to find some presents to send home to Hope and Mom and everybody. In fact…" She nibbled on her bottom lip for a moment. "I might even pick up a baby present to send Jessie and Drew."

"Over my dead body!" Jared began. She grabbed him by the front of his sweater.

"I'll take your body about any way I can get it, mister," she teased. "Come on. We'll have them ship a plaid bib and a pair of booties and then—"

"Then what?" Jared demanded darkly.

"We'll go be party animals, Dr. Butler. I might even live dangerously and get a lemon in my tonic water instead of a lime. And who knows?" She flashed him a come-hither smile that almost dropped him to his knees. "You just might get lucky after all."

TWO HUNDRED YEARS of peat smoke had seasoned the rough wood beams of the Royal Stuarts Public House. Dusty stuffed fish were smattered on the gray walls among World Cup posters and beer signs. The massive stretch of bar, polished by the hands of generations of patrons, gleamed softly in the dim light, the evening crowd gathering around wobbly tables.

Emma tried to claim a couple of tables in the back corner, but the proprietress, a stocky woman with a ruddy face and a wealth of ice-white hair, gave her a look that stopped her in her tracks.

"Sorry, miss, but that table is occupied," she said.

Emma frowned at the chairs. "It looks empty to— Don't tell me!" she exclaimed, with a sudden burst of excitement. "You have a ghost! Some soldier from the seventeen-hundreds who followed Bonnie Prince Charlie to the battle of Culloden Moor!"

"No self-respecting Jacobite would ever get near that table." Jared took her elbow, guiding her firmly away. "Snib would have driven them away years ago."

"Snib?" Emma wrinkled up her nose.

"That's the ruddy bastard's table. He brings Widow Steen trout once a week in the season and she holds it for him."

Emma pulled a face. "*Please* tell me it isn't trout season!" She cast her gaze heavenward. "Hey, God, if you want to give me a birthday present, keep that man and his demon dogs away from here!"

Jared surprised her, slipping an arm around her in spite of the students' watchful gazes. "Don't worry," he murmured, his breath tickling her ear. "I'll protect you."

Emma figured he could start by deflecting the daggers Veronica was shooting out of her eyes. But before Jared could see the woman's reaction, Veronica plastered an oh-so-helpful smile on her face.

She brandished a disposable camera. "This is my present to you, Emma," Veronica said. "Pictures of one of your last weeks in Scotland. I'll be sure to write everyone's name on the back of the photos. You can't be expected to remember little details like that when you go back to Hollywood."

"I'll remember," Emma said, looking around the bright faces of the students she'd come to love and the man she wished could be the love of her life.

But not this life, she admitted with a sudden ache. Jared belonged to another life. One an A-list actress would never be able to have.

In spite of the enmity she'd sensed from Veronica, Emma couldn't help but be grateful for her camera. It would be good to have pictures of Davey and Beth. Pictures of Jared. She imagined his fierce green eyes staring at her from his warrior's face in a frame set beside the one of her family. Reminders of what really mattered, the people she loved.

One of the boys ordered a round of drinks and the party ensued. With a laugh, Emma refused to drink anything but tonic water, for self-preservation she insisted since God knew what would fall out of her mouth after a few drinks.

The kids teased and begged until Davey finally convinced them to surrender, insisting no power on earth would get her to change her mind. Emma watched Beth try her best to flirt with a blushing Davey while the other boys turned their energies to showing off for the girl students, downing shots that should have knocked out an elephant. Seamus Jones was on his fifth by the time the pub door swung open to reveal the last person on earth Emma wanted to see.

Snib MacMurray stomped in like a little black cloud, the pockets of his tweed jacket bulging with what looked to be old tin cans, a smelly stringer of glassy-eyed fish dangling from his hand.

It took a moment for the farmer to realize his pub had been invaded by Jared and his much-loathed students. Once he recognized their faces he might as well have been some medieval pope seeing Jerusalem being desecrated by infidels. Jared folded his arms over his chest and met the old man's gaze as if daring him to ruin Emma's birthday party. Suddenly a mere toothpick impalement from Hope's Twinkie cake seemed uneventful compared to the threat of an all-out brawl.

The Captain would have been in hog heaven, Emma thought with a chuckle. The old man would've delighted in emptying a can of gasoline on this particular fire. Considering how Jared's eyes blazed, her grandpa wouldn't even have needed a match to start things burning.

The best Emma could hope for was Snib being so disgusted with their presence he'd turn on the heel of his mucky boots and stomp out. But before the farmer could make his escape, the barkeep bustled out in a swirl of faded tartan skirt and stale lavender perfume that only made the stench of the fish more nauseating.

"Have you brought a treat for your Flora, you dear man!" The woman snatched the stringer of fish as if it were a dozen roses.

His Flora? Emma tried to register the words as the kids all around her giggled and nudged each other.

"Friday, isn't it?" Snib said gruffly, patting an old tin can bulging from his jacket pocket.

His cheeks actually looked redder than usual. Windburn, Emma figured.

"Always bring the fish by on Friday," Snib continued. "When you said you wanted it, as I recall."

"But you never fail, do you?" Flora crooned. "Why, I can count on you regular as lilies at Easter, Snib MacMurray."

"I can't believe it," Jared muttered in Emma's ears. "The woman acts like he sailed on a log raft clear to the Amazon to catch them for her."

Emma grimaced. "She's obviously pickled her brains with

too much good Scotch. Or maybe she's blind. I'd better check to make sure Snib's Flora didn't miss any giant furry spiders in the bottom of my glass. One thing is certain." Emma pinched her nose and pulled a face. "The woman's olfactory cells must have been burned out years ago or she wouldn't be putting Snib and lilies anywhere near each other in the same sentence!"

Jared roared with laughter, giving her a quick squeeze. "Well, we'll not be letting anything spoil our evening." He turned to the students. "Will we, mates?"

Cries of agreement rang from the pub's oak rafters. Snib seemed to take it as a personal challenge, digging in at his table like a World War One doughboy in one of the trenches. But only Emma seemed aware of him as he munched on the fish and chips Flora set before him, his gaze following the older woman over the rim of his glass. Was it possible Snib had a soft spot for Flora after all? And if that was the case, maybe he wasn't as reprehensible as he seemed.

Right, Emma thought cynically, *and Snib's collies had just been greeting Captain with an overenthusiastic hello that first day! The man threatened to shoot your dog!*

Even so, she could test the waters, couldn't she? What did she have to lose? Maybe she could soften him up a little, get him to let them dig on his land.

But she had to get rid of Jared first. An hour had passed before she saw her chance. Jared was laughing at some joke one of the soccer boys told when Emma noticed Sean fleeing toward the loo with a decidedly greenish cast to his cheeks. She nudged Jared.

"Don't you think you'd better check on him?" she asked, putting on her worried face. "I'd go, but…"

"Poor lad would never survive the humiliation." Jared slid his big body out of his chair with an animal grace. "Here, now. The rest of you—slow down, won't you? No more shots or you'll not be fit for work tomorrow. Davey, lad, tell Flora to break out her finest bottle of whiskey and some fresh glasses. We'll toast our birthday lass once I get Jones settled, then it's tonic and lime for the lot of you!"

"Take your time," Emma said innocently. "No hurry. That poor, poor boy." *Listen, God,* Emma bargained, *if you keep Jared in that bathroom for a half an hour I'll give up Reeses Peanut Butter Cups for a month.*

The moment Jared's broad back disappeared down the narrow hallway, Emma pretended to follow him. Once in the shadows, she slipped over to Snib's table, the man finishing his own pint along with a malt vinegar-smeared chip.

"Mr. MacMurray," Emma exclaimed with forced brightness. "Good to see you."

"Well, it in't good to see ye, Miss High and Mighty film star. Yer a pain in me backside, so ye is. So why don't ye take yerself back over to yer own side o' the pub."

"It's a free country," Emma said. "At least, I'm pretty sure it is. You know, I think Flora over at the bar's got a thing for you. I never guessed you'd be such a ladies' man. But then, that just goes to show you first impressions can be deceiving."

"Humph!" the old man snorted. Emma couldn't help staring at his front teeth, which wobbled when he spoke. Yep. They were false all right.

"Whole village knows the woman's out of her mind," Snib grumbled but Emma caught a glimmer of something in the old man's eyes.

"Of course." Emma laid one finger along her jaw, considering. "It does make one wonder what she sees in you."

"She's after me money, she is."

"She'd earn every penny of it putting up with you," Emma said cheerily. "She'd also keep you a whole lot warmer in bed than all that cold hard cash." An unfortunate picture of Flora and Snib doing the dirty deed flipped into Emma's mind and she couldn't help but laugh.

"Sex an' loose morals! That's what I'd expect o' someone like ye!" Snib blustered. "But Miss Flora, she's a decent woman, so don't be filthying up her name talkin' like the scum ye are!"

"Hmm." Emma considered for a moment. "I'm not sure which you were most set on—insulting me or defending her. Better be careful, Snib, or you'll lose your bad name."

"Don't be twisting my words!"

"Into something almost human? All right. We'll stick to basics, then. You've got a rotten attitude, Mr. MacMurray."

"Keeps undesirables away. *Most* of 'em at least."

"You're going to have to do better than that if you want to get rid of me. You don't scare me a bit."

"That so? You were shrieking like a baby over that mongrel dog, when I had every right to do away with him. But I'm not worried too much. He'll get loose sometime, thieving devil that he is, an' me an' me collies will be waitin'."

Emma forced herself not to think about how close Captain had come to courting just such a disaster. She tipped her head, seeming to give his threat consideration. "You know, now I've spent more time here in Scotland, I can see where a stray dog could cause trouble for a *gentleman* farmer like you. You have my word I'll keep Captain under lock and key." *Maybe Jared has a medieval straitjacket tucked away somewhere. Yeah, that should keep Captain from getting away again.* "Can't we settle this thing like reasonable adults? I'll keep my dog off your property and you...well, maybe you could be pleasant for a change."

"Pleasant! I'll give yer pleasant!" He made a vulgar gesture with his hand. "What do yer think of that?"

Emma feigned a yawn. "Listen, Mr. MacMurray, I've

played to way tougher audiences than you. My grandfather—
now *he's* tough. Took down a whole gang of thugs back in
my hometown. And when it comes to words, well, compared
to him you sound about as threatening as an eighty-year-old
schoolmarm."

Snib swore a blue streak.

"Don't feel bad that you're not having the impact you
want," she empathized when he stopped to take a breath. "It
takes a lot to impress me."

"It's harassing me you are!" Snib sputtered. "Just because yer a celebrity doesn't mean I can't have ye thrown
out on yer arse!"

"But I'll just keep coming back. See, I'm determined to
finance an archaeological dig on your property."

"What! Did Jerry Butler put you up to this? Hiding behind
a woman's skirts! I'll see him in hell before I let him—"

"This isn't about Dr. Butler. It's between you and me.
Frankly," she lied, "I want the publicity for my movie and I'm
willing to pay whatever you want."

"And it's all about money with you Yanks these days, isn't
it? Money and teats and arse. You tart yourself up and come
over here, sure you can get your way. Think every man has
his price. What about honor? Eh? A man's got his pride!
What would the likes of you know about either one o' those?"

Emma pinned him with the Captain's glare. "Try me."

"Pah! You've got all the spine o' these worms here." He
grabbed the tin can from his pocket and dumped it on the
table. The liveliest worms squiggled into the spilled loam to
hide. He was trying to gross her out, Emma knew. But her
grandfather had taught her to handle worms and snakes and
anything else that usually made little girls scream.

She picked up the nearest worm and coiled it in the palm
of her hand. It felt moist, crumbs of dirt still clinging to its

skin. "Cute little fellow. But he's almost dead. Now that you're done fishing for the day I suppose you're going to set his little buddies free. You being such an animal lover and all."

"Animals are for food or work an' that's the end of it. You do-gooders should be grateful yer at the top o' the food chain, not complaining about us who take advantage of it."

"Well," Emma said, prodding the worm gently with her finger. "I suppose you could have Flora fry this little fellow up for you, but he'd barely make a mouthful."

"I'd eat 'im raw, so I would! And many the more like him."

"Emma?" Jared's voice cut in sharply. The big Scotsman stalked toward them, his boots hitting the floor so hard the whole room shook. What had she called him when she first met him? MacTavish the Pissed Off Scots Giant? He was doing a great imitation of the guy right now. "It's time for your birthday toast," he snapped.

"I was just having a little conversation with our neighbor here," she said sweetly. "Talking about how dangerous first impressions can be."

"The man threatened to shoot you. I'd say that's pretty clear as far as impressions go."

Snib swore, but Jared continued as if the old man hadn't said a word. "Let's head back to the table. I'm buying another round. The best Scotch Flora has."

"A Butler buying his own drinks!" Snib jeered. "Your ancestors must be heaving in their graves. They'd con the life out'a folks here to get their drinks, the Butlers would. Generations of 'em. But the blood's too thin now." Snib curled his lip at Emma. "Might as well be Yankee lasses like you."

"They didn't con anyone," Jared defended. "They earned their drinks."

"Earned them?" Emma's question was lost in Snib's cackle of derisive laughter. "How?"

"Singing mostly. And fiddling." Jared was hedging. She could feel it. "Now, let's get back to…"

"That's a prettified tale!" Snib scooted his chair, blocking Emma's path. "What about the rest o' it? Tell her what you did when you were fourteen or so!"

"You could drink when you were fourteen?"

Jared stiffened. "I was with my da and…it doesn't matter. Ms. McDaniel doesn't want to know about any of this nonsense."

"Oh, yes she does," Emma said. Tension swirled around the two men, a Mexican standoff of mammoth proportions. She knew in her gut that if she left the field of battle now, before somehow piercing Snib MacMurray's armor, she'd never get another chance with him. The crusty old man would make sure of it, just as her grandfather would in the same situation.

"What kind of talent did Jared use to earn his drink?" Emma asked Snib. "Singing? He's got a lovely voice."

Snib howled. "His voice was crackin' like an old woman's back! Sounded like a cat bein' dragged through a knothole."

"Damn it, Emma—"

She cut Jared off. "Did he do a little soft-shoe?"

"He took a dare to earn his drink, so he did!"

"I should never have done it."

Emma looked from one man to the other, their faces livid, tempers hot.

"It was stupid," Jared snapped.

"Aye, it was stupid all right, Butler," Snib crowed. "Can't wait to see yer fancy lady's face when she hears what ye did." He puffed out his chest, positively gleeful. "He ate a worm!"

"Oh." Emma's stomach wobbled. She fought to keep her attitude in place. "That's a…a nice talent, too."

Snib's beady little eyes narrowed. "Yer not foolin' me for

a minute, lassie. You'd never have the grit to do something like that. Not near tough enough, with yer pretty little smile and yer dainty little—"

"Don't say it, old man," Jared warned, fist knotting, "or I'll knock out the rest of your teeth!"

"Poor lass needs you to defend her? Way she talked, claimed she was made o' pure steel. Well, she's two strikes against her then, doesn't she? Just like a pampered wee movie star an' just like a Yank."

Damn, but the jerk was jumping up and down on her very last nerve. "No woman, especially no *American* woman, would have the nerve to eat a worm. Is that what you're saying?"

"Emma, for Christ's sake, who gives a damn what this sodding fool thinks?"

"Yer lady friend does, 'parently." Snib grinned with satisfaction. "Now if you earned your drink the way little Jerry did so long ago, well then you'd be earning my respect."

"But Jared didn't earn your respect doing that years ago," Emma reasoned.

"He was too young and too stupid for it to matter. Lads that age, they'll do anything."

"But I'm different. Is that it?"

"Grown woman, with all yer fancy Hollywood ways."

Emma looked down at the worm in her hand. "You think I'm too pampered. Too squeamish. That I wouldn't have the nerve."

"That's the way of it."

"Stop trying to bait her!" Jared raged. "She's not about to fall for your—"

"Jared, this is between Mr. MacMurray and me."

"Mr. MacMurray…" Jared sputtered in rage.

"This is all about respect, right, Mr. MacMurray? That's what matters to you."

The farmer's grizzled chin jerked up a notch. Emma half

expected Jared to swing his fist and knock it back down. "Nothin' matters more to Snodgrass Begood MacMurray."

Oh, God, Emma thought. That was his full name? No wonder the man was so crabby!

"Exactly how did…does one do it?" Emma asked, eyeing the worm dubiously. "Is there some trick to this?"

"Emma, don't be ridiculous. You're not going to—" Jared tried to grab her hand, but she elbowed him smack in the stomach, his breath going out in a whoosh.

Snib looked as pleased as if he'd done the elbowing himself. "People said the Butler trick was to stick the damned squiggler at the back o' your throat and think o' Bruce and Bannockburn. Then gulp a glass o' whiskey to chase it down."

"I don't drink whiskey, actually. The stuff tastes horrible."

"Emm…" Jared wheezed.

But she'd already dodged his grasp, fetching her tonic water from among the glasses of whiskey he'd ordered for the toast. Jared's students spilled off the chairs, realizing something was up. They trailed after her, jabbering among themselves as they watched with saucer-wide eyes.

Her thoughts raced. If she went through with this, Emma knew she'd damned well have gotten Snib's attention. It would give her an opening, at least a chance to change his mind. But she would also have swallowed a worm.

No, she thought. Don't think of it. Think of the stone circle. Sir Brannoc's gauntlet. Think how badly Jared wants to dig there….

The worm stirred against her palm.

Maybe…maybe I can't do this… she thought wildly. Wait a minute! She berated herself. She wasn't some—some fluffy. She was the Captain's granddaughter. A McDaniel. McDaniels didn't back down.

Fixing her eyes on Snib, she raised her glass. "To Bruce

and Bannockburn." Flashbulbs popped, Veronica taking pictures in quick succession. In went the worm, down the hatch poured the tonic water, a fizzy gulp that all but choked Emma. *She would not* throw up. *Would not.* She'd die before she gave MacMurray the satisfaction. Instead, Emma leaned past the stunned Jared and patted Snib's smelly cheek. "Have a nice day," she said brightly. She walked slowly, deliberately toward the table where the empty toasting glasses stood waiting.

She grabbed the full bottle around the neck, downing its contents in blazing gulps.

"Emma, you bullheaded, daft woman!" Jared laughed until tears ran down his cheeks, the students all cheering—with the notable exception of Veronica. "You're magnificent. There's not a woman in the world like you."

"Thank...God for that." She choked, coughed, Jared smacking her on the back in an effort to clear her throat.

"I thought you didn't drink," he teased.

"Maybe..." Emma gasped "...I do...drink whiskey...after all."

Chapter Eighteen

FLORA THE PUB KEEPER really should get her boyfriend Snib to nail down this floor, Emma thought as she made her way toward the bathroom. A person could get hurt with the hallway moving all over like a fun house at the county fair. Then again, maybe Snib had taken a hammer to the boards already to sabotage the place in the hopes that Jared would break his neck. She concentrated on putting one foot in front of the other. Now, where was she supposed to be going again? The bathroom. She was trying to find the bathroom.

No. They didn't have bathrooms here. *The W.C.* Wasn't that what the Brits called it? The water closet. Absurd name. But at least it made better sense than "the loo."

There! She stumbled to a halt, triumphant. That was a water closet-y looking door if she ever saw one! She squinted at the sign, making out the letter. "G," she said aloud. "G is for girl." She flattened her hand and tried to aim for the damned thing. But her arm was stopped dead mid-shove.

Hey! Some jerk had hold of her! Her hair tumbled into her

eyes as she spun around, ready to knee him in the groin to make him let go. Her captor evaded her trick move with practiced skill. "Whoa there, your ladyship!"

"Jared!" she exclaimed in complete surprise. "Did you have to go to the bathroom, too?"

"You don't want to be going in this door, love," he warned, his eyes twinkling. "That's the gents."

"The gents?"

"You know. You're a lady. I'm a gentleman."

She roared with laughter. "I'll tell you this for nothing, Butler. You're no gentleman. It's one of the qualities I like best about you. Besides how good you smell. And your mouth…that mouth of yours is a genuine work of art. But it's not purely decorative. You *way* know how to use it."

She grabbed on to him, pressing herself tight against him. "Lord, you feel good." She sighed. "So—so big and…er *bigger.*" She made a sound low in her throat and wriggled against the ridge beneath the fly of his pants. "Wonder just how…big…I can make you."

Jared took a deep breath, and she reveled in the power she had over his body, even when she was drunk. "How about if we try that little experiment later?" he suggested, putting her firmly away from him. "Wouldn't want to be giving the children any ideas."

Emma pouted. "They're in college, sweetie, not in preschool. In fact, I'd bet nine out of ten of 'em have hooked up with somebody this summer. Don't tell me you were a monk at that age. I bet you were hot."

Jared chuckled. "I bet you were hotter."

"Nope." Emma frowned. "No hotness allowed. Just lots of sweet an' thoughtful. *Bor-ing.* And as if Drew wasn't *sweet* enough, now I get men my stepfather picks out."

Jared got that "I don't like what you're saying" dent

between his eyebrows. Emma loved it. It was so darn cute, made him look all dangerous.

"I thought you said there weren't any other men," he challenged.

"Gotta have some kind of escort to all the premiers and junk I have to go to." She giggled as Jared's dent got deeper. "You know, the kind of guy who can kick paparazzi ass if the need arises but still looks good in a tux. For the last year and a half Jake's been setting me up with the stud-li-est bodyguards he can find. And background checks? These guys are so clean they'd make Mother Theresa look like a suspicious character. Yep. My stepdad the matchmaker."

She made her expression go all smoky and seductive. She knew exactly how to do it, had had to practice in the mirror until her face hurt to get it exactly right before the first Jade movie. "I don't suppose you'd consider doing a little moonlighting as a bodyguard at this charity gig I've got coming up, would you, Jared? We could even try to find some filthy-rich contributors to help you keep the site open. A cool gazillion dollars and some loose change. That would be worth the agony of a night with London's high society, wouldn't it?"

"Don't need it since I've put up with you the past month. The salary Barry Robards paid me for training his Lady Aislinn will keep the castle afloat a few years longer."

"But there's so much more to do! And Snib's stone circle…"

"That circle is a historical monument!" Jared snarled, suddenly surly. "It doesn't belong to anyone. Especially not Snib MacMurray!"

"*Snodgrass* MacMurray. I still haven't given up on getting my paws in that dirt. I mean, it's hardly fair. Captain got to dig away in it, but—I know! How about if I go down to Snib's for tea and worms and you sneak over and—"

"Destroy the site? I'd think your time at the castle would

have taught you that an archaeological dig has to be executed precisely, recorded meticulously."

"So you're saying I'd better be prepared to eat a lot of worms, eh?"

"More than even you could stomach."

She wriggled her eyebrows, grateful to feel herself sobering up, at least a little. "That depends. What's it worth to you?"

Jared ran his teeth over his tongue, and she heard a sudden seriousness in his voice. "More than I could ever afford."

"A few hours in a tuxedo and dress shoes escorting me to a gala? Being charming to people even when their boring conversation is turning your brain to mush?"

"I doubt I could manage it, even for digging rights. I tried to keep my mouth shut once. When they told me I'd lost the grant. But I told them to stuff it."

"That's my darling boy. You could tell people at the gala to stuff it. My grandfather did once when I took him…well, it was the most entertainment I ever had at one of those deadly dull parties. Speaking of entertainment, maybe that's what I could do to lure you into my sparkly little high-society web. The party might suck, but once it was over we could have a party for two. I promise I'd make it worth your while."

Jared's dent got even deeper. If he kept it up he'd end up with a hole right through his head. "Me at some gala? That would be a stellar idea." He grimaced. "My being such a people person and all."

"You wouldn't have to say a word, just lean against the wall and look all sexy and brooding." She sighed. "Oh, well. Far be it from me to inflict that kind of torture on you. But I *so* don't feel like another of Jake's *this-is-not-a-date* deals. I guess I'll just have to call him and tell him to make sure the new guy looks like Barney Fyfe."

"Barney who?"

"A big purple dinosaur. Or…oh-oh." A wave of urgency hit her anew. "I really do need to…um, go…"

Quick on the uptake, Jared steered her across the hall and opened a door. She'd just have to trust that it was the right one. She lurched into the room, rushing past someone in her desperate quest to get to a stall. A few minutes later, Emma collected herself and crisis abated, made her way to the sink. She leaned over the basin, splashing cold water on her face until her head cleared at least a little. Now if the coffee Jared had exchanged for the whiskey a while ago would just kick in, she'd be back to her old self in no time.

A paper towel magically appeared in her hand. Amazing service here in Scotland, she thought, dabbing most of the water off her skin. She turned, half expecting to see Jared and his adorable dented forehead, ladies room or no. Instead, a different familiar face popped into Emma's line of vision.

"Beth?"

"Hi, Emma." The girl was sitting on a stool, looking so woebegone it drove back the worst waves of Emma's dizziness.

"How long have you been in here?" Emma asked.

"Oh, awhile. Forty-five minutes or so."

Guilt jolted Emma. She hadn't even noticed the kid was gone from the table. "Are you feeling sick?"

"No. I don't drink."

"That's good." Relief flooded Emma. "Don't start. Especially not with whiskey straight from the bottle. That stuff'll kill you."

Beth shoved her bangs back from a face incredibly young, full of tenderness and intelligence and empathy rare in someone her age. "You were so awesome, what you did out there," the girl said, her eyes brimming with admiration. "Facing down Snib like that! I could never be that cool."

"I'll let you in on a little secret." Emma smacked her lips, still tasting dirt on the back of her tongue. "Eating a worm is one form of cool I could have gone my whole life without."

"You wouldn't say that if you'd seen Dr. Butler's face," Beth exclaimed. "He just…just lights up whenever you're in the room. And I've never heard him laugh like that. Not ever. Neither has Davey and he's known Dr. Butler for years."

Emma leaned against the nearest wall, grounding herself. The room cooperated and stilled for the most part. *Good room*, Emma praised as if it were Captain. *Sit, room. Stay.* "You like Davey a lot, don't you?"

Beth stuttered a denial, her cheeks turning pink. Oh, yeah. She had it bad for the guy. "We're just…well, he's the greatest friend…"

"Friend? My uunt Fannie's ass!"

Beth choked out a stunned laugh. "Oh, my God! I can't believe you said that!"

"Neither can I." Emma raked her curls back from her face. "Especially since I don't even have an Aunt Fannie."

She wanted the girl to laugh. Instead, Beth looked more wistful than ever. "No wonder Dr. Butler's crazy about you. You're so funny and smart and…and gorgeous."

Beth crinkled up her freckled nose and looked at her reflection in the mirror with patent disappointment. "If I looked like you, then maybe Davey would…"

"Would want to be more than friends?" Emma supplied.

Beth picked at a thread on her butter-yellow sweater. "Sometimes I think he…well, it's all so confusing. I'll catch him looking at me, and I'll think, *he's going to do it. He's finally going to kiss me.* And my heart starts pounding and I close my eyes and…and lean toward him and…"

"He bolts like you just set his hair on fire?" Emma supplied.

Beth nodded, swiping at her eyes. "I feel like such an idiot. Veronica says he must be gay or something."

"He's far from gay," Emma said. "Not that I'd care if he was. He'd still be the same wonderful, bright, kind…" She stopped herself mid-tirade, focusing instead on the girl before her. "Beth, I'm going to give you a little advice about men."

Beth's eyes lit with eagerness and Emma's heart twisted, remembering her own first love. She hoped Beth and Davey's path would have a far happier ending. "I'll do anything you tell me to!" Beth enthused. "Maybe you could tell me how to get my hair cut, or put on makeup, or…we could go shopping. I don't have a lot of money to blow on clothes, but—"

"This solution won't cost you anything but guts," Emma cut in.

"Okay." Beth straightened her shoulders like a soldier waiting to receive her marching orders from General Patton. "What is this advice you've got for me?"

Emma crossed her arms, her eyes narrowing. "Sometimes in life, you just have to swallow the worm."

Beth's eyes bulged. She pressed both hands to her stomach. "Oh, no offense, Emma, but…but I don't think I could."

"I meant it figuratively, not literally. You know. Take the bull by the horns. Steal control of the situation. Get the boy's attention."

"I've been trying to get his attention all year. Short of running through his tent in my underwear—" Beth stopped, horrified with herself. She nibbled at her bottom lip, so nervous and unsettled Emma wanted to hug her. But the girl didn't need comforting. She needed a strategy to break through Davey Harrison's reserve.

"He won't kiss you?" Emma challenged. "Fine. You kiss him."

"What if he doesn't like it? What if—"

"He runs screaming into the night?" Emma joked.

"Something like that."

"Kiss the boy," Emma insisted. "See what happens. I bet you'll be surprised."

Beth's face lit up with a mixture of dread and hope. "Do you really think so?"

She wanted to put the poor girl out of her agony and tell her Davey adored her, but it felt like a betrayal to expose the lad's secret. Let him be the one to have the pleasure of seeing the joy in Beth's eyes when she found out he was crazy in love with her as well. Emma settled for giving Beth a smile of encouragement.

"Summer's almost over, sweetie," she warned. "What have you got to lose?"

Beth's decision hung in the balance. Shyness warred with desperation. Silence stretched between them. Then suddenly Beth squared her shoulders. "You're right. I'll do it."

"Sure you will." Emma hugged her. "Now get out there and kiss that boy senseless. The poor lad doesn't know who he's up against."

Beth flushed, giggled. "I'd sure like to be up against..." She started out the door, banged it up against something solid. Jared's pained oath echoed in the hallway.

He swung the door the rest of the way open and Beth brushed past him.

"I was just about to come in there after you," he groused, rubbing a knot on his head. "What the devil were you doing in there so long?"

"It's top secret. I can't tell you or I'd have to kill you." Emma ran her fingertips down his chest, her voice dropping low, seductive. "Jade Star, woman of mystery, doing what I do best."

"And what's that?"

"Saving the world one worm at a time." Emma flounced past him. They made their way back into the light. Emma blinked hard, noting the determined look on Beth Murphy's face as the girl maneuvered to get a seat close to Davey Harrison. Emma bit the inside of her cheek, considering. She'd better get Jared to beat feet out of here before he saw the way Beth was gobbling Davey Harrison up with her eyes. Butler was completely capable of grabbing the nearest fire extinguisher to put the flame out.

"Jared?" Emma said, nuzzling against him.

"Hmm?" Jared reached for the carafe of coffee he'd ordered while settling the liquor bill.

"What do you say we get out of here?" Emma murmured in his ear. "You know. Howl at the moon. Leap tall buildings in a single bound."

Jared grinned. "You're sure your family's not Scottish?"

"Why?"

"We Scots have this strange compulsion. Whenever we've been drinking we want to climb up really high places."

"High places like the Knight Stone where I saw you fighting?"

"Something like that." She knew the moment he recognized the devilish intent in her smile. He tugged a lock of her hair. "*Please* tell me you're scared of heights."

"Not in the slightest." Emma moistened her lips, slowly, seductively, knowing exactly what she was doing to him. Hunger flared in his eyes.

"Bloody hell, woman," he groaned. "Have mercy!"

"That's the last thing on my mind when I think about you. And I think about you a lot. Fantasy after fantasy…"

Jared's breath quickened, a flush staining the blades of his cheekbones. She could feel how much he wanted her. "Fantasies, huh?" he said. "Want to tell me about 'em tonight?"

"I don't want to *tell* you about them at all. I want to make them come true. And we're running out of time."

Impending loss hit Jared harder than he expected. He glimpsed an answering ache in the curve of Emma's mouth. He wanted to drive the inevitable away with a kiss, but that would have to wait until he got her alone. "Your wish is my command."

"Then I wish we could go to the Knight Stone. Make love there as if we had forever."

But they didn't. Jared thought of the magazine spreads Veronica had flashed about. Emma, exquisite in satins and jewels, sailing through a sea of shouting humanity and flashing cameras, journalists and fans salted through with unscrupulous bastards like Joel Feeny. A world he didn't understand, could never feel comfortable in. A sharp reminder that any life with Emma would always be completely beyond his reach.

"I've never taken anyone else there," Jared hedged. "It's slick. Dangerous."

If he took her to the stone in the water, his secret place, he knew in his soul that her essence would remain there, seeped into the ancient pillar forever. That every time he set foot upon the stone, he would feel her in his heart's deepest core.

Emma slid her hand down and twined their fingers together. "I'm not afraid."

"I am." Jared lost himself in her eyes. He slipped his arm around her shoulders as if to steady her. "I'm taking Emma back to the castle so she can sleep off the Scotch," he told the group. "You all stay and have fun."

He led her out the door to a chorus of good-nights. They drove back to the castle, exchanging fire-hot kisses at every stop sign, hands too eager to wait catching bare skin under shirts as they drove. Castle Craigmorrigan loomed against the sky, a pagan goddess turned to stone. She whispered love charms as they made their way to the cliff's dizzying edge.

Anticipation sang through Emma's veins, honed by a fine edge of danger and the ache of knowing their time was running out. The sea crashed and roared, the stones slick beneath her feet, the untamed wonder of this place and the man who had brought her here soaring her spirits higher, ever higher. Emma almost expected Jared to speak some incantation, to make a silvery path appear upon the water for them to cross.

But at the last possible moment, she glimpsed the faint shelf of stones the sea had not yet crumbled away. In a few hundred more years, she thought, this bridge of Jared's would have vanished, eaten away by time, just as the curtain wall in the castle above had crumbled. No one would ever know that once, a man and a woman had loved here.

But she would know, Emma thought. She would remember this night for the rest of her life. Jared, so strong and sure, guiding her by instinct along a path no one but he could see. Leading her to the one place in the world that belonged to him alone.

Salt spray dampened her face, the beating of waves against rock feeding passions centuries old. Craigmorrigan's own brand of magic… What else could it be? Enchantment, its pull more primal than anything Emma had ever known.

The wind sang the wild song of the standing stones, the sea ballads of Lady Aislinn's love. But the sacred Knight's Stone whispered of loves beyond memories, beyond poems, beyond bard's tales. Fairies older than time, dragons who ruled men's fears and warriors pagan still.

Emma embraced it all with sweet abandon, wishing she could hold this man—this madness—for all eternity.

Jared laid his worn leather coat down, then his bulky blue sweater to make her a bed.

"The stone is rough…" He hesitated before he moved to cover her with his body. "I don't want to hurt you."

"You won't." She looked up at him with eyes filled with

strength, courage, love. "I'm strong enough to take whatever you're willing to give me."

Was she? Jared wondered, knowing she spoke of far more than hard rock and sex with all pretense of the civilized stripped clean away. Was it possible she was strong enough to take him as he was? Rough-edged and temperamental and self-centered? A man far more comfortable with facts than with feelings?

He stripped away her clothes, kissed her creamy skin. She felt so damned small beneath him, so delicate, so...fragile? But he couldn't wait. He drove himself deep into her welcoming heat, felt her surge up against him, sea to his cliff, soft to his hard, in a sensual battle as old as time.

He marveled at the power of her as she took all of him, body and soul. Emma fragile? She was fire beneath him, storm, like a wild witch borne in from the sea. As they made fierce love there upon the stone, she took as much as he did, demanded as boldly, reached as deeply and when the climax came, she cried out, and clung to him so hard his ribs ached almost as much as his heart.

How on God's earth was he ever going to let her go?

What other choice did he have?

He closed his eyes, remembering the magazine picture Veronica had flashed in front of him, the red satin, the polished smiles, the delicate stiletto heels.

A world where he was doomed to fail. But did he have to? Couldn't he even learn to like the diamonds and satin if he were the lucky sonofabitch who got to peel them off of her at the end of the day?

Right, and then the two of you could dash off to the baby minder's and pick up the kids.

Cold sweat broke out on Jared's nape. Don't be a fool, he told himself. Love her if you have to. But never forget that differences wider than the world will always keep you apart.

You might as well be the sea and Emma, the moon...

He looked at the scrap of horizon where the two bled together, moonshine and the water's reflection...seeming to touch, but their joining not real. An illusion. Something no man could keep, hold. Like this time he and Emma shared.

"Emma, promise me something," Jared said, feeling like a fool, unable to stop himself.

"Anything."

Stay here with me. Make your life this castle. Turn your back on the craft you love and the children your heart longs to have....

For what? A man so selfish he'd take all that from her to keep her in his world?

No. Even he wasn't that selfish.

"Jared?" She cupped his face in her palms, tipped her head in gentle query. He knew she left her handprints on his heart. "What is it?"

"Promise I'll be able to sense you, feel you...after you're gone. Here at the stone. Come back and haunt me."

Her eyes filled with love and loss and longing. Impossibility an alchemy that made the moment all the sweeter.

"You already haunt me." She kissed him gently on the lips. "You'll be there, Jared. Every time I close my eyes. I'm counting on it."

Jared's throat burned. He climbed to his feet, turned his face into the wind for long, silent moments, the familiar lash of sea spray and isolation encasing his emotions as he shuttered the pain away.

When he'd hidden them deep enough, he turned to Emma, forcing a smile.

"Come along with you, then," he said, extending his hand to pull her up. "It's time we get up to the tower. Morning will come plenty early."

He helped her dress and clothed himself, then tucked his jacket around her to keep her warm. He led her along the stone bridge, losing himself in the magic of this one night, how right it was. Perfect. Inevitable. Fleeting. She followed him across the stones as if she, too, had known where the footing lay from the dawn of time.

When they reached the cliff top, Jared paused, looking down into her face. A face a little too pale, eyes still a little red from the whiskey she'd drunk what seemed an eternity ago. He brushed her hair back tenderly. "We'll be stopping at my office first, before we're off to the tower."

"Whatever work you've got left will still be there in the morning."

Jared laughed, reaching past the ache to the amusement Emma so often inspired in him. "You think you've left any strength in me for work, woman? I'm half dead from having my way with you. We'll be going after the paracebo I keep in my desk drawer."

"Parace...? You mean, aspirin?" He saw her eyes go wide, her expression adorable. "Jared, did I, um...hurt you?"

"It's not for me, treasure. It's you who'll be needing it. You're going to have the devil of a headache come morning."

He chuckled, running his thumb along the fullness of her kiss-stung lower lip. "It's a rare fine birthday you had for yourself here in Scotland, Emma McDaniel. If you're lucky, by tomorrow you won't remember a thing."

"Until I read about it in the morning papers," Emma quipped wryly.

Jared's jaw set, grim. "That's one thing I can promise you won't be happening. Not while I'm on watch."

He drew her into the crook of his arm as they walked down the path toward the main camp, reveling in the weight of her, the warmth of her against him. He didn't hear the footsteps in the shadows behind them. Didn't see the white gleam of a hunter's smile.

Chapter Nineteen

THE TRAILER DOOR STOOD open to the night, the metal panel thudding in a hollow rhythm against the structure's outer wall. Jared eyed it in surprise. "I thought I locked that before we left for the pub."

He felt Emma stiffen against him. "I'm sure you did. You dropped the keys and we both made a dive for them. We clunked heads and couldn't stop laughing."

She was right. Wariness stole through him. "It's probably nothing," he attempted to soothe her. "Kids bent on mischief."

"Or someone trying to get the dirt on me."

He bristled at the idea. "That's breaking and entering. It's against the law."

"Only if you can prove it. Feeny and his buddies would tell you sometimes it's worth taking a chance."

Jared ground his teeth. "If those bastards so much as set foot on castle property, I'll call the police."

"Don't be dragging the poor cops away from their coffee

and donuts just yet." Emma grimaced. "I'm probably just being paranoid. It's not like we've got some front-page-worthy story we're hiding around here. I mean, I think you're plenty newsworthy, Butler, but the rest of the world would like it better if you were married or something."

"Stay back until I see what's going on," he ordered as he stepped through the opened door into the dark trailer and fumbled for the light. He should have known she'd still follow right behind him.

Jared found the switch, the bulbs glaring to life, blinding him for a head-splitting instant. He heard Emma's involuntary groan, could imagine what the flash had done for her whiskey-fogged head.

Jared scrubbed the back of his hand against his eyes to clear them. He heard Emma gasp.

"Davey?"

Jared's sight popped into focus, zeroing in on the dispirited figure huddled at his desk. The rims of the boy's eyes shone red, his face etched with silent misery. A misery deeper than any Jared had seen since the day Davey had told him about the stable job. What the hell? The boy had seemed fine at the pub. Almost…well, cheery, laughing and joking, basking in all the attention Emma gave him. Her influence had smoothed things out with the other kids, too, from what Jared had been able to see.

Last time Jared had seen him, Beth Murphy had been sliding into the seat beside the kid and Davey had looked like he'd won the lottery.

"Cheers, there, boyo." Jared crossed the space between them. "What are you doing here so late?"

"Why can't everybody just leave me alone?" Davey said bitterly. "You're not supposed to be here. Why didn't you just…just stay away, up in the tower with Emma? Shagging each other's brains out like the rest of the normal people in this damned camp?"

Jared heard Emma's breath catch. This edginess—it didn't even sound like the Davey Jared knew. From the moment Emma had set foot on the site, Davey hadn't been willing to tolerate any disrespect to her. And now he was sniping about sex in front of her with something near rage in his voice?

"Davey," Emma said gently, disregarding his sharp words. "What's the matter?"

The boy turned to her with a miserable groan. "Oh, God, Emma! I'm such…such a loser! The lads are right! I'm a stupid, dickless loser!"

"I don't believe that for a minute, and neither does anybody who knows you."

"You weren't there…you didn't see…I made such a mess of everything!"

"Just tell us what happened," Jared soothed. "Start at the beginning."

"She kissed me! Beth kissed me! Right on the mouth! In front of everybody!"

Had it been some sort of a dare? Some cruel joke that had shaken the boy so? Jared would find whoever was behind it and make them so damned sorry they'd never try a trick like that again. "Who put her up to—" Jared began but Emma cut him off.

"I thought you wanted Beth to kiss you." Confusion rippled through Emma's voice. "You were just too shy to kiss her yourself. That's why I told her to try it."

Suspicion raked Jared. "What the hell?"

Emma bristled, defensive. "Beth was moping in the bathroom, as miserable in love with Davey as he is with her! I told her that if *he* wouldn't kiss *her*, maybe *she* should kiss *him*."

"Ah, God save us," Jared swore roundly. "Words of wisdom from a drunken fool!" She winced as if he'd slapped her. "I told you to keep the hell out of this."

"I wasn't too drunk to see what was right under my nose!" Emma raged back. "He's in love with her. Didn't you hear that?"

"Jesus! Love?" Jared kicked his desk in frustration. "He's nineteen years old!"

"I do love her! I love her so much!" Davey turned to Jared, anguished wonder in his eyes. "Oh, God, Dr. Butler. I didn't think there was a chance in hell she'd love me back."

The words ground deep, echoing doubts Jared understood far too well.

"Then what's wrong, Davey?" Emma broke in. "You're not making any sense."

"Haven't you done enough damage here?" Jared snapped. "Why don't you let me handle this?"

Emma faced him down, hands on hips. "You want me to sit here and watch you teach this amazing, wonderful boy how to shut himself off from life like you've done for so many years? Because it's safer? Because you aren't sure he's strong enough? No way, Butler. Davey deserves better!"

"It's not like I don't have cause for concern. Can't you see how upset he is?"

"Davey, you love Beth and she loves you back," Emma said, ignoring Jared's retort. "Do you have any idea what a miracle that is? How precious? You're an amazing young man, David Harrison. With a huge heart brimming with passion for work that both you and Beth love."

"She doesn't...doesn't know...who I am. If she did...she wouldn't want me."

"She *does* know you," Emma insisted, touching Davey's cheek. "She knows she can trust you. Knows you would never hurt her."

"No!" Davey protested. "Nobody here really knows me.

Not even Dr. Butler. I've made sure of that after what happened ten years ago. You don't know what it was like, the way people looked at me. I couldn't bear it if Beth ever looked at me that way. I'd want to die."

Jared's muscles clenched at the boy's words. He was more aware than ever of the scars on Davey's wrists, the life those wounds had almost cost him. "Davey, you're the finest young man I've ever taught," Jared said. "Just tell me what's troubling you. We can work it out." Christ, how bad could it be? And yet, whatever it was, it was eating Davey up inside. "Just tell me what happened that's upsetting you so."

"The accident. But it wasn't an accident. He did it on purpose."

"Who did what, Davey? I don't understand." Emma looked from Jared to Davey in confusion.

"Mum tried to stop him. But he beat her and—and I was so scared. I thought he'd killed her!"

Jared's throat closed. Images flashed through him—the one time he'd met with Mrs. Harrison, the scars that marked her face. It was from an accident, Davey had later explained, obviously unnerved by them. Now Jared suspected that she hadn't run into another car. She'd run into Davey's father's fists.

"Who hurt your mom?" Emma asked.

"My father. He…oh, God. Her face!"

Jared broke in. "You said your mother tried to stop him. From what?"

"He took the car…they were getting off work. People crowded on the corner at Fulsom Street, waiting for the light. When his boss walked out, my dad…he floored the accelerator and ran the car into the crowd to reach him. All those people, six hurt, eight dead."

Jared couldn't breathe. Headlines ten years old flashed

into his mind, the sensational case that had horrified all of Britain.

"Your father was Ralph Dempsey?" Jared tried to wrap his head around it—studious, gentle Davey Harrison the son of the roaring monster who'd reveled in the carnage he'd caused, gloating before the cameras as he was dragged away.

"See?" Davey grieved. "Even after all these years you know who he was, what he did! In court, he said he was glad he did it! Hoped when I grew up I'd be man enough to…to stand up for myself and…do the same thing if some sodding rag head tried to rob me of the promotion I'd earned. I shouted that I never would hurt anybody like that, but he laughed in my face as they dragged him away. Said not to be so sure. I was his son. His blood would be in my veins forever."

Davey paced the small space. "And he was right. The blood of a monster! Who beat my mum…and killed all those other people…people he didn't even know… He didn't care if they died, as long as—as his boss died, too."

Jared ached for him. "Why didn't you ever tell me?"

"I didn't want you to know. I didn't want it to change the way you look at me. Have it make you sick at your stomach…every time you looked at me, thinking about all those bodies he left broken on the street."

What the hell could Jared say? His stomach *was* churning, the thought of Davey carrying such a burden repulsive, unthinkable.

"That's what I was afraid of," Davey said, gazing, helpless, into Jared's eyes. "The way you're looking at me right now."

"I just… I hate knowing you have to carry this with you. I want to fix it."

"I did, too. Wanted to fix things for Mum. I tried to be perfect for her," Davey continued, sorrowful. "I tried not to let him be…inside of me. *That's* why I cut my wrists the first time… I was trying to get his…his blood out." Davey's voice cracked. "Stupid, wasn't it?"

"I'm only glad you stopped yourself before it was too late." If the brutal man hadn't been killed in prison, Jared would have hunted Ralph Dempsey down and beaten him to death for leaving such a legacy for his wife and the boy Jared loved like his own.

"So now you know," Davey said. "The whole awful truth. Can't you just leave me alone?"

Davey made to leave but Emma cut the boy off, blocking the open door. She grabbed him by the arms, held on tight. "No," she said. "I'm not going to leave you alone. I know exactly how you feel."

"Sure you do." A hopeless laugh rose from the boy's throat. "I hate when people say that, as if—as if everybody in the world knows how it feels to have a father who did something so terrible you want to throw up every time you think of him."

Jared waited for Emma to resort to any platitude she could think of to make the kid feel better, that poor baby sympathy shite that in the end proved simply worthless. Instead she looked into Davey's face, her eyes suddenly grown old.

"Everybody in the world *doesn't* know," she said. "But I do. Just as sure as I know that you're nothing like your father."

Something in Emma's voice stopped Jared cold. It was as if he were standing on the opposite side of a wall only Emma and Davey could see, cut off from their pain, their touch.

"What happened on that street corner is *your father's* crime," Emma insisted. "*His* anger. *His fault.* Not yours. You don't have to pay for the rest of your life for what that man did."

"Right, Emma," Davey scoffed, too caught in the claws of his own anguish to see pain in anyone else. "That's what the counselor the court assigned me tried to say. Just add your bill to his. Maybe you can use all this angst crap in your next role."

"Watch it, lad," Jared cut in, brows lowering in warning. "She's trying to help."

Emma laid a hand on Jared's arm. "No, Jared. Really, it's okay. I don't blame him for thinking I'm just bullshitting him, trying to make him feel better. But I'm not."

"Then what—?" Jared started to ask, then stopped when Emma pressed her fingers to his lips to silence him. He surrendered and she gave him a heartbreaking smile.

"Davey, sit down," she said, turning back to the boy, and indicated Jared's chair. "I'm going to tell you something I've never told anyone else in the world. Not once in my whole life."

Davey sat as she asked. He peered up at her, held by the spell of her voice.

"It's a secret my family discovered when I was sixteen. And Drew…you know, my ex-husband? He was at this…this class reunion thing when it…well…"

She hesitated, biting her lip.

"When it what?" Davey asked. Jared could feel the kid's fragile hope.

"When the secret blew up in my family's face." Emma's features tightened with pain, with old horror, the secrets that put the shadows in her eyes. "You know that my mom raised me alone."

"Like me and Mum. We talked about it before."

"That's right."

Davey was responding to Emma's honesty. Jared could feel the boy hanging on her every word.

"She was just a kid herself when I was born," Emma confided. "Everybody in Whitewater thought she'd gotten what she deserved. They labeled her the town slut. You know how nasty kids can be."

Davey nodded, and Jared wondered what cruelties he'd endured at the hands of children after the crime his father had committed. Far more often than adults wanted to admit, the *Lord Of The Flies* gang won over a classroom's better nature. The biological microcosm that proved only the strong survived.

"Not even my grandpa or my uncle guessed that Mom wasn't nearly as tough as she looked," Emma said. "Not only wasn't she the town slut, she'd never had sex in her life until the night she got pregnant with me."

Jared sensed where the story was heading. Wished he could stop her. Stop her from talking about it, stop her from knowing what had happened.

"My father was some big-deal jock. The captain of the football team. He took her out on a date, then up to this make-out place back home and she thought…well. She thought he loved her. He wanted sex. She wasn't ready. When she said no, he raped her."

Jared couldn't breathe, imagining Emma at sixteen, so innocent, so loving, hearing about how she'd come to be. An incident so brutal, so full of betrayal it had to brand itself forever in her darkest dreams. She glanced up at him, as if she'd heard his thoughts, as if she knew how much he hurt for her.

"Sometimes I still have nightmares about my mom trapped in that car, trying to fight him, get him off of her." Emma swallowed hard. Jared could almost feel her gorge rise. "I can feel him…hurting her," she said. "And then, how scared she must have been when she felt me growing inside her."

Davey stared at her, anguish and understanding stark in his face. Silent. Why the hell wouldn't he be? Jared thought. There wasn't a damned comforting thing to say.

"It hurts so bad, you know?" Emma confided, looking from one to the other. "I wish…wish I could just wipe all

Mom's pain away. I still wonder how she could ever love me so fiercely in spite of all that."

Jared didn't wonder at all. How could anyone not love Emma, down to the last atom of their heart?

Emma hugged herself tight. Jared wanted to slip his own arms around her, knew he didn't dare. She was drawing on every bit of her strength, reliving her private hell for Davey's sake. She had to stand through this alone.

"Mom says she loves me, not *in spite* of what I did to her life," Emma said, "but *because* of it. She had to fight for survival for both of us. She told me the most beautiful thing, Davey, the day all hell broke loose and she had to tell me about the rape. The bright thing, the real thing I take out and hold when the dark of my father gets too heavy to bear. Mom said…" Emma's voice hitched. "She said I was the making of her. The magic of it is that I can look back over all those years Mom and I struggled and survived and I know it's true."

Davey scraped the back of his arm across his eyes. "My mum loves me. But she's scared for me. I see it, sometimes. She doesn't want me to hope for too much out of life. That's what made my dad angry, she said. Wanting things he could never have."

Jared thought of Angus Butler's rugged face, his callused, laborer's hands that had never been too busy to untangle a fishing line, never lashed out in anger at a child or a woman. Angus, who loved and hoped and dreamed in the face of all the world had done to harden his heart.

Jared's eyes burned. How many times had professors and colleagues called him brilliant—Dr. Jared Butler, a master in his field? So why had he been too damned brainless to realize how damned lucky he was to have a father like that?

"You know what I used to do?" Davey whispered, reaching for Emma's hand. Emma enclosed it tenderly in hers, feathering her healing touch over the scar on the boy's pale wrist, evidence of Davey's quiet despair.

"What?" she asked.

"I'd pretend I was Dr. Butler's son. In the summer it almost seemed real. But then, when I started loving Beth…it all came back. You know? My real dad, with his fists like hammers and…I couldn't pretend anymore. I had to see things for real, and know how…how bad it would be if she found out the truth. That's when I knew what Mum meant…about wanting something…too much. I can't have her, Emma. Not ever. She'd find out someday and…"

"And what?"

"She wouldn't want me. How could she want me?" Davey pulled away from her, clenched his hands into fists, misery gray in his face.

"You don't know that," Emma said. "She loves you."

"They're only nineteen," Jared protested, not even sure that he meant it as an excuse anymore.

"That doesn't mean their love isn't real," Emma said. She took the boy in her arms, hugged him tight, then drew away, gazing into his eyes with pure love, utter faith. "Davey, I can't promise you Beth will be strong enough or wise enough to know how lucky she is to have won a heart like yours. But sometime you're going to have to take a chance. Tell someone you love the truth or else your father wins."

Jared winced. Damn her for being right.

"Talk to Beth," Emma said.

"It's too late. I acted like…like such a jerk. Emma, I shoved her away from me in front of everybody, made her cry."

"Your boss here has made me cry a time or two." Emma flashed Jared a glance. "Not when he was looking, of course."

"Of course," Jared said, hating the fact that it was true.

"What will I tell her?"

"Do you love her?" Emma asked.

"I do."

"Then tell her all of it," Emma urged.

"Maybe that's not such a good idea," Jared began but his protest was lost in Davey's reply.

"No! I can't! Not yet…" Panic flared in the boy's eyes. "Just thinking of people here knowing…" He shuddered, looking so damned young, so damned brittle it scared the hell out of Jared.

Emma just hugged the boy closer. "You don't have to tell Beth right now if you aren't ready. Your secret's safe for as long as you need it to be."

"Safe? It's never safe. Not for Mum or me. It's always there, on the edges, waiting to come out…"

Emma's gaze darkened with understanding. And Jared thought of the weight she'd carried all these years. The dread that must always haunt her, that scavenging pigs like Joel Feeny might stumble onto the truth about her own father and make it front-page news.

"No one here knows about your father but Emma and I," Jared said. "And we'll never tell a soul."

"Never," Emma said, giving Jared a solemn smile. "Can I give you just one more bit of advice, Davey? Because I love you so much?"

She did love the boy, Jared knew, a lump in his throat. It was in every line and curve of her beautiful face. Davey flushed, nodded.

"Just make sure that when the truth *does* come out to the woman you love, it comes straight from you. My mom's courage in revealing her secret to me is something I'll never forget."

"But once she told you, then you had that burden to carry," Jared objected. "Something you couldn't ever put down."

Emma shrugged. "Not talking doesn't change the truth. It gives the dark things more power. In the end, I was glad my mom told me about what happened to her. It hurt to know…but she didn't have to carry that horror around with her anymore, all alone. I knew the truth and Jake, my stepfather, knew. Uncle Cade and Aunt Finn and my grandpa. We shared the pain of it, divided the sadness. That's part of loving someone. Letting them see the ugly bits."

"Nothing is ugly about either one of you," Jared bristled.

Davey rolled his eyes. "This from the guy who thinks mummies are beautiful." Jared's throat constricted with gratitude, seeing Davey's spirit come back to him.

Emma laughed.

Davey's answering smile faded, his features dead serious. "I still don't know if I can risk it," he said. "Tell Beth my father's a murderer…like you told Dr. Butler and me about your mom."

"If Beth is worth loving, it will only make her admire you more. The way you've struggled, triumphed, in spite of everything. But you've got plenty of time to decide. Tell her when you're ready." Emma brushed the lank hair back from Davey's forehead. "There is one thing I need to ask you before you go."

"What's that?"

"To keep my story secret, even from Beth."

Davey nibbled at a hangnail, doubt clouding his eyes. Jared could almost hear the boy thinking. Hadn't Emma just said that secrets were ugly things? Talking about them stole their power?

"I'm not ashamed of who I am, Davey," Emma said firmly. "If the story only concerned me, I wouldn't care if you told Beth what happened to my mom. But people I love would be hurt if that tale went public. My mom and Jake. My little sister."

Jared thought of the family in the purple glitter frame, knew just how much Emma loved them, how deeply she must fear for them. The risk she'd taken in trying to make Davey Harrison's heart whole.

"And my birth father—" Emma said. "He'd be damaged by the story, too."

"You want to protect the guy who raped your mom?" Davey exclaimed, amazed.

Jared stared at her, stunned. He figured with Emma's temper she would have handed the guy his front teeth.

But Emma only shrugged, looking a little sad, a lot disillusioned. "He asked me to meet with him once when he was flying through L.A. a few years ago. He's not evil, you know? Just kind of…pathetic. Said that he's sorry. He was just a stupid kid. Well, rape's rape, right? What he was *really* scared of was that I'd announce the story to the press. He didn't want his wife and daughters to know. It didn't take me long to figure out that's what the whole 'come meet your daddy' bit was about."

"The selfish son of a bitch!" Jared muttered.

"I got through the meeting just fine," Emma assured him. "I just hit instant replay on the scene Drew described to me from the night of Mom's class reunion. The guy announced he was going to move back to Whitewater, where my mom would have to see him every day. Jake took a baseball bat to good old Dr. Farrington's Porsche in the parking lot. And guess what? Daddy dearest changed his mind."

Jared liked Emma's stepfather already. At least he *would* like Jake, once he stopped setting Emma up with those irritating bodyguard/this-is-not-a-date deals. But that wouldn't happen anytime soon, since the woman still needed the protective escorts Jake provided. In fact, Jared thought grimly, once audiences saw Emma's brilliant portrayal of Lady Aislinn, she'd need protection more than ever.

"I'll never tell anyone," Davey promised with aching sincerity. "I swear, Emma. And never…never tell anyone about me either, promise? About my dad? I'd die if…if the whole world knew I was his son. I still wish there was some magic, you know? To make that part of me go away."

Jared looked at the boy he loved, humbled by all Emma had given him, wanting to give Davey something to carry away as well.

"Davey," Jared said gruffly. "You're not his son. Not anymore."

Emma and Davey turned to look at him. Jared took a penknife from his desk, flicked it open, then slit his own palm. Pain burned away the darkest shadows on his heart.

"Jared!" Emma cried. "What on earth?"

"What did you do that for?" Davey exclaimed, stunned.

"You're not that bastard's boy," Jared said through clenched teeth. "Not anymore. You're *mine* from now on. You understand?"

Jared took Davey's hand in his, made a gentle nick in the boy's skin. Jared watched a bead of blood well up, then pressed their two cuts together. "When you think of a father's blood inside you from now on, lad, you think of me."

Davey stared at the place where their wounds were joined, a drop of blood trickling, red against Jared's skin. Davey's smile dawned, so bright it almost blinded him. "I love you, Dr.…uh, sir."

"I love you, too, son," Jared rasped. Davey hugged him fiercely, then swept Emma into a bone-crushing embrace.

"Emma," the lad choked. "I don't…know what to say."

"Don't waste your time talking to me!" She kissed him fiercely on the cheek. "Go find Beth! Tell her you love her. Even if you aren't ready to tell her about your father yet, those three words can heal more wounds than you'll ever know."

Davey bolted out the door they'd left open, the portal

swinging wildly on its hinges as he clattered down the metal stairs in search of the girl he loved. Jared watched him go, wondering at a night that had seen so many changes it seemed to last a thousand years.

Jared braced himself on the doorframe, drinking in a lungful of sweet Scottish air, watching shadows shift in the night. A shape moved off in another direction, some night creature finished hunting, heading back to find his mate. Like Jared had, somehow, if he only dared believe it.

He turned from the star-spangled night back to Emma. She sagged against the wall, her hair a straggly mess, bruised circles under eyes far too raw from secrets stripped bare.

She'd never looked more beautiful to him.

"What you said to Davey…" she breathed. "About loving him, and…" She took Jared's hand in both of hers and gently kissed the wound he'd made. Salt stung the cut. The sting, Jared knew, came from Emma's tears. Washing wounds away. Tears of healing, tears of sacrifice, tears of love.

"You are such a fine man, Jared Butler," she whispered. "A true knight, slaying Davey's dragons. I wish I could give you something even half as precious in return."

Jared stared down into Emma's face, thought of Davey's courage, the chance the boy was willing to take for the girl he loved. Jared remembered the fierce determination in Emma when she'd insisted she wouldn't let Davey be like Jared—shutting himself off from love.

Maybe it was time Jared took his own leap of faith. Stepped out of the cave where he'd buried his emotions so long. Let Emma and Davey lead him toward something brighter.

"How about we face down some dragons of our own?" Jared asked her, stroking her hair. "What do you say I go to this party of yours?"

"You'd go to the charity event?" she asked, so carefully it

made his heart ache. "With all those people screaming and the whole media circus? It's going to be insane."

"Are you trying to get me to change my mind? Because if you don't want me to go, just tell me."

"No. That's not it at all." She looked suddenly serious, bruised, as if remembering old wounds. "It's just, it can be so overwhelming. Once you're officially linked to me, you'll be big news, at least for a little while. People prying into your life, asking questions, poking around. It's possible they'll dig up things you—you've tried to bury. Your mother leaving. Jenny's plane crash."

"Maybe they won't," he said. And yet, the possibility seared like acid. His past, exposed….

"It's a risk, Jared. One bigger than you know."

God, don't look at me like that! he thought. For the first time fear haunted his valiant Emma's eyes. *Don't let me fail her,* he prayed. The way he had failed Jenny. The way he'd failed his father.

He hid the hammering doubts behind a shield of humor. "I don't suppose I can wear my cargo pants? I'm a firm believer in that Thoreau quote: *Beware of any enterprise that requires new clothes.*"

"I don't care what you wear, as long as you're there with me," Emma choked out, tears shimmering again in her eyes.

"Then what's this all about?" He scooped the drop from her lashes.

"I'm just—just scared. The press takes things you don't want to give them, Jared."

"I'm not afraid." He echoed what she'd said to him hours before. But it wasn't true. He was just more afraid of losing her without ever trying to make their relationship work.

She cupped the rough skin of his cheek with her palm and he knew she'd left her handprint on his heart. "Just don't hate me, Jared. I couldn't bear for you to hate me because of what they might say."

Davey's feelings, Davey's fears. Fears she'd sought to comfort.

"What the press does or says isn't your fault, Emma. You're not responsible. And as for hating you? I could never—"

She pressed her hand to his lips, cutting off the words. "Don't say 'never.' I've heard *never* so many times before. Just promise it won't change the way you look at me. The way it changed Drew."

"I'm not Drew."

"No." She peered up at him with eyes that spoke of coming home. "No," she said with certainty, moving into his arms. "You're so much more."

She burrowed against him, trusting him, believing in him, all the way down to her beautiful soul. He felt her to the core of his own.

It wasn't as if he were promising her forever. It was only one night in a tux and dress shoes that would probably pinch his feet. And the possibility of fielding a few questions he'd rather not face. How would she react if he asked for more? Asked her to stay with him? Told her how he felt.

A fragment of a Burns poem his father often read aloud whispered through Jared's memory, the familiar lines biting deep with new meaning, terrors, hopes.

As fair art thou, my bonie lass,
So deep in luve am I;
And I will luve thee still, my dear,
Til all the seas gang dry.
Til all the seas gang dry my dear,
And the rocks melt wi the sun.

And I will luve thee still, my dear,
While the sands o' life shall run…

He closed his eyes, forcing himself to remember the children she wanted. Could Jared ever dredge up enough courage to give them to her?

No, the old voice cried out inside him.

I don't know, a more honest one echoed. And yet, he'd meant what he'd said to Davey, taken the wounded boy as the son of his heart.

It's not going to matter whether or not you've the courage to breed! a voice disturbingly like Snib MacMurray's mocked in his head. *Once the woman takes you out in public she may never speak to you again. What will a plain Scottish bogtrotter like you have in common with the folks that will fill up that fancy room?*

Emma will be there, Jared answered fiercely, *and just the sight of her will fill up the heart of me with more than I can hold.*

This is a mistake, Snib warned. *One giant massacre at Culloden Moor of a mistake.*

He's wrong, Jared's father's voice echoed in reply. *Not loving, son. Now that would be a mistake worth fearing….*

No, Da. You waited forever, your love was so strong. I swore that I'd never let myself hope that way, risk myself hurting that way, take the chance I might lose that way. That was always my greatest fear. Loving a woman the way that you did.

And my greatest fear, lad, Angus Butler whispered tenderly out of time, *was that you never would.*

Chapter Twenty

IN THE SHADOW OF the six-foot-tall bank of purple and white flowers was a decent enough place to stay out of the way and watch Emma in action, Jared thought with a resigned smile as he leaned against the wall of the Dorchester ballroom. Sleek, sophisticated, so exquisite she didn't even seem real, Emma moved through the adoring throng of London's A-list like a wayward goddess strayed from the heavens.

Turquoise satin draped her curves, the creamy tops of her breasts just peeking above the V-shaped neckline, her hair tumbling in smooth, soft waves down her back. Sapphires dangled from her earlobes. Her grandfather's diamond star winked in the hollow of her throat, so subtle only Jared could see it, and a square-cut sapphire worth more than Jared made in five years glowed just above the shadow of her cleavage. But in spite of the finery that felt foreign to Jared, the animation in her beautiful features shone every bit as bright as it had during those precious, intimate hours they'd driven through the countryside so he could show her more of

Scotland. And the smiles she flashed him whenever she caught his eyes were full of the memories they'd made, a light and life that was all Emma's own.

It had even been worth it to fasten himself up in the tuxedo, considering the heat that had flared in her eyes. Of course, his trip to the barber had been a less successful venture as far as Emma was concerned.

Ohmigod, what did you do to your face? hadn't exactly been the reaction Jared was looking for when he'd returned to the five-star hotel where he and Emma were staying before the event, but even now, hours later, the memory of her expression still made him laugh.

Your hair, it's all cut off...and your beard...well, not a beard exactly, but that delicious scruffy stuff all over your jaw. It's gone....

I thought you'd like it if I got cleaned up a little.

Well...you look so different, I... She scowled playfully, leveled him a measuring glance from head to toe. *You'd better kiss me so I'm sure you're not a rogue reporter possessing my man's body or something.*

They'd spent a precious hour when Emma was supposed to be what she called "turning into Cinderella going to the ball" exploring possession of another kind. Emma had been totally unconcerned about putting off her preparations for the dinner but her "glamour team" was summoned to the room so late that the lot of them went into artistic hysterics as they attempted to do her hair and makeup and zip her into a designer dress the blue of a Grecian sea.

The minute the waiters carried away the last of the plates, Emma had leaned over, whispered in Jared's ear. *"Newsflash! Emma McDaniel manages to get through the meal without spilling something down the front of her dress!"*

Dinner was over, thank God. The endless stream of

courses, the mysteries of multiple glasses and more silver-ware than Jared had ever seen, had been navigated success-fully. The dinner conversation? Dogs, horses and gardens. Smiling and making small talk. Avoiding probing questions. And being damned grateful he wasn't seated where the board members and major contributors were. Journalists from various society magazines and newspapers were sprinkled among them at two different tables.

He'd almost come unglued when Joel Feeny gave him a smug wave from one of the tables, but Emma had kicked Jared in the shin, leaned over and whispered, "The whole point of these galas is to get publicity for the charity. Be *glad* the press is here!"

"But that jerk—"

"Will write a huge spread in the *Independent Star* that will bring in even more donations. So either ignore him altogether or else *be charming,* Butler. Got it? Don't let him bait you into saying something you'll regret."

He'd eyed the teensy evening purse she held in one ring-bedecked hand. "Charming, eh? I don't suppose you've got a stapler in that purse of yours. Maybe if I stapled my mouth shut, I'd at least stand a chance."

She'd laughed out loud, then. That all-the-way-to-the-bottom-of-her-belly laugh that he adored, the whole room craning their necks to see who had delighted the elegant Ms. McDaniel so deeply. Jared had actually felt his chest swell with pride. Wanted to stand up on the chair, announce to the lot of them, *That's right, mates, it was me. The daft woman's mad in love with me, can you believe it?*

Jared glanced at his watch for about the hundredth time since the driver had dropped them off, counting the minutes until the night would be over and he could have Emma all to himself again.

But the truth was, he admired the hell out of her for what she was doing here tonight. She'd been tireless, enchanting everyone until Jared was certain that when it came time to open the checkbooks, the evening's take would be tremendous.

Baby Steps... He read the banners decking the walls. *A pathway to bright futures...*

Around the ballroom, photographs of mothers painfully young, babies themselves with babies in their arms. Above the podium, a billboard-sized blowup of a photograph that could only be Emma at about two years old, a fairy child, perched on the lap of a girl who might have been her older sister.

Jared's heart lurched, wondering if *his* daughter would look like that, a winsome, wee, otherworldly thing, with eyes that pierced his soul. The daughter who would never be.

His gaze shifted to Emma's mother's image, Deirdre McDaniel worlds different than the beaming woman in the purple glitter frame. Defiant blue eyes were framed by catlike features, a fierce protectiveness that did nothing to conceal an underlying fear. Fear Jared understood far too well—that she would fail her child. That she wasn't good enough, wise enough, strong enough to be the mother baby Emma deserved. That she was one heartbeat away from running...her daughter better off without her.

Jared tried to shutter his thoughts away as someone approached. Feeny. Jared gritted his teeth. Hearing Emma's warnings in his head. *I have to go be brilliant. Play nice with the other boys and girls....*

Easier said than done when just the sight of Feeny made Jared want to strangle the guy with his necktie.

"Well, well, if it isn't Dr. Butler."

"Feeny."

"Hard to believe you came down out of your intellectual

ivory tower. But then, a few nights alone with Jade Star would be worth it." He licked his lips, sending Emma a lust-filled stare. Feeny was trying to goad him, Jared knew. It was working. It took every atom of Jared's willpower not to snap the asshole's head off. "So, Butler, tell me. Is the luscious Emma McDaniel half as good in bed as she looks? Inquiring minds want to know."

"This event is for a worthy cause, Feeny. Why don't you cover it and get your mind out of its usual place in the gutter?"

"Right," Feeny jeered, drawing a miniature tape recorder from his tuxedo pocket. "All these worthy people with all their worthy money playing dress-up and spending their trust funds. It's usually so boring I want to shoot myself. But tonight—well, tonight promises to be a whole lot more interesting."

"I'm thrilled for you, Feeny," Jared drawled, wanting to sound bored out of his mind. But something in the bloody sod's busy eyes set Jared's nerves on edge.

"That's mighty generous of you, Butler, all things considered. But then, if you're going to be our Emma's new boy toy, you'd better get used to life in the spotlight. Or, should I say, on the front page of the *Independent Star.*"

Jared thought of Jenny, the airplane crash, the ugliness between them that plenty of people who'd known them could expose if they chose to. He didn't want it to become public knowledge, but if that were the price of being with Emma, he'd just have to deal with it. "I think I can handle anything you can dish out, Feeny. The lady is definitely worth it."

"Of course she is." The guy stared at Emma as if the recorder was a hand grenade and he couldn't wait to pull the pin. "Just ask her ex-husband."

Jared's jaw clenched so hard his teeth should have cracked. "If Lawson couldn't stand the pressure, that was his problem.

Hell, you people are so deep in lies and twisting the facts around I wouldn't believe you if you told me the sky was blue. It would be pure accident if you ever hit on the truth."

"But it has been known to happen, once in a great, great while." Feeny's lips curled in a nasty smirk. "Are you willing to go on record then, that you and Ms. McDaniel are seeing each other?"

On record? Hell, that sounded official. He didn't care. "Ms. McDaniel and I are seeing each other. On the record."

"Brilliant." The journalist gloated. "See, Butler? Nothing like a little persistence and a little bit of luck to make a man's fortune. This will be a night everyone here is going to remember."

A woman in Chanel and pearls swept up to the podium, her cultured voice rippling out of speakers as she leaned toward the microphone. "If everyone would return to their seats, I'd like to introduce our esteemed guest and spokeswoman, Ms. Emma McDaniel."

Guests abandoned conversations midsentence, eager to hear what Emma had to say. Chairs scraped across floor, dresses rustled, conversation dropped to a low rumble of whispers. Then silence, the whole room on the edge of their seats.

Jared joined Emma at the table they'd shared for dinner. Saw her, just a little stiff, a little nervous. Her hand sought his under the table and hung on tight.

It didn't seem possible. A talented, self-possessed actress nervous when speaking before a crowd?

"You'll be brilliant," Jared whispered. She bit her lower lip.

"It's just so important. I think about my mom, how alone she was, and I want to do her story justice, you know? Make people understand how much courage she had, what a difference a program like Baby Steps could have made for her. For both of us."

Jared thought of the tale Emma had told, the harrowing way she'd been conceived, the loneliness, the poverty, the pain. The young mothers in the pictures that decked the room stared out at the world with the same haunted eyes.

"You'll never make your mother anything but proud," Jared told Emma. When Emma's name rang out, she stunned Jared by leaning over, kissing him full on the mouth in front of the whole damned world. Flashes popped, journalists crowding to get the perfect shot.

She swept to her feet, so graceful, so poised. He watched her mount the stairs to where the podium stood. Cameras closed in on her and broadcast her face onto giant screens around the ballroom for everyone to see.

But as Emma began to tell the audience what it had been like for her mother, Jared's chest ached. It wasn't the polished actress who held the crowd spellbound. It was *his* Emma. Baring old wounds, jarring people out of their safe worlds, making them not only see, but *feel* what it must have been like to try to build a decent future for a baby you hadn't planned on but loved more than life.

"We can make a difference, through education, through child-care programs and mentoring these young mothers. They want to support themselves and raise their children, give their babies futures bright with possibilities and build productive, independent, fulfilling futures of their own. Look around you at these photographs featured here. Each face tells its own story. And they each have a happy ending because of Baby Steps."

A slide show commenced, flashing photographs of graduations, the young mothers who had seemed so overwhelmed, so young and frightened, moving into a new and far more promising phase of life. Emma told of college degrees earned, teachers, doctors, solicitors now in the workplace. Mothers who managed to study and thrive. Music welled in accompaniment, jazz sung in a soulful, mellow voice that had more than one society lady dabbing at her eyes with her cloth handkerchief.

Someone to watch over me... The singer's haunting voice held the plaintive strains of Cole Porter's masterpiece.

On the giant screens the image changed. Jared heard the collective gasp as the image of baby Emma and her mother flashed up in counterpoint to a far more recent photo of Deirdre Stone cradling a microphone in her hand while she sang her heart out before an audience of entranced clubgoers.

As Emma looked up at the images, she glowed with love and pride and hope enough to light the whole world. She fairly beamed, her own voice cracking with emotion as she made her final plea. In the end, this event wasn't about Emma's fame, what Emma had achieved. It was about her mother, who'd faced far more hideous dragons than the rest of the world would ever know.

This charity so dear to Emma's heart was her personal tribute of love and admiration and faith in a mother who had shown the courage to face her mistakes and try to make things right. Redemption, clean and sweet. A second chance. The same gift Emma was mad enough to offer him, Jared realized.

The ballroom erupted in deafening applause, the crowd leaping to their feet. A standing ovation that rocked the whole room. Emma deserved it and so did the remarkable woman who had raised her. Jared wondered if Deirdre McDaniel had ever heard what her daughter had to say about what must have been painful years, years that had, by love alone, still managed to provide some of Emma's most cherished memories.

He wanted to meet the woman responsible for that simple triumph.

You? Going to America? Meeting the family? Christ, boyo, you've got it bad. Just marry the girl and be done with it....

Shock jolted through him. *Well, why not?* a voice demanded in his head. *You love her, don't you?* As for his wariness about having children—hell, if Deirdre McDaniel, seventeen, brutalized and so damned scared, could manage not to ruin her daughter, Jared reasoned, he must have at least a decent chance with a child of his own. Especially with Emma by his side to show him how to live…how to love…how to dare and dream.

The applause died down at last, the woman in pearls taking the microphone for a moment, opening the floor to questions.

You'd think the bloody reporters' butts were equipped with springs. They bounced out of their chairs, arms waving, voices crying out. "Emma! Emma, over here!"

"Patience," she said. "Patience. I'll get to all of you, I promise. This cause is so important to me and the coverage you all will supply matters so deeply, I'll stay here all night answering questions if I need to."

And she meant it, Jared knew. She fielded questions brilliantly, had the reporters eating out of her hand. The woman was so skillful, so animated, by turns so amusing and heartwrenching in her sincerity that it awed him.

But something was amiss. Something about the smirk on Joel Feeny's sly face. At last the reporter raised his hand and Emma couldn't avoid acknowledging him. "Mr. Feeny."

"Let me join my colleagues and the rest of your esteemed guests in thanking you for your heartfelt words about a problem that concerns us all."

She gave him a smile, but Jared could see a touch of suspicion in it. "I'm honored to be here."

"Because of your mother's tragic story."

"My mother's story is hardly tragic. It's a triumph."

Damn right it is, Jared thought. You tell the jerk.

"So you say, so you say all the time. She was an inspiration to you, your mother."

"That's right."

"What about your father? I assume you know who he is? This mystery man."

Emma's smile turned brittle. "My father has never been a part of my life."

"You're certain of that? Wasn't there one brief encounter back in Whitewater, Illinois? An incident where someone vandalized a car?"

The floor seemed to cave in beneath Emma. She saw Jared's face turn white, prayed he wouldn't leap out of his chair. A scene would only make things worse.

Where had Feeny gotten that information? Emma wondered, terrified. If he'd dredged up that much, the rest wasn't far beyond his reach.

An image flashed in her head—the interior of Jared's trailer. She'd bared the whole ugly truth there, things no one but her family knew... She felt her gorge rise. Had Davey... *No. Davey would never have betrayed your secret. Get a hold of yourself, Emma! How could anyone have hidden in that tiny space? Or heard... Feeny has clearly been digging around for info about your father for years. Just fight this one step at a time....*

Feeny glanced down at some notes. "I have it on good authority that your stepfather took a baseball bat to a red Porsche. Do you have any comment on that?"

"I hate to disappoint you, Mr. Feeny, but if you check insurance records, you'll find that the authorities never found the vandals. It was a random act. Perhaps we should get back to the cause we've gathered tonight to champion."

But Feeny wouldn't be shaken.

"I've been able to confirm that a Dr. Adam Farrington, the

owner of said car, had just closed a deal to buy the local medical practice before the incident occurred," Feeny claimed.

He approached the podium where he'd be able to see her every reaction. A fiendish imitation of the hide-the-thimble game Aunt Finn had used to keep the twins busy inside on rainy days: You're getting hotter, you're getting colder. Right now, Feeny was burning up. And more terrifying still, he knew it.

"Dr. Farrington announced his impending return to his hometown at the reunion. Do you have anything to say about that?"

Emma blinked, doing her best "innocent and confused." "I can't imagine why I would."

Feeny regarded her with laser-beam eyes. "Sources say that people saw one Jake Stone leave the auditorium a few minutes before your boyfriend told Dr. Farrington of the vandalism."

"Again, I'm in the dark here," Emma said. "But Jake was a private investigator at the time. It's only natural that he would look into any trouble that arose."

"He has a notoriously quick trigger finger. Jake Stone. Lost his police badge for killing an unarmed suspect, didn't he, Emma?"

Jake. So brave. So honorable. So strong. A real-life hero who'd loved her mother back to life. Emma wanted to scream at Feeny, rage. She wanted Jared's hand to hold on to, anchoring her in this storm. Instead she drew herself up stiffly.

"Even good men make mistakes. Jake regrets his. He's paid for it the best way he knows how, by living a life any man could be proud of."

"A baseball bat from the gym was found the next day in the bushes near the car. How do you explain the fact that Farrington didn't want to pursue the matter, even though the possibility of fingerprints—"

She thought she glimpsed Jared in the crowd, tall, powerful, edging toward her. "If Dr. Farrington didn't consider the incident important enough to worry about, I can't imagine why you would. As a doctor, he knows malpractice suits have swelled insurance costs until it's almost impossible to practice medicine. If he chose to absorb the cost himself, more power to him."

"Chose?" Feeny queried incisively. "Or was blackmailed into it?"

Fury jolted Emma, the people she loved threatened. "Even if what you're hinting at is true and this man is my father, the possibility that he and my mother got carried away in a car when they were teenagers is hardly a cause for blackmail. I'd tread carefully if I were you, Mr. Feeny. A libel suit could tie you up in court for a very long time. And I would happily spend every penny I earn to see you silenced if you try to hurt the people I love."

"A libel suit would be impossible to file in this case, I'm afraid. You see, I have a source willing to go on record. Overheard quite a conversation in a..." He checked his notes. "Trailer that serves as Dr. Butler's office."

Lady Maria Clark, chairman of Baby Steps in England, swept up to the podium in a whirl of indignation and pearls. "It is hardly suitable to be harassing our guest of honor," she said icily.

But Feeny cut in. "You'd spent the night at a local pub and had too much to drink. Do you have anything to say about that, Emma?"

The other reporters scented blood in the water. Emma could see their eager, burning eyes. Panic, ice-cold, sucked her under.

Feeny knew it all. Knew about the rape. Knew about Davey's father...a mass murderer so vile no one in England could ever forget....

Emma didn't stagger, struggled not to shatter.

"During the time of this conversation you were speaking to one David Harrison, a student who has quite an intriguing line of parentage himself, telling him how your father raped your mother."

"Mr. Feeny," Emma said, her voice a hollow roaring in her ears, "perhaps we could finish this in private?"

At that instant Jared surged through the crowd, taking the microphone from her hand. "Ms. McDaniel has no more to say at this time."

Emma almost sagged in relief as Jared curved his arm around her, guiding her toward the door, his massive shoulders keeping people away.

The horrified hostess apologized as she tried to facilitate their retreat. A cacophony of voices erupted around them, people shouting, people shoving, trying to get near Emma. But Jared held her tight, navigating her toward the private sitting room set aside for her use.

"W-wait," Emma said as he swung open the door. "I have to meet with Feeny."

"Talk in private with that scheming bastard? Are you mad?"

She pulled out of Jared's arms, glared up at him, more desperate than she'd ever felt in her life. "You think I don't want to run?" she cried. "But I can't. Did you hear what he said?"

"He can go to hell!"

"I have to do damage control. Maybe I can keep the focus on—on me. At least shield Davey and maybe dodge the question of the rape. If I bolt, Feeny is in charge of the story. He'll make it as horrific as possible. Is that what you want?"

"Of course not! I—"

"You can't stuff a secret back inside a bottle. Not once you've been fool enough to let it out. I have to do the best I can to shield the people I love."

Jared shot her his warrior's glare. "I'm staying with you."

"I want you to. Just—just don't make it worse. He'll be trying to get a reaction out of you. Please, Jared. Help me. I need you."

A few moments later, a discreet knock sounded at the door. The badly shaken hostess of the dinner ushered Feeny into the room.

"Ms. McDaniel," she stammered, "I'm so very sorry."

"None of this is your fault," Emma said quietly. "Now, if you would be so good as to leave us alone?"

The woman bowed out of the room, looking painfully relieved to be escaping the scene to come, while Feeny swaggered toward Emma, the journalist gloating with triumph, the tape recorder whirring in his hand.

"You can't use any of this information," Jared growled at the man. "You were trespassing on site property. Emma had expectation of privacy."

"Nice try, Doc. You might even have a case if I was the one who heard the conversation. But I didn't. One of your students did."

Jared swore. "Who the hell was it?"

"I can't tell you. A journalist is honor-bound to protect his sources." Feeny shrugged. "The student had every right to be at the dig site and reported the door to Dr. Butler's office was wide open. Hardly expectation of privacy."

Emma fought to drag air into her lungs, afraid she was going to pass out. She reached deep for inner strength she feared might fail her, managed to raise her chin.

"There are some points I'd like to clear up for the story tomorrow," Feeny said. "Can you give me some details, Emma? Was your mother injured in the rape?"

"She put it behind her years ago. I'm begging you, Feeny. Don't print this. You've got a big enough story, unearthing my father's identity after all this time. I'll give you an exclusive.

Answer whatever you want if you'll just keep the rape out of the story. Stay focused on me."

"The focus *is* on you," Feeny said. "Anything the public can get their hands on about the rich and famous Emma McDaniel. You should know that by now."

"That doesn't mean it's right. Have a little human decency. I've got a little sister. You'll turn her life into a living hell."

"A necessary risk of a free press. Unless you believe in censorship."

"You arrogant bastard—" Jared grabbed the tape recorder out of Feeny's hand, smashed it beneath his heel. "If you think I'll stand by and let you—"

"You just made this an even better story. Exactly who are you trying to protect, Dr. Butler?"

Jared shoved his way between them. "Get the hell away from her!"

"Have it your way, then, Dr. Butler. I've got a few questions for you as well. Records reveal this boy you've been mentoring—this David Harrison—he spent some time in a mental hospital. Were you aware of that?"

Jared swore, murder in his eyes.

"Suicide attempt," Feeny pressed. "Nasty business, that."

"Leave Davey out of this!" Emma cried. "I'm begging you. He's just some poor kid who had the rotten luck to know me."

"That's not quite the whole story, is it Emma? The kid is the son of the Fulsom Street murderer. But you tried to save him by baring all your own wounds. The public will eat it up."

Bile rose in Emma's throat. "Please, Feeny. I'll pay whatever you'd get for the story. If you'll just keep it out of the press…"

"But that would be extortion. Even we reporters have lines we won't cross. Unlike David Harrison's father. Quite a burden the lad carries, doesn't he? His mother's face slashed by a broken bottle when the boy's father went on a rampage? Eight people crushed to death on the pavement. David's father yelling out in court that his son would grow to be just like him. Dr. Butler, would you care to comment on that? Have you noticed any tendencies toward violence in the boy?"

Jared cocked back his fist, but Emma grabbed his arm, held on with all her might.

Feeny didn't flinch. "Hit me, Dr. Butler. A few bruises on my face will make the story sell for that much more."

"He's right, Jared," Emma said in utter defeat. "There's nothing we can do. Nothing we can say. No way to stop it."

Jared whipped around to glare at her, argue. But what could he say? Emma felt the truth slice through him. The horror. The futility of fighting. This man who'd battled Davey's demons, thought he'd destroyed them, watching them spring back to life like a mythical army from dragon's teeth. A foe not even the knight of the sea could keep from devouring the boy he loved, stripping Davey's worst fears naked before the world.

And why? Because of Emma. Because Jared had been reckless enough to love her and Davey had been naive enough to trust her. Like her mother had the day she'd told Emma about the rape.

"We're getting out of here," Jared growled. He grabbed Emma, swept her past the gloating Feeny and out of the room, then down some back stairs to the car that had been waiting since the end of the program.

"Floor it," Jared ordered the chauffer. With a dismayed look at Emma's stricken face, the man peeled away from the curb, obviously sensing the urgency of the situation. Jared glanced back through the tinted rear window, saw the reporters scrambling for cabs and cars of their own to chase after them.

"Turn right," Jared ordered, and the driver complied, the tires screeching in protest. "Now left." The instant Jared was sure they were out of sight, he ordered the driver to stop. Jared flung the door open before the vehicle had slammed to a complete halt. Jared helped Emma out, then turned to the driver. "Keep driving north," he instructed the guy. "Lure them the hell away from her."

"Right, sir."

He hustled Emma into the aperture between two buildings, hiding them as other cars began to squeal down the street in search. Fearing someone might glimpse her pale skin or the blue of her dress, Jared sheltered her from view with his big body as he moved her deeper into the shadows.

His blood boiled with the lust to kill any reporter who dared come near her or was coldhearted enough to print anything about Davey. But what the hell could he do? Emma was right. Nothing on God's earth could stop the story from breaking now.

He curved his arm around Emma, hurrying her toward the sliver of street light on the opposite side of the building, hoping when they emerged they would be far from the hunting reporters.

But before he could test his theory, she stumbled. Her knees struck the concrete with a force that must have scoured the skin off of them, the blue gown pooling on the filthy ground around her. Horrible sounds rose from her throat as she braced herself on hands and knees, shaking so violently it terrified him. He knelt down beside her and caught her hair back, murmuring futile words of comfort to her as she retched. Exhausted at last, she leaned against him, shattered, her face damp with cold sweat as he gently wiped her mouth with the handkerchief from his tuxedo pocket.

"Oh, my God, Jared…" she choked out, searing him with anguished eyes. "What are we going to do?"

He swathed Emma in his jacket, trying to warm her. "I'm going to find whoever contacted Feeny from the site. Then I'm going to throw them off Craigmorrigan land bodily."

"But it won't matter," Emma mourned, clinging to the front of his shirt with one clenched hand. "It's too late. By tomorrow it will be all over the news. We've got to get to Davey before the story breaks. The press will be all over the site. I'm sorry! So sorry."

But sorry didn't matter, Emma thought in despair. Tomorrow her mother's rape would be front-page news, Davey's past exposed to the whole world. Her head filled with images—Davey's scarred wrists, Jared's knife wound, still healing. Her mother, trying desperately to explain the unthinkable to innocent little Hope before the jeering began, the kids in her classroom teasing, the grown-ups in Whitewater gossiping.

Emma had betrayed them all, even if she had told Davey the tale for only the right reasons. She'd wanted to heal the boy, soothe his fears, his feeling that he was the only one who knew that kind of pain. But she'd ended up wounding him far deeper than his brutal father ever had.

She shuddered, even Jared's arms small comfort as Davey's anguished words echoed in her mind. *I'd rather die than have anyone else know what kind of man my father was. I'd rather die....*

Jared sneaked them into the back entrance of the hotel, then up to their room. He helped her shed the designer gown, abandoned it and his tuxedo jacket on the floor. She dragged on black leggings, Jared tossing her his blue sweater before he tugged on his leather jacket, the nondescript clothes disguising them at least a little. Taking nothing but his car keys and her giant black carry-on bag, they climbed down the stairs to the parking garage in an effort to avoid being sighted.

Jared Butler with his honor and his in-your-face ways hiding, sneaking, slinking away from the ugly glare focused on her.

She barely noticed when Jared loaded her into his car, steered it out to the street. A streetlight blazed, casting Jared's rugged face in sharp relief. Wariness and alarm deepened the lines and grooves. His green eyes were filled with the desperation of quarry.

She had done this to him, Emma knew. Put him in the hunters' sights. Without her, no journalist would torment him.

Emma huddled against the passenger door as Jared drove like a fury, leaving the bright blur of London's city lights behind. Jared, racing back to his castle, back to his cliffs, back to the boy he'd fought so hard to save.

Emma closed her eyes, too filled with pain to look at Jared's beloved face. Drew was right, she thought in anguish. It *was* dangerous to be close to her.

She left everyone she loved bleeding.

Chapter Twenty-One

RAIN SLASHED FROM the sky, obscuring the rising sun and slowing the car's climb up the treacherous mountain roads. Aching from driving all night, Jared gripped the steering wheel in white-knuckled ferocity, the elements threatening to pull the vehicle out of control in an eerie echo of the way he felt inside.

As if he were coming apart. Crashing and burning in a conflagration even more soul-destroying than the one that had killed his wife and unborn child ten long years ago. Because he hadn't loved Jenny. Not the way he loved Emma. And he hadn't ever gotten to know or grown to cherish his coming child the way he cherished David Harrison.

A man was supposed to protect the people he loved, Jared thought. Stand between them and all the pain the world could hurl their way. He was supposed to be strong enough, wise enough, brave enough to hold fast, like the mountain cliffs even time could not wear down.

But he was failing. Failing Emma. Failing Davey. Just as

he'd failed Jenny and his father years before. What could he do to hold back the forces that threatened to overwhelm them? Drown them in shame and guilt, regret and betrayal, shattering any delusion that their world could be safe again….

Jared swerved onto the lane that led to the castle, the cluster of tents a white smear. The students were doubtless hunkered down to begin the day's work, cleaning small finds, catching up on paperwork or research or, in the case of Davey, catching up on the moves most teenaged boys had mastered a long time ago. Pleasures Jared knew would be all the sweeter because Davey had waited for love.

Jared winced, remembering the wonder that had lit the lad's face the morning after the heartrending revelations in the trailer. An elation that had left Jared little doubt that Beth Murphy had not only forgiven Davey for the scene at the pub, but had stolen away with the boy to some secret hideaway in the night. A place that, come morning, David Harrison had left a man.

Changed utterly. Forever. The way Jared had been when he'd first made love to Emma. Jared glanced across the car's interior to Emma's heart-shaped face, so pale it terrified him, her eyes huge and bruised, even though the worst blows hadn't yet been dealt. She hadn't yet told Davey his secret was out. She hadn't warned her mother about what was to come.

I need a secure landline… Emma had said when he offered her his mobile phone. *Something no one can intercept…when I tell Mom….*

He'd been afraid she'd start to retch again, but she'd pressed her hands against her belly, holding her emotions in by force of will—all her horror, all her rage, all her fear of facing her family after what she'd accidentally betrayed to the world.

Not "betrayed." No. Secrets the world had stolen from

her, ripped away and thrown into the glaring light for the salacious to gloat over. Matters that should have remained private becoming fodder for gossip in offices and restaurants all over the globe.

I'm afraid... her voice echoed in Jared's heart from the night he'd offered to go with her to London. *The press takes things you don't want to give them....*

They'd exposed the pain of her divorce, flaunted her ex-husband's baby when Emma's arms were empty. But even that humiliation paled in comparison to what she faced now.

"You'll want to ring up your mother right away," Jared said. "The telephone in the trailer should be secure."

"No. Davey first. It'll take time for the media to pick up the story in the States. But the press could stampede the castle anytime."

The trailer was probably the logical place to meet with Davey, too. Private with doors that would conceal what happened inside, if you remembered to close them. But Jared passed the structure up. He couldn't stomach returning to the setting where the boy had bared his secrets and Jared had cut his hand, bonded them together, promised to be Davey's father. Made the boy feel safe.

Davey should have *been* safe. But Jared couldn't shield him from the train wreck that was barreling his way. Couldn't protect Emma any more than he'd been able to pluck Jenny's plane safely from the sky.

Truth was, Jared had been right all along. There *was* no safe place. Not when you loved a woman this much. And yet...

The castle... He peered through the rain, making out its beloved warlike silhouette. To Jared, Lady Aislinn's tower had always seemed strong enough to withstand the pounding of enemy blows.

A moving shape caught the far edge of the headlight beam, a student in a dark green slicker on the way to God knew where. Sean. The lad came up to the car, drenched, but enjoying the storm the way kids often did. The way Jared had when he was a boy, roaming out in the wildness, the crash of thunder like the long-ago battling of Celtic war gods.

Jared rolled down the window, chill rain pelting the side of his face as the boy loped up to the car.

Sean grinned, looking far less green than he'd been in the pub's W.C. "I don't have to ask you how the party was, Dr. Butler." He tried to swipe rain from his eyes. "You look like Emma dragged you behind the car the whole way from London. Should have taken the advice you gave me at the pub and laid off of the whiskey."

"Send Davey up to the tower," Jared cut Sean off sharply.

Sean's humor faltered as he became aware of the edge in Jared's voice. "Davey? He and Beth were running some tests on... It's something bad, isn't it?"

"Just send him. Don't let him know anything is wrong. Understand?"

"Right," the lad agreed, but his face paled. Jared's heart ripped at the sudden protectiveness transforming the gregarious boy's usually carefree features. Emotion grudgingly won by the quieter Davey...and far more valuable than the hail-fellow-well-met camaraderie of the football boys. Respect. Would it remain once Sean and the other students learned the truth?

Jared pulled away from Sean and drove up to the tower, parking as close to the castle door as possible. Emma climbed out of the car as he jammed the gearshift into Park. Rain battered her, streamed down her face, soaked her hair as he turned off the ignition and got out himself.

The waves the stylists had pressed smooth with some kind

of heated contraption rebelled, twisting into their natural riotous curls as she staggered toward the door.

Jared moved to steady Emma but when he tried to take her arm she yanked away as if he'd pounded on an exposed nerve and the merest touch might shatter her. She looked so small engulfed in the folds of his sweater, her eyes burning in a face white as parchment.

How many times had he climbed these stairs with her in the past weeks? Waiting to love her? Fight with her? With swords, with words? Challenging her mind, her heart, her body's thunderous response to his?

But today the stairs were gravestone cold, the walls hopeless gray, the dream they'd woven here together torn down like the vibrant tapestries that once covered the castle walls, leaving desolation.

Jared had always sensed that this reckoning would come. The end of summer. Happiness all too fleeting. He'd just never known they would face such wanton destruction when it did.

They mounted the landing, Emma retreating to the alcove and the table where her family picture sat in its place of honor. A purple frame full of beaming McDaniels. Would their smiles ever be quite so open again, once the whole world knew secrets that should have stayed their own?

Jared's hands clenched at the thought of Emma's mother fielding questions about the rape. Emma herself, pounded by vultures like Feeny: How does it feel to know that you're the child of a rapist who attacked your mother when she was sixteen years old?

Poison. Pure poison. As toxic and potentially deadly to the spirit as the poison David Harrison would be forced to swallow all too soon.

Jared grabbed the coverlet from the bed and started to

wrap it around Emma's shivering body. He swore when she tried to thrust it away. "You're soaking wet!" he insisted, forcing her to accept the warm folds he swirled around her shoulders. "You'll catch your death of cold. That won't help anybody."

She huddled on the bench, rainwater dripping from her soaked hair onto the picture in her grasp. Jared saw the hand-painted decorations start to smear, the glue dissolving, sloughing off glitter as it ran. Moisture seeped under the edge of the glass and a water spot bloomed in the photograph's corner, damaging it the way the family it captured would soon be damaged forever.

Jared grabbed a clean T-shirt from his own stash of clothes and blotted the worst of the rain from Emma's hair and face. She let him. Her sudden stillness terrified him more than the moments when she wouldn't let him touch her.

Footsteps.

Jared's muscles clenched as he recognized the galumphing rhythm all Davey's own, accompanied by the tick-tick of claws and Captain's enthusiastic yips as lad and dog rushed up to the tower. The terrier racketed into the room first, flinging his furry body against Jared in canine ecstasy. Jared scooped up the dog, tried to put the terrier into Emma's arms. But Emma refused even that small comfort.

She took the animal and laid him numbly in the crate near her bed, then waited for Davey to come in.

A moment later, Davey's lanky frame filled the door, his oiled canvas coat dripping, his eyes shining. Jared scarce recognized the boy. Davey seemed taller with his new confidence, awed by his newfound love, basking in an unexpected peace with the world that had once excluded him.

"What are you two doing back?" Davey exclaimed, obviously glad to see them. "I didn't think you were leaving

London until—" He suddenly sobered, looking from Jared to Emma and back with searching eyes. His voice sharpened with unease. "What is it? What's wrong?"

Jared clamped his hands on the lad's shoulders, shoulders far too narrow to hold up under the burden Jared was about to shift onto them. "I'm not sure how to tell you this," Jared began.

"Is it Mum?" Davey squeezed the words through a tight throat. "Is she sick? Was there an accident?"

"No!" Emma said.

"Your mother is fine," Jared assured him. *But she won't be for much longer…not after the headlines run in tomorrow's* Independent Star.

The boy hitched out a breath, his eyes only a little less filled with alarm. "If it's not Mum, then what is it? You look horrible."

Jared struggled to find the right words, knowing all the while that there were none. But Emma beat him to it, gazing up at Davey with banished fairy eyes.

"Someone overheard us the night Jared and I found you in the trailer," she explained.

"You two find me in the trailer a dozen times a week," Davey protested in blatant denial. "Which night are you talking about?"

"The night we went to the pub," Emma said. "When you told us about your father."

Davey curled into himself, as if trying to ward off a blow. But there was no shield for the kind of sword Feeny wielded. It cut without steel and you bled where the damage couldn't be seen with the eye, only felt in the heart.

He swallowed hard. "Who heard? It was Veronica, wasn't it?"

Emma stiffened at the mention of the grad student's name. Jared's eyes narrowed. "Why would you say that?"

Davey twisted his fingers together, pacing as if the walls

were closing in on him. "I passed her that night when I was running to Beth's tent." The kid froze, looking scared out of his wits. He turned to Jared. "Oh, God— Is Veronica going to tell Beth about my dad? They're friends and—and maybe to warn her…"

That would be difficult enough for Davey to handle, Jared thought. But he would have welcomed it in comparison to what the boy faced now.

"It's worse than Beth knowing," Emma said softly.

Davey spun toward her, his voice rising in panic. "There *is* nothing worse than that! It's the most awful thing that could happen!"

Christ, if the boy only knew. Jared sucked in a steadying breath. "It appears Veronica kept in contact with that reporter I had thrown off the property the first week Emma was here."

"That Feeny jerk? Why would she do that?"

"To get me out of the way," Emma explained flatly. "Veronica knew Jared wouldn't tolerate the uproar of the press swarming all over the site. And she'd be paid God knows how much money for feeding him information. The problem is that, in the process, something else leaked out. How my mother was raped and…" She faltered. Jared jumped in, his rugged features stark.

"Davey, the truth about your father is going to be front-page news come tonight—if it isn't already."

Davey backed away, banging into Emma's arm. The frame slipped from her rain-slick fingers. It crashed to the stone floor, glass shattering, wood miter joints jarred askew. "That's…that's impossible… Beth doesn't…doesn't…she can't know I'm—"

"There's still time to tell her," Emma urged. "I'll send you and your mother away for a while. Someplace safe until this all dies down. Anywhere you want to go. Maybe Egypt, to see the pyramids. Or Pompeii or Troy. Some ancient city you'd love and where no one will find you."

A ragged sob tore from Davey's throat. "You promised no one would find out!" he accused her. "I trusted you!"

"Emma had no control over what happened," Jared started to defend her. But Emma cut in.

"I know you trusted me, Davey," Emma said, picking up the fallen frame and pressing it against her chest. "I'd give anything to stop this. But the story about your father became big news since Feeny tied it to me."

"What do you mean, tied it to you?"

"Veronica told him that I was…trying to comfort you when I told you about my mom. They'll make it something ugly."

"How do you make it any uglier than it is?"

"They'll say I told you my story out of pity. That I…felt sorry for you. They'll make it seem like…"

"Like you're some kind of freaking saint, scraping the pathetic spawn of Satan out of the sewer? I'm a charity case?"

"You know that's not true." Emma laid the frame down on the table with trembling hands.

"Well, nobody else will!"

"Easy, lad!" Jared warned, trying to temper Davey's panic. "Don't forget, they'll be blasting Emma's story over the airwaves, too. She's a victim here."

"A victim?" Davey cried wildly. "She's the star! The great famous Emma McDaniel who…who made some poor sod like me actually believe I was…worth something. Could crawl out of my father's shadow. But I can't. Not now. Not ever!"

"Davey, that's not true!" Emma protested, but Jared felt the boy's words strike her like a dagger to her chest. "I know it doesn't seem possible that things will ever be all right again," she said, "but we'll get through this somehow. We don't have any other choice."

Davey braced himself against the table. The sun broke out, its sudden rays piercing the window and ruthlessly baring the torment in the boy's thin face. As if Feeny's betrayal had peeled back any scar tissue Davey had managed to grow over the wounds the murders had left in him. Every shard of agony and guilt and horror naked again, and new.

"Davey, this doesn't change the truth—that your father's crimes weren't your fault."

"Right, Emma." Davey gave a wild laugh. "Tell yourself that if you need to!"

Emma approached him. Jared could feel how badly she wanted to hold the boy, comfort him. "Jared and I love you."

"No one else ever will!" Davey cried. "I can't live like this! I told you…"

Davey didn't say the words. He didn't have to. They thundered in Jared's mind and Emma's heart, filling the room with terrifying possibilities.

I can't live like this….

A white scar gleamed in Jared's memory.

Emma tried to enfold Davey in an embrace. He shoved her away, racing blindly toward the door. Emma lost her balance, careening against the table. Jared swore, diving toward her, but she fell, cracking her head against the corner. Davey was too distraught to notice as he fled down the stairs.

Jared caught her in his arms, a thin trickle of blood crimson against her white brow. He grabbed his damp T-shirt, put pressure on the inch-long wound, crooning words to her, his heart breaking—torn between Emma's pain and the boy's.

Head wounds always bled a lot, he tried to assure himself. But they healed quickly. Far more so than the kind of wound Davey had carved into his wrist in despair.

Fear surged, ice-cold, through Jared, Davey's voice echoing from that night in the trailer.

I'd rather die than have anyone know who my father is.

No. Jared wouldn't believe the boy could be made that hopeless again. Davey had grown stronger under Jared's watch. He loved his work. He had a future Jared would make damned well sure was bright.

"G-go after him," Emma tried to struggle dizzily to her feet. "We have to stop him before he…he hurts himself."

Jared heard the car engine fire up below. Hell, had he left the keys in the ignition? No, but he'd always entrusted Davey with his spare set.

The worst of the storm had stopped, but the roads would still be slick, the curves far too dangerous for a boy half out of his mind with grieving. For the love he thought he'd lose, for the life he'd thought he built, for the mother he knew would suffer.

Jared tried to dab at Emma's cut, torn by indecision. But Emma had clamped her hand over the cloth and was already heading for the stairs, oblivious to the lump forming on her forehead. "We have to stop him before it's too late."

It took too damned long to slog through the mud to the camp at the other end of the curtain wall. Then they had to find another car and rummage a set of keys from the Peg-Board in Jared's office.

A cluster of students with worried faces spilled around them, Veronica conspicuously missing from the group as they begged to know what was wrong. Beth's plea more heart-wrenching than any other. "Where's Davey? Sean said something's wrong."

"Do you love him?" Emma demanded as she made her way around the car.

Beth gaped at her, stunned.

"Do you love him?" Emma repeated fiercely.

"Yes!"

"Now's your chance to prove it."

The girl stumbled back a step, her face pale with alarm as Emma slid into the seat. Jared jumped behind the wheel.

"Buckle up," he said, doing the same one-handed as he gunned the engine. He saw Emma fumbling with the seat belt as they sped to the main road. Tires squealed. The car started to slide sideways on the pavement. He felt Emma brace herself. Jared's muscles went rigid as he eased the steering wheel the other way to compensate, slowing down just a little as the car gradually pulled out of the slide.

Jared let a breath out. Emma didn't even seem to care that they'd almost rolled the car.

"Which way would he go?" she prodded. "North or south?"

"I don't know." Jared repositioned his hands on the wheel. "He's spent his whole life trying to get back *to* the castle. Not running away *from* it."

But gut instinct made him turn south, toward town. Maybe Davey would go to the pub. Some whiskey—hell, Jared could use a dram or two himself. The three of them could sit at Flora's bar and figure out some way to fight through this. He and Davey and Emma.

He sped down the road, the standing stones a blur on the rain-drenched hill, Snib's cottage hidden in the valley below. The countryside whizzed past them, no sign of the car or boy in sight. He was questioning himself, almost ready to turn around when the road banked left.

Emma screamed as a cloud of panicked sheep flashed up before them in the middle of the road, bleating hysterically.

Jared slammed on the brakes, the car weaving madly, slamming to a halt just before he struck the animals. He laid on the horn, trying to scare the lot of them off the road, all the while cursing Snib and his bloodthirsty collies. Why the devil wasn't he keeping his gates locked and the flock under control?

"Oh, God! The fence!" Emma's cry jolted Jared. He looked in the direction she pointed, his gaze finding the scattered stones. Frightened sheep fled, revealing the break in the centuries-old fence, deep tire ruts dug in the turf, smoke billowing from a ditch beyond.

"Davey!" Emma screamed, and Jared knew her gaze found the wreck almost concealed by the lip of the ravine at the same second his did. Jared slammed the car into Park and flew out to the crash site, Emma in his wake.

"Stay back!" he shouted, wanting to spare her if Davey—bright, shy, earnest young Davey—lay dead.

No. Jared wouldn't think that. He couldn't or he'd be no use to the boy or Emma. But he'd seen wreckage like this the day Jenny died. Her plane had crashed barely a mile from the airstrip where he'd been waiting to pick her up. His gut clenched, nightmarish images pouring through him. His feet pounding as he ran toward the crash site, his lungs filling with smoke, twisted metal splashed with flame and death he couldn't hold back....

Jared found the shattered window, peered into the car's interior. Davey slumped against the wheel, his skin gray, drenched with blood.

Emma caught up to him just as Jared pressed his fingertips to Davey's throat, searching desperately for some faint flutter of life.

His voice tore on a sob.

"Oh, God, no," Emma cried. "Don't let him be—"

"He's alive!" Jared grabbed the handle, he and Emma struggling to wrench the door open. It gave with a teeth-grating screech, sending them both tumbling backward. Jared smacked his elbow on a stone, heard Emma's breath whoosh out as she hit the wet earth as well. But in a heartbeat they were scrambling back to their feet.

Jared poked his head into the car, heard Emma's gasp of horror as she saw it, too. On the side farthest away from them, Davey's left arm twisted at a gut-churning angle, bone piercing skin. Blood flowed from the wound in a deadly stream.

"We need something to make a tourniquet," Jared said.

"Your shirt," Emma said, taking over putting pressure on the wound.

Jared wrestled off the garment, tore a strip from it. They worked together to tie it, thrusting a thick branch through the knot to help twist it tight as they could, praying they could exert enough force to stop the bleeding. The stream slowed but didn't stop.

"We need help," Jared said. "I don't know how much blood he's lost." He patted his pockets, searching. "Damn it, where's my mobile phone?"

"You tossed it on the dashboard after you offered it to me to call my mom. Even if we could find it, the thing has to be crushed to bits from the accident."

"One of us has to go—"

"I'll go!" Emma cut in, backing away from the wreck. "I'll take the car back to the castle."

"No! The MacMurray place is closer. But your head—are you—"

"I can do this. Stay with him. If he wakes up he'll need you."

Need you. The words pierced him. Had anyone ever needed him this way? Needed his strength, his love the way Davey and Emma did? It made him feel humble, afraid and so damned grateful. He searched her face. She was strong, his Emma, the cut on her forehead no longer bleeding, her eyes almost clear.

"Ring up the medics." Jared eased his body close to Davey's in the car seat, holding the tourniquet tight. "Tell them to hurry."

Emma nodded, then climbed back up to the street, her feet slipping on the wet turf. She leapt into the car, wheeled it in a U-turn and headed back up the road, searching for the entrance to Snib's farm, praying she wouldn't be too late.

Her mind filled with Davey's wound, the bright red blood on the seat. Jared's tortured face.

This is my fault. The truth hammered in her head as she glimpsed a mailbox with *S. B. MacMurray* painted on it in awkward letters and wheeled down the lane. *If it weren't for me, Davey wouldn't be lying there bleeding, maybe dying. He'd be safe. And Jared wouldn't face the possibility of losing him....*

Jared would never forgive her, Emma thought, hopeless. And how could she blame him? She would never forgive herself.

The dilapidated farmhouse reared up before her, Snib's collies racing around the corner, barking as if bent on murder. Emma didn't care. She climbed out of the car and ran to the front porch with the dogs snapping at her heels. She pounded on the peeling paint of the door with both fists.

The door flew open. Snib was savage as his dogs. "What the devil are ye thinkin'? Runnin' from me dogs like that! Yer lucky they didn't tear out yer throat!"

"Thank God you're here!" Emma sobbed, clutching the front of the old man's shirt. "I didn't have to break through the window..." Snib grabbed her wrists but not to thrust her away.

His scowl turned to alarm as he felt the stickiness of Davey's blood on her hands, saw the dark red stains.

"Did those beasts hurt you? By God, lass!"

"No! There's been an accident!"

"Butler?"

"One of the students. Davey Harrison. We have to call for help."

Snib guided her through the dim house to his kitchen and pulled out one of his mismatched chairs.

"Sit ye down, I'll be ringing Fergus Campbell's lads up. They'll be there in no time. Where's the wreck?"

"Just a few miles south of here. There's a ravine. He shot off the road and…broke through the fence."

"By the standing stones, then," Snib said. "They'll see the hole where he went through."

She expected him to start swearing about his sheep, about his fence, about the plague of reckless drivers among the students Jared had brought to the castle.

Instead, while telephoning in the alarm, Snib filled a dented copper kettle and set it on the Aga in the corner. By the time he was off the phone, he'd spooned tea leaves out of a tin container into a fat brown ceramic pot. He poured in the boiling water, covered it with a stained tea cozy and rummaged for a mug on one of the chock-full shelves.

"Damned Butlers—left the whole place stuffed with crockery. Couldn't take it with 'em to the smaller place. But at least I've got something fit to serve a lady." He finally settled on a cup old enough for her aunt Finn to love, with pink and yellow carnations on it and a chip out of the rim.

"This'll put the heart back in yer chest," he said, straining her a cupful of tea and adding a generous slug of whiskey from a dusty bottle on the countertop.

Emma surprised herself, smiling at him as he pressed the cup in her hand. "Thank you," she said, her whole body shaking. "But I have to—to go back to help. Jared—"

"Butler will be making enough trouble all by himself for the medics up there. You'll be nothin' but in the way."

"No! He—he needs me."

"Sure and he will. Soon as ye've got yer feet back under ye, I'll take you to the hospital. Ye'll be waiting when they come. Drink up, now. That's a good lassie. Every drop of it."

Emma started to argue, then realized he was right. She drank, the tea and whiskey scalding her throat.

"There now." He actually patted her shoulder. "That's the magic brew we used when we were taking France back from the Nazis."

"You were a soldier?"

"A long time ago." His eyelids dipped down, hiding thoughts too grim, memories too bloody. Emma could see him driving back the demons, just like the Captain sometimes did.

"Mr. Snib, before we leave…may I make a phone call? To my mother. There's something I have to tell her."

"Call America?" Snib's eyes widened in surprise. "Does yer mum know this boy somehow?"

"No. It's…the press. They found out something awful. I have to warn her. I'll pay for the call."

"Devil you will! Ring up yer mum fer as long as ye need, but catch your breath first or ye'll scare the poor woman to death."

Emma's bottom lip wobbled in gratitude at his kindness. He gave her shoulder a hearty squeeze.

"Ye'll get through whatever tempest those sneakin' papers are going to stir up. And so will yer mum. That's what folks do when they have grit like ye," Snib encouraged.

"But Davey—"

"The boy will be fine as well, if that scurvy Butler is with him. Stubborn enough to wrestle the devil himself for the lad, if he needs to."

Emma almost managed to smile.

"There now, lass," Snib encouraged. "Bottoms up. Ye'll be back in fighting form before you can say Snib's-your-uncle. 'Course, my magic brew is missing one vital ingredient, I'm afraid."

"Really?" Emma gulped the last dregs in the cup. "What's that?"

He smiled, a real smile, bracing and surprisingly sweet. "I'm a little short on worms this time of day."

Chapter Twenty-Two

MACHINES WHIRRED, tubes snaking across the hospital bed where Davey lay unconscious, his arm in a white plaster cast, his bandaged face swollen and misshapen from where he'd hit the steering wheel, a neat row of stitches marching across the cut on his left cheek.

The students had practically come to blows over who would donate the blood Davey needed so desperately. But surprisingly it was Emma and Jared who'd been the perfect match. They'd lain on the gurneys beside each other, willing their life force and love for the boy into every drop of blood the nurses drew.

But even that hadn't been strong enough. For three days Davey hadn't wakened. Just lain there, so white, so helpless, so young. Until Davey regained consciousness, there was no way to tell how bad the damage would be. Whether that hungry mind of his would be as broken as his arm. Whether he'd ever recover enough to go back to school, to earn his degrees, to work at Jared's side in the science that he loved.

Either way, Emma resolved that Davey would never want for anything. She'd make sure he had the finest doctors in the world, whatever he needed. The best of everything. But even her promises to take care of the boy financially hadn't driven the darkness from Jared's eyes or the anger from Mrs. Harrison. The woman telling Emma what she already knew: that all the money in the world couldn't undo what Emma had done. Even the famous Emma McDaniel couldn't piece together her boy's mind if it was shattered.

Emma's own family's reaction to the press scandal had been typical McDaniel. Fury, outrage on Emma's and her mother's behalf, then closing ranks against the enemy. Emma's cell had fielded supportive McDaniel phone calls at least once a day, and only fear of dragging even more vultures down on the hospital where Davey was fighting for his life had kept her family on the other side of the ocean.

Her mother's reaction still broke Emma's heart, Deirdre's courage and love unfaltering. *In some ways it'll be a relief once this media frenzy is over. I've always suspected the story about the rape would come out sometime since there were witnesses when Jake smashed up Adam's car.*

But I was the one who blabbed it, Mom, Emma had cried.

It's not your *fault or mine,* Deirdre had said fiercely. *We're the victims here, and don't you forget it. We'll get through this, Emmaline Kate.*

But Hope… Emma had faltered. *She's so little.*

Her mom's voice got a little quiet, a little sad. *I do wish Hope were older but you've taught me to have confidence in my daughters' strength. And she'll have the whole family to love her and help her cope. You're the one I'm worried about. Promise you'll come home, Emma. As soon as you can. I won't feel right until I can hug you in person.*

Tears had streamed down Emma's face. She'd closed her

eyes, imagining her mom's arms around her, the smell of Deirdre's shampoo, the mother-grizzly-bear protectiveness Emma loved so much.

Emma, I want you to listen to me right now. I love you for trying to help that poor boy. You did the right thing. This Joel Feeny and that bitch Veronica what's-her-name did the wrong thing. I hope neither of them ever come around Jake. He's just itching to take a baseball bat to the assholes' cars. But he'd have to get the bat away from me first.

Emma had hung up the phone feeling a little better, loving her family more than ever. She wished Davey and his mother had people they could depend on half as much.

But they did. They had Jared. And they had her, even though Davey's mother might find help from her hard to swallow.

Emma hovered in the hospital room's doorway, not wanting to upset the woman further as she watched the doctor update her on the boy's progress. Saying the same thing he had said so many times before. Surgery had saved the boy's life in the agonizingly tense hours before Mrs. Harrison had been able to reach her son's side. Now if Davey would only wake up....

What would it feel like to know your child had skated that close to death? Emma wondered, hugging herself tight. But that kind of love, that danger of loss was something she would never experience. Drew was right. Who would bring an innocent child into this kind of insanity? The hospital grounds swarmed with reporters and photographers staking out every possible exit route, hoping to snag Emma as she left.

One had even managed to slip past the hospital's security, belting out questions when Emma had gone to the vending machines to buy a can of soda.

Is it true the Fulsom Street murderer's son tried to kill himself again, Emma? The story surfaced because of you. How do you feel about that?

"How do you think it feels, you bloodsucking son of a bitch?" she'd yelled back, hurling her pop can against the wall. Wishing she could pound the man, hurt him as badly as his kind had hurt her family and the boy who still lay fighting for his life. Fists knotted, she'd stalked toward the journalist, but Jared had dived between her and the goggle-eyed reporter before it was too late. Scooping her into his arms, he drove the reporter away and the guy fled. It seemed even bloodsucking sons of bitches had survival instincts.

"Don't listen to them," Jared had said, keeping a tight hold around her fury-stiff shoulders as he led her back to the waiting room. "It's not your fault."

But Emma knew for damned sure that no one else in the crowded, dreary room had the same opinion. A stack of weekly magazines littered the waiting room table. The lurid headlines might as well have been written in Davey's blood. *Emma McDaniel child of rape. Star bares darkest secret to Fulsom Street murderer's son....*

Even the studio's PR department had its hands full trying to put the right spin on the story. But Barry Robards' edginess was the least of Emma's worries. The effect of this disaster on the people she cared about hurt her far worse.

The kids haunted the hospital waiting room as stubbornly as Jared and Emma did as the days slipped past. Sitting so quiet and pale in small clusters, they treated Emma almost as coldly as they had treated Veronica before the doctoral candidate had fled back to St. Andrews, more than a little horrified at what she'd done. Not only hurting Emma, but Davey—someone she'd worked with, laughed with, someone innocent and fragile.

She'd turned up at the hospital with a check for Davey's mother, donating the money the paper had paid her to the boy's medical fund. But that fixed nothing. Veronica would still have to spend the rest of her life looking in the mirror, knowing what she'd done in a fit of jealousy. Knowing she might as well have shoved that car off the road, shattered Davey's arm, battered his head. She'd live with it forever, just as Emma would. Maybe that was punishment enough.

Emma would face the same thing. She didn't blame the kids for treating her like a pariah. Watching Beth was hardest of all. Veronica, Beth's best friend, had betrayed the boy Beth loved. And because of Emma's fame the whole world knew it.

The teenager wept silently and mumbled prayers by turn, breaking down whenever she sighted a camera. "Make them go away!" Beth finally shrieked at Emma, driving her from the room. "Why don't you make them go away?"

Beth was right. That was at least one thing Emma could do. Draw the paparazzi away from the hospital doors. Once she left Scotland, they would follow her.

But she'd have to leave Jared. Leave Davey before he woke up. Before they knew if Davey's mind was still bursting with potential and the wires and tubes were swept away. Before his mother could hold him in her arms again. Before Emma could tell him how sorry she was.

At least Davey's fears about Beth would be banished for good. The girl not only still loved him, she loved Davey all the more. If Davey woke up…no, *when* he woke up, he'd be fine, Emma told herself. He and Beth would be happy together. Someday marry, have the babies Emma never would. They'd spend summers with Jared, digging for treasure. And he wouldn't be alone.

That would have to be enough. She'd make that be enough.

Emma shook herself from her thoughts as she saw the doctor shake Jared's hand. The doctor patted Mrs. Harrison's shoulder, tucked his charts under his arm and headed for the door. He was so preoccupied, he almost ran into Emma. "Ms. McDaniel!"

"Is there—is there any change in Davey?"

He gave her an encouraging smile. "Some signs look hopeful. We just have to have patience and let the body heal itself."

"Right."

"Quite a carnival around here with you in town. I nearly ran over a reporter when I pulled into my parking space."

Emma winced. "I'm sorry."

"I'm not. Of course, I wish we'd met under different circumstances. But my boy is a huge fan of yours. He's probably watched each Jade Star movie forty-eight times."

Oh, God. Her stomach sank. "Then he needs to do something else with his time."

Great idea, Emma. Piss off the guy who's going to be sticking needles in Davey's arm.

She tried to backpedal. "I'm sorry. I haven't slept much the last four days."

"Of course. It was insensitive of me. But Allan's fifteenth birthday is coming up. You know how hard it is to find a present at that age."

She thought of her cousins, Will and Amy, hinting at what car they wanted. "I know."

The doctor hesitated, then obviously decided to go for it. "If I could get your autograph it would be the best birthday Allan has ever had. He'd be thrilled."

Emma closed her eyes for a moment, pulling in a weary breath. "Of course."

The doctor pulled the DVD of the last Jade Star out of his lab coat pocket and handed her a permanent marker. Nothing like coming prepared, Emma thought. She scrawled *Happy Birthday* and her name across the plastic cover.

"Grand!" the doctor said as she returned it to him. "I've seen all your movies—of course, not as often as my son has! I hear you'll be making one here in Scotland during this year.

The story of our own Lady Aislinn. The whole town has been in a dither of excitement about it."

Emma swallowed hard. Looking through the doorway at Jared, at Davey, everything she could never have. "There's been a change of plans," she said. "I'm going back to America. Tonight."

It was all arranged. Snib, who had guarded her in the days since the accident as if she were one of his lambs, had promised to take her to the airport, where a private plane would be waiting. But first she needed to collect the only things that mattered from the tower room. The scrappy little terrier and the battered purple-framed picture of the family she still had to face.

She ached to hold Captain in her arms, bury her face in his fur and cry out her pain, the hopelessness raging through her. Her little buddy would keep her from falling apart in the years to come. Someone who loved her, who would be waiting for her when she came to whatever home she made for herself somewhere.

And her family—they had to keep on loving her, in spite of what she'd done. She was a McDaniel. Emma's stomach twisted. Had the barrage of headlines started hammering them yet? How was her baby sister really holding up? Hope's voice had sounded so small the times Emma had talked to her. But Jake would be standing guard over his family. And as long as Hope had her tap shoes, Jake would be able to get his daughter's mind off the trouble, at least for a little while. And it seemed the rest of the family would soon be distracted as well.

Last time Emma had talked to her mom, Deirdre Stone had been packing. Uncle Cade planned to load the whole extended family into one of his planes to fly them to his best friend's ranch in Montana for a few weeks. Jett Davis knew exactly what they were up against. The plane-crazy actor had spent years building walls around his life to keep the world out. The McDaniels would be safe behind them.

Emma would join the family there, stay until things cooled off enough for them to come back home. To March Winds with its gazebo and the antique wedding dress she'd never wear. To Jake's craftsman-style bungalow, every board lovingly restored by his own hands. To a mother with her own ghosts and shadows, who understood the pain of hurting the people you loved most, regretting words you could never take back.

I'm sorry, Mama… I'm so sorry….

"Emma?" Jared's voice, right beside her. She hadn't heard him approach.

She glanced up at the clock on the wall. Snib would be pulling up to the service entrance any minute now. She'd put off the inevitable long enough. She had to tell Jared goodbye. She looked into eyes green as a Scottish glen. Eyes that had known so much loss, so much pain. She couldn't imagine her life without him.

"There now," Jared said, drawing her into his arms. "What's this? My brave lass in tears? There's to be none of that now. Davey is going to wake up and start demanding his trowel. Complaining summer is not yet over and there are treasures still to be found."

Emma caught her lower lip between her teeth, reaching for strength she wasn't sure she had. "I'm sure he will. But…Jared, I…I have to leave. This is insanity, all those cameras crowding the hospital. The press."

"Sure, you need a break. It's no wonder. I can't leave Davey. But Seamus can sneak you out for a bit. It'll do you good to get some air."

"It's more than that. I need my family. I've held them off this long, but if I don't fly to them soon, they'll be charging in here, wanting to make sure I'm all right."

She saw Jared's shoulders tighten, knew the battle he waged. Needing her, but wanting to give her what she needed even more. "They love you," he said after a moment. "You can come back once you've rested."

His selflessness wrenched her, so far from the gruff, prickly, temperamental man who'd met her in the airport five weeks ago. But she couldn't let that weaken her resolve. Emma stiffened and pulled away from him. "I won't be coming back to Scotland. Not ever."

"What?" Jared paled. "But the movie—what about—"

"I rang Barry Robards this morning. I pulled out of *Lady Valiant*."

"Emma, no!"

"He was relieved, really. He liked the fact that I could do my own sword-fighting stunts, but he didn't have a lot more confidence in my performance than you did when I first came to the castle. Besides, with all the negative publicity surrounding me at the moment, he'd just as soon not have me attached to the movie. This gives him the perfect excuse to wait for his wife to heal."

"For God's sake! You can't—"

"I have to do this. For Davey's sake. And yours. Don't you see? If I leave, the story dies. There's not enough to keep the press here. But if I'm in Scotland, filming, the story will take on a life of its own. They'll never stop, Jared. Never."

"They can go to bloody hell!" Jared raged. "Lady Aislinn is the role of a lifetime! What you've always wanted, Emma! And you'll be brilliant at it. You can't do this!"

"It's already done."

Jared's jaw knotted. "And us?" he demanded. "What about us, Emma?"

Emma drew on every ounce of will she had. "We're impossible as a couple, just like you said. We always were. You want to live the rest of your life with men like Feeny thrusting cameras into your face? You want to live in fear of what new headline will be blazed across the gossip rags? That I'm cheating, you're cheating, whatever lie they want to print to sell copies?"

Jared's chin jutted out in stubborn denial. "We'll know it isn't true."

"And what about next time someone else gets caught in the crossfire? What if some kid like Davey gets killed? What if next time, the child lying in that hospital bed is our own? A son or daughter I was selfish enough to bring into the world so they could be hunted, their every move stalked?"

"Other actors and actresses manage somehow. We would too. Emma you're exhausted. Half out of your mind with worry. It's no wonder you're—"

"No, Jared. I'm thinking clearly for the first time since we made love and I...spun all those crazy dreams. There's nothing you can say to change my mind."

Jared's throat convulsed. His eyes filled with pain. "But I love you."

A sob strangled her. She forced it back. "I'm sorry for that, too." She tried to turn away, but he caught her in his arms, compelling her to meet his soul-searing gaze.

"No, Emma. Don't be sorry. Not for that. Not ever." He kissed her cheeks, her lips, her hair, his body so warm, so familiar against hers. Her heart broke, knowing she'd never feel the solidness, the strength of him again. "It's not over, Emma," Jared growled. "Damn it, I won't let it be over."

She stiffened, made herself draw away. "It's not your choice to make. It's mine. And you know...know how stubborn I am once I decide."

A low groan came from Davey's room. Mrs. Harrison

cried out, "He's waking up! Thank God. Dr. Butler! My boy is waking up!"

"M-Mum?" Davey's voice. "What're you doing here? Summer's not…over yet."

Emma wept with relief, joy driving some of the shadows from Jared's face as Mrs. Harrison cried, murmuring something to her son.

"Where's Dr.…Dr.…Butler?" Davey asked groggily. "Some…thermo-dating Beth an' I need to get for him…soon as poss—ouch! My arm hurts. My head…" Alarm threaded through Davey's faint voice. Fear only Jared could calm. "Dr. Butler…where is he?"

"He's calling you," Emma said, gratitude and loss warring inside her.

"Emma, I have to… I can't…"

"Go to him," Emma said.

But Jared grabbed her arms, so obviously torn it made Emma ache for him. "Wait for me," he pleaded. "Just until tonight. At the castle…we'll talk about this at the castle."

Davey's voice came from the room. "Mum… Dr. Butler…where's Dr…"

Emma nudged him toward the room. *"Go."*

"Stay," Jared begged her, a lifetime of heartbreak in his eyes, his mother disappearing, his father still loving her. Countless Christmas gifts under a tree, waiting for a woman who would never come.

"Please, Jared. Try to understand," Emma whispered.

"Emma." Jared's voice caught, ragged in his throat. "Don't do this."

She buried her face in her hands, the familiar yearning filling her, the desperate need to bury her face in Captain's fur, feel his warm, wet tongue lap the tears from her cheek.

She'd only wanted to love Jared, but in the end she'd made

his deepest fears come true. "I wish you had your magic sword," she said, lifting her face from her hands, memorizing his beloved features so she could take them out in her mind's eye on the long lonely nights to come.

"I don't need its magic anymore. Now I've loved you. Even after this—after everything that's happened, I'll never regret you, Emma," he swore. "Do you hear me? Never. Don't leave me like my father, waiting all alone."

She closed her eyes, heard him turn, heard him go.

Ae fond kiss and then we sever, Ae fareweel and then— forever... Robert Burns's plaintive poem echoed in her head, mingled with the image of Jared's gentle father, singing to his motherless son.

Jared's plea struck right through her. *Don't leave me like my father...* Leave him waiting all alone? No. She couldn't do that to him. She had to find some way to fill the space she'd carved out for love in Jared's heart. But how?

Her mind filled with images of Jared trying to work, his unexpected laughter, his affectionate grumblings as Captain frolicked around him, pure devotion sparkling in the little dog's mischievous eyes.

Loss jolted through Emma, followed by resolve. She'd leave her knight of the sea, her slayer of dragons, her solitary hero someone who loved him to the heart...almost as fiercely as she did.

And once she did, there would be only one more thing she could do for Jared, one last thing for Davey. Give them something to dream on.

Clinging to that last hope, she left the hospital, slid into Snib's car and took hold of the old man's hand.

SHE WAS GONE.

Jared struggled to remember how to breathe. How to keep

his heart pumping as he picked up the letter she'd left on the table where her purple frame had been. Captain howled piteously from his crate in the corner, the dog intuitively knowing the people he loved were shattered. Jared wished he could do the same.

His fingers clenched on the parchment—part of the writing set he'd put together for Emma when he'd been sure she was a piece of Hollywood fluff he'd be able to scare off from his castle in no time.

Before she'd thrown him in the middle of a dogfight, flashed her perfect breast to get her sword to his throat, swallowed a worm, drawn him to the Knight Stone to make love on a magical, sea-swept night.

How on God's earth could she be gone? Gone like the sword he'd lost while saving her. Gone like the laughter she'd pulled from him. Gone like the light she'd loved back into his soul.

He scanned her writing, scratched with the quill and ink, blotted here and there by her tears. He could see her bent over the table, her hair falling in a veil about her shoulders, her bottom lip caught between her teeth as she wrote.

By the time you read this, I'll be on my way back to the life I chose. And you'll be busy trying to get the students back to work, excavating your dream castle, helping Davey and the other kids heal.

They respect you so much, Jared. More than ever now, after all you did for Davey. They need you here, with your hands all dirty and your forehead dented in when you concentrate too hard. I'll miss seeing your dastardly scowl. But this is the way it has to be.

I'm who I am. A celebrity. God, what an awful word. And you're a scientist, a teacher who chose a path so much wiser than I. You're so gifted at the work you do, but you're not good at taking care of yourself. At laughing and playing and taking time to enjoy little things like the wind in your hair when you're riding or a dog licking your face. That's why Captain is staying here to love you. With him, you'll never be alone.

The dog scratched at the floor of his crate, whimpering. Jared crossed to the bed and sat down, laying one hand on the dog's scruffy head.

You'll be receiving a visit from Mr. MacMurray soon. Try not to drive him off with that temper of yours. He has a story to tell that's worth showing a little self-control to hear. The standing stones are yours, Jared. All their secrets left to tell. I wish—

She had crossed these last two words out. And Jared could feel her surrender, her regret. He could almost sense the burning of tears in her eyes.

I know you'll be brilliant. And someday you'll know what happened to the fairy flag and to your valiant lady. Don't come after me. I've made my decision. And you know how stubborn I am.

Emma

Jared let the parchment fall from numb fingers. She was gone. Really gone. She'd left him. Captain scratched and scuffled, doing the impossible, scrambling over the top of the crate. The dog found one of the medieval gowns Emma had worn and tugged it down with his teeth. He dragged it across the floor to dump it on Jared's lap.

Captain sat down, pawed at the dress, then Jared's leg, whining. As if he could make Emma reappear out of thin air. Somehow, the dog's misery made Jared's even more painful. There was no way to tell Captain that Emma wasn't coming home. The terrier would spend the rest of his life waiting…like Jared would.

He gathered up the dog's wriggling, warm body, buried his face in Captain's rough coat and wept.

CAPTAIN ERUPTED like fireworks, barking as Jared's office door swung open three days later and Snib MacMurray limped inside.

Jared raised his head from where he'd propped it on one hand and tried his best to glare the surly old bastard down. "Have you ever heard of knocking?" he demanded.

"A time or two, perhaps. But I faced a bit of a dilemma coming here and that's a fact. Always swore I'd cut off my hand before I knocked on a Butler's door. Seems I like my hand too much to be parting with it, even for that feisty Emma McDaniel."

Emma. She'd said Snib would be coming. Chided Jared not to lose his temper. Hell if he could muster the energy to get a good mad on, anyway. "I suppose you're here for a reason?"

"Other than irritatin' the snot out of you?" Snib shifted an awkward bundle in his arms. "Been my favorite sport for years now, tormentin' you. Told Emma it was going to be hard to give it up. But there's no arguin' with the lass."

Snib thumped the bundle onto Jared's desk, raining dried dirt down on the papers he'd been working on.

"Damn it, old man! Those were important!" Jared tried to slide the papers from beneath the bundle, but Snib slapped his hand down on top of the canvas-wrapped parcel, trapping the documents even more securely.

"I suppose ye've been caterwauling and moping around like that da of yours did," Snib groused. "Fat lot of good that'll do ye."

Jared lunged to his feet, rising to the crotchety son of a bitch's bait. "I don't know what the hell kind of business you've got here, but say another word about my father and I swear—"

"I wouldn't advise makin' a threat ye can't keep, lad. Consider my own little knocking dilemma and learn from it if ye can. I'm going to say plenty about Angus and yer mother."

"What the—"

"Should've known better than to be spoutin' it off to our Emma on the way to the airport. But I would've done nigh anything to take her mind off of leavin' ye. And once she heard it, she'd give me no peace. Swore to me ye'd listen to the story I tell. For her sake if nothin' else. Or is endurin' me for twenty minutes more than the lass is worth to ye?"

Jared clenched his teeth. "Get on with it, then."

Snib nodded in satisfaction. "You know they used to go courting up by the standing stones? Your ma and da. Before he took her away to the city. He'd dig about and find her treasures, pretty flowers, rocks with prints of leaves and ferns in 'em."

That was how Jared had fallen in love with archaeology, wandering with his father, the big man pointing out shells and fossils and finding musket balls and buttons from Jacobite uniforms and such.

Snib patted the bundle on Jared's desktop. "He found this on one of his thievin' trips, when ye were a tiny lad. Tried to take it off me land, but I caught him at it. Angus ever tell ye about it?"

"He said he'd found something wonderful, but he hadn't really known what it was. It started to crumble when he touched it so he merely wrapped it in his shirt to carry it home. He meant to take it to one of the professors at St. Andrews. Da said you were going to toss it in the ocean."

"I meant to, but I had my sheep to look after first. So I took it and stuffed it under me bed. Just never got around to giving this lot a toss in the end. I didn't want the filthy thing, ye see. I just didn't want Angus to have it. Not when he'd already stolen Mary."

"My mother?"

"I had a ring all ready for her finger when Angus caught her eye. Spoutin' poetry, talkin' all soft and gentlemanlike when he was just a grimy-fisted sot no better 'n me."

"Da never said anything about you and my mother."

"He never knew. Nobody did but Mary. When he took her away, I—well, I wanted to take whatever else I could from him. Pounced on this land when he was fool enough to let it go 'cause of the way Mary hated it."

"That's why you bought it? For some kind of twisted revenge on my father?"

"What else did I have t' do with me life, with Mary gone? And don't be lookin' at me so superior, young Jerry. You did the same—got hard and mean and selfish when yer wife crashed in that plane."

How the hell could Jared argue when he knew what Snib said was true? "My flaws have nothing to do with my father. He was a good man. A decent man. He never let life make him hard like we did."

"He might as well have been Bonnie Prince Charlie, he was so goddamned perfect. Bonnie Prince Charlie with a shepherd's crook."

The historian in Jared couldn't keep from pointing out, "Actually, Charles Stuart turned out to be a self-indulgent ne'er-do-well who deserted his men at Culloden Moor and—never mind."

"My point is that your father was so perfect it put me off my feed. I knew Angus would regret losing the farm for the rest of his life. Drivin' him off it was a pleasure after Mary left him. Gave me hope, don't ye know, that between faithless Mary and I, we could make him feel what the rest of us felt. Jealousy. Hate. Bitterness. And when I caught him with this bundle, actin' like he'd found the holy grail, I threatened to call the authorities if he didn't hand it over. Asked how he'd like it if his boy added a daddy in prison to his whore of a mother."

"You bloody rotten—"

"I'm tryin' to make it right before I die, if ye'll let me, ye damned fool! When I talked my fool head off to Emma about the bundle, she said goin' to the grave with somethin' this cold on yer heart would be a terrible thing. Humph. Would've sworn I didn't have a heart anymore, until that lass rushed in like a bulldozer an' knocked all my rocky parts away."

Jared's sharp reply died on his lips. He looked away, suddenly quiet. "She's good at that, Emma is."

"So, man, the long an' short of it is this. Ye can dig on my land if it'll make Emma happy. As long as ye don't worry my sheep."

Jared gaped. He should have been elated, his dream of excavating the area around the standing stones coming true. Emma's gift to him. But even this triumph seemed hollow without her.

She'd given up her own dream to protect him and Davey. Her chance to prove to the world the truth of who she was— a brilliant dramatic actress with a soul so deep Jared's beloved Lady Aislinn shone through her eyes. God, it didn't seem fair that she'd gifted him with this and surrendered so much herself.

Snib scowled at him, nudging the bundle in disdain. "This thing—well, it's a lot of nothin' if ye ask me. If ye want to find yerself a treasure, ye fecking eejit, go after that lassie with the eyes that love you fierce."

"Don't you think I want to?" Jared snapped. "But I can't leave until the site closes down for the winter and Davey is back on his feet. And even if I do, she may not have me. She's dead stubborn and she thinks…"

"Thinks she's ruined yer life, almost killed that boy. Well, from where I'm sittin', looks to me like she's waked ye up from one o' those fairy spells, where a man spends his whole life asleep. I don't know what the devil she sees in ye—scurvy Butler that ye are—but yer a fool if ye don't go fetch her."

"What am I supposed to do if she won't change her mind?"

"A stout highland lad like yerself? Fling 'er over yer shoulder and drag her back here if ye must. Tie 'er to yer bed an' get a child in her. That's the way our ancestors did it. A rough wooing."

"Right, man. That's a fine idea. I'll just march up to her home, grab her by the hair and haul her off right under her family's noses."

"Can't see a problem with it. The lass'll probably be so happy t' see ye, she'll beat ye to the bed, once she gets over the mad of it. No man would ever force that prime little ewe to do anything she didn't want to. And she wants *ye,* Butler. God help her. On that ye can depend."

Jared stared at the old man who had been his enemy for so long. "Why are you here? Doing this for me?"

"Not doin' it fer a thievin' Butler. Doin' it fer her." Snib scuffed the floor with the toe of his boot. "Can't seem to help meself. The damned woman swallowed a worm."

Jared chuckled wanly.

"Gets a man's attention, that does. An' she did even worse before she flew off in that fancy plane."

"What's that?"

"Made me promise I'd look in on ye. And then…" Snib shook his head in wonder, his false teeth rattling. "Kissed me, square on the mouth she did, an' told me I was a gentleman. Snodgrass Begood MacMurray, a gentleman!"

Jared laughed out loud.

"Gives a man somethin' to aspire to, that McDaniel filly does. More grit in her than sense."

"That's the truth."

Snib patted the bundle again, raining dirt all over the desk. "Tell her this is her wedding present. From me. If yer man enough to win her."

Snib spun on his worn-down heel and stalked out the door. Paused to glare back at Captain, who was busily sniffing at the contents on Jared's desk. "I'll *still* shoot that devil of a dog if he comes on my land. Guess I just can't shoot you. Can't have our Emma picking buckshot out of your arse."

Jared listened as Snib's truck fired up and the old man drove away. He peered down at the bundle, remembering the day Emma had clasped his hand through the hole in the stone that was supposed to bind true hearts forever. Was it possible, just possible that Craigmorrigan had some magic left…for them?

Chapter Twenty-Three

JARED PULLED HIS RENTAL car into the gravel driveway and looked up at the Civil War era house looming against the horizon. Destination by default. He wasn't even sure the family would be here at the moment. But he knew eventually at least one of the McDaniels would have to show up at the bed-and-breakfast Emma's mother and aunt ran.

He remembered the way Emma's face had shone when she talked about how much her family loved this place with its vast kitchen and treasure-trove attic, its welcoming veranda and the stained-glass window with a peacock displaying jewel-toned feathers. Emma's smile had warmed with affection as she'd spoken of the ghost she'd believed in as a little girl. But Emma's eyes, those beautiful dark banished fairy eyes, had shone even brighter as she'd shared the memories she and her mother had made from the time Emma was ten, the six years they'd lived in the private section of the house.

He scanned the grounds. The driveway was empty, late-September breezes riffled the white lace curtains at the open front windows. The garden to the right of the house welled up with fall hues. Jared saw the white gingerbread trim and the wooden spire atop what must be the gazebo where Emma had tried unsuccessfully to seduce Drew Lawson, the fool. Jared wouldn't give a damn if the whole world caught an eyeful today—if Emma would only let him love her.

He slid out of the car seat, nabbing Captain's leash just in time as the little dog jettisoned himself out of the car. Looping Captain's leash over his wrist, he concentrated on avoiding the terrier dodging under his feet while he popped open the trunk and extracted the crate he'd hand-carried all the way from Scotland to L.A. and then to Illinois. The "wedding gift" Snib had sent to the Yank lass who'd eaten a worm, toasting the Bruce and Bannockburn.

Jared's chest still swelled with wonder every time he thought of what marvels the crate held. A gift that would stun Emma, amaze her. And maybe, please God, maybe give her faith in the power of love and hope enough to change her mind. Trust in loving. In trying. In a dramatic triumph she'd surrendered and a future she didn't believe they could have.

And just where would that future be? his old doubts mocked him. *I don't know,* he answered himself. At least coming here was a start. Seeing her world for the first time— a place that might have jumped right out of the pages of the Mark Twain books he'd read as a boy—he wondered at the courage Emma had shown, facing him down at the castle. He was the outsider here. He hoped when he entered the world that was hers, he'd show half the resourcefulness she had.

Jared started toward the front door, but Captain would have none of it, the terrier straining so hard on his leash that Jared feared he'd drop the crate. Grimacing, Jared surrendered to the hardheaded animal, letting Captain tug him toward the rhododendron bush that marked the entry to the garden. The back door would do as well as the front, he figured. At that moment Captain wrenched his head right out of his collar.

Jared swore as the terrier darted off. A curse erupted from the vicinity of the gazebo, a man of about ninety emerging from beyond the white gingerbread rail. He brandished a garden spade at the yapping dog.

"Back to your own yard, you little fluffy! There'll be no digging in Finn's rose beds on my watch!"

The dog stood his ground.

"Not your fault, poor little bugger," Spade Man groused. "When I find the moron who owns you I'll take it out on his hide!"

"He's Emma's dog."

The old man looked up, impaling Jared with a vivid blue gaze designed to peel away layers and unearth what a man was made of inside. "Emma's?" the old man repeated. Good Lord—was that a gold hoop glinting in his left ear?

"That's right." Jared stepped to the wrought iron table where a glass of some kind of fizzy drink sat, ice cubes melting in the sun. He slid the crate onto the table. "At least, he used to be her dog. She left him behind for me."

"Left him where?"

"In Scotland."

Razor-sharp intellect burned lines in the old man's leathery face. "You the man who stood by and let my grandbaby eat a worm?"

Bloody hell. Jared should have guessed he was face to face with Emma's legendary grandfather. The man was hefting the shovel in his hands as if it were an M-16 and he was trying to figure out where to spear Jared with the bayonet. But damned if Jared was going to back down.

"Nobody could make that woman do anything she doesn't

want to!" He grabbed Captain and refastened his collar, then tied the leash to the nearest table leg, well out of the old man's range. "If you don't know that about Emma, you don't know her very well at all."

Captain McDaniel rocked back on his heels. "Oh, I know her plenty. Right down to her stubborn little toes. What the hell are you doing here?"

Jared's chin bumped up a notch. Why not say it right out loud? "I've come to marry her."

"Didn't they teach you to read in that fancy university you went to?" Captain McDaniel's scowl could have leveled a city like a nuclear blast. "She won't have you. She said she made her feelings clear in that letter she wrote."

"I don't care what she wrote." Jared stared the old man down. "I'm not leaving here without her."

The Captain guffawed in disdain. "Emma made up her mind she won't see you. What are you going to do? You and that fluffy little dog you've got there going to howl outside her window?" The terrier showed his teeth in his most convincing I'm-not-scared-of-you growl.

"Show a little respect," Jared said. "She named this fluffy little dog after you."

"Did she?" Captain McDaniel eyed the scruffy rat of a terrier with new interest, then turned his attention to the wooden crate. "What's that thing you've got scratching up my paint job on the table?"

Jared crossed his arms over his chest. "It's for Emma."

Without so much as a by-your-leave, the old man set his spade aside and wrestled the top off the box. He tossed the lid to the ground. The terrier dodged under the table with an offended yelp.

"Ratty old canvas and a bunch of dirt?" McDaniel complained. "Some gift to bring to a woman. Ever hear of flowers or candy over there in Scotland?" He poked the oiled canvas with his finger. "What is it?"

"That's for Emma to know. This was buried beneath the standing stones near the castle."

"That's just what the girl needs," Captain McDaniel scoffed. "More old junk to moon over like that stuff in the attic, where she's been spending all her time. I was just about to haul her out to help me with the garden. All that brooding is no good for the girl."

So Emma was here! Jared's heart skipped a beat. She was close, so damned close.

But her grandfather bristled with hostility, looking so much like Captain the dog, Jared might have laughed if the situation weren't so dire. "I don't care if you brought her the tail from King Tut's monkey," the Captain said, drawing himself up to his full height. "You made my grandbaby cry, you low-down son of a bitch. Damned if I'm going to let you upset her again!"

Jared's mouth set in a thin, hard line. "There's no 'let' about this, Captain McDaniel. I don't want trouble but I'll go through you if I have to."

"You can try." The old man cocked his fists up, ready, blue eyes filling with exhilaration.

Jared groaned inwardly as the old man called his bluff. What the hell was he supposed to do? Emma would hate him if he broke the old man's hip. He'd just have to grab the old guy carefully and try not to hurt him when he moved Captain McDaniel out of his way.

Jared started toward McDaniel, looking for someplace on that thin body he wouldn't break. In a flash, the Captain grabbed his wrist. Pain shot through Jared. He dropped to his knees to keep his wrist from breaking. Another flick and SMACK! Jared lay flat on his back, the wind knocked out of him, a boot sole balanced oh so delicately on his windpipe, the *frail* old man beaming down at him in triumph.

The terrier yapped frantically, trying to snap at the old man's leg, but unable to reach. He set to lapping the bare patch of ankle where Jared's pant leg had ridden up.

"Now, young man," the Captain said. "Are you going to go away like I told you?" He took his foot off Jared's neck so he could answer.

"No," Jared said hoarsely, gently nudging the dog off him.

"No?" McDaniel echoed, staring.

"That's right. I said *no.*" Jared rubbed his throat with his left hand as he climbed to his feet. "I hope you're ready for a very long battle of wills, Captain McDaniel, because I'm not going anywhere until I see Emma." Jared narrowed his eyes in grim determination. "You do what you have to do, guarding the gates to the citadel or whatever. But I'm just going to keep on coming at you until I get through."

The old man frowned. "Is that so?"

"It's so." Jared pushed up his sleeves, then rolled lightly onto the balls of his feet, ready to lunge, dodge, evade as he searched for an opening in the old man's defense. He braced himself for another onslaught, praying he wouldn't hurt the old man by accident. The Captain's arm swung in a hearty arc, but not to knock Jared back to the ground. This time Emma's grandfather smacked him on the back in unmistakable delight.

"I'll be damned!" McDaniel said. "I can finally die in peace."

"Die?" Jared echoed, alarmed, thinking what such a loss would do to Emma. "Are you sick?" The thought of Emma facing such an illness when she was already so emotionally battered turned Jared's stomach. He eyed the Captain sharply, his mind racing. The man didn't look sick. Okay, he looked ninety-something years old, but if the grip he'd dropped Jared with a few minutes ago was any indicator, he was a whole lot healthier than he appeared. Or at least a whole lot craftier.

"Hell no, I'm not sick!" the Captain scoffed. "Couldn't afford to be. I had to hang on long enough to make sure my girl would be taken care of."

"Sir?" Jared rubbed his temple, confused. Had he bumped his head harder than he thought when Captain McDaniel had dropped him like a rock?

"You're just what my granddaughter needs! That Drew Lawson—" McDaniel made a face like he'd just gulped down sour milk. "Everybody thought he was Prince Fucking Charming. *I* knew he was all wrong for my Emma from the first. But what can you say? I'm just one old man and the rest of my family was thrilled. *Such a nice boy, Drew,*" he mimicked. "*Such a gentleman.* A gentleman for my Emma? Bah! What that girl needs is a man she can't push around!"

Jared grinned into the Captain's wizened face and the hawk-sharp eyes, knowing exactly why Emma loved her grandfather so much. "Even with me, she tries."

"That's good. That's good." Captain McDaniel puffed out his chest and for a moment Jared saw the man he'd been fifty years before. "Taught her everything she knows. I've been waiting twenty-eight—no, twenty-nine years now for a man to come along who deserves my diamond in the sky." He gave Jared a long hard look from head to toe. "If you carry that girl off and give me a *great*-grandbaby before next summer, you just might do."

Jared laughed out loud. "You know, you're the second old man who's told me to kidnap the woman and get her pregnant. Don't you think I should show a little more finesse than that?"

"Finesse, my ass!" The Captain pretended to glare. "Are you a fluffy or are you a man?"

Jared planted his fists on his hips, loving the old man already. "I'm no fluffy."

"No, you're not, by damn." The Captain slapped his thigh heartily. Then he sucked in a deep breath. Jared's heart tugged as he saw tears in the old man's eagle eyes, Captain McDaniel's voice soft with gratitude. "No, you're not."

"Thank you, sir." Jared thrust out his hand, Captain McDaniel taking it in a viselike grip.

Sparkles danced back into the old man's ornery eyes. "Don't be thanking me before you've lived with her awhile," he warned. "She's got a damned foul temper and she's stubborn as…well, as me." He shrugged thin shoulders, a little sheepish. "The rest of the family's off at some dance rehearsal for Hope. One of those fluffy tutu things on a McDaniel!" He shook his head, screwed up his face. "Never thought I'd see the day. But I won't hold it against her, long as her daddy keeps teaching her tae kwon do as well. Girl's got to defend herself, you know. Never know what kind of renegade she might run across."

Jared chuckled, remembering the times Emma had bested him, the times she'd battled him. The times she'd loved him. "That's a dead cert."

McDaniel jerked his head toward March Winds' open back door. "Emma's alone up in the attic with all that old trash she loves so much. Might as well take that bundle of dirt you carted all the way from Scotland to add to it. Head up to the second floor. It's the third door on your right. If you see lots of cobwebs and trunks, you're in the attic. If you bump your head on shelves full of towels, you're in the closet."

The corner of Jared's mouth ticked up in a smile. "I'll keep that in mind." He started to reach for Captain's lead. But Captain McDaniel stopped him.

"How about we give you a little privacy? Might as well get acquainted with my namesake, here."

"Only if you promise not to bite each other."

Captain McDaniel flung his head back and laughed—Emma's laugh, belly-deep and clear—as Jared headed for the door.

"Hey!"

Jared stopped at the Captain's brusque cry. He turned to see the old man giving him a glare that would have made armies back down. "Hey what?" Jared asked.

"You hurt her, I'll break every bone in your body, got it? I'm not dead yet."

"Emma thinks you're going to outlive us all."

"I might." The Captain flashed his pirate grin, his gold hoop gleaming. "I just might after all."

RAIN DRUMMED SOFTLY on the attic roof, filling March Winds with the magic that had been so much a part of Emma's childhood. Dress-up clothes spilled across the wooden floor where Hope had left them. Treats from an impromptu tea party set up under the window had been decimated. Hope had dashed off to the dress rehearsal for her recital hours ago, insisting Emma remain in the attic until she an' her daddy were gone. The costumes, sewn by her mom and Aunt Finn, were supposed to be a surprise.

It was good to be home, Emma thought. The past month in Whitewater had healed her in ways she'd needed far too long. It was amazing—the resilience of the McDaniel clan's spirit. Hope had navigated the playground minefield with aplomb, reminding anyone who teased her exactly how good her daddy was at swinging a baseball bat.

Former classmates of Deirdre had been surprisingly kind, a few even apologizing for being such jerks when she was pregnant and alone. Deirdre had accepted their apologies with the dignity that was all her own. Not that she had needed their empathy. Jake had convinced her a long time ago that she wasn't responsible for what Adam Farrington had done to her in the backseat of that car.

One of the few things that actually gave Emma a bit of grim satisfaction was imagining her birth father having to explain the bad press to his wife. Unfortunately, Farrington's daughters would have to learn the truth, too. The crime of rape was an ugly thing to have to connect to your father. Emma knew that all too well.

But of all the things that had happened since she'd been back in Whitewater, the most surprising had been the day Drew had shown up at the door. His face shadowed with guilt, his eyes pleading. *I just wanted to let you know I refused to talk to the press when they wanted to interview me about what your father did and that night at the reunion when Jake smashed up the car. I'm sorry, Em. About…about this mess. About everything. Jessie and I…we loved the bear you sent from Scotland. The ba—* He'd stopped, as if knowing mention of the child Emma had wanted to have with him would hurt her.

It's okay, Drew. You can say it. Baby. See? I didn't break into a billion pieces. Not one tear. We were wrong for each other. A baby wouldn't have fixed that. It still doesn't mean you weren't a jerk. But maybe that's a good thing. Makes you almost human.

He'd left soon after and Emma suspected that, in time, the "three musketeers" might even be able to be friends again. Not as close as they had been. But friends, nonetheless. It was something to hope for.

She curled up in her favorite spot near the window, where the crooked brick chimney sheltered the keeper of her most precious memories of all. Treasures not to be dragged out and played with, but rather to be lifted out reverently, one at a time, and smiled over, wept over, scattering their unique spell.

Emma opened the trunk and leaned over it, remembering how it felt to be a child looking into it for the first time. The March family's keepsakes from the Civil War had filled it then. Emma had added heirlooms of her own.

Uncle Cade's lucky shirt with the diamond shapes Emma had cut out of it the day she'd made him so furious and they'd first met Aunt Finn. The tattered blue play script of *Romeo and Juliet* that Emma and her mom had found when she was sixteen and so in love with the stage, with hearing a live audience gasp or cry or leap to their feet in a standing ovation.

Between the pages of Grandma Emmaline's playbook, Emma had discovered the letter that had changed all of their lives forever. Scraping bare the unhappiness of her grandparents' marriage, the secret of her mother's birth. But in the storm that followed, Deirdre McDaniel had found something precious as well. She'd found Jake.

Emma trailed her hands over the treasures tucked in the chest, talismans that reminded her no matter how bleak things seemed, the sun would shine on her beloved family again. Her childhood journey was stowed away here—full of wonder, full of hope—when she'd still believed with all her might that people you loved and lost would somehow find their way home.

And they had—her mother, her aunt Finn. Every McDaniel woman had built the home they'd always dreamed of, the family they'd always longed for. Every McDaniel woman but Emma.

Jared wasn't coming.

She'd told him not to. Was still determined to stand by her decision. And yet as weeks passed she realized that somewhere, in some secret corner of her heart, she'd hoped one day she'd turn around and see his face. But he was gone from her life for good.

Tomorrow she'd be on her way to a new life as well. Away

from Aunt Finn's pitchers of lemonade in the kitchen of March Winds when the bed-and-breakfast guests had left for the day. Far from Uncle Cade's log cabin beyond the picket fence and the Captain's adjoining apartment snuggled up to the building's east wing. Gone from her room at Jake's bungalow, the special addition he'd built in spite of the fact she'd left for drama school in New York before it was finished and he knew she never planned to live back home again.

But more than anything, she'd miss her mother's unfailing love and strength, the mental toughness that had helped Emma survive the pain of what had happened in Scotland.

It was time Emma showed the same grit. Put her life back together and get on with things. As her grandfather told her: There wasn't a man on earth good enough to merit making his grandbaby cry.

But for once, the Captain was wrong. Jared was worth every one of her tears. The brawny Scotsman hadn't just captured her heart. He'd stolen it altogether, until every time she closed her eyes she could see him. On the night wind she could hear him. In her dreams she could feel him—his callused workman's hands on her bare skin, his mouth hot on hers, demanding she give herself to him completely. His big body bearing her down as he drove himself inside her so she could know....

Know what all those words meant in the wedding ceremonies she'd heard. Two becoming one....

But once that happened, once you were joined with a man that way—in your hearts, if not in some church—could you ever be whole again without him? Or would you always feel his loss, like the phantom pain that came when an arm or leg was torn away?

Strange, even when Drew had left her she'd never missed him this way. Never felt bound to him, soul to soul, the way she did to Jared Butler.

She leaned into the trunk, took out a soft bundle wrapped in acid-free tissue. The antique wedding dress she'd never wear. She fingered a sleeve that peeked out of the wrapping. Thistles... Mariah March had embroidered thistles on the sleeves of her gown, in honor of her bridegroom's country. Another man from the wild shores of Scotland. Emma's heart squeezed, as if Mariah March were reaching out to her through time.

A wedding dress...such a silly thing, really, Emma had told herself after Drew had walked away. A costly white dress a woman wore just one day, then packed up in a blue drycleaner's box and stuffed in an attic to yellow with age, then sent to Goodwill once the divorce papers were filed. And yet Mariah's gown was different. All those stitches taken so carefully, every thread dipped in a bride's sweet dreams.

Emma fingered the tiny mother-of-pearl buttons and wondered. If she'd married Jared, would she have worn this historical artifact? No, the archaeologist in him would be horrified. Not to mention, the gown was too small. Would she have dragged out her lucky diva dress, the simple black gown that had replaced the similar one she'd used both for auditions and her elopement to Drew?

Or would she have slipped on the surcoat and silver-tissue undergown she'd worn as Lady Aislinn? The dress Jared had stripped from her body the night he'd saved her on the cliff, made love to her. The night all the walls between them tumbled down at last.

Her throat tightened. She swallowed the lump of pain. *No.* What dress she might have worn didn't bear thinking about. That wedding would never be.

She should have tucked the dress away, but she couldn't stop herself from spreading the tissue back from the gown she and Aunt Finn had found when everything still seemed possible, even someone you loved coming to find you.

Emma had already had that dream come true once. Her mother coming back to love her. It was a precious one, even more so since the maelstrom of guilt and pain and publicity had battered Emma and Deirdre Stone.

But McDaniels never surrendered to defeat. Her mother standing strong. Her stepfather right behind her. Little Hope trying to understand. Even Hope would be okay, Emma knew. The child was certain of the one thing that really mattered: Her mother and father loved her. And so did her big sister.

Someday Emma would watch Hope float up to the gazebo, thistles embroidered on her sleeves, as the wedding dress made another McDaniel bride's dreams come true.

Emma would make that be enough.

SOMEONE WAS COMING. Emma climbed to her feet at the sound of footsteps on the attic stairs and brushed the last of the tears from her eyes. She didn't want anyone to see her cry. Especially not now, before she had to leave. For New York, a new audition. Please, God, a fresh start somewhere on the stages of Broadway where her dreams used to live. She turned, expecting to see her mother's catlike face and flyaway hair.

Instead, dimly filtered light revealed a Scottish warrior's face stepped out of time. Her heart tried to beat its way out of her chest and run to him. She wanted to knock the wooden box out of Jared's arms and fling herself against his broad chest, wanted to hold him and be held. But that would only make the inevitable harder. Nothing had changed since she'd left Lady Aislinn's castle for good.

His eyes ate her up with that hungry look that had always made her want to fill his soul with everything he needed. It took every atom of self-control not to give in to it. "What are you doing here?" she asked, wiping her dusty hands on the legs of her jeans.

He carried the box to an old desk, set the crate down. "Bringing you a wedding present from Snib."

Grief pressed tight on Emma's heart. "You'll have to return it," she said. "I'm not getting married. Not ever."

"So you said in your letter." Pain flashed into Jared's beautiful eyes. Emma knew she'd put it there. "You should have waited for me, Emma," he said softly.

"And you should have let me go."

"That's what I figured you'd say." Jared ran his fingers through his hair. The weary laugh he gave tore at Emma. "In fact, I've been getting plenty of advice about how to proceed here. Davey says I should take the advice you gave him. Tell you I love you. But I've already done that."

Emma winced, the words slicing deep. She'd found out the hard way that sometimes love wasn't enough.

"How is Davey?" she asked, trying to switch to a safer subject.

"Appalled that we were afraid he'd driven off the road on purpose. The crash was an accident. He wasn't trying to kill himself as we feared."

"Thank God," Emma breathed.

"He and Beth were inseparable while he was recovering. They finished this summer's dig in fine style. After the truth about his father broke, well—she clung to him more fiercely than ever. Who knew the girl had that kind of backbone, facing up to something like that? They're engaged."

Emma's eyes widened. "Engaged?"

"He says he knows she's The One. I think he's too damned young, but what the hell do I know? If I learned one thing this summer it's that love doesn't always happen on a convenient schedule. Hell." The old impatience crackled in his voice. "There's not a damned thing convenient about love at all, come to think of it."

Emma's mouth curved in a half smile. "I'm glad for Davey."

"Then, after I got pointers from a nineteen-year-old, I got hammered by two old men. Snib and your grandfather both told me I should throw you over my shoulder and have my way with you to change your mind. In fact, Captain McDaniel had specific interest in a great-grandbaby. After he kicked my ass."

"He what?" Emma froze in surprise.

"Dropped me like a rock on the garden path before he let me in here."

She smiled. She couldn't help it. Not with the funny expression on Jared's face. The Scotsman flushed just a little. "Of course, I *was* trying to be gentle with him."

Emma chuckled. "I'll bet."

Jared's eyes darkened. All humor fled. "Emma, I would have let him beat the hell out of me a hundred times if I had to. To get to you." She saw him swallow hard, his voice catching in his throat. "Marry me. Let me love you the way Robert Burns described. *'Til all the seas run dry, my dear, and rocks melt wi' the sun.*"

"Poetry," Emma breathed, her chest hurting. "Burns is beautiful, Jared, but it doesn't change anything. Didn't you see what our lives would be like during those days at the hospital? Nothing would ever be easy."

"Maybe it doesn't have to be. Maybe that's what makes every minute I spend with you so damned sweet."

He reached out, touched her face. She bit back a moan, knowing how much she'd missed this—the rough tips of his fingers, the warmth of them on her skin. She forced herself to pull away.

"God, Jared. Don't…"

"We're not the first ones to face challenges. Hell, next to what Lady Aislinn and Sir Brannoc faced for love, this is nothing."

Even through her pain, Emma started. "Sir Brannoc? You mean Lord Magnus. You've got your history mixed up." '

"No." Jared's eyes shone the way she loved so well, intense, intelligent, filled with awe at some small find. "I've got it right for the very first time. Lady Aislinn's husband was a scheming opportunist who poisoned her father on the night before the wedding."

"But…but why?"

"He only wanted the fairy flag—to add its magic to his family's bloodline."

"But how could anyone prove that?"

"Magnus's first wife died in an *accident* to clear the way for the alliance with Lady Aislinn. On the eve before the wedding, Sir Brannoc met with Lady Aislinn's father in secret. He'd ridden across Scotland at breakneck speed, bringing the maid who'd seen Magnus throw her mistress off the cliffs to tell her tale of murder. She'd heard the man say once he'd got a brace of sons on his new bride, he'd do the same to her as well."

"But helping anyone this way is completely out of Sir Brannoc's character. Why would he bother to do such a thing? Not out of the goodness of his heart. Every source I've read claims he was Scotland's most infamous mercenary. Did he want to marry Lady Aislinn himself?"

"Certainly not. After the meeting, Sir Brannoc left the castle with a hefty reward for saving Lady Aislinn from such a fate. But later that night, when her father called Magnus in for a private meeting to tell him there'd be no wedding, Magnus poisoned him, killed the maid and blamed Sir Brannoc for their deaths."

"But didn't Sir Brannoc defend himself?"

"The gold that had been Brannoc's reward was missing from the coffers. Magnus said Sir Brannoc stole it after he committed the murders. No one in Scotland would believe Sir Brannoc's tale, save his own loyal men. Who in power would take a renegade knight's word against a noble lord's?"

The truth sank into Emma. "What did Brannoc do?"

"Sailed off to the continent to sell his sword to the highest bidder and vowed that as soon as he was strong enough, powerful enough, he'd go to Craigmorrigan to take his revenge."

"And Lady Aislinn?"

"The wedding took place the next day, supposedly to fulfill Lady Aislinn's father's wishes. Lord Magnus insisted that Lady Aislinn needing protecting from the evil knight who'd murdered her father."

"But how…the story wasn't that way—not in any of the texts I read. Not even in your book! How did you find all this out?"

"Snib."

"The standing stones? You excavated and found—"

"Not me. My da dug up a cache of things while he was on MacMurray's land. He had a gift for it—finding old pike blades and soldiers' spurs and such. Da figured the things belonged to whoever cared enough to find them. Snib caught him with the finds and confiscated the bundle Da put the things in. Snib took it just for spite. It's a miracle he didn't burn it." Jared's voice hushed. "Thank God he didn't."

"But where…where did your father find them?"

"We'll never know for sure. But I'd wager within two meters of where your little rogue of a dog found the gauntlet."

"Jared… Oh, Jared!" Emma flung her arms around him in elation. He hugged her for a moment before she came to her senses and drew back.

"These things all have to go to a museum once I've shown them to you," Jared explained. "But…Emma, I've read the words Lady Aislinn left behind." He unfolded the oilcloth. Emma gasped at the sheen of carved ivory.

"My God, Jared! What is it?"

"Her book of hours. Apparently she could read and write after all. Before she fled the castle, she penned their love story, squeezed it between the lines."

Emma reached out to touch the edge of the battered cover with her hand. "However did it survive?"

"There were metal fittings from a series of different document boxes in the bundle and fragments of cloth. My guess is that they wrapped each layer in oilcloth to seal it. Then wrapped the whole thing in oilcloth again. Lady Aislinn wanted to make sure this record of their story survived. She wanted the world to know."

"Know what?"

"The truth. And it is true, Emma! The part of the tale I always doubted. Sir Brannoc and Lady Aislinn and the swords. But he wasn't just taunting her while Magnus was off fighting for the thieving English as history says. After he took the castle to avenge himself on Lord Magnus, he saw scars on the Lady. He knew her husband beat her. It was a husband's right in those days. I don't know why Brannoc decided to school her in swordplay—because she'd won his respect during the siege or to pass the time and be a thorn in the side of his old enemy." With exquisite care, he opened the book to the middle and Emma stared in awe at the page, the elegant scribe's hand and Lady Aislinn's far more crude one.

"Whatever his reason," Jared said, "Sir Brannoc's goal was to teach Lady Aislinn how to fight back. He didn't expect to fall in love. But it happened." His voice lowered, still amazed. "Just like I fell in love with you."

Emma touched the bit of parchment, marveling. "It's so hard to believe. Six hundred years he's been cast as a villain. Now all of a sudden…"

"He's just a man who loved his woman enough to give up everything."

"No wonder he went mad when Lady Aislinn disappeared…" Emma said, sorrow weighing down her heart. "And we still don't know what happened to the fairy flag."

"But that's the best part of the tale!" Jared said. "When Sir Brannoc returned from hunting, the whole castle was weeping. A boy searching the cliff for bird's eggs had found the lady's favorite coronet caught on a piece of branch partway down the cliff, and clinging to one of the enameled flowers, a scrap torn from her gown. The whole castle believed he was so obsessed with her that he threw her off the cliff rather than surrender her to Magnus once they heard news of the lord's return."

"But Sir Brannoc—he wouldn't have let that monster take her!"

"Lady Aislinn was Lord Magnus's by church law, and no man could stand against it. And Lord Magnus marched at the head of an army that would have crushed Sir Brannoc's forces in a day. Sir Brannoc ordered his men to take their plunder and leave. Then he haunted the tower room, touching her clothes, pressing his face to her pillow, breathing her in from the things she left behind."

"Him smelling her clothes was all in the book?" Emma asked, astonished.

"No." Jared's cheeks flushed. "But I know it's true. That's how I tried to hold on to you."

Emma's eyes burned, the image of this proud man alone, touching things she'd worn, trying to feel close to her.

"Sir Brannoc went mad and might have thrown himself to his death also, if it weren't for his lady's last request. One she had made him swear to see through is ever she died. She must have feared it would be at Lord Magnus's hand. Brannoc swore, no matter what, he would…"

"Would what?" Emma asked, breathless, spellbound by a fairy tale ages old.

"Would take his sword and go to the standing stones. Pledge in that ancient holy place that he'd avenge her. Kill the husband who'd made her so desperate. He was kneeling at the stones, swearing his oath when she stepped from the shadows. She'd been waiting for him all along."

"Wh-what?"

"When Lady Aislinn got word of her husband's return to Scotland, she took the fairy flag and slipped from the castle gates, telling no one."

Emma imagined the Lady in her silver gauze gown, slipping from behind the standing stones to offer herself to the man she loved. A man who'd suffered, believed her crushed on the rocks, carried out to the sea beyond the Knight Stone.

"But why didn't she tell Sir Brannoc what she planned to do? Why put him through that torture, making him believe—?"

"To save his life, and hers. His grief was the only way to make certain the castle folk would believe she was dead. And their believing was the only chance she and Sir Brannoc had of escape. If she'd been discovered and dragged back to Craigmorrigan, her husband would have put her to the sword."

"For loving another man?"

"No. To keep his bloodline pure. He was obsessed by his lineage, wanting a son to carry it on."

"But Lady Aislinn was barren." Emma's breath caught. "Oh, God! With the fairy flag gone Lord Magnus would have no reason to keep a barren woman as his wife."

"That's right." Jared smiled at her, admiration in his eyes for her insight. "For years he'd blamed Lady Aislinn for no heir being conceived. But in the end, it wasn't her fault." Jared's voice dropped low. "There was a far more precious reason she had to make certain the world thought her dead. Lady Aislinn wasn't barren after all. She was carrying Sir Brannoc's child."

"The child she'd wanted for so long," Emma whispered, feeling her own empty arms, her womb's hollow ache.

"She and Brannoc pledged their love with none but the stones to hear them. She wore a ragged gown her maid had given her, no bridal finery but the fairy flag veiling her hair. But she wrote that she was garbed in something far more magical and precious—her bold knight's love."

"But if they had a child, why didn't their descendants tell what really happened? Years later, after Lady Aislinn and Sir Brannoc had died and they were out of danger?"

"The lovers would have had to shed their identities and remain anonymous on pain of death. Lady Aislinn still being married in the eyes of the church, their child would have been a bastard. Even so, maybe one of their grandchildren did try to set the story straight, but we Scots do love our tragic folklore. And the original version made a better tale to hand down."

"A little like the paparazzi, huh? Scandal's much more interesting than happy endings." Suddenly Emma's pulse quickened. "Oh, Jared! You have to tell Barry about what you've discovered. *Lady Valiant* will be even more amazing than before once the script's rewritten to tell the truth."

"Robards knows all about it. I went to see him first, with the proof of the story and a briefcase full of videotapes Davey took while you were training."

"You what?"

"I made Robards watch the tapes right then and there. Told him this discovery made *Lady Valiant* the film of a lifetime. The whole world knows about his demand for excellence. The best—scripts, actors, set designs. I told him that if he didn't cast you in the lead, he'd regret it the rest of his life."

"Jared, you're crazy! You can't just—"

"He actually called his wife to come see the videos as well. She said the same thing. Without you, Emma, *Lady Valiant* will never be everything it could. Angelica Robards said your portrayal of Lady Aislinn had Oscar written all over it. And Barry would be a fool if he didn't move heaven and earth to get you back."

Emma's head reeled, her hands trembled. "They really…they thought…"

"He'll be calling you tomorrow. Would have called sooner but I convinced him to let me tell you—about the true story, about you playing the part. You will, won't you? Bring Lady Aislinn to life? My lady? And yours?"

"But Davey—the publicity—"

"Doesn't matter a damn. The boy is dying for you to come back to the castle and so is the rest of the town. If Feeny and his like want to stalk you, they're going to find it rough-going around Craigmorrigan. Snib alone ought to scare them to death. The man's got a mean pair of collies to sic on them."

Emma tried hard to believe what Jared said was true. To star in *Lady Valiant*. To go back to the castle…it seemed like a miracle.

But it still couldn't wipe away the things that separated her from the man she loved. Because of who she was. What that might cost anyone near her.

Jared grasped her shoulders, looked down into her face, his beautiful mouth tender with love for her. "Just think about Lady Aislinn and her knight. They had so many battles to fight, Emma. But in the end what really mattered was only that they fought them together."

Panic jolted through her, mingled with desperate longing. She'd made up her mind for the best, she reminded herself ruthlessly. What was best for Jared. For the children they'd never have. But it hurt. God, it hurt. "I'm sorry, Jared," she choked out. "I can't…"

"Don't tell me you can't," he said fiercely. "I don't believe it." He cupped her face in his big, warm hands, his eyes bright with love for her. "There's nothing on this earth you can't do if you put your mind to it. Get a sword to my throat. Make me want…"

"I want, too," Emma cried. "But wanting something doesn't mean we can have it."

"Tell that to the little girl who won't let me sleep at night. The one brandishing a wooden waster while I'm teaching her to sword fight. Tell that to the little lad with your eyes who knows his mum will be there to open the gift he made her come Christmas morning. Tell that to my heart, Emma, where those babies you made me want so badly already live." His eyes shone, bright with tears. "Damn it, woman, marry me out of mercy if nothing else! They're half McDaniel, you know. They'll give me no peace!"

Emma stared at him, the desperate need plain on his face, so many shadows vanquished at last. What had it cost him to risk what he feared most…to challenge his darkest demons for her? For children that might never be. Love… She'd heard it bite through his husky Scottish burr. He loved them already. Just as she did.

Emma brushed a stray leaf from his hair, imagining him facing down the Captain, determined to love her. Such courage deserved honesty, whether it terrified her or not.

"They've been busy, those babies," she confessed. "They've been haunting me, too. But I thought…my life…it's still so complicated."

"I don't care," he started to argue. She laid her fingers over his mouth, a gesture so familiar, so right, his breath warm and moist and infinitely precious feathering against her.

"I do care. I've had time to think about what I really want, Jared. I'm going to try doing live theater."

"*After* you star in *Lady Valiant*," Jared cut in, the dent showing in his brow.

She couldn't help grinning, he looked so determined. "Right. After," she said. "Theater is what I really wanted all along. I was going to head to New York tomorrow, audition for a show on Broadway, but London...London has some of the best theater in the world."

Jared closed his eyes, caught her hand, kissing her fingers. "We could winter there, in the city. Maybe I could get a grant to work with the British Museum. And in the summer, we could go wherever we wanted, excavate sites together. Unless you want to keep doing films once the world sees what you can do in *Lady Valiant*. Then we'll work it out somehow. I won't have you giving up part of yourself for me."

The words filled Emma with hopes she hardly dared hold. "And I'll be pestering you on dig sites until I'm eighty. Asking you questions. Dressing up in medieval costumes."

"And I'll be stripping them off you whenever I get the chance."

She sobered suddenly. "Jared, I can't promise there won't be men like Feeny in the future. But in theater I won't be as high-profile as on the screen."

"It won't matter a damn which way you choose to go with your career. Feeny and his kind trade on tragedy and scandal. And we'll be so happy there will be no heartbreak for them to find."

"We can't know that. What life might bring."

"It doesn't matter," Jared said fiercely. "We'll always know what's real, Emma. My love for you. Your love for me. We don't need a Scottish fairy flag or a wedding dress sewn in your Civil War to bless our future. We'll have all the magic we need in each other. Best of all, we know we'd both rather die than surrender. You and I can keep the dragons at bay."

Emma felt fear melt. What else could it do in the face of such a valiant knight?

"I already convinced your grandfather I mean what I say," Jared insisted. "I'm not leaving without you."

"Is that so?"

"Yeah. And this whole marriage thing—I'll even fight you for it. Me and you. A couple of swords. If I win, you marry me."

"I don't know, Butler." Emma's lips warmed into a smile. "You've lost to me before."

"Not this time, lady. This time I know what I'm fighting for." He glowered at her, his fierce warrior's face. *"Marry me!"*

"All right. I surrender." Emma slid into his arms, laughing. "You win."

"No." Jared's mouth found hers in a kiss fierce with love, sweetened by awe, his quest achieved at last. "This time we both win. Forever."

Emma melted against him, slid her hands under his sweater, felt the hot, hair-roughened warmth of his skin. She kissed him with hope, with faith, believing in miracles, the way she had when she was ten. Before she sneaked through the broken place in March Winds' picket fence and her life began to brim with people who loved her.

"Listen, Emma, there's one more thing we need to discuss. The whole flight over here I've been thinking…"

"About what?"

"About what I'd do with you once I got you into that gazebo. That's where I'd hoped to do my 'rough wooing' if it came to that. You know. Throw you over my shoulder, ravish you until you swear your undying love and all that."

"You hardly have to go to that much trouble, Butler. I thought we already did that—the swearing and all."

"I know, but I got kind of turned on by the idea. Unfortunately, the gazebo's a little crowded at the moment with your grandfather and Captain out there."

"Captain!" Emma exclaimed.

"Oh, no. I never should have mentioned the damned dog. I don't mind the two of you having a tender reunion after I'm done with you. But until then—" He frowned, the dent in his forehead delighting Emma to her soul. "Maybe I could bribe the two Captains to get lost. A few dog treats, an opportunity to get in a lovely fistfight. I could get that lad I saw driving the tractor a mile back to come and call them both fluffies. That should keep them busy."

A cacophony of noise erupted in the kitchen, a racket of familiar voices and furry Captain's eager bark making Emma's heart well up with gratitude for all the treasures she'd found. Her mother and Jake. Cousins Will and Amy and little Deirdre Skye. Uncle Cade's gruff affection. Aunt Finn always trying to make peace in the raucous clan. But it seemed that peace in the McDaniel family was once more in short supply. Hope's high-pitched voice pierced right through the other sounds.

"Grampy said that bad man came who made my sister cry! I'm going to kick him right in the—"

The last words were muffled, doubtless by the nearest grown-up's hand. Deirdre Stone's admonition echoed up the landing. "You're supposed to be a ballerina today."

"I'm not a ballerina!" Hope exclaimed fiercely. "I'm Red Riding Hood and my daddy's the big bad wolf. And there's not anybody we can't beat! We're McDaniels, right, Daddy?"

"Some of us are." Jake's laugh echoed up the stairs. "Almost makes me feel sorry for this Butler guy. Almost."

Emma leaned back in Jared's arms and flashed him a devilish grin. "Looks like it's time you meet the rest of my family."

Jared winked at her, the castle's magic sparkling in his eyes. "I can't wait."

* * * * *

If you've enjoyed Kimberly Cates's
THE WEDDING DRESS, don't miss the author's
next enchanting romance set in Whitewater, Illinois,
THE PERFECT MATCH,
available December 2007, from HQN Books.

REQUEST YOUR
FREE BOOKS!

2 FREE NOVELS
FROM THE ROMANCE/SUSPENSE
COLLECTION PLUS 2 FREE GIFTS!

YES! Please send me 2 FREE novels from the Romance/Suspense Collection and my 2 FREE gifts. After receiving them, if I don't wish to receive any more books, I can return the shipping statement marked "cancel." If I don't cancel, I will receive 4 brand-new novels every month and be billed just $5.49 per book in the U.S., or $5.99 per book in Canada, plus 25¢ shipping and handling per book plus applicable taxes, if any*. That's a savings of at least 20% off the cover price! I understand that accepting the 2 free books and gifts places me under no obligation to buy anything. I can always return a shipment and cancel at any time. Even if I never buy another book from the Reader Service, the two free books and gifts are mine to keep forever.

185 MDN EF5Y   385 MDN EF6C

Name _____ (PLEASE PRINT) _____

Address _____ Apt. # _____

City _____ State/Prov. _____ Zip/Postal Code _____

Signature (if under 18, a parent or guardian must sign)

Mail to **The Reader Service:**
IN U.S.A.: P.O. Box 1867, Buffalo, NY 14240-1867
IN CANADA: P.O. Box 609, Fort Erie, Ontario L2A 5X3

Not valid to current subscribers to the Romance Collection,
the Suspense Collection or the Romance/Suspense Collection.

Want to try two free books from another line?
Call 1-800-873-8635 or visit www.morefreebooks.com.

* Terms and prices subject to change without notice. NY residents add applicable sales tax. Canadian residents will be charged applicable provincial taxes and GST. This offer is limited to one order per household. All orders subject to approval. Credit or debit balances in a customer's account(s) may be offset by any other outstanding balance owed by or to the customer. Please allow 4 to 6 weeks for delivery.

Your Privacy: Harlequin is committed to protecting your privacy. Our Privacy Policy is available online at www.eHarlequin.com or upon request from the Reader Service. From time to time we make our lists of customers available to reputable firms who may have a product or service of interest to you. If you would prefer we not share your name and address, please check here. ☐

BOB07